The Gathering Storm

The Gathering Storm

The Chronicles of the Raven
Book I

DAVID DOERSCH

CORVUS
Enterprises, LLC

THE GATHERING STORM
The Chronicles of the Raven, Book I

ISBN 979-8-9879819-0-0

Cover and illustrations © 2023 Duncan Eagleson
http://duncaneagleson.com
Interior design by Corvid Design.
http://.corviddesign.com

Published by Corvus Enterprises, LLC
125 S Lexington Ave., Suite 101, PMB 131
Asheville, NC 28801

For the Raven is a cunning bird,
that bides twixt spirit and clay.

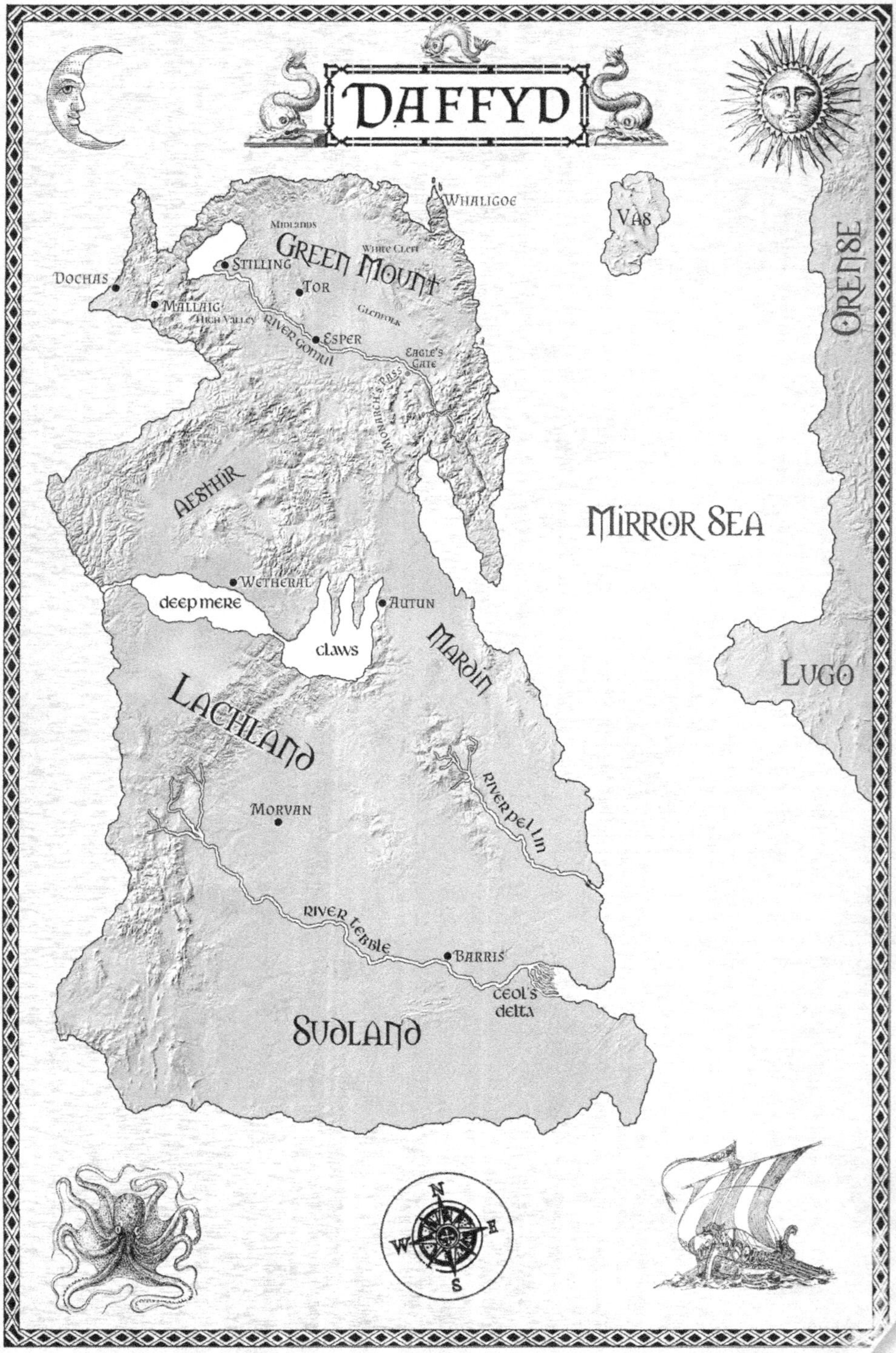
DAFFYD
WHALIGOE
VAS
ORENSE
MIDLANDS
GREEN MOUNT
WHITE CLEFT
STILLING
DOCHAS
TOR
MALLAIG
HIGH VALLEY
GLENFOLK
RIVER GOMUL
ESPER
EAGLE'S GATE
MONARCH'S PASS
AESTHIR
MIRROR SEA
WETHERAL
deep mere
AUTUN
claws
MARDIN
LUGO
LACHLAND
RIVER PELLIN
MORVAN
RIVER TEBBLE
BARRIS
CEOL'S delta
SUDLAND
N
E
W
S

Prologue

The Year 545 HR (Highland Reckoning)
Palace of the Silken Emperor
Near the Fayoum Oasis, Fezzan Province, Asland

Coinneach

"But Amiri, if this continues, he'll die!"

Coinneach could hear his teacher's urgent whisper, though the blood flowing from his scalp in his eyes prevented him from seeing the sword master.

"It is his choice," the Prince responded, loudly enough to ensure Coinneach himself heard clearly. "He may yield my brother's blade at any time."

Lacking the strength to respond verbally, Coinneach merely shook his head, wiping the blood from his eyes where it streamed from his scalp wound.

"Continue." The Prince's cold voice echoed in the darkened chamber.

Coinneach stood slowly on trembling legs, his sword arm dangling limp at his side, useless and dripping blood. Gripping the precious captured blade with his left hand, he wiped his eyes again with his forearm and turned once more to face the giant. He had wounded him, but not enough. The colossus still smiled through bloody lips, hefting his great khopesh lightly and preparing to charge.

Despite the dizziness that kept the chamber spinning, Coinneach calmed his breathing, settled into Willow stance, and prepared himself for the huge eunuch's attack.

With a shout, the giant rushed at him, sweeping the oversized, wicked, hooked blade at the Highlander's head. As the willow bends in the wind, Coinneach arched his back and relaxed into the movement. He avoided the vicious cut by mere inches, then with an effort that drained him of his last reserves of strength, he sprung back with the elasticity of a bent sapling, burying his blade to the hilt in the chest of the onrushing behemoth. The giant's momentum bore his mass forward onto him, their bodies falling in a heap. Coinneach heard, rather than felt, the bone in his left arm snap under the weight of the eunuch and all went dark.

Desert sunlight sparkled through a series of dangling glass baubles suspended before the arched windows of his room. Coinneach flexed his left arm, finding it mobile. He then did the same with his right, inspecting the long, jagged scar the eunuch's khopesh had made. It had been almost two months since his trial and ordeal. The royal physicians had tended him as closely as if he had been the Emperor himself, and though he had lost much muscle during his convalescence, both arms had healed fully, as had the broken ribs. More worrisome to him had been the gash down his back that had come close to severing his spine. Standing in the flowing silken garments of his convalescence, he stretched and moved gingerly, testing each injury. The scar on his back felt tight and his weakened limbs trembled, but nonetheless he began moving through his forms—Badger, Willow, Mountain, even the lengthy Ocean form—testing his range of motion, his power, his speed. Pleased with his returning mobility, he executed a rapid open-hand strike series from Badger form, noting that while his arms trembled with the effort, his strength too was returning. The physicians had worked a miracle—several, to his mind.

"Well, that is progress, I think," a grinning Yazid said from the doorway, where he stood holding a tray of hibiscus tea and a steaming bowl of rice porridge spiced with cinnamon, cardamom, and nutmeg. He had also brought a small pitcher of fresh goat's milk to pour over the porridge. The smell made Coinneach's mouth water immediately and he was surprised by how hungry he was. He smiled ruefully at his friend.

"I suppose I've managed tae hold off Fel's hand for another day," Coinneach responded, sitting on the edge of the bed.

"You were looking rather, how is it you say, *peely wally?*" the jovial Aslene said, setting down the tea service and sitting beside him.

"Ach," Coinneach said gripping his side. "Dinna make me laugh, you great bawface bòidheach! I'm still recovering!"

Yazid's rumbling laughter filled the room as Coinneach desperately tried not to join in, grimacing, holding his healing ribs, and swearing colorfully at his friend.

Swordmaster Ashahl's entrance interrupted them. Though small of stature, he had a regal bearing and natural grace that seemed to fill the room.

"I am pleased to see you smiling," the stoic master said by way of greeting, his voice deep and mellifluous.

"Master," Coinneach said, rising with Yazid's help. "You honor me with your presence."

"Sit before you fall," the sword master told his student gently. He strode gracefully to the window and began to examine a sapphire-blue piece of cut glass with an uncharacteristic absent-minded air. Coinneach knew it to be affectation, as his master was anything but absent-minded.

Yazid helped him to sit once more and he waited respectfully for several moments, a stone of dread resting in his stomach. He sensed from Ashahl's posture that the man bore weighty news. His teacher was doing everything in his power to seem casual, but Coinneach noted the tension in the fist held tucked into the small of his master's back. He was a man of iron discipline, and a rigidly stoic demeanor. That fist, clenched so tightly that the knuckles whitened, belied an inner storm raging. Ashahl continued casually inspecting the blue bauble, turning it to catch the morning sun. Finally, Coinneach could bear the suspense no longer and asked, "Is there word from the Prince, master?"

Lifting his head and gazing across the lush gardens of the palace, Ashahl responded thickly without turning. "The Prince has decreed your banishment. You must leave this land. Forever."

Coinneach's head bowed and he leaned forward, placing his elbows on his knees as he absorbed the edict; the stone in his stomach turned into a black void that threatened to swallow him. He had been expecting this, or worse, but had desperately hoped Ashahl might persuade the Prince to allow him to stay and continue training. He had learned so much, and was on the cusp of understanding so much more. Yazid squeezed his shoulder in brotherly reassurance.

"I was able to convince him not to have you executed," said the short sword master in his rich voice, his words tight and clipped.

"How soon, my master?" Coinneach managed.

"There is a caravan departing tomorrow evening." Ashahl turned and looked meaningfully into his protégé's eyes. After a long moment, he turned and strode from the room, his fist still clenched tightly at his side.

"Here," Yazid said, wiping his brow with a brightly colored kerchief. "Let me help you up."

Coinneach paused before mounting his camel to take in the view, one last time. The fabled palace of the Silken Emperor. He shook his head in wonder at the twists of fate that had brought him here. The setting sun painted the white marble walls and pointed arches a brilliant red-orange as the evening birds that made their home in this oasis came alive.

"Will I ever see it again, Yazid, d'ye think?" Coinneach asked his friend quietly.

"Who knows the paths our lives will travel?" His friend responded. "Who could have ever predicted that you would see it even once? It is a wonder it has been your home these two years, I think."

"Aye," Coinneach said, smiling at Yazid. "True enough." He turned and gripped the saddle, preparing to mount.

Ashahl's voice stopped him. "Ajnabi, a moment." Turning, he saw the sword master striding toward him across the manicured gardens.

"Saydaa," Coinneach said, placing his hand over his heart and bowing deeply as his teacher approached with three attendants trailing after him, each carrying silk-wrapped bundles.

"Is all in readiness for your departure?" Ashahl asked formally.

"Yes, my master," Coinneach said, glancing at the pack camel that Yazid had just finished loading. "We depart with the sunset."

"Good, good," his teacher affirmed stiffly. He was a man who was uneasy showing emotion. In the two years that Coinneach had studied with him, he could count on one hand the number of times he had seen the man smile, and only once had he heard him raise his voice in anger.

"I have some things which must accompany you," his teacher said, breaking the awkwardness.

"Master, I…" Coinneach started to object, but was silenced by Ashahl's raised hand.

"You may examine them at your leisure as you travel. But there is one detail that has been overlooked."

Coinneach looked from his master to Yazid quizzically.

"It is customary," Ashahl said, taking a long, wrapped bundle from an attendant, "that when a student attains the rank of master, through training, trial, and ordeal, he is to be given a new name. And though your training here has been truncated, your mastery of the forms you have learned is clear."

Coinneach's eyes flew wide in surprise and he dropped to a knee.

"Though our Prince has decreed that these lands are forever forbidden to you," Ashahl continued, with ceremonial formality and in a clear voice, for all present to hear, "he has grudgingly accepted that you have earned the right to carry this blade. None can deny your skill—your mastery of the blade and the forms." His master unwrapped the bundle in his hands as he spoke, revealing the very sword that Coinneach had seized from the dead hand of the Prince's brother in the desert.

Nodding to Coinneach to stand, Ashahl presented the elegant weapon to him, the curls of its intricate handguard and the scallops along its blade glinting orange in the rays of the setting desert sun.

"No longer will you bear the name Coinneach MacLir. From this day forward, you shall be known as Corvus Corax, the Raven, both the harbinger of death, and the messenger of the ancestors.."

Coinneach, now Corvus, looked from the beautiful weapon in his hands to his master, whose eyes were moist.

"May the Ancestors guide you in all things, my friend," Ashahl whispered.

Chapter 1

Most men dreaded standing in the shield wall—the cries of anger and pain, the smells of sweat, piss, blood, and shit overwhelming the senses in the tight, breathless scrum of bodies as feet stumbled on the rising mound of the fallen and dead. The screams of the injured blended into a horrific cacophony of human suffering that seemed to linger in the ears for months after battle. Blade movement was restricted in the press of bodies, limited to only short thrusts and jabs over and beneath one's shield. Indeed, most men described the shield wall as utter hell, glad to have survived it but praying never to have to enter one again. But Corvus Corax was not most men. Corvus Corax, the Raven, né Coinneach MacLir, reveled in it with a deep, soaring euphoria that seemed to give him strength and stamina beyond expectation. Those who knew him and fought alongside him told of the signs—the grim, determined battle grin that came upon him, the keening song, so terrifying and fascinating to hear—and they spoke in tones of awe at his deadly prowess. Though he was a man who yearned and fought for peace, in his most honest moments of self-reflection, he was shamed to admit that there was no place he felt so alive as he did in the clutch of battle.

— *The Chronicles of Corvus*
as told by Piper the Bard

569 HR
The Glenfolk region of the Green Mount

Corvus

Over two weeks of marching and fighting, the two battles and countless skirmishes had gone well strategically for Corvus and for the allied forces of the Green Mount, over which he had command. But the cost had been high. Of the two thousand members of the fyrd he had led to join with the armies of the White Cleft and the Glenfolk, over eight hundred had been killed or wounded. The armies of his allies had suffered similar casualties, and though the enemy had been bloodied, they were still able to field over fifteen hundred wild barbarians, and with their backs against the merciless and raging Gomul River, he knew the fierce Barbárs would fight like cornered wolves. But he also knew he had to end this here. The enemy force had invaded the Green Mount with just over three thousand warriors near Midsummer, and had quickly cut a rapacious swath through the southern foothills, burning and pillaging as they went. They seemed intent on moving quickly, pausing only for a few days before the fortified town of Esper, King Mannon's seat, before choosing to eschew a lengthy siege and instead continuing northwestward toward the High Valley, the large unincorporated region of farming communities in which Corvus had made his home. Since returning from Asland, he had built a house high on a rise overlooking the cliffs and moors. It was a sturdy home built of expensive quarried granite blocks, imported walnut bannisters, and oaken stairs. Though the house had many appointments that were beyond the means of others in the village of Dóchas, it was not ostentatious; it was comfortable, solid, and tasteful. Here, Corvus had married his wife Greer and had two sons, whom he had raised with the help of his Aslene friend Yazid after Greer had died. Despite the hole left by her death, it had become a home filled with laughter, story, and song. The villages and towns of the High Valley would be unprotected if the allied forces allowed the enemy to get past them this day. He shuddered to think of that cost.

A Young Glenfolk Soldier

The young soldier stumbled and swore under his breath. He glanced back accusingly at the large root that had caught his foot, and scratched at his thin beard, chasing a louse.

"You'll learn to pick up yer feet, lad," Alasdair told him with a wry smile from his position in the ranks. "Now, step up before the sergeant sees ye."

The young soldier hurried his pace and glanced at the older man marching alongside him. He liked Alasdair. Unlike so many of the veterans of the Glenfolk army, the older man had a gentler approach to coaching the new recruits. Rather than just ridiculing or barking orders at the youths struggling to pitch a tent or stay in file, Alasdair's comments usually came in the form of encouragement. He'd served King Mannon since he was a lad, and looking at his grizzled beard and the wrinkles by his eyes, the young man could only assume that had been a long, long time.

The young soldier was about to ask Alasdair something when three men on horseback thundered past their line, startling him. The three riders mounted a small rise on the side of the road and reined in to survey the passing armies and, no doubt, confer out of the hearing of the common soldiers. He recognized King Mannon as one of the three, his bearlike stature and dark hair and beard were distinctive, but the other two were unknown to him. One of the men bore a golden circlet on his brow, a fine flowing scarlet cape, and had a bold, red beard that covered his throat. He assumed that would be King Fergus of the White Cleft. The third man, who seemed to carry himself so assuredly and rode a dappled gray stallion in the lead of the two monarchs, was dressed simply. He wore all black with breeches and boots—a woolen shirt with long sleeves, over which he wore a fitted black leather doublet. He was not overly large, but from a glance, one could tell he was extremely fit and rode with a masterful touch, as though born to the saddle. He was bald, with a tightly trimmed dark beard, just beginning to gray. But what struck the lad most about him was his dark countenance. The man had piercing, intelligent eyes and a brow that the lad's gram would have described as "stormy." Instead of a great sword strapped to his back in the Highlander fashion, he bore a curved blade at his hip with an ornate handguard that shone in the afternoon sun. The style of the sword was unfamiliar to the youth.

"Who's that on the dappled horse, yonder?" the youth asked Alasdair.

"That there?" Alasdair replied with a light laugh. "Why, that's Himself, lad. Corvus Corax."

"Really?" The youth couldn't stop staring, open-mouthed, as they neared the rise on which the commanders stood.

"'Tis true," the veteran affirmed.

As they marched past the rise, the lad's head finally turned forward once more. But the older man must have noticed the quizzical look on his face.

"Ask your question," Alasdair offered gently.

"'Tis a strange name, isn't it?" the boy mused. "Corvus Corax. I've ne'er heard the like."

"Aye, 'tis," the older man agreed. "From a long dead language, I heard. That of scholars, sages, and—some say—wizards."

"Really?" The youth glanced up at Alasdair in surprise. "What's it mean?"

"His name?" Alasdair clarified. "I'd think you'd know it by his banners with the great black bird. It means the Raven, lad. And 'tis true, the very sight of his banner can make even savage Barbárs soil themselves." He chuckled again.

"Oh..." The young soldier nodded thoughtfully before continuing. "I tho't he was bigger than that." The comment elicited a laugh from Alasdair. "I mean, dinna get me wrong, for he cuts a fine figure, but the stories I've heard…"

"Campfire tales are quick to grow to legend," Alasdair cautioned wryly. "But where he is concerned, muckle's the tale that's true, lad." The boy could hear the reverence in the older man's voice. "Ye'll ne'er see a deadlier swordsman on the battlefield than Corvus. Can be frightening at first, I'll warn ye."

"Sure?"

"Aye," Alasdair confirmed. "I've seen him single-handedly take doon a dozen men, all with nary a scratch. And as quick as I'm tellin' ye now."

"No!" The boy searched Alasdair's face to see if he was having him on, but there was no twinkle in the older man's blue-gray eyes. Instead, his mind seemed to have drifted into memory and when he spoke again, a quiet awe colored his tone.

"I fought my share of times in the shield wall," Alasdair said, "and I've come to know that there's no man I fear, in battle or brawl. They all die when you put a blade in 'em, no matter how great, strong, or savage they be. But that man… Och, lad, he fights like a divil. And 'tis said he has a sorcery of sorts, something mysterious he learned during his sojourn in faraway lands, long ago."

The boy stared at Alasdair, rapt, and hanging on his every word.

"I canna say if 'tis true or no, but right glad I am that he's *our* divil. I've never seen a man move like him, his blade weaving a web of blood and protection. The enemy canna touch him, sure."

"That wee blade?" the youth asked, incredulous. "It's curved and too thin! A great sword would cleave it in two! No?"

Alasdair chuckled. "That's the mistake every man makes when they take his measure." Then the veteran nodded, a look of grim respect on his face. "I've seen that blade take blows from axe, hammer, and great sword that would fell a tree, and come away with nary a mark on it. I'll tell ye true, lad, that sword has killed more men than ye can count. I dinna know if it be true or no, but I've heard that it was a great king's sword, forged from a fiery meteor that fell to earth in the distant past." He looked sidelong at the younger soldier and shrugged. "Who knows? But I can say that it is a named sword."

"Aye? And what's the name?"

"Raven's Tooth," Alasdair said, grimly. "Pray to Ilian that you ne'er have to face it in anger."

Corvus

Corvus and his son, Cailean, rose before dawn to begin their preparations for battle. Before putting on their armor, they knelt, prayed, and burned an offering at the small altar in Corvus' tent. The Highlanders honored a variety of gods—some looked to Feryn, goddess of luck, some to the one-armed god, Nuada, whose willing sacrifice reminded the people of a balance in all things, and some looked to Cruim the Clever to help solve their problems with a clear mind. Most revered was Ilian of the Golden Hand, the noble and chivalrous patriarch of their pantheon. Though it must be said that on a day of battle, all feared and gave homage to the hand of Fel the Reaper. The grim god of death was capricious and hungry and knew no favorites. He had long ago turned against the other five gods. He would exploit any weakness or opening if it meant wholesale slaughter. Corvus and Cailean dutifully honored Ilian, in their family's tradition, burning sacred herbs in a small brazier and saying the ancient words to invoke his wisdom and ask his blessings and protection. In the red glow of the brazier, Corvus looked across the altar at his son, and swelled with pride as he watched him dutifully recite the prayers of his ancestors. Then, as all Highland warriors did on a day of battle, they lit the black candle, touched the brass charms on the altar, and begged Fel's mercy in the coming conflict. Corvus sat back on his heels, having completed his supplications to the dark god, and watched as Cailean completed his. The boy was only fifteen, unbearded, and yet he had already earned the respect of his peers for his courage and his prowess with a blade. With moist eyes, Corvus uttered one more silent entreaty to Manu, mother goddess and wife of Ilian, asking her to watch over his son. *Keep him safe, Mother. Love him as I do, for his heart is pure.* Opening his eyes, he nodded to Cailean to extinguish the candle and prepare for the day.

Corvus' knees creaked as he rose from the floor, earning a derisive chuckle from Yazid, who had completed his prayers in the Aslene tradition and had been quietly watching Corvus and Cailean finish theirs. In response to his friend's chortle, Corvus shot him a warning look and raised a finger, saying, "Not a word from you, old man."

The jovial Aslene raised his hands in mock surrender.

As they dressed for battle, Yazid asked, "Which banners shall we fly today? The Raven or the solid black?"

Corvus answered with a question. "Did you see what they did to those poor people at Cairgean? Two thousand slaughtered." It would be the black banners today—no mercy, no surrender.

Yazid nodded in understanding.

Corvus arrayed his fyrd in the critical center beneath solid black banners while the stalwart Mannon, King of the Glenfolk, took the southernmost flank. With green and gold banners flapping defiantly, Mannon expertly arranged his troops in a wide arc to protect against a possible ambush from the thick woods in the hills that bounded the southern edge of the valley. King Fergus of the White Cleft took the northern flank, arranging his forces up against a deep ravine known as the Burn of Woe; his garish yellow-and-red checkered banners were positioned in a proud line with their leftmost edge abutting the nearly sheer drop.

Having donned his armor, Corvus strapped on his shield, stepped out of the tent into the pre-dawn chill, and prepared to join the men and women of his fyrd. The traditional great swords carried by most Highlanders were useless in the crush of the shield wall and remained in their sheaths, strapped to the warriors' backs, while the shorter, lighter seax did its deadly work. Unlike his fellows—each carrying two swords, both a great sword and the smaller seax—Corvus carried but one: the prized cutlass presented to him by his master, Ashahl, decades earlier. As he drew Raven's Tooth, he paused to listen to its characteristic bell-like ring. With a smile, he indulged in his pre-battle ritual of examining the blade that had become so familiar and comfortable to him over a score of years. The intricate handguard and the graceful sweep of the still razor-sharp sword, scalloped along its false edge, were so unlike the weapons of Daffyd. He remembered well the raucous ribbing and teasing he received when first he had showed it to his fellow Highlanders upon his long-awaited return from the deserts of Asland.

"Only a dafty would fight with a wee, curved lady's blade like that!"

"Somethin's stuck in me geggy! Ho there, can I use yer wee blade to peck my teeth?"

But in bout after bout against men wielding traditional Highland weapons in villages and towns throughout the High Valley, he had prevailed, and his blade's speed and maneuverability earned first the grudging acceptance of the Highlanders, and eventually their admiration. Though it was only two fingers wide at its thickest—as opposed to the four-finger width of a great sword—it was made of a steel unlike anything in his homeland, well balanced, fast, and graceful, yet strong enough to parry the fiercest blows from hammer, sword, or axe. Earning the right to wield it had cost him much blood, suffering, and months of recuperation, but despite these difficulties, the blade had proven to be a treasure worth the cost.

He glanced at the sky. A light rain was falling. *No archers today, strings will be wet,* Corvus thought ruefully. *'Twill be butcher's work, then.* Looking at the now forming shield wall before him, his face took on its customary battle grin as he moved through the ranks of his troops and anticipated the grisly work ahead.

"Right then, Niall," he called, as he gently pushed his way through the throng, working his way to the front line. "You've got my right side today, eh?"

"Sure and I do, Corvus," responded a grinning young man with crooked teeth and dark, unkempt hair, clapping his hand on his leader's shoulder proudly. "'Tis my pleasure!"

"And Quinn, you've my left?" Corvus asked Niall's grinning brother, who nodded proudly.

"Well, aren't I just the rose among the thorns, then, eh?" Corvus laughed and slapped Quinn's shield fondly.

Stepping out in front of the line and turning to face the troops, he flashed a quick smile and wink at Yazid, who was adjusting his helmet; it never seemed to fit his large head. The corpulent man always looked haphazard when he dressed for battle—leather chest guard, gorget, and greaves strapped over his customary white Aslene robe, which seemed to blouse from every joint like an overstuffed sausage bursting from its skin. But regardless of his almost comical appearance, there was no man Corvus would rather have at his back in a fight. Yazid carried no sword, his skills being primarily with polearm weapons: staffs, spears, halberds, guisarmes, and the like. He would stand in his usual position, directly behind Corvus, thrusting his spear with deadly precision over his friend's shield into the faces of the enemy. They were a lethal pair in battle, each sensing the other's movements and rhythms and instinctively reacting, providing cover and openings wordlessly. It was said among the fyrd, that as long as he had Raven's Tooth in hand, and Yazid at his back, nothing could stop them.

Corvus paused and looked over the expectant faces of the men and women he had trained. So many—like Cailean—were young, barely old enough to stand in the wall. Some were still nursing wounds from the previous battles and skirmishes, but insisted bravely that they were still fit for combat. Some were old and long of tooth and should rightfully have been quietly tending their lambs on their farms. He knew the name of each and every one, what village they lived in, their occupation. He loved them all, and would fight like the devil for and with them, and he knew they felt the same.

Unlike the professional soldiers of the Glenfolk, Midlands, or the White Cleft, the fyrd was comprised of farmers, coopers, blacksmiths, and potters that rose to fight for the common defense. In other countries, fyrds were generally less well trained and equipped, and were usually considered only supplemental or support troops to back up the professional soldiers. Often, a fyrd was simply sent into battle as bodies to absorb arrows or broaden the battle lines, while the soldiers did the real fighting. In the High Valley, however, the fyrd under the tutelage of Corvus and Yazid had become a treasured military force that had proven its value repeatedly over the past twenty years. This hadn't happened by accident. As a youth, Corvus had seen his people humiliated and butchered on battlefields facing the Mardish, and ever since, it had been his dream to create an effective defensive force fielded by the High Valley. In the long nights of their captivity among the dreaded corsairs of the Mirror Sea, he had spoken to his friend of this dream. He had found in Yazid not just a sympathetic ear, but a spirited and gifted partner with significant talents in planning, training, and pedagogy and a natural empathy that seemed to transcend cultural and national boundaries.

"People are all alike," Yazid had said one night. "They wish for simple things: respect, pride, and peace. They will sacrifice the third if you can guarantee the first two. And to somehow give them all three would make you a god among men, I think."

The young Corvus discussing these dreams with his friend knew with the fervor of youth that his hard-earned martial lessons in the many battles he had seen in the deserts of Asland, coupled with the extensive and powerful training at the hands of Ashahl—sword master to the Silken Emperor himself—had prepared him to lead effectively. But how, he had wondered, could he inspire the disparate villages and communities of the High Valley to mount an effective fyrd? Yazid had seemed to understand, instinctively, what Corvus desired to accomplish and the two of them, each encouraged and inspired by the other's insights, spent those long nights dreaming together, planning how—if ever they could escape their captors—to inspire an entire region and forge a fighting force from farmers and shepherds.

When eventually they won their freedom, and more, from the corsairs, they spent most nights on their months-long journey back to Corvus' homeland around their campfire, scheming and talking for hours. Though Yazid had never been to the Green Mount and didn't know its people or their culture, his innate understanding of human nature, coupled with an uncanny ability to plan for the long game, convinced Corvus that it could be possible.

Upon their return to Dóchas, Corvus and Yazid had set their plan into motion. It didn't happen in weeks or even months. But over years of continuous effort, each encouraging the other when spirits flagged, they began to see results and all of their careful planning and labors started to yield fruit. It had taken years of work and training, teaching recalcitrant weavers and masons how to hold a sword, demonstrating proper stances, balance, and so much more. There was travel to distant communities, spirited discussions and arguments with stubborn locals, and more than a few bouts and duels to prove their individual mettle. But, step by step, progress was made. All of this was helped by the significant amount of silver and gold that Corvus had spent commissioning the creation of weapons and armor from smiths, wagons from wainwrights, barrels from coopers, as well as tents and other materiel that an army would need. He had returned from his adventures among the corsairs laden with chests of treasure, and he intended to use the riches he and Yazid had accrued for the good of the fyrd. His largesse had encouraged the ofttimes stubborn Highlanders to hear him out, and between his skills and clear vision—and Yazid's disarming charm and affable nature—the communities of the High Valley had been convinced one by one of the importance of this great project. The fyrd had started to take shape. Not the fyrd of old, the desultory, frightened amateur warriors that had been so shamed by the Mardish. No, a new fyrd, a proud fyrd. One capable of standing side by side with the professional soldiers of the White Cleft or Midlands, or even those of the mighty Glenfolk.

Respect. Pride. Peace. Yazid's three cornerstones. Corvus and Yazid had promised them the first two, and through those, they could earn the third, but only if they worked hard, trained tirelessly, and never forgot what it meant to be from the High Valley. In time, this new force under Corvus' command had earned a place of respect among the allied commanders, standing defiantly against the Barbárs, even when the soldiers of the Midlands broke and ran, and eventually finding their uncontested position in the center of the line, under Corvus' Raven banner.

It had become tradition that once the snow had melted, each village yielded up a number of men and women to train for three continuous days every two weeks with Corvus and Yazid. The drill days were intensive and included everything from foundational weapons skills to working together in formation to basic soldiering—pitching a tent, setting defensive perimeters, guard duties, etc. These citizen-soldiers took growing pride in their skills and continued training with their fellows in their home communities between drill days. It soon became a mark of honor for a village to have a member of their community selected to stand in the front line of the fyrd. Some villages boasted more than a dozen, and universally the people of the High Valley came to understand the importance of martial excellence and value it highly. The fact that the fyrd now enjoyed the place of pride at the center of the line of the Green Mount forces was a flower in the bonnet of the people of the High Valley, and not one that they would readily yield. Respect. Pride. Peace. Corvus and Yazid had helped them find the first two, and now they fought for the third.

With a breath, Corvus returned from his reverie and a hush quickly fell over the fyrd—a sign of the silent bond they shared with their commander. He addressed his troops.

"'Twill be grim work we do today, my friends," Corvus shouted. "Some of you have not stood in the wall before, having just been moved up from the reserves. And some are old, grizzled veterans like Ogilhinn here… and myself, to be fair." There was laughter from the men as Ogilhinn took feigned umbrage at the comment. "But fear not, friends," Corvus continued. "Your training is sound. We are highlanders! And these bastards need a sound thrashing! This ends here, today, with the death of every loupin' Barbár that dares set foot in our valley! Today, we send a message to all: The Green Mount will not be conquered! And should you dare to invade our lands, you may be lucky enough to face the Glenfolk or the White Cleft or the Midlanders, but pray to the gods you dinna face the fyrd of the High Valley!"

A roar went up from the entire fyrd as his forces banged their swords on their shields and shouted their defiance to the enemy, each striving to be heard over the tumult. Corvus joined the sound, smacking Raven's Tooth against his shield over and again. When the clamor finally died down, he spoke in a more businesslike tone, though still using his battlefield voice.

"Right, let's form up. Dinna forget yer training!"

"May the Ancestors be with us," Yazid said softly as he moved into position behind Corvus, placing his left hand on his friend's shoulder and hefting his spear in his right.

The Barbárs formed up some hundred yards from the Highlander line, their shields creating a wall similar to that of the allies. As in his earlier encounters with these barbarians, Corvus was struck by the unusual uniformity of their coloring. The bare-chested warriors—male and female—had pale, almost translucent, skin which was tattooed in elaborate, swirling patterns. Their eyes were so dark as to seem almost black, and they wore their near-white hair in long, knotted ropes adorned with beads, trinkets, and human bones. Something in their diet—or perhaps it was an affectation they adopted for battle—dyed the insides of their mouths black, and the savage creatures waggled their tongues before a fight, rolled their eyes wildly, and howled like dogs to intimidate their enemies. Given the slope of the land and the positioning of the enemy troops, Corvus couldn't see much beyond the enemy's front ranks. Something seemed off to him, yet he couldn't discern what it was that had him uneasy. He needed a better vantage point to see the disposition of the Barbár troops, but he knew he didn't have time to leave the front of the fyrd to climb the steep hillside on the southern flank and read the battlefield from its heights.

The Eagle sees far, and climbs above obstructions.

The words of his teacher came back to him, just as they had many times over the decades. *Eagle form*. One of the twelve secret forms of the Aslene martial mystics. Though he had only worked with the revered sword master to the Silken Emperor for two years, those years had been filled with endless, exhausting days of intense, demanding, and rigorous discipline that had shaped the rest of Corvus' life. He remembered the first time he saw a demonstration of Eagle form from one of the masters, and how taken he had been with the power and elegance of it—the unexpected angles of attack, the manipulation of an enemy's balance, the intrinsic gathering and unleashing of one's ruhon, or spirit. This was a form only learned after many years of training, demanding explosive power and balance, unparalleled grace and fluidity. Even then, very few ever unlocked the more arcane gift of the form, Longsight. Corvus had humbly begged his master to introduce him to the form and its mysteries. Ashahl had cautioned him that Eagle form was something only masters could attain, and usually only after a lifetime of intense work and practice. Corvus' training to that point had been focused on the first four of the twelve forms—Willow, Badger, Mountain, and Ocean—and to study Eagle would be to learn a form out of order, which would be unheard of. But something in the earnestness of Corvus' entreaties, perhaps coupled with his unique aptitude, had persuaded Ashahl, and the teacher had eventually relented. Determined to prove his worthiness to his master, Corvus would regularly stay hours into the night, practicing the nuances of this new form in the training ring after a day full of the routine of drills in the other forms. He recalled how amazed Master Ashahl had been at his student's almost instinctive grasp of the new postures, strikes, and blocks. The great master had been dumbfounded when this young, gifted foreigner had been able to access Longsight after only a few weeks of introduction to the form. Sadly, Corvus' training with Ashahl was cut short just as he was beginning to make great progress in the ways of the Eagle. Separated from his master's tutelage, Corvus' skills with the form had stalled, yet he still made time each day to meditatively move through what he had learned of it. Surprisingly, he was still able to achieve Longsight, albeit for only brief periods which were followed by disorientation and dizziness.

He shifted his weight onto his left foot, and pulled his right foot back, toes just touching the ground. He quieted his mind, opened his arms, swelled his chest and—with a breath—felt the world drop away beneath him. The clamor and tension of his fellows faded as Corvus' breath took on the rhythm of the wingbeats of a great bird of prey rising from a strike. He once more felt the familiar sense of soaring euphoria as his vision gained new perspective. He looked down upon the battlefield from a great height, his eyes sharpening to take in distant particulars. He could make out details in the enemy line, seeing deep into their ranks. The center of the Barbár formation looked strong, as he predicted, but for some reason, they seemed to be concentrating their forces on Fergus' side. The enemy troops facing Mannon looked thin, barely strong enough to hold for long. *He means to try to turn us on the north... but why would he assume weakness there?*

Corvus knew he could only maintain this Longsight for a few heartbeats, so he quickly sought out the enemy commander, focusing on him. Finding their leader was not difficult as the Barbár chief sat astride a gray-and-white dappled stallion positioned beneath a huge wooden banner pole with a crossbar, on a small rise at the rear of his forces. The banner pole was adorned with a large, black ram's skull with great curling horns, tufts of fur clinging to still-rotting flesh on its face. Strings of human skulls dangled from the cross bars beside it. The commander himself was tall, wiry, and lean, a full head taller than the tallest man in Corvus' ranks. Despite his slender build, he bore a great, double-headed axe strapped to his back. There was a scar on the left side of his face that ran from just above his left eyebrow, down through a milky-white eye all the way to his jawline. The man seemed agitated about something on the northern flank, and was in a heated discussion with an advisor about it, pointing and shouting. Corvus watched, curious, as the enemy leader dispatched runners to ferry messages along his line, the majority of whom seemed focused on the Barbár right—the northern flank. *What is he so fascinated by to the north?*

Suspecting some flaw or weakness in the White Cleft position, Corvus had started to turn his focus toward Fergus' line when his concentration finally failed and suddenly, with a disorienting sense of falling, he was back in the ranks with his men. He blinked his eyes several times and had to concentrate firmly on the ground beneath his feet for a dozen or more heartbeats to ward off the nausea that always followed his use of Longsight.

Sensing that time was short before the opposing forces converged, Corvus called over his shoulder to his son, who stood several rows back among the fyrd.

"Here, Da," Cailean responded promptly. Though only fifteen summers old, he was broad of shoulder and tall, well-muscled for his age. He was, as always, eager to please his father, and his clear blue eyes shone from beneath his helmet.

"Gather the reserves, and position them behind Fergus' line," Corvus commanded.

"But…" Cailean began.

Corvus cut him off. "No time to argue, boy. Do it now!"

He regretted taking such a peremptory tone with Cailean. He knew his son would assume that he was pulling him out of the fight, putting him with the reserves to protect him. But in truth, Cailean had a natural gift for command, and the rest of the fyrd respected him, despite his youth. Corvus knew he could rely on his son to follow the order and position the reserves as requested. He hoped the maneuver would prove sufficient to counter whatever stratagem the enemy had in mind, but there was no time left to worry about the enemy's machinations. The armies were preparing to move.

Corvus looked to the left edge of the Highlander line, where he caught the eye of King Fergus, his red beard jutting proudly from beneath his helmet. The two men nodded at each other in grim understanding of what lay ahead. Turning to his right, Corvus repeated the process with King Mannon. Looking back to their foe, Corvus silently settled into the quiet place he occupied before battle. Breathing deeply to shake off the last of the nausea, he concentrated on the soft breeze blowing down the mountains to his right, scented with heather and gorse. Despite the cacophony of the enemy's howls and jeers, he allowed himself to become aware of the roar of the mighty Gomul to his left. Shifting his weight, he felt the spongy response of the peaty soil beneath his boots. This was *his* land, *his* home, *his* people. No enemy would conquer here, not while he lived.

A great horn sounded raggedly from the enemy lines, pulling him from his thoughts. He watched as the enemy began to advance. Cinching the strap of his helmet, Corvus turned to his banner carrier and shouted, "Right, let's to it then." From the rear of the fyrd, commands were shouted and rows of pipers began to skirl their dreaded battle songs defiantly, the unearthly sound echoing off the mountains. As one, the banners of the Glenfolk, the White Cleft, and the Raven dipped forward and the allied lines began to move. The Highlanders were marching to war.

It always seemed to take a lifetime to cross the final yards before the shields met. Corvus was again surprised by the discipline shown along the Barbár line. Given their appearance and behavior, it would be easy to dismiss them as unruly savages—dangerous, yes, but not a focused, military force. But over many battles, Corvus had learned to respect this enemy, despite his abiding hatred of them. Though brutish and wild in many ways, they understood warfare, and they were a foe to be reckoned with.

It took training and discipline for a shield wall not to break formation in the last rush before the opposing forces converged. Each side hoped to slam into the opposing wall with enough power to gain advantage, but if the line became ragged on the charge, the integrity of the shield wall would break down, and the line would crumble. It was in these last moments of convergence that the discipline and training of the troops proved critical. All too often, ill-trained, over-eager, or nervous soldiers rushed or lagged, causing the line to falter or become ragged with disastrous results. Corvus felt a surge of pride at the disciplined advance of the fyrd. Yazid seemed to feel it as well, for Corvus felt the hand on his shoulder give an encouraging squeeze. As the walls converged, Corvus' vision misted red and he began to involuntarily keen his battle song. With a crash that thundered and echoed from the surrounding mountains, the lines came together and Corvus began his slaughter.

He was deep in his battle fugue, his eyes seeing red as his dark, wordless song of death emanated from him. Raven's Tooth seemed to move of its own accord, finding openings in the legs, groins, and stomachs of his opponents as Yazid thrust his deadly spear over Corvus' shoulder at their faces and shoulders with almost surgical precision. Together, they butchered and felled enemy warriors almost as quickly as the Barbárs could fill the gap created by downed barbarians. With Yazid at his back and the two of them surrounded and supported by his fyrd, Corvus felt the years melt away from him. He was once more a force of nature.

Yazid's hand on Corvus' shoulder was a constant reassurance upon which he had come to rely. It told him wordlessly that his comrades were with him, and allowed him the indulgence of slipping deeply into his fugue, doing the bloody work at which he was so very skilled. But now there was a sudden difference in Yazid's grip on Corvus' shoulder. Urgent, demanding of his attention. Shaking himself out of his trance, he heard his friend shout, "Fergus' line is breaking!"

Signaling to Niall and Quinn to fill the gap and for Yazid to stay with the fyrd, Corvus pulled out of the front line, his men expertly flowing in around him, just as he had drilled them for countless hours. Forcing his way to the rear of the fyrd, Corvus quickly assessed the battlefield. There was indeed chaos on the northern flank, the checkered banners of the White Cleft falling as Fergus' well-ordered shield wall dissolved into a mob. A small force of Barbárs led by a handful of their dreaded Räuber shock troops, had somehow gotten behind the White Cleft soldiers and surprised them in their vulnerable rear. He stood for but a moment taking in the sweep of battle as the chaos turned to a rout. Fergus' desperate troops found themselves between the hammer of the warriors behind them and the anvil of the heavily reinforced enemy shield wall. In an instant, Corvus understood what he had seen with Longsight. The enemy had secretly positioned a strike force among the tangled thorns and sheer sides of the burn. *He must have positioned them in the dark of night,* he thought. Once battle had been joined, the enemy commander had sprung his trap, and his shock troops had roared out of the ravine and attacked the White Cleft soldiers from behind.

As Corvus had commanded, Cailean had positioned the fyrd reserves—a mixture of green recruits and those too wounded to stand in Corvus' primary force—directly behind the White Cleft. As Corvus watched, a great surge of Fergus' soldiers broke and flooded toward his son's position. Corvus had seen moments like this on many a battlefield. The routed troops, desperate for safety, would overwhelm the integrity of the reserve shield wall as they pushed their way into its ranks, and unless the pursuing enemy were slowed in their chase, they would fall upon the confused mass and destroy them all.

Cailean flashed a nervous glance in his father's direction and Corvus gave a quick hand sign, telling his son to form up the line quickly. Then the Raven strode with purpose toward the chaos, as if he alone could stop the rout and salvage the day. Something about the situation, the exhaustion, and the unexpected peril to his son and his beloved fyrd pushed him to the edge. He would not see his people—his boy—fall to these wild, arrogant invaders. Charging forward, Corvus wove through the fleeing White Cleft troops like a salmon swimming upstream. Instinctively he breathed in Badger form, a vicious and quick fighting style intended for encountering multiple foes, and the world around him slowed to a crawl. His eyes raced from one enemy to the next, sighting openings, vulnerabilities. Moving with surprising speed, he crashed single-handedly into the pursuing Barbár soldiers. He shed his shield as he rushed forward, drew his long knife in his left hand in addition to Raven's Tooth in his right, and waded into battle. He fought as the vicious badger—as Ashahl had taught him years before—spinning, slicing, ducking, spinning again, and thrusting. As quickly as he spotted a vulnerability, his blades followed, taking exposed knees, necks, arms; every opening was exploited.

Within moments, he left a score felled in his wake, dead or wounded. His mad, whirling attack so surprised the charging enemy that they actually paused in their pursuit of Fergus' fleeing men, buying the White Cleft troops the critical moments they needed to safely integrate with the Raven's reserves. Even the massive Räubers—the giant-like elite troops of the Barbárs—fell like wheat before him, shocking and immediately demoralizing the enemy's troops. But eventually, the bemused Barbárs surrounded the single crazed man, forming a wide circle with shields to stop his advance and prevent any further casualties from his whirling blades. Corvus paused, knowing that every second he commanded their attention was a critical moment in which the White Cleft troops could meld into the reserves. A spear was hurled at him from behind the protection of the shields. Still breathing in the form of Badger, Corvus watched the spear's slow movement through the air. It was a simple thing to avoid, and he batted it away with Raven's Tooth almost casually, his blade shattering the thick oaken haft as it passed. The Barbárs exchanged glances with one another, apparently in wonder at the preternatural skill and power of this madman. He stood alone, seemingly untouchable and unfazed by the hundreds who faced him. Corvus knew it was only their shock at the brazenness and early success of his attack that held them at bay. They could easily overwhelm him with sheer numbers, but he had to hold their attention a few moments more. Every second was critical.

"Come for me, you wild bastards!" he shouted at the enemy in defiance, his dark eyes glowering from beneath his helmet.

The circle of shields stood firm, muddy Barbár faces looking at him in much the way they would a trapped bear or a rabid wolf. Despite their numbers, they were chary of coming within reach of his whirling blades. His skilled eye noted their shifting feet, knuckles white on the grip of their weapons as each one rallied his courage to charge. Despite their numbers, none seemed eager to be the first to rush in against him. He noted a great Räuber's stance shift an instant before the brute threw another spear with enough force to impale a war horse, and once again with a casual movement and a defiant laugh, Corvus batted the hurled weapon aside. Silently he thanked Ashahl for the countless hours he had spent on the training grounds, avoiding and batting away the spears and javelins hurled at him.

Despite their clear trepidation, he could see in the stances of the enemy that a charge would come soon and they would rush him, ending his mad exploits. He only hoped he had given his son enough time to organize a new wall. With a whispered prayer to Ilian to protect this land, he lowered into Willow stance and prepared for the end. Just then, the reserve troops—with young Cailean leading them—crashed forward into the Barbár circle, seizing their attention away from Corvus. Looking quickly at the shield wall, he saw King Fergus standing shoulder to shoulder with the proud, grinning Cailean. The White Cleft monarch looked battered and bloody and had a nasty gash down the right side of his face, but he was holding his shield firm as his men slammed into the enemy warriors. The surprised Barbárs quickly began to pull back and form a new shield wall, facing the reserves. This allowed Corvus time to rejoin his troops, sheathe his long knife, and take a shield proffered by a terrified young recruit—who was all too happy to yield his armament to the legendary Raven and step toward the relative safety of the rear. Squeezing between his son and the wounded King, Corvus paused to say lightheartedly, "Cut yourself shaving, did you, Fergus?"

"Well," the red-headed monarch replied with a twinkle in his eye, "I was in a wee hurry. Couldn't let you have all the fun. Though I see your dance steps have improved!"

"Not much to do in the High Valley," Corvus responded with a wink, "but lay about, dance, and sing songs all day."

Fergus' face wrinkled into a broad, appreciative grin—which his bleeding wound caused him to immediately regret.

Now it was the Barbárs' turn to mill in confusion as they rushed to form a new wall. Without hesitation, Corvus raised his sword, and leading the charge, cried, "No mercy, today, lads! We fight for the Green Mount!"

As the line began to jog forward, he noted that the largest and most savage of the brutes had positioned himself directly in front of him. It was clear that the enemy warriors looked to this one as a leader, and trusted that if anyone could stop Corvus, he could. He was a Räuber, by the look of him. The brute stood nearly seven feet tall, with shoulders that seemed nearly as wide. He had a golden ring through his left nostril. His left arm held his shield, and with his right he held a long, curved, and barbed sword high above his head, point downward. The brute opened his mouth wide, wagging his black tongue defiantly as the distance closed between them. Corvus saw that his opponent planned to use his height to thrust downward over the shields as the crush of bodies came together. With the pressure of the mass of troops pushing from behind, Corvus knew his body would be momentarily pressed flat against his shield as the forces converged. A downward thrust from the brute at that moment would be lethal.

The waves are inexorable, irresistible.

In the midst of the charge, time seemed to stop as Corvus heard his master's voice from so long ago. He remembered the first time he had seen Ashahl demonstrate the power of Ocean form. He had stood in the center of the training ring, twenty students facing him in a group, four abreast and five deep. They were braced and standing firmly, arms on each other's backs ready to resist any force. After his explanation of the technique, Ashahl had begun moving through the form, his hands together and arms creating a circle that flowed and pulsed in a wavelike motion. Ashahl closed his eyes, and Corvus knew he was summoning and focusing his ruhon. His breathing and body fell into the rhythm of the waves, and he stepped toward the massed students, his feet sliding on the ground, drawing semicircles in the sand of the ring. On an exhalation, he suddenly sank more deeply into his battle crouch and extended the circle of his arms forward, hands still touching. Corvus remembered being amazed as the entire mass of martial trainees were shoved back as though by the force of a great wave. The front few ranks were knocked entirely off their feet, landing in a dazed, tangled mass on the ground, while those further back had staggered, off-balance, barely remaining upright. He had been equally surprised when months later, he found himself able to tap into that same power as he trained in Ocean form, first felling a single opponent, then two, then five as his ability to focus his ruhon increased. Since that day, Corvus had continued to practice Ocean form as part of his daily morning exercises, finding inner peace and balance in its graceful, slow movements. Over the years, he had become intimately familiar with the powerful sensation of drawing, focusing, and unleashing his ruhon. But he had never attempted it in battle; the rush and press of bodies would present a challenge greater than he had ever imagined. However, looking at the savage Räuber's blade—poised to lash downward in a fatal, unforgiving thrust—he knew he had no choice.

Time seemed to resume its normal flow as the opposing lines converged. Despite the turmoil of the rush of the wall, Corvus breathed into his center, his feet immediately changing their pattern from the uniform quick march of the line, to a semicircular glide. He felt the tension in his body release and he took on a peaceful, calm demeanor as he felt the familiar swell of the Ocean began to build within. Just as the shield walls came together with their characteristic thunderous crash—the bodies behind pressing in furiously to try to push the enemy off balance and create an opening—he released the pent-up wave of his ruhon, the circle of his arms pushing forward impossibly against the opposing masses. A shock wave of force seemed to emanate forward from him. His giant opponent staggered back several steps, momentarily off-balance, while those behind him—several ranks deep—were thrown back in disarray as the combined force of charging Highlanders and Corvus' ruhon washed over them. Still apparently hoping for his planned quick kill, the hulking brute thrust downward with his wicked blade, but his sword found only the open space in the center of the hoop of Corvus' arms.

Immediately releasing the force he held, Corvus allowed the pressure from behind to slam his body forward, trapping the enemy's blade between his torso and the back of his shield. In the same moment, Raven's Tooth found its opening and snaked upward between the enemy's displaced shields, through the yielding flesh of the tall warrior's exposed belly and directly into his heart. Like a bull struck with a pithing rod, the Räuber fell. The Barbárs behind were still struggling to regain their balance after the unexpected wave of force, and the hole in the line created by the giant's death provided the opening into which the charging Green Mount line surged. Within moments, the organization of the enemy wall devolved into chaos and the struggle turned into butchery as the fierce enemy was overrun by an amalgam of Corvus' green recruits and White Cleft soldiers who now fought to recapture their dignity after suffering the earlier rout.

Fel was fed that day until Death himself was sated.

In the aftermath of the battle, Corvus and Mannon stood together, conferring quietly and watching as Fergus' wounds were tended to nearby. Given the events of the day and the enormous expenditure of ruhon in the Ocean form attack, Corvus was beyond exhausted and he was thankful that standing was all that was required of him at the moment; he knew that if he sat down, he would likely pass out. Cailean was busy helping at the healers' tents with the fyrd wounded. Yazid was overseeing the fyrd as they worked with the other allied forces to round up and dispatch the enemy survivors. No mercy. No surrender.

Corvus looked up wearily as Niall and Quinn, accompanied by six other members of the fyrd, dragged forward a tall, lean Barbár who was thrashing and struggling against them. They threw him face down on the ground before the three leaders. The group of fyrd fighters looked pleased with themselves, and Corvus noted that Quinn was dragging a great double-headed axe in one hand. Niall wiped his brow, smearing mud and blood into his dark hair and said, "We found this knob hiding in a cleft by the river, whimpering like a wee barra and soilin' himself. I think he's the last of them."

Corvus nodded his thanks to the men as the Barbár raised himself to his knees and faced his captors defiantly. Corvus knew him instantly. That scar, the milky-white eye. This was the enemy commander. With a rush, the prisoner leapt to his feet and charged at Niall, attempting to seize his sword from its sheath. Before he could take two steps, however, Niall's brother clubbed him in the back of his head with the flat of the great axe, dropping the Barbár like a stone.

The two kings both looked to Corvus, deferring to his judgement as to the disposition of this sole survivor. A mixed crowd of soldiers from the three forces had now gathered around to see what was to become of this final Barbár. Corvus stood for a moment, staring at the prone man, just breathing and trying to muster whatever reserves of energy he had left. Finally, he shook his head and stepped forward over the unconscious man before raising his eyes to the gathered troops who were watching him expectantly.

"This is their commander," Corvus said, using his battlefield voice and holding his helmet in the crook of his left arm. "Rather than bravely lead his men in the line, he sat in the rear astride his pony. And when the battle went against him, he hid in fear, cowering and hoping he wouldna be found." Turning to King Mannon, he asked in a clear voice, "Who among your brave forces, King Mannon, would you single out for honor this day?"

Without hesitation, Mannon gestured to a stout female soldier with a freshly bandaged leg standing just behind him. "Morag fought as bravely as any man, felled three of their great brutes once the lines broke, and personally saved me when I found myself in difficulty."

Corvus placed his hand over his heart, acknowledging Morag, who returned the gesture.

"And you, King Fergus," Corvus said next, turning to the other monarch. "Who among your people would you single out for honor?"

"There are too many to count, my friend," Fergus said in a loud voice. "Every man and woman among the ranks of the White Cleft deserve my thanks this day." A cheer went up among the watching troops at the unexpected praise. Everyone present was aware that the White Cleft ranks had broken. Regardless of the cause, it was a shame they would bear. But Fergus' words seemed to go far to heal their collective wounded pride. "But if I were pressed to choose," the red-bearded King continued, "I would have to say that Aillig, my banner carrier, today earned the greatest honor." A hush fell over the assembled White Cleft troops as the other soldiers looked on, confused. "Sadly, he fell against the enemy. But to his last breath, I saw him struggle to hold our proud colors aloft."

"A worthy choice, my friend," Corvus said. "Does Aillig have any kin among your ranks?"

"H-here, my lord," said a sheepish voice as an unbearded youth stepped forward.

"Your name, lad?" Corvus asked gently.

"I am Brochan," the youth answered. Corvus couldn't tell if that was his name or if the young man was making a statement of his grief, for the name meant "broken." But he nodded to the boy.

"From the ranks of the fyrd," the Raven said loudly, "I would put forward all of you, for I have never been so proud of the men and women of the High Valley as I am today. In our tradition, I would ask the warriors of the fyrd to put forward someone deserving of honor before the sun sets. Talk amongst yourselves and decide whom you believe to be worthy."

He met the solemn eyes of the members of his troops. They seemed to understand the gravity of the moment, and he trusted that they would reach a consensus without his request devolving into a contest of popularity.

Corvus looked at the prone Barbár before him, and fought down rising nausea at what he knew he must say next. This was the aspect of command that he least enjoyed, yet he would not shirk from this, nor show the slightest hesitation to the people under his care. He was weary to the bone, and longed for nothing more than a hot meal, a strong drink, and his bedroll. But this was part and parcel of the robe of responsibility that he had figuratively chosen to wear when he had first set out on his mission with Yazid those many years earlier. *Come weal or woe,* he thought, *I must see it through.*

"We remember the poor souls of Cairgean," Corvus pronounced loudly, "that this monster slaughtered and raped. We remember the fallen members of our ranks, who died in the forest, or along the river near Gillock, or here today, protecting hearth and home." He used his foot to disdainfully roll the man's limp body onto its back. "This creature shall be gelded," he said, "blinded, and using his own axe, his hands and feet shall be removed. Then, at dawn tomorrow, he shall be cast, by the designated heroes of our three forces, from the heights of Monarch's Pass down into the Devil's Hoof where his corpse shall be a warning to the enemy that the Green Mount will never be their next conquest."

A grim and determined silence gripped the gathered forces. Corvus saw young Brochan's face blanch and, a moment later, watched as the fierce Morag stepped up to put a reassuring hand on the youth's shoulder.

"We take no joy in butchering this, or any man," Corvus continued, "but a firm message must be sent. This enemy must understand that our homes and our land is sacred. The black banners flew today, my friends. No mercy. No surrender."

"No mercy!" the allied troops shouted back as one. "No surrender!"

Looking to the group that had dragged the prisoner before him, Corvus said quietly, "See it done." Then, as he felt his knees almost buckle with fatigue, he nodded his respect to the two monarchs and left to find Cailean and Yazid, and hopefully wash away the disgust he felt at his own pronouncement by wrapping himself in the loving balm of family and sleep.

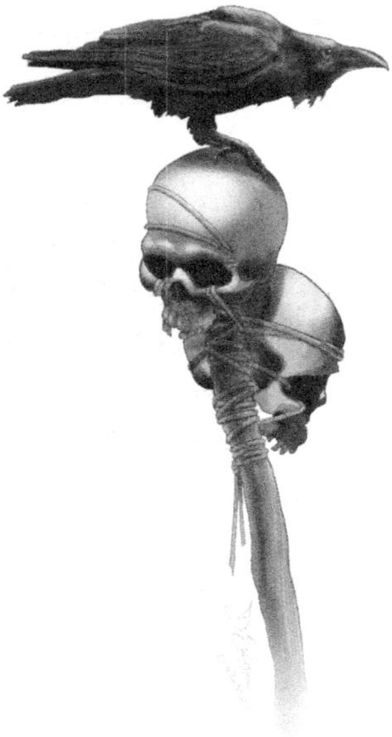

Chapter 2

The Great Steppes: the nearly unbounded grasslands that stretch through most of Orense and Ludo eastward, skirting the northern half of Angor and on to the western edge of the Free Territories and their delta. From this endless ocean of grasses sprung two great peoples, the Orensians and the Barbárs, as well as countless smaller independent crossbred tribes known collectively as the Szövetség. Dark of skin and hair with almond-shaped eyes and typically smaller stature, the Orensians were prone to forming large settlements, engaging in agriculture, animal husbandry, and trading, whereas the Barbárs were a tall, fair people—nearly albino in coloring—with a long, savage history of violence and cruelty, and a social pattern of raiding and stealing. In near-constant warfare, these two cultures, like steel and whetstone, sharpened and toughened one another over the generations. The nomadic Barbárs, raided and pillaged the settled trading society of the Orensians, while the Orensians, with their vast, well-organized military, sought to drive out their wilder siblings—though it must be said that internecine discord within the Orensian Kingdom, and a failure to unite the scattered tribes of the Szövetség, kept them from driving away the Barbárs for long generations. It was only under the leadership of King Fajsz that the Szövetség were finally brought to heel, spreading the hegemony of the Orensians well beyond the Ezüst River and establishing trading outposts near the Free Territories. But it was under his ambitious daughter, Queen Zsoka, that the Orensian Kingdom truly became an empire, filling most of the continent and finally driving the Barbárs eastward. For reasons unknown, Zsoka's reign was cut short by a palace coup and her cousin assumed the antler throne shortly into her reign.

— *A Brief History of Trade Across the Mirror Sea,*
by Nigel Fawnworth, DDL

573 HR - *Midwinter*
Isle of Vas, off the northwest coast of Orense

Zsoka

Empress Zsoka sat brooding before the enormous fire pit in her great hall. Her dark hair bore a streak of white from her right temple that her people called the "Mark of Mennykő," assuming her to have been touched by the storm god at birth. It was a fitting story, given the storms that customarily raged in her violet eyes. Despite the blaze before her, she felt chilled, and irritably adjusted the wolf-fur cloak about her shoulders. Is wasn't just the cold of the year's end; she always felt chilled on this godsforsaken island. Her breath steamed in clouds before her, and despite the thick, ermine gloves she wore, her fingers tingled with the cold. They always tingled with the cold. In the seven years since her imprisonment on the rugged Isle of Vas, she had never been warm.

Empress indeed, she thought darkly. *Empress of this miserable island, surrounded by sycophants and servants. Monarch of bears, wolves, mountain goats, and human chattel. Unable to return to what is rightfully mine.* She shook her head in disgust as she opened the scroll that had just arrived once more, squinting in the dim light to try to re-read the message.

"Bring more torches!" she snapped at the servants, who scrambled quickly to obey. It wouldn't make a difference, she knew. The black stone from which the chamber had been carved seemed to drink up all light, no matter how many torches, candles, and braziers they lit. Deep beneath the mountain known as Könyörtelen—"Merciless"—the rock of the chamber radiated a constant, bone-chilling cold that seeped into everything. Even hot meals cooled within moments of being served. Her attendants stood bundled in layers of wool and fur, until they appeared more bear-like than human.

"Úrasszony," a female attendant bearing two torches said with a curtsy, "the emissary's ship has landed. He should be here shortly."

Zsoka nodded acceptance and dismissed the girl with a curt wave of her hand.

Let us see what news he brings, she thought, scanning the scroll again, searching for any clue as to his intent.

"Do not waste our time, priest!" the Empress said harshly, dropping all pretense of the courtly diplomacy with which the audience had begun. The emissary from the foreign church had spouted no end of diplomatic drivel since the moment he arrived. Flattery. Gods how she hated flattery! Her foul mood was getting fouler with every word from this tedious man's lips. "If you have something of interest to say, then say it!"

"Of course, Majesty," the cleric responded smoothly. "Forgive me. I am a diplomat at heart and old habits die hard." He flashed a charming smile. "Let me get directly to the point, then," he continued. "You are aware of the legend of the Four Gates and their Lost Keys?"

"Myths and stories for children, yes," she said curtly. "Surely, you have not sailed all this way and braved the treacherous seas in winter to spout childish nonsense to me?"

"I assure you, Úrasszony," he said in a low voice, "this is no nonsense, and the news I bring could be of great interest to you."

She noted that he had used the honorific of her people when addressing her. He was indeed a diplomat at heart. The priest—he bore another title from their bizarre faith, "Archbishop"—inclined his head respectfully as he spoke, yet the gesture carried no feigned obsequiousness. It felt more like an invitation to something mysterious, something grand. Perhaps she would hear him out.

"Very well," she responded after a moment's further consideration. This man had a confidence, an almost regal bearing that she found strangely appealing. "Tell me your tale, and why it should be of interest to me." Turning to her attendants, she called for mulled wine to be served and a seat to be set near the fire for the archbishop.

Hours later, she sat alone, wrapped in her furs, staring into the now-dwindling fire. Her irritation was gone, replaced by an emotion she hadn't felt in seven long years. Hope. Hope for an escape from her exile. Hope for the chance to reclaim her birthright… and more. There was a warmth in the pit of her stomach like a dying ember fanned back to life, and she felt it radiating heat and purpose throughout her. That cinder warming her from within was the chance she finally saw for revenge. Revenge on those who had cursed her, dethroned her, exiled her, and ignored her lineage and rights. Revenge on her so-called allies who had turned their backs on her in her time of need. Yes, revenge on the very gods themselves!

"Shall I stoke the fire, Úrasszony?" her attendant asked, timidly. Shaking herself from her reverie, Zsoka, Empress of the Steppes, Lady Monarch of the Orensian People, Defender of the Silver Flame of the Szövetség, and eldest daughter of King Fajsz the Cruel, rose from her throne, shucking off the heavy fur cloak and ermine gloves for the first time in memory.

"No, I think not," she said, with a barely masked fervor in her voice. "It is warm enough here." And she stared once more into the heart of the flame, her violet eyes dancing with an inner fire brighter than the reflection of the blaze before her.

Chapter 3

Though many credit the rise and teachings of the heretic Amal min Alma' for the Great Schism, this is incorrect. For as we see clearly in the salt carvings of Baalu, the Schism was already some three hundred years past when min Alma' began luring his followers away from the teachings of the Faithful. In fact, little is written of min Alma'—or, perhaps more truthfully, little that was written has survived. For in the broad sweep of history, his impact upon the Convocation of the Faithful was minimal at best. He was but a momentary boil upon the lip of the True Faith, and once that boil was lanced, it left virtually no mark. Now, the Schism, however... that produced more long-lasting results, and we know next to nothing of its provenance. We cannot say, with certainty, the cause or origin of the Divide, and lacking any further evidence, we must assume that it developed as the Ancestors directed and intended. That what we are left with is what should be. Hikmat al'ajdad.

The contemporary records, you see, which presumably told of the development of the Divide—its political and theological antecedents, the theosophic tropes which underpinned such an iconoclastic tumult to the body faithful—were all lost to the winds of time, and those few documents that we believe did survive the passing of the Third Millenia, were lost between the conflagration at Waaladi and the concurrent subsuming of Atal. But whatever its genesis, the Schism tore asunder that shared duty—violently, one must suppose. It had been a shared responsibility for countless generations prior, a tree with two interwoven branches but only one root, you see. Indeed, as early as the seminal teachings of Harilal Tiana, in the pre-Dynastic epoch, the Subjection of the Five Eternal Constants was a subjection carried by all followers. But after the Schism, we see the rise of the different schools, the rise of the Path of the Divine Halls, mainly populated by female devotees, and the Way of the Hand, a predominantly male martial pursuit that developed in the mountainous southern regions. Of course, I am guilty of neglecting their many attendant denominations and bifurcations, but in my defense, discussing them thoroughly and with didactic authenticity would keep us here through the spring. And as much as I enjoy the dialectical discourse here amongst you, the festival season is upon us, and I, for one, am eager to return to my Zawja and her cinnamon rice. But as I said earlier, without clear documentation, we must assume that the outcome of the Great Division, the Schismatica, is as the Ancestors directed and that our path forward is true and appropriate. Hikmat al'ajdad!

— Excerpt from a lecture given by the Most Elevated Samal bin Malik at the University of Rawafid, in the fifteenth year of the reign of Her Most Serene Beneficence, Djamila aibna Rayan

574 HR - Last month of winter
Qat Province, Deserts of Asland

Mama

Priestess Warad of the Path of the Divine Halls, "Mama" to her votaries and the people of her village, sat alone by the dying embers of the small fire among the low, scrub covered hollows. The beginning of the year usually brought the heaviest rain, but tonight the sky above her was clear and the air was still. She had followed the caravan route northward until she reached the Camel's Humps, two small hillocks that resembled their namesake a day's walk from her home in the village of Jado, in the province of Qat. She had received a cryptic note that morning instructing her to come alone to this place before the moon set that evening, near midnight. At first, she had been tempted to discard the strange note, thinking it merely a clumsy attempt by bandits to lure her away from the safety of the village—though for what purpose she could not fathom, as she led a simple life, teaching and tending to the needs of her community. But the handwriting had been flowing, elegant, and somehow familiar, and the parchment on which it was written bore the subtle scents of sandalwood and cedar, immediately pulling her thoughts back through the years to a time of innocence, youthful passion, and stolen love.

It couldn't be, she thought. *But if he has need...*

"Nabila," said a deep, familiar voice from the darkness.

Mama gasped involuntarily and her eyes filled suddenly with unbidden tears as she raised a hand to her mouth. Though she intended to rise from the flat-topped stone upon which she sat, she found that she suddenly couldn't stand and her hands shook visibly as she nervously straightened her robes, searching the gloom at the edge of the firelight for the form of her visitor.

A figure stepped forward, wrapped in the humble traveling robes of a caravan trader. But nothing could disguise his natural elegance and grace, the almost regal bearing that made his small stature seem so magnificent. Despite the intervening decades, she recognized him in an instant.

"Ashahl," she whispered, her face melting into tears. She covered her eyes with a hand and sobbed quietly.

The Way of the Hand weapons master quickly set down the staff he was carrying and rushed to her side. Crouching gingerly, he wrapped her in his arms and rocked her gently, kissing her forehead as she whispered through her tears, "Habiy ya habia"—*My love, O my love*—over and over again.

When her tears had subsided, and the surreal nature of the meeting had finally begun to settle back into reality, she pulled away from him enough to search his eyes. There he was. Ashahl ben Qadir, sword master to the Silken Emperor himself. She noted the wrinkles that now feathered those beloved eyes and the white of his neatly trimmed beard, but it was still her beloved Ashahl, her habibi, the man for whom she had almost abandoned her calling to the priesthood. Seeing the intensity with which he gazed into her eyes, she nearly melted into tears once more. Instead, choosing to pull away and catch her breath, she busied herself with the struggling fire.

"I'm sure the need must be great for you to reach out to me, after all these years," she said, breaking the last meager twigs she had brought with her to feed the flame.

After a long pause, Ashahl sighed and spoke, his mellifluous voice rich with all the poetry and unnerving elegance she remembered from so long ago.

"I could spend a lifetime sitting here by this fire," he began softly, "sharing with you the countless times you have filled my thoughts, and still it would not be enough. The memories of you have been the lodestone of my life, guiding me and giving me strength, while cutting as deep as any blade. I have never forgotten you, though the Ancestors forced our paths apart."

"The Ancestors," she said with acid in her voice, "and your father."

Apparently realizing the futility of rehashing their painful parting, the sword master paused a moment before continuing. "Nabila," he said, his voice filled with a quiet urgency, "there is a terrible danger upon us all. I cannot explain now, as I fear I may have been followed. I need your help." Mama Warad turned back to look quizzically at Ashahl. Here was the only man in memory to have mastered all Aslene martial styles, sword master to the Emperor, and personal instructor to the Prince. A cupbearer among the Elevated of the Way—though from what she had heard, his refusal to write a concordance of his practices was what kept him from his final elevation to Water Giver. Though she had not seen him in over thirty years, his legendary reputation, military conquests, and martial accomplishments were famous throughout all of Asland, and beyond. He was easily the most self-assured man she had ever known, or could ever hope to know. The idea of him asking her for help with this clandestine urgency simply did not fit with the Ashahl she knew.

Clearly reading the confusion on her face, Ashahl continued. "Time is pressing, but suffice it to say that a great evil has arisen and is gathering its power in the north. If its progress is not slowed, it will wash across the sea and our people will be overrun."

"Has Holy Vision revealed this to you?" Mama asked in a quiet, businesslike tone. Being a priestess of the Divine Halls, she was well acquainted with visions, dreams, auguries, and other methods of guidance from the Ancestors. The Divine Ones had spoken to her and her protégés often and clearly, so the possibility of a mystical visitation or message was not a question, though she knew the followers of the Way of the Hand eschewed the divinatory arts, viewing them as parlor tricks and—even worse—delusional.

In lieu of an answer, he glanced over his shoulder momentarily at a distant sound before reaching back to fetch a large piece of what looked like driftwood. "The priests of the Temple believe this staff to be a Blessed Tool." At those words, Mama reflexively touched her right hand to her heart, then her lips, and then gestured to the sky, palm upward.

Ashahl waited for her to complete the brief obeisance before continuing with gravity, "I have stolen it from the Great Temple."

"Ashahl, no!" Mama exclaimed in shock.

The sword master held up a hand to restrain her protestations. "There are Great Mysteries in your tradition, as there are in mine," he said, with a firmness borne of a lifetime of martial study. "I know, beyond question, that this is no Blessed Tool of the Prophets, but is, in fact, one of the Lost Keys to the Wheel."

"How…?" she began, but he continued before she could complete her question.

"I am sorry, my love," he said, with an earnestness that pulled at her, "I simply don't have time to explain. You must take this staff to a land far away. To a place called the Gate of Eagles in the land of Daffyd, where you must search out my former student, Corvus Corax, the Raven."

"Daffyd is across the sea," she protested. "A journey of many moons and great hardship."

"I know, Nabila," he answered calmly. "And I would not ask this of you if there were any other way. But the urgency is great. You must bring this to the Raven by the Fall Equinox, or he will have no hope of slowing this great evil."

"That is eight moons," she calculated quickly, "to journey across the sea, find a single man in a foreign land, and deliver this staff to him." She was utterly bemused. "Ashahl, thirty years have passed between us. I haven't seen your face, nor heard your voice in all that time, and now... now you come to me and ask *this*?"

"My love." Ashahl sank to his knees and took both her hands in his, kissing them. When he looked up again, his eyes were filled with uncharacteristic tears. "There is so much I would do differently, if I were given the chance again. You are the only one I can trust with this. The palace is filled with vipers and scorpions, and I have sacrificed much to bring it this far." He released her hands, and cupped her face gently as a single tear tracked down his cheek. "I pray that we will be reunited in the Divine Halls, where I will devote my next life and all the lives that follow to you."

She leaned back in surprise at his reference to the Divine Halls and rebirth. These were anathema to the followers of the Way of the Hand. He could be put to death by the brothers of his order just for saying those words. He evidently saw her confusion at his remarks.

"You know me," he continued. "And you know I do not ask lightly. This is a task I cannot do, and it *must be done*. Even if you are successful, there is no assurance that it will be enough to stop, or even slow, the darkness. But if we are to have any hope, any prayer, the Key must find its way to Corvus."

Dozens of questions rushed through Mama's mind, each struggling for preeminence. She trusted his word that they didn't have time to discuss this; his occasional glances over his shoulder revealed how conscious he was of their limited time together. She searched those familiar eyes for answers, but knew that ultimately, it would have to be a decision based on her faith in him. He was right. Though it had been thirty years, she *knew* this man, and trusted him with the assurance of a soul bonded to his, beyond life itself. He had never asked anything of her. In truth, it was not in his nature to ask anything of anyone. Nor had she ever known him to be moved to tears, except for that fateful parting beneath the cypresses so long ago.

"Oh, Ashahl," she whispered, shaking her head slightly in amazement at the conclusion she was reaching. "Yes, of course. I will do this."

With a grim nod of appreciation, the sword master stood, wincing slightly as he did. He helped her to her feet, then kicked dirt onto the fire, extinguishing it, before whispering, "I am afraid we are out of time, my love. My pursuers will be here shortly. Take the Key, and go with my love and blessings. I'll hold them off."

A frisson of danger passed over Mama at his words, and she stooped to gather her satchel. It had been a long day of travel through the desert to this place, and now she faced a long night of hiking back to her village without rest. Having passed her fiftieth rain, her body was already rebelling at the thought of walking the miles back, but she dutifully accepted the unusual, tall staff from Ashahl without complaint.

With a resigned sigh, and a fond look back at her old love, she walked into the darkness.

Ashahl

He watched Nabila Warad walk away into the night. He noted that she bore a slight limp, and that the years of privation and religious service had not been kind to her. To her congregants and votaries, she was a powerful woman with a fierce and undeniable demeanor, yet he still saw in those eyes the sweet, innocent flower that had so captivated him all those years ago. For a long moment, he allowed himself to drift back to the jasmine-scented gardens and stolen moments of their love. Despite the cruelty of their parting, and the long intervening years, he had never loved another, choosing instead to devote himself to an ascetic and celibate life, dedicated to martial study. *So many regrets.*

With a sigh, he offered a silent prayer to the Ancestors that she might succeed in her quest. A sharp pain lanced through his side as he turned to the northeast, to face the pursuers he knew would arrive shortly, the cloaked assassins sent to stop him. Touching his side with his left hand, he could feel the blood that was oozing from his wound. The arrowhead was still buried within him, and he felt the jagged edge of the shaft where he had broken it off as he fled the palace, bearing the staff.

"Just one more fight, my Fathers," he whispered fervently as he drew his sword. "Let me prevail in but one more fight, and I will come home."

Chapter 4

The village of Dóchas was a small rural affair. Situated on the western edge of the High Valley region of the Green Mount, perched at the high southern end of the moors that abutted the famous west-facing seaside cliffs from which the settlement gained its name. The village itself, comprised of some five hundred souls, was a cluster of modest residences that were mostly wattle and daub, with solid foundations of stone. Toward the center of the village there was a busy market area with several small lanes—muddy paths, if truth be told—that wound among the various stalls and shops selling pottery, modest jewelry, produce, tallow candles, meat, and, most importantly, woolens. The weavers of Dóchas were famed for their soft woven goods and the subtle dyes that colored them, made from the plants and flowers that grew on the nearby hillsides.

The Circle of Grievance was located near the market, just in front of the Smithy. It was the dueling ground for settling scores and exacting justice. An unassuming fifteen-foot-diameter area of well-tended sawdust. It was a place of long-standing tradition. Every community throughout the High Valley had such a Circle, some larger, some smaller, the traditions stretching back to antiquity. It was as much an idea as a location. Any aggrieved party could call out another to the Circle and know that their fight would be a fair one.

No one could interfere with a duel in the Circle. It was sacrosanct. Others could watch, but none could violate the ring once a duel began.

– *The Chronicles of Corvus* as told by Piper the Bard

574 HR - First month of summer
(on what would thereafter be known as "The Day of the Seven")
Dóchas, The High Valley region of the Green Mount

Corvus

Corvus was shirtless and sweating in the garden behind the stone house, working through his morning routine, when Cailean turned the corner, his face flushed and a look of alarm in his eyes.

"Da, come quick," the breathless young man said. "It's Dallin."

Corvus didn't pause to ask what the nature of the problem was. Dóchas was not a large village and Corvus felt close to everyone in it, but Dallin was like family. Since childhood, she had been the very closest friend of his younger son, Ligulf. Their gentle and lasting bond had shaped both of them for the better. Li seemed to find in her a confidante and trusted ally as he had struggled his way through the difficult time of his puberty, while Dallin seemed never to tire of his quick wit or his beautiful voice and clever skill on the cittern, pipe, and drum. The two had been nearly inseparable since their early years. Corvus had fond memories of them as children bounding together into the stone house to grab a quick snack before heading into the fields on some adventure or another, Li's high laughter teasing Dallin's playful outrage. As young teens, they had carried their loads of laundry down to the river together to do their chores, and Corvus had invited Dallin, Kamdyn, and Dallin's father Lundy to dinner at their house many times, before Lundy's passing—convivial dinners filled with gentle laughter and light gossip. Over the years, Corvus had come to regard the girl as a daughter or niece.

No natal day or high holiday would pass without him presenting Dallin with a gift, like a true daughter.

Grabbing his shirt, he told his son to lead the way and the two dashed to the Moor, where they found Davonna and Kamdyn, Dallin's mother, kneeling over the girl's prone form. Her body was covered with the torn and soiled remnants of her dress and a shawl Corvus assumed came from Kamdyn. A small cluster of three or four concerned villagers stood nearby, shading the girl's face from the bright sun. *Oh Gods, no! Not Dallin!* Rushing into the cluster, Corvus took in the horror of the scene quickly. Dallin lay on her back. The sweet girl was bloody and sobbing, having been ravaged by some bastard.

Who would do this? Here in Dóchas? Though in his heart he already knew the answer.

Ten days ago, a group of traveling traders had rolled their wagon into the village. The strangers—a group of six men, all under the age of thirty—claiming to hail from the town of Plockton, situated in the far northeast of the Kingdom of the White Cleft, and had set up a merchant stall on the southern end of the market row, selling sundry goods. As was customary, Corvus and Yazid had accompanied Davonna, the village leader, and her husband Toren, as she greeted the newcomers and asked their business. A gangly young man with greasy, unkempt black hair had introduced himself as Brodie, the leader of the group. Something about him had set Corvus on edge from the moment the young man began speaking. He had a skulking posture, a conspiratorial grin, and shifty eyes that often failed to make contact with those of whomever he was addressing. None of the other men in the group had stepped out to meet the delegation of elders, instead busying themselves setting up their wares in a makeshift stall that seemed hastily put together. Davonna had extended her usual warm welcome to the travelers, but, perhaps influenced by the group's behavior and Brodie's uneasiness, she had stressed that Dóchas was a peaceful village and would brook no trouble.

"Sure, ye'll have no trouble from us, ma'am," Brodie had muttered, looking at his feet. "We're just traveling throughout the Green Mount selling our wares." As he finished speaking, he had looked Davonna in the eyes—seemingly with great effort—and flashed a smile that disappeared too quickly. After a pause, she had accepted his assurance and the delegation of elders moved on with their business, leaving Brodie and his gang to finish setting up shop.

"We must keep an eye on them," she said to Corvus and Yazid afterward. "They could be trouble." Corvus and Yazid had nodded in unison, assuring her that they would be extra watchful as long as the young men were in town.

Corvus had reached out to Niall and his brother Quinn, Gordon and his wife Nathaira, Yazid's promising protégé Bradana, and a handful of other reliable men and women in the village, asking them to spend the next several evenings at the Golden Swan tavern to keep an eye on the strangers. Corvus and Yazid spent those evenings there too, sitting and chatting at a corner table where they could observe the room. The strangers were a rowdy bunch, more boisterous than the locals, and they had watched as Smitty—the son of John the smith—was drawn like a moth to the flame of their drunken laughter and coarse talk. The smith's son had few friends in the village. Handsome, tall, and strong, one would think he had all the advantages and should be admired by his peers. But Corvus had noted early on that Smitty was a grandstander, seemingly desperate for attention and approbation. Overly competitive, the lad was known to use his size unfairly in footraces against his fellows, shoving or tripping them to gain advantage. Petty in defeat, boastful in victory, Smitty had alienated most of the young men and women in the village. Some said it was his father's constant disapproval that had steered the boy wrong. Some said he was just a bad seed. Corvus didn't know the cause, but had watched the boy warily as he grew to manhood. During the most recent fyrd selection and placement, Smitty had been the odds-on favorite to be selected for the front line, given his size, strength, and skill. But two days prior to the event, he had been accused of theft in the market by Maire, the potter—an old and dear friend of Corvus. Smitty had denied any wrongdoing, but in doing so, he had slandered Maire, loudly denouncing her as a mad and ugly old hag. He had shown such a paucity of dignity in the proceedings that Corvus had decided then and there that this young man had no place among his troops, where trust and mutual support were critical.

When Corvus told him that not only would he not be selected for the front line, but that he would not be welcome in the fyrd at all until he learned to show respect and value others, Smitty didn't take it well. He stopped attending training sessions, and began bullying and picking fights at the tavern. Twice, Corvus and Yazid had been forced to break up altercations between Smitty and Gordon the shepherd, a reliable, longtime veteran of the fyrd who would not suffer arrogance. In the last such altercation, Smitty had broken Gordon's nose and had even taken a wild swing at Yazid when the Aslene had stepped between the belligerents. Smitty had been so drunk and bellicose that Corvus had been forced to draw his long knife and warn the young man of dire consequences if he did not calm down and go home immediately. With hurled insults and threats of retribution for his wounded pride, Smitty had staggered off into the night. That had been a fortnight ago.

In this group of strangers, the smith's son clearly saw a fresh opportunity to make an impression with his imposing size and good looks. Brodie's band had readily welcomed him, and he had taken to returning to their camp each evening after tavern hours, where they would continue their carousing until the early morning. Other than being noisy guests, they had not truly violated the peace until a few nights ago when they had provoked a tavern brawl.

Smitty had been regaling the group with the tale of his recent altercation with Gordon—whose nose was still healing—pointing over his shoulder at the grim veteran who was sitting at a nearby table with Nathaira and Muireall. Muireall was a one-armed weaver who had lost her limb serving in the fyrd, at the battle of Gillock. She had a sharp wit and a commanding voice, and was intolerant of rudeness. Tired of the group's stolen glances and obvious snickers at Gordon's expense, Muireall had stood and approached their table, scolding them for their ill-manners. A slender and disheveled member of the gang with uneven eyes and an unfortunate mass of curly hair had sprung up and shoved her back, telling her to mind her business and leave them be. That was all it had taken for Gordon and Nathaira, along with Bradana and six or seven other townsfolk, to leap to her defense. Fists flew, and chairs and bottles were broken. Corvus and Yazid had quickly jumped in to try to calm the erupting donnybrook, separating the combatants and angrily ejecting the strangers from the tavern. Each day since, there had been some additional problem with the newcomers, from minor vandalism of merchant shops to the overt bullying of young boys and lewd comments and leering at the young women.

Finally, Davonna and the delegation of elders had notified the strangers that they were no longer welcome in Dóchas, and should plan to leave the next morning. After finding that pleading innocence got them nowhere, Brodie had sullenly assured the elders that they would indeed depart the next day. That had been the night before, and the strangers spent the rest of yesterday packing their wagon and preparing to depart. Later in the evening, after once more causing a stir at the Golden Swan, they were chased out by Aftyn, the meek tavern keeper's diminutive yet fierce and fearless wife. That Dallin had been attacked shortly afterward could be no coincidence.

Corvus' mind struggled to fathom the brutality of the act. Violence against women was largely unknown in the lands of the Green Mount. While many towns might have a king, war chief ,or other male leader, an equal number of villages and towns—if not more—were guided by a matriarch. The people of the Green Mount worshipped the five gods and had many affinities, but universally, they revered Manu the Mother. She it was who turned the Great Wheel, changing the seasons and telling the snows to fall or the grass to sprout, or the delicate heather to flower and paint the hillsides purple. Women were honored throughout the Green Mount, and so it was that Corvus looked with confused horror at what had been done to sweet Dallin.

Kamdyn and Davonna gently prepared the girl to be carried back to her house by Yennel and Flynn, affable brothers from a neighboring farm who had come running to see if they could help. The brothers were experienced members of Corvus' fyrd, and quickly created a field stretcher out of their shepherd's crooks and the canvas from a tent they carried when tending sheep across the glen. As they busied themselves, Corvus squatted next to where Dallin lay, gently stroking her battered face and pulling a stray ringlet of hair back behind her ear.

"Dallin, darlin'," he said softly. "Who did this to you? Hmm? Can you tell me?" His voice was gentle, and he repeated his questions without urgency, stroking her hair paternally as he waited for her to respond. "Can you tell me, darlin'?"

Her only response was to groan softly.

The field stretcher's construction completed, the two brothers helped Corvus and Kamdyn place the girl on the canvas and, without a word, lift the fragile bundle together. Davonna and Kamdyn positioned themselves on either side of her, each holding a hand, their presence surrounding the injured young woman with matronly reassurance and protection.

Just as they began to carry her back to her home, Dallin's hand shook free of Davonna's and flailed by her side as she moaned with some urgency. Corvus thought he heard his name from her ruined lips and he rushed forward to her side, the stretcher bearers pausing on their way.

"Corbus…" she moaned again, her swollen lips making her words hard to understand.

"I'm here, child," Corvus said as he gripped her hand firmly. She opened her eyes and stared urgently at him. The cornea of her left eye was entirely bloodshot and red, while blood and snot ran freely from her broken and misshapen nose.

"Bwodie and Shmitty…" she managed, eventually. "All of dem." Corvus grimly nodded his understanding, then she released his hand and seemed to fold inward upon herself as brutal sobs wracked her body. She covered her face with one hand as they carried her away, the other bouncing limply from the side of the stretcher with the steps of its bearers.

Corvus watched them leave, his breathing growing increasingly urgent, his jaw clenching with barely suppressed emotion, and his brow knitting and unknitting as he remembered the child, laughing and chasing Li after some playful slight. Dallin had a reputation for fearlessness, after having single-handedly chased off a pack of wolves circling her flock one evening. But no amount of courage could have protected her—surprised and alone on the moor—from Brodie's pack.

With a deep breath, Corvus immediately turned back toward the village center some two hundred paces distant, a dark fury in his eyes. "Fetch my sword," was all he said to Cailean as he began striding purposefully toward the market.

Cailean

It was not yet nine in the morning, yet the summer sun was already high in a clear sky, promising a hot day. A light sheen of sweat covered Cailean as he burst through the solid oak door into the stone house, surprising Yazid, who was leaning over a pot suspended near the fire, a spoon of the morning's porridge near his lips. The burly Aslene looked at Cai, and gestured quizzically, turning the palm of his free hand upward. Fetching the sheathed sword and belt from its customary place leaning against the hearth, Cai answered Yazid's silent question with one word only, "Trouble." Then he dashed out of the house to try to catch his father, Yazid dropping his breakfast to follow close behind with his stout staff.

Without pausing, Cailean opened the top button of his shirt to combat some of the building heat of the day as he rushed over the cliff tops, where gulls swooped and cried out on the ever-present ocean winds. He could see Corvus near the southern edge of the moor, now nearing the village, the sweat on his bald head and bare chest visible even from a distance as they reflected the morning sun. Cailean could also see the horrible, puckered scars that striped his father's back, which he knew had been earned during Corvus' great sojourn in his youth. Cai's father was a private and modest man, and it was unusual for him to be seen in public without a shirt, but now, he seemed to wear his scars proudly, like a warning to any who might oppose him. Though only a little above average height, in moments like this, when he moved with lethal purpose, his father looked to be a colossus. Cai felt a swell of pride that this scarred and terrible giant of a man—a storm of righteous fury about to break upon the unsuspecting village—was his father. And he ran all the faster to be by his side when the storm broke.

Catching up to him, Cai handed over his sword and belt. Without breaking stride, Corvus took the weapon and strapped it on with practiced hands, dark eyes still focused on the nearby market as he crested the natural berm at the edge of the moor. His eyes searched the merchant stalls and shops for his prey, but Cai spotted them first, standing in a gaggle near the morning lineup outside the bakery. He pointed them out to his father, who nodded grimly.

Corvus

"Brodie!" he shouted at the cluster of men standing with cups of morning ale in their hands. All seven of the group, as if instructed to do so, turned inward toward one another and ignored his call, snickering at some private comment made by their leader.

"Brodie, you viper!" Corvus' fury was barely contained as he came within two yards of the men. "You face me, boy. Now."

"Yeah, old man?" Brodie's insouciant posture when he looked up seemed affected and overly innocent. "What do you want?"

"Dallin," was all Corvus said. A single word that bore the weight of a full accusation under his eyes that glowered with rage, and the rhythmic clenching of his jaw.

"Who's that?" Brodie asked, in a way that made clear he knew very well, as his co-conspirators snickered and whispered amongst themselves. Even from this distance, Corvus could see that the shifty younger man's face bore a streak of angry-red scratch marks—no doubt from Dallin's efforts to resist their attack the night before. Fury filled him.

"I'll not mince words with you, whelp," Corvus responded loudly. "All six of you and Smitty, to the Circle, now!"

All seven of the young men's faces, as one, looked up in shock and bemused surprise. By calling out the entire group, Corvus was challenging them to a series of one-on-one duels until all seven had fought him. The idea of one man, even if he was the famed Raven, fighting seven duels in a row was unheard of, and these young toughs clearly fancied themselves the equal of any older man, even one with Corvus' reputation.

We should have expelled this lot when they first turned up, Corvus chided himself as he turned and stomped toward the Circle. *I should have trusted my instincts.*

But the customs of hospitality had been too strong, and he hadn't expelled them, and now it had come to this.

"What is the cause, my friend?" Yazid asked under his breath, having caught up to his friend's side, brandishing his staff.

"It's Dallin. They *abused* her," Corvus said through gritted teeth. "Beat her bloody, and… more." His throat tightened with emotion.

"Oh, I see." Yazid responded matter-of-factly, but Corvus could sense his friend's hands tensing on the staff. "Well, whatever you don't finish, I will, I think."

Corvus nodded curtly in silent acknowledgement.

"Smitty, too, eh?" the Aslene asked, receiving only another nod from Corvus. "Shame."

"They're a pack of wild dogs that need to be put down," Corvus said as he stepped into the carefully tended circle of sawdust in the center of the village. Removing his sword belt, he drew Raven's Tooth from its sheath and then carelessly tossed the belt aside.

A murmur rippled through the gathering crowd. Having suffered countless minor indignities at the hands of the young men, the community was aware they had been told to depart, and, on the whole, was happy to see them go. But this turn of events was unexpected. The murmur grew into excited whispering as people tried to establish exactly what was happening.

"Who was Corvus calling out?"

"Which of the men?"

"To the death?"

"What happened?"

"Something to do with Dallin."

"He called out all six?"

"Smitty too?"

"He's challenged seven?!"

"Look after Ligulf," Corvus growled over his shoulder to Cailean, as the first of the young toughs eagerly removed his shirt to reveal a pale, slender chest, and stepped into the ring.

"Da..." Cailean began, but stopped as Yazid placed a hand on his shoulder.

"Not now, boy," the Aslene cautioned. "He's got the storms within him, I think. There's no calling him back."

The first man to enter the Circle was a tall, ill-favored man with crooked teeth and a shock of red hair that seemed to sprout in all directions. Seemingly the clown of the group, he had typically been the loudest in the tavern, his braying laugh cutting through the gentle din of conversation between customers. More than once, Aftyn had scolded him for standing on chairs or even a table, breaking mugs carelessly as he animatedly regaled his comrades with some ribald tale or other. He laughed loudly at some parting words from his mates and gripped an antique great sword loosely with both hands. The weapon had obviously seen better days—though from the look of it, Corvus judged it had never been a fine sword. It looked poorly balanced and the rust on the blade showed it had not been well cared for. Indeed, it looked to be little more than pig iron inexpertly shaped like a blade with a handle and rough cross guards, but the young man seemed not to care. Prancing about from side to side, he taunted Corvus, spitting at the ground in front of him.

"You understand what's at play here, boy?" Corvus asked, not moving.

"Sure," the young man spat. "An old geezer is about to get filleted!" He laughed a rapid-fire laugh that sounded not unlike a donkey, and looked to his friends for support. As a group, they urged him on, eager for blood.

Davonna, who had just returned from seeing Dallin to her home, adopted her customary role of duel officiant and stepped into the center of the Circle, between the two combatants. She looked to each of them, before speaking ceremonially.

"State your name and your purpose in this ring," she said first to Corvus.

"Corvus Corax of Dóchas," he said, using his battlefield voice so that all gathered might hear. "Accusing this man, and all seven of that group, of the brutal attack and defilement of Dallin, daughter of Kamdyn."

There were gasps of horror and dismay among the swelling crowd.

Davonna then turned and said the same to the red-headed man who looked at her with a mocking expression before responding.

"My name's Ian," he barked loudly, "of no town in particular. And I deny this old man's claim."

With a solemn bow of her head, Davonna said, "Let the truth be known through this trial." She then backed out of the ring to stand beside her husband.

Wasting no time, the younger man stepped forward and took a wild swing at Corvus with the heavy weapon, missing him by a foot. Perhaps he was wary of his opponent's vaunted skill after all, and didn't want to get too close. Corvus did not move nor flinch as the blade passed, his own sword tip still resting in the sawdust at his side, his eyes seeing only Dallin lying beaten and bloody on the moor. *Her blood...* As Ian wound up for a return backhand swing—this time a little closer—Corvus launched forward suddenly, his left hand jamming the handle of the attacking blade as he thrust Raven's Tooth through the chest of the still-grinning younger man. Ian's face slowly registered shock and dismay as the razor-sharp sword pierced him, and protruded more than a foot out of his back. He looked quizzically into Corvus' merciless eyes, as if to ask why Corvus would do such a thing. As if to say, "We was only having fun."

"Did you rape her, Ian?" Corvus asked coldly as tears fell down the younger man's shocked face. "Speak truth before you die, man."

Ian's eyes wandered a moment, and Corvus doubted he would answer, but then the red-headed man looked at Corvus and nodded slightly, tears of pain and despair rushing down his cheeks. His lips moved as though he were trying to say something, but his knees started to buckle, then his eyes opened wider still in surprise as Corvus slid the blade out of him quickly. No words came as the young man fell to the ground like a marionette whose strings had suddenly been cut.

A shout of outrage went up from Brodie's gang. Corvus looked over to see Smitty standing among them, looking as disappointed and angry as the rest. Despite the fact that Corvus had spoken quietly, the crowd of onlookers had hushed at the suddenness of his strike and in that momentary stillness, all had heard the question and seen the nodded response. Horrified by what they had witnessed and the implications of that nod, the accusing eyes of the spectators shifted to the pack of men who were alternately shouting defiance at Corvus and whispering urgently amongst themselves. The villagers began to back away from the group, clearing an area around them. The gang became suddenly aware of the dark mood of the crowd, and they pulled more tightly together, facing outward as if expecting to be attacked by the mob.

"Which of you is next?" Corvus asked, breaking the tense silence. "You there?" He pointed the tip of sword at a hirsute, swarthy member of the gang who happened to be standing nearest the edge of the ring. The man had dark hair and eyes and wore no shirt. Instead he had a leather vest which was open, revealing a chest and stomach covered in black hair. He wore a braided copper torc, which had stained the skin of his neck green.

Startled at being singled out, the man looked back at Corvus, who saw despair in his eyes. Brodie clapped the man on his shoulder and encouraged him to "Teach the old man a lesson, Ewan." His fellows echoed Brodie's cheer, and several hands urged him forward. With a resigned sigh that seemed to suggest he would rather be anywhere but there, he stripped off his vest and stepped unarmed into the Circle.

"Pick it up," Corvus said, indicating the sword that Ian had used, still lying in the dust. Seemingly afraid to commit to the contest, Ewan shook his head, staring dumbly at the bulky weapon.

"I said pick it up," Corvus repeated, "or so help me, by Fel's teeth, I'll gut you where you stand."

"Come on, Ewan," Brodie called from the side. "Stick the old man and everything's fine. You can do it."

Ewan didn't turn at Brodie's words, but something in them seemed to light a fire in him. By the Law of the Circle, Brodie was right. If Ewan prevailed, he was technically innocent, his good name restored—at least by tradition, though they would never be welcome in this community again. Hope seemed to flare to life in the man as he crouched to collect the sword. He frowned at its poor balance, but he was stronger than his friend and after a few test swings, which Corvus indulged, he seemed ready.

The two began circling, Corvus taking nothing for granted; he had fought enough opponents in his life to know that anyone could be dangerous in the ring, regardless of the weapon. This young man was thirty years his junior, strong, athletic, and fighting for both his life and redemption. He'd be dangerous. Ewan feinted twice with the heavy sword, seeming to test Corvus' reactions and whether he could bait the older man into responding. Corvus continued circling, unfazed by the maneuvers, dragging the tip of Raven's Tooth lazily through the dust of the arena. It was a signal understood by swordsmen that the fight was to the death. To hold the tip of the blade up off the ground, whether it be in a guard posture or merely held ready, was a sign of respect for your opponent. Letting it drag in the dirt signaled that, regardless of the outcome, you hoped to at least cause infection or even poisoning by dirtying your blade. It was an old custom, but one that Corvus understood, and from the look on Ewan's face, the young man did as well. His eyes hardened, and he attacked.

As Corvus expected, it was a vigorous and well-executed sequence beginning with a downward arcing blow intended to cut from the right side of Corvus' neck to his left hip. He had predicted the blow based on Ewan's guard stance, and gracefully stepped to his right, raising his blade in a guard known to the Aslenes as the "feather guard," so named for the fact that the blade seemed to float upward to meet the incoming attack. Raven's Tooth rang with a bell-like tone, sharp and clear in the morning air, as the blades connected—a distinct difference from the undistinguished clack produced by the pig-iron sword. Rather than stop or reverse his swing, as any clumsy, novice swordsman would, Corvus was impressed to see that his opponent continued his momentum, spinning and lashing out with a savage cut to Corvus' right side. The force of the cut was impressive, and had the blow landed, even the dull blade would have done permanent, possibly fatal damage. With a simple flip of his wrist—an Aslene maneuver called a *tahuna*—Corvus translated the force of Ewan's first cut against the feather guard into a lightning quick, powerful block on his right side. He stepped into Ewan's attack, and his left hand struck the wrist of Ewan's sword-arm in a forceful open-handed check, disarming the younger man and sending his sword spinning into the dust.

Ewan stopped for just a moment, his face inches away from Corvus' with a look of shocked surprise. The older man allowed himself the slightest hint of a grin, then he struck Ewan with a powerful backhand blow with his left hand. Ewan fell to his back, his nose and lip bloody as his cheeks flushed bright red from the impact. Dazed, the young man lay there for a moment, clearly expecting his death.

"Pick it up," Corvus growled.

Apparently surprised by the courtesy, Ewan blinked several times before scrambling to his feet to retrieve his sword. Scooping it up, he spun just in time to parry a fierce series of slicing attacks, which drove him back to the edge of the Circle. Corvus wasn't going in for the kill yet, just testing his opponent and keeping him off-balance. He knew that the illusion of dominance was just as effective in the ring as true skill. The more Corvus appeared confident, relaxed, and completely in control, the more these young men would be nervous or fearful and, consequently, off their game when they faced him.

Stepping back to the center of the ring, he turned casually back to Ewan, his arms open wide, inviting an attack. Egged on by his mates, Ewan answered with a series of quick thrusts, executing them fairly well considering the weight and imbalance of the weapon. Corvus parried each of them almost casually as he allowed himself to be driven back to the opposite edge of the Circle. Perhaps perceiving an opening from Corvus' retreat, Ewan threw his force into the last thrust of his combination. Corvus, though, was waiting for just such an over-commitment, as it would force Ewan to pause for a moment afterward to regain his balance. That moment was all Corvus needed. Using the false edge of his blade, he parried the final thrust to his right side, and with a quick tahuna, he brought his much lighter, well-balanced sword down in a vicious cut to Ewan's exposed neck with breathtaking suddenness. The young man fell in a fountain of blood, his lunging leg sliding forward out from under his weight and putting him into an undignified split as his torso collapsed forward onto the ground. His splayed body lay there as a shocked and almost reverent hush fell over the crowd. There was no sound for a moment but the incessant waves against the cliffs in the distance and the cries of gulls.

Corvus looked down at the ruined corpse as two men from the crowd dragged it out of the ring. Without moving his head, his eyes flashed up at the dwindling gang to see who would be next. In two bouts that had lasted mere moments, a brace of the strangers already lay dead, and Corvus was barely winded. There was much agitation among the young men as they furiously whispered to each other, fiercely debating who should step forward. Their panicked eyes looked frantically around the crowd, seeming to hope for some help in their predicament. But they found only icy and accusing glares facing them, and so the pack returned to their furious discussion. Finally, a slender young man stripped off his shirt and produced two short swords from a burlap sack nearby. They were a matched pair of seaxes, the type of short swords used in the shield wall, though it was rare to see someone fight with two of them at once. The lad sauntered into the ring with an irregular, almost insect-like quality, spinning the blades confidently. He had an unusually large nose and a scraggly wisp of sandy-colored beard that struggled to find purchase on his chin. He had bright hazel eyes, and Corvus noted the left one had a dark spot in the lower iris. Corvus remembered him from one of the tavern incidents. This was the rude young man that had pushed Muireall, provoking the first brawl. Corvus had heard his fellows refer to him as "Mop," presumably for his bushy shock of curly hair.

Keeping his posture relaxed, Corvus took a quick swig of water from a skin offered by his son, and watched the cocky young man prepare for the fight. He remembered the look on this loudmouth's face as he had shoved Muireall—an indignity that the respected woman did not deserve. Corvus' mind went to Dallin's blood-red eye and her ruined nose, and his jaw clenched once more with a new wave of barely suppressed rage. Glancing over his shoulder, Corvus caught Muireall's eye. She was standing just behind Yazid, and when she gave him a grim nod, he inclined his head slightly in response. Then, flashing a quick reassuring glance to Yazid and Cailean, he turned back to his foe.

"Ready, Mop?" Corvus said in a low voice, settling into Fortress stance—a flexible defensive posture that could flow easily into Badger, Willow, or even Mountain Form.

Giving no response, the young man began to circle, and Corvus countered, allowing his opponent to choose when to attack. Mop continued to circle until he had the morning sun at his back, then paused just a moment before attacking. The attack came as a furious and devilish sequence, the two blades seeming each to have a mind of their own; as quickly as one would cut, the other would thrust, and vice versa. Though with Fortress stance, Corvus had positioned his blade and balance advantageously, he was still forced to give ground before the onslaught, parrying each attack just in time. The blinding sun prevented him from seeing the attacks initiate early and thus mitigated any advantage gained from his stance. He chided himself for committing the type of mistake a raw recruit makes: allowing the opponent to put the sun in your eyes. *Stupid!* He scolded himself, as he barely managed to counter the final thrust of the series and escape a few feet around the circle, the chimes of Raven's Tooth's parries still ringing in his ears.

Mop's two-handed assault had been skillful and complex. The final thrust from his right hand had come hard on the heels of a quick attack with the other sword aimed at Corvus' left hip. A lesser swordsman, or one wielding a heavier blade, could never have made the transition from the downward block which protected his hip to the immediate backhand check with the false of the blade that was necessary to avert the thrust aimed at his right eye. But Corvus had made the parry gracefully with a deep lunging step to his left, though he had only just escaped the blow. The force of his check had momentarily thrown his assailant off-balance. The two of them took a moment to recover before they faced off once again. Corvus and Mop now stood in a north-south orientation with Corvus' back to the moor just north of the village, where Dallin had been found. *Dallin!* A stone of despair sank in Corvus' stomach at the thought of her savaged and left behind like refuse.

He was keenly aware of the disadvantage he had in only one blade versus two, as well as the fact that he still had four more fights to go and couldn't afford to draw this out. He switched from Fortress stance to the more flamboyant and less predictable Eagle form. He attacked in a sequence that varied from broad slices to arcing thrusts as he leapt gracefully from side to side, never allowing his opponent the chance to counterattack. Mop was clearly thrown off by the unfamiliar fighting style and backed up furiously, his blades thrashing wildly at the incoming attacks that seemed to come from every possible angle. Seeing his opponent's concentration thrown, Corvus diverted one of his strikes at the last moment, aiming for the fingers of Mop's exposed hand rather than allowing the man's blade to affect the block. A seax had no handguard and featured only minimal cross guards as the blades were intended for close work in and around shields; any cross guard might catch on the edge of one's shield and foul an attack. The hand wielding the weapon was therefore exposed. This vulnerability was not something an attacker could normally exploit if wielding a great sword, great axe, or hammer. Those weapons simply weren't responsive enough for such a subtle maneuver. But Raven's Tooth was another matter. The light weapon was quick and agile, and it took only the slightest flex of Corvus' wrist to redirect his blade. The famed cutlass effortlessly sliced into Mop's right hand, separating the last two fingers at their knuckles. The severed digits landed with a wet plop in the sawdust.

With a cry that sounded like a scared child, Mop dropped the sword, clutching the wounded limb to his belly and covering it with his other arm. He staggered back toward the edge of the circle, the sun now fully in his face as he looked at Corvus with tears and snot streaming down his face, rage and accusation forming in his eyes. "This is your fault, old man!" he screamed. "Everything was fine until you stepped in! Y'old cuif!" He spat and then ineffectively tried to wipe his streaming nose with the sleeve of his injured arm.

Corvus decided that he'd heard enough. Knowing that he now had the sun to his back and that his opponent would be momentarily blinded by it, he struck before Mop could spout off anymore. Stepping forward, he raised his sword high on his left side and with a quick tahuna flipped the blade to suddenly attack from the right, cutting directly through Mop's exposed throat faster than the injured man, struggling to see into the sun, could react. A fountain of blood erupted from Mop's ruined throat, the force of which tilted his head backward. The crowd gasped audibly as his almost headless torso collapsed into the sawdust, and Corvus casually stepped to the side to avoid being sprayed as the corpse fell forward. He looked expectantly at Brodie.

After they recovered from their collective surprise, there was an immediate uproar among the spectators as they voiced their approbation for the decisive blow. Muireall's cheer was loudest of all. Brodie's group too was growing increasingly agitated, and more furious whispers were exchanged, until a decision seemed to be reached and the next opponent raised his hand and bent to retrieve his weapon. He was the largest of the bunch: Smitty.

The morning sun was high and hot, and Corvus could feel the skin of his bare chest reddening beneath its glare. Despite his air of dominance, sweat dripped off his chin as he watched the bold youth confidently enter the ring. Though he had dispatched the previous three opponents without suffering an injury, he knew this one would not be as easy. This would be no contest of swords. Smitty was taller and broader than the rest and was carrying a well-crafted war hammer. It was a fearsome weapon, no doubt made by his father, with a handle of leather-wrapped ash over four feet in length. The hammer head was a vicious-looking foot-long rectangle of iron with a wicked six-inch hook on the back side that arced downward toward the handle. The head of the weapon was studded on all sides with two-inch iron spikes that glinted darkly in the morning sun. It was a weighty weapon meant for shattering shields, armor, and any limbs that might get in its way, and yet the big lad hoisted and spun it effortlessly as he stepped forward.

"You can do this, lad," a voice called out for Smitty from the dwindling gaggle of young men that Corvus had challenged. The Smith's son flashed a smile back at the group and called back, "Sure, not a problem."

"Shield," Corvus called to Cailean, who—characteristically—had already anticipated the need and quickly produced a solid oaken shield for his father. It wasn't Corvus' personal shield, the one that bore his crest and had a padded leather backing—that was still back at the stone house—but it was solid, heavy, and well-built, and he wasn't about to delay proceedings while his personal shield was fetched. Smitty waited, a condescending grin on his face, while the older man strapped the shield onto his left arm. Corvus nodded to Cailean gratefully before turning back to meet his well-muscled opponent.

Remembering the fight against the giant eunuch before the Prince of the Silken Court, Corvus took up Willow stance. He opted to place his shield side forward and hold his sword low and behind him to provide the greatest number of counterattack options. Having seen Smitty fight many times over the years, he knew there would be a vicious opening assault. Willow stance had always been Ashahl's recommended stance against heavy weapons, as the shield or left-hand blade—if fighting two-handed—could absorb or block the enemy's initial attack, the defender bending like the willow before springing forward to counter.

Smitty paced out of range, sizing Corvus up, and seemingly trying to decide on his best line of attack. Before he could settle into his own stance, however, a disturbance among the spectators broke the combatants' concentration. John the smith, a huge bear of a man, pushed his way through the crowd and into the ring. It was a rare breach of the protocol of the Circle, and John no doubt knew he could be punished—even exiled from Dóchas—for it. But the smith's face was filled with tortured emotion that seemed beyond his endurance. Gasps erupted from the spectators as Corvus backed up a bit and pivoted slightly to face this new threat.

"Corax, you'll no' be killin' my boy!" John roared as strode into the ring, a finely made great sword gripped in his left hand, feather-light in his massive grip. His bald head was grimy with sweat and ash, and his great, bushy eyebrows were raised high emphasizing his point. His leather apron was filthy and sweat-stained, and his massive hairy shoulders bulged out on either side, exposed by a dirty sleeveless shirt that may once have been white.

"John, step out—" Corvus began, but was quickly interrupted by Smitty.

"Da!" the young man yelled. "No!"

"Quiet, boy," the smith growled over his shoulder, not taking his eyes off of Corvus.

"No! I'm no bairn! This is my fight," the muscular youth argued. "You'll no' take it from me!"

There was a pause as Corvus eyed John and his son warily. Voices from the crowd called out in outrage at the smith's breach of tradition, urging him to step out. John ignored the rising chorus, staring intently at Corvus, his eyes wide, seeming to dare the Raven to disagree with him. Over the years, Corvus had relied heavily on the big man to help arm his fyrd, and he had always ensured that John was well paid for his work, both in silver and in praise; his workmanship was excellent. While Corvus couldn't say that he and the surly smith were close, they had worked together many times, and Corvus had always felt that the relationship bore mutual respect. But blood is thicker than water, and John's face showed no sign of relenting as his eldest stood accused in the ring, despite the cries of indignation from the crowd growing louder.

"John, please," Corvus said. "You know the Law of the Circle. These men—Smitty included—must be punished for what they've done to Dallin."

"Da, you're muckin' it all up," Smitty protested from behind his father. But the smith's eyes were still locked, unyielding, on Corvus.

Toren, Davonna's husband and the respected hunt master of the village, stepped in front of Corvus and slowly approached John, placing a hand on his shoulder. The large smith looked imploringly into the eyes of the tall huntsman, whose only reply was to shake his head. The smith then looked past him at Corvus, with a pleading desperation in his eyes. Corvus returned the gaze with implacable determination. After a long, tense moment, John's shoulders finally slumped and his eyes cast downward. He took a few deep breaths, then looked first to Toren, then to Corvus once more. His eyes were moist and filled with rare emotion—Corvus would pay a price for this, he knew. John turned to face his son, sword still held loosely in his left hand. Silently he stood face-to-face with his eldest boy, searching his eyes, seemingly memorizing his face. Smitty was resolute as he returned his father's gaze. After a few more silent breaths, John placed his right hand on his son's chest and patted him twice, sighing. Then he turned to leave the Circle, a massive weight on his shoulders, his hand falling to his side defeated. Without a word, he pushed his way back through the crowd, returning to his smithy.

His son watched him go, his face a mixture of regret and sadness. John was a stern man, not prone to showing emotion or affection, and Smitty seemed to have long since given up trying to gain the man's approval, seeking praise elsewhere. This moment of connection clearly had an effect on the young man. As he stared at his father's disappearing back, he raised a hand to his chest, where his father's hand had been but a moment before.

With a huge sigh, the lad shook his head, blinked back a tear, and turned once more to Corvus. He dropped into a fighting stance, his left hand holding the end of the handle of the weapon and his right cradling it mid-haft.

"You see the heartbreak you've caused?" Corvus said, looking from Smitty to the remaining three youths grouped together. "John is a good man…"

"Shut it!" screamed Smitty as he launched a furious sweeping attack. Just as he had done with the eunuch years before, Corvus avoided the blow, slipping just out of range and arching his back—bending as the willow. The hammer missed his chin by a hand's breadth. Corvus saw his opening, and his explosive Willow form response would easily have plunged his blade into Smitty's chest before the young man could wind up for a follow-on attack. But in that instant, Corvus hesitated. He remembered Smitty as a vulnerable boy, obviously hurt by his father's ongoing disapproval, desperate for attention, boasting among his fellows—not at first out of spite or meanness, but a simple longing for love and respect. The moment of recollection allowed Smitty the time to continue the sweep of the hammer, bringing the weighty weapon around for a powerful descending blow. Corvus' rear foot was at the edge of the Circle and Smitty was crowding him, preventing any sideways escape. Cursing himself for his hesitation, Corvus knew there was nothing for it now but to crouch suddenly, raise his left arm and take the heavy blow on the shield—not his preferred choice by far, but in the moment, his only option.

A great crack resounded as the hammer hit, echoing off the steep hills that bordered the village to the south. Corvus' left arm exploded with pain. The stout oaken shield disintegrated with the force of the blow and Corvus was pitched into an ungainly roll to his right. In addition to the injury to his arm, the force of the strike had driven the lower edge of the shield into his ribs, and he felt a sharp grinding in his side as he tumbled away.

Shucking off the splintered remains of the shield as he came out of his awkward roll, he flicked his blade forward and up. Not a serious attack by any means, but a quick searching move that somehow managed to find Smitty's left cheek just below his eye. The big youth staggered back, surprised by the cut, aborting a follow-up attack with the hammer and giving Corvus critical time to assess his own injuries.

His left arm hung useless, numb, and limp at his side, and his breath caught in his ribs. *Broken arm? Possibly. Broken ribs? Maybe. Well then, no time to dally.*

He attacked. His flurry of cuts and thrusts were effectively fended off by Smitty, who shifted his hold on the weapon to a staff grip, deftly blocking blow after blow with the leather-bound haft. Corvus closed rapidly on the youth with each attack, seeking to get inside the long reach of the hammer where Raven's Tooth could do its work. Smitty was good. Quick for his size, and while he ably countered each blow, he continued to give ground around the circle, keeping the older skilled swordsman at distance.

Corvus felt off-balance. Customarily, he relied on his left arm as a counterweight for his flamboyant blade work, but the limp limb offered no support for his attacks, and he could feel each blow pulling him over his balance point, slowing the flurry as his body adjusted to the unaccustomed extra dead weight. Desperately attempting to close with his foe, Corvus ended his attack series with a high right thrust, which Smitty once more fended off in staff grip to his left side. Seeing the lad's arms both committed to his left to affect the block, Corvus stepped in and across with his left foot, closing with his opponent. He spun to deliver a crushing elbow to the face of the taller lad and felt the crunch as Smitty's cheekbone broke. As the youth staggered back, his right eye quickly swelling shut and streaming with tears of pain, Corvus reversed his spin, ducking into a deep lunge and barely slipping under a sloppy backhand swing of the hammer, before he once more flicked out with his blade tip for a quick cut. This time it was aimed at the belly, and he sliced a short, shallow cut just above the hip. Again, it wasn't a killing blow, but it was enough to further shock the previously unscarred young man and give him yet another injury to assess.

Blood flowed from Smitty's cheek, nose, and stomach as he looked down at the shallow new cut. Corvus stood from his lunge, pausing to experimentally flex the fingers of his left hand. The pain that shot from elbow to shoulder told him that while the arm was likely not broken, it may be days before he had full use of it again. *Lovely.*

Behind the swelling, Smitty's eyes filled with newfound rage and he thrust the hammer head unexpectedly at Corvus' chest, striking him with force. It felt like being kicked in the chest by a warhorse, and Corvus staggered back, off-balance. Deftly switching his grip, Smitty reversed the weapon to present the spike and, with a raking motion, ripped Corvus' left leg out from under him, opening up a sizable gash down his left calf. Corvus hit the ground hard. Stars spun in his vision as he gasped for breath and struggled to focus on the incoming hammer. Another quick hand-switch by Smitty, and the weapon was coming down to finish the older man in a mighty vertical chop.

Corvus reacted instinctively and tucked his injured left leg under him, exploding up and forward into a kneeling posture, well inside the arc of the hammer, which found only sawdust as its target. Using his momentum, Corvus thrust into the lad's left side, piercing Smitty's belly just below his previous injury. The blade stopped only when it hit the pelvic girdle on the opposite side. Smitty staggered back, and the blade pulled out of his body with a sucking noise. A squirt of black blood accompanied it, mixing with the brighter red blood flowing from the shallow, earlier cut. Smitty stared at the wound in horror, his left hand cupping the injury and coming away painted with a swirl of black and red. Apparently knowing his time was near, the younger man roared and swung a wild, vicious downward blow at Corvus, lunging in on his right leg as he attacked. Slipping right to avoid the blow, Corvus placed the sharpened false edge of his blade on the backside of Smitty's lunging right knee, and pulled, slicing deeply to severe tendons and the artery. The youth collapsed, releasing the hammer and clutching his leg with both hands to try to stanch the pulsing flow of blood.

Both the thrust through Smitty's side and the slice to his leg were mortal wounds, though the hole in his belly would take agonizing days before fever, infection, and blood loss took him. The arterial slice to the leg, however, would be a much quicker death—though not as quick a death as the blows to the previous three had been. Corvus stepped back, gasping for breath, as Smitty began frantically crying for help from his fellows or from any of the community watching. The ringing of John's hammer in the smithy stilled as his son called desperately for aid. But no help was offered, and his urgent, tearful calls gradually lost strength as he bled out, hands pressed against his leg in a futile effort to stop the flow. The villagers looked on in cold, harsh judgement as the young man thrashed and cried and eventually stilled. After a long moment, the sounds of the hammer in the smithy resumed.

Corvus watched from the edge of the Circle nearest to Cailean and Yazid. He cursed himself for allowing sentiment to almost get him killed as he panted shallowly, his bruised chest reminding him painfully of the hammer thrust with each inhalation, and his grinding ribs restricting his efforts to catch his breath. His left leg was on fire from the gash, so he balanced on his right leg as he shook his left arm, hoping for some recovery of use. He was rewarded with an explosion of needles stabbing up and down the length of it. Yazid handed him a waterskin, which he gratefully accepted after shifting his sword to his nearly limp left hand and taking the skin in his right to drink deeply. As he passed the skin back, Cailean handed him a rag to wipe the sweat away. The rag smelled of oil and metal and smoke, and Corvus reckoned it had probably been dropped by John when he had entered the circle, fresh from wiping down a blade. A group of villagers dragged Smitty's limp form out of the ring, piling it unceremoniously on top of the those of the previous three.

Corvus was startled out of his moment of rest by the sudden roar of three voices as Brodie and the remaining two gang members, Lyall and Mac, rushed together into the ring, blades out. The spectators erupted in shouts at the violation of tradition that a three-against-one fight represented and Davonna made to enter the ring in objection, but was held back protectively by Toren. Corvus suspected that the men didn't care about the crowd's reaction. If they could survive this event, they would no doubt flee the village for good. He assumed that, for them, breaking tradition and living as outlaws would be preferable to what they had just seen happen to four of their fellows.

Lyall circled left, cautious. He was a short and dirty brute, bare-chested with close-cropped dark hair, a thick mustache that drooped below his chin, and a silver earring dangling from his right ear. He was wielding a bearded axe in his right hand and carrying a shield in his left. Lyall's caution encouraged Mac to check his initial charge and so instead his pale friend—with a full, dark beard and eyes as black as midnight—countered him, circling right. He stood tall, still wearing his homespun shirt and holding Ian's rusty great sword with both hands. He laughed tauntingly as he moved, daring the injured older man to commit to an attack.

Brodie stood directly across from Corvus, barely inside the circle, also still wearing his shirt and vest. In each hand he held a long knife, and twirled them with menace. He was a slender and gangly youth with a darkly mischievous smile. His slate-gray eyes still shifted uneasily away from eye contact with the older man, and his head jutted forward as he snickered at Corvus' discomfiture. Corvus stared at the streak of red welts marking Brodie's face.

Let's finish this, he told himself. *For Dallin.*

"What now, old man, eh?" Brodie taunted from a distance, as Lyall and Mac positioned themselves on either side of Corvus. Being at the center of three attackers, Corvus adopted a modified Badger stance, with his weight on his forward right foot, his sword pointed low, and his center toward Brodie. Normally, the assumption of Badger stance would slow the world to his eyes, enabling him to see vulnerabilities and incoming attacks with the speed of thought. But the sharp pain from his injuries and the corresponding lack of balance prevented this effect. He could feel the blood flowing down the back of his left leg, and he knew that the gash from the hammer's spike had been deep. That leg would not bear much weight, and could betray him at any moment. In a true Badger stance, the combatant would hold his empty hand forward and parallel to his sword hand, feet side by side, ready to lash out in any direction, but after his encounter with Smitty, his wounded left side was of little help.

Corvus heard a brief commotion behind him, and was heartened to see Cailean and Yazid had stepped into the Circle, flanking him protectively. Cailean stood to his right and faced Mac, armed with a seax and shield, while Yazid, in his flowing Aslene robes, stood to his left, armed with his ubiquitous staff. He twirled it effortlessly, grinning in anticipation and maintaining eye contact with Lyall.

Now finding themselves without their presumed advantage, the three men exchanged nervous glances; Lyall and Mac looked to Brodie for direction, while the greasy youth began backing away, out of the circle.

All at once, Brodie turned to flee but stopped suddenly, a knocked arrow poised mere inches from his face. Toren, who had anticipated the gang's treachery and repositioned himself around the spectators, and now stood pointing his fearsome longbow at Brodie. The huntsman said nothing, but quietly shook his head, denying the gang leader escape from his fate. Correctly assuming that trying to avoid Toren's deadly aim would be futile, Brodie stamped his foot in frustration and spun back toward Corvus.

"Spit the bastards!" the shifty-eyed leader shouted to his comrades, then advanced cautiously toward him, letting Lyall and Mac engage Cailean and Yazid first.

Lyall swung quickly for Yazid with his axe, but the big Aslene was—despite his corpulence—a flowing and graceful opponent, deadly with the staff. Within moments, Yazid had disarmed Lyall, breaking the young man's wrist with a sharp downward blow, then swiftly sweeping his legs out from under him. No sooner had his opponent hit the ground than the fore end of Yazid's staff found Lyall's left temple in a stunning blow that ended the trader's fight. Lyall still lived, but Corvus knew Yazid's strength; a blow like that could well damage the man's mind permanently.

Concurrent with Lyall's efforts, Mac raised the great sword and charged Cailean. Corvus did not fear for his son's safety. The lad had trained tirelessly with a variety of weapons, and over the years Corvus had introduced him to many of the martial techniques he had learned from Ashahl. In single combat, Cailean was the equal of almost any man. And indeed, by the time Corvus looked back from Lyall's defeat to check on his son's progress, Mac was already disarmed and bleeding freely from a grievous arterial wound to his inner thigh. Corvus grinned appreciatively. *Good choice, lad.* Cailean's posture was relaxed as he carelessly kicked Mac in the chest, sending the taller man sprawling onto his back. Mac struggled to find the pig iron sword he had been wielding, but a cruel punch with the edge of Cailean's shield silenced him, leaving him with a broken jaw and very few teeth remaining. Corvus suspected Mac would bleed out from the leg wound before ever recovering his wits. Corvus took no small measure of pride in his son's battle prowess, sparing a quick wink for his son, who flashed him a bright grin as he and Yazid backed to the edge of the Circle. Their work here was finished.

Corvus now turned his attention to Brodie. He could feel his right leg beginning to quiver, unaccustomed as it was to bearing his full weight for so long, and the injury to his left leg continued to burn like a streak of fire down his calf. Sweat and blood streamed freely into his boot. But, no matter his injuries, this last fight would be his own. Corvus shifted his weight slightly, adjusting his blade to directly address the greasy young man.

"No escape now, you vile whelp," Corvus said in a growl, his eyes intent on the claw marks raked across Brodie's face. "You've brought evil to our village."

Brodie's only response was to sneer and spit at him, his eyes glancing nervously around the Circle. The villagers, as one, pressed forward, making clear to the gang leader that there was no escape from the arena.

Brodie began to dance lightly from side to side, apparently gauging Corvus' injuries and the limitations of his movement. He then maneuvered to Corvus' left, forcing the older man to shift and pivot painfully on his injured leg to continue facing him, and attempted a series of quick, uncommitted little attacks with the blade in his right hand to test Corvus' mobility. The older man's left arm still hung dead at his side, his elbow pressed tightly against his ribs. His breath came in short, quick gasps and his face was blanched and sweaty from the pain and exertion. His left leg extended behind him, toes lightly touching the ground; clearly it could bear no weight. It seemed obvious that a quickly pressed attack would force him back onto the wounded leg and yield an opening for Brodie's blades.

How did you find yourself here, old man? Corvus silently scolded himself. *You've fought far better swordsmen and beaten them easily.*

With a yell, Brodie rushed forward, thrusting first with the blade in his right hand then slashing savagely at Corvus' right leg with his left. Roaring defiance, Corvus planted his injured left leg firmly behind him and rocked back onto it. Waves of agony roared up the irate limb and stars exploded in his vision, yet—digging deep and finding some remaining reservoir of strength and endurance—Corvus allowed the leg to bear his weight for just a moment longer. With a quick block of the first knife, Corvus swept his sword back and down, meeting Brodie's wrist just before the expected slash arrived. Brodie's left hand, still clutching its long knife, was severed from his arm and skidded harmlessly into the sawdust. Corvus staggered back, quickly getting his weight off his agonized left leg, and gasping for breath against the searing pain in his chest and ribs.

The realization that his hand was gone seemed to dawn slowly on Brodie's face as he backed up toward the onlookers around the Circle's edge. Then he let out a low, long scream,-which shifted suddenly to a high, pinched sound as a knife blade from behind him thrust powerfully up into his groin. Brodie's head twisted back in agony and his brow furrowed in disbelief at the sight of his attacker. Then he pitched forward, squirming into the dust with the blade handle protruding between his legs. Dallin stood behind him, her swollen face bandaged and her mouth open in a silent scream of rage, revealing broken teeth and mangled lips. She fell on him from behind, ripping the knife from his crotch with a strength born of years of difficult farm work and the passion of revenge. Kneeling over his prone form, she plunged the long knife into his back repeatedly, sobbing with each strike. No one moved to stop her from exacting her vengeance. She continued to stab the body long after life had left it, her arms and face spattered with Brodie's blood.

A hush fell over the crowd and Corvus closed his eyes, knowing the ordeal was finally over. He inhaled a long, slow, and painful breath as he attuned his mind to the sounds around him: Dallin's sobs, the dull thudding sound of the blade hitting Brodie's corpse over and over again, a hammer ringing with unusual intensity at the smithy, and the ever-present gulls calling mournfully over the crashing waves below the cliffs of Dóchas.

Chapter 5

The city of Deep Mere was situated on the eastern end of the eponymous lake, just on the north side of the Mere Canal—an artificial waterway constructed by Isador's great-grandfather, Armel III, to connect Deep Mere to the busy commerce of the Claws. The Claws were a chain of three long, thin, parallel lakes that resembled a great claw scratch across the landscape beginning in the south of Aesthir in the Hawless Mountains and cutting southeastward across much of Lachland, even into the western edge of Mardin. Countless towns and cities had sprung up along the edges of the Claws and merchant ships, barges, and pleasure boats plied the lakes from early spring until well after the first snows. The Mere Canal, thanks to its ingenious lock system, connected the once small and isolated town of Deep Mere to the rest of the kingdom. After its completion, the town grew rapidly, fueled by the trade of its rich resources, which were now accessible.

King Armel III, a man of vision and legendary stubbornness, had always planned to move his capital to Deep Mere, but until his two great projects were built—the Mere Canal and the majestic Wetheral Castle—it simply wasn't practical. To Armel's dismay, the construction of the two projects lasted most of his thirty-two year reign, with the canal finishing some ten years before his death and the castle only being completed in time for the King to die and be buried in it. Indeed, his last official act was to officially move the seat of government from the city of Morvan in the south to Deep Mere and Wetheral Castle.

– *Encyclopedia Daffydia,* Third Edition

574 HR - *Second month of summer*
Somewhere near Deep Mere, Lachland

Darienne

The clash and clangor of the blades rang out with fierce intensity in the vast cavern, echoing and rebounding from the stony walls. Darienne and her scarred opponent both circled one another with a similar feral grace on the sandy shore of an underground lake. The darkness of the subterranean space was broken only by the reflected light from the cavern's overgrown and narrow entrance, some hundred feet distant, and a single lantern perched on a boulder near the combatants. Darienne's unbound auburn hair offset her pale complexion and whipped about her as she fought, like the flame of a torch dancing in the wind. Her mother, Queen Isador IV of Lachland, insisted that Darienne braid her hair and wear it in a more seemly, feminine style, which was precisely why the defiant Princess wore it down and free—just as she so often preferred the comfort of men's clothing over expensive gowns. The Princess fought with a curved cavalry saber and dagger, while her assailant held a straight-bladed rapier in one hand and his own dagger in the other. The sparks from the clashes of their furious blades reflected on the otherwise still, black water. The only sounds within the cavern were their labored breaths and the ringing of their Aesthirian steel blades.

Darienne's long leather coat swirled as she avoided a killing blow, spinning suddenly to a knee and slashing viciously with her saber across her opponent's midsection. The cut would have killed the man, had he not anticipated such a move and spun himself just barely out of her reach. As it was, the saber opened a gash across the front of his embroidered military vest, a silver button spinning away to splash far out into the water. Unfazed by the close call, her assailant's attacks redoubled and Darienne deftly rolled out of the way of a vicious dagger cut, springing back to her feet just in time to deflect his incoming rapier. With a roll of her wrist and a sudden circular flash of her blade, her attacker's sword spun out of his grip and landed softly in the sand nearby. A slight grin flashed over the man's scarred face as, without the slightest pause at losing the weapon, he thrust with his dagger at her belly. Reacting instinctively, Darienne surprised him by dropping her own dagger and blocking his incoming strike with her left hand, grabbing his wrist in a viselike grip. With a grunt of surprise, her attacker pivoted toward her, slamming his right shoulder into her left, only narrowly avoiding her saber's counter thrust and grabbing her sword arm with his free hand. Thus locked together—each with one weapon, while their other hands grasped their opponent's weapon arm—the two struggled for a time, each striving for leverage and advantage in an almost choreographed dance of death. Finally, Darienne found her moment, and managed to jerk her opponent's upper body toward her slightly, affecting his balance for just a split second. It was all she needed. She slipped her leg behind his and with a sudden buck of her knee into the back of his leg, followed by a daring tumble into the sand, she threw her attacker violently onto his back. Despite being thrown, the man maintained his grip on her arms and the two tumbled over one another until Darienne ended up kneeling on top of him, her saber blade against his throat, his hand no longer gripping her wrist.

"Yield, Kaiso," she said, breathing heavily, her voice echoing in the cavern's stillness. "You're beaten."

"Am I?" The mercenary captain glanced down toward her unguarded stomach, the prominent scar on his cheek turning his slight grin into a sneer. Looking down, she saw that the captain still held a knife—one she hadn't accounted for—and it was pointed directly at her heart.

"Shit," Darienne muttered, leaning back and absent-mindedly tucking her auburn curls behind her ear. "Where did that come from?" Shaking her head, she stood and offered him a hand up.

"Always have a backup plan, Princess," Captain Kaiso replied, accepting the hand and standing. He slipped the knife back into its hidden sheath beneath his vest with a click.

"Whee! Such fun!"

A high voice accompanied by the sound of clapping surprised them both, and they spun to face the sound, weapons up once more. Silhouetted against the light from the cavern entrance, Darienne could just make out a wiry, ragged man perched atop a boulder. Moving closer to get a better look, she saw that he had a wild mop of unkempt hair and was dressed in torn, motley trousers that came to his mid-leg with a matching motley vest over an otherwise bare chest. It was hard to judge his age—he could have been thirty or sixty—and he was giggling manically in delight at the display of sword work, clapping his hands and his bare feet together. A small and rather mangy dog sat by his side on the rock, and it yipped animatedly along with the man's laughter and antics.

Kaiso looked to Darienne quizzically then back to the intruder, unsure of what to make of him. The captain cautiously bent to collect Darienne's dropped dagger. The princess, meanwhile, strode calmly over to Kaiso's fallen rapier. Slipping the toe of her boot beneath the forte of the blade, she deftly kicked the weapon high into the air, where it arced—handle first—right at the captain. Just before the blade arrived, Kaiso tossed her dagger to her. Both caught their weapons effortlessly in almost synchronized fashion, and after brushing the sand off of them, returned them to their sheaths.

"This is a private place and a private matter," Kaiso said menacingly, stalking toward the intruder.

Darienne's voice stopped his advance. "Peace, Kaiso. Latrans is a friend—a strange friend, but a friend."

"We are discovered," Kaiso hissed back at her, never taking his eyes off the odd, unknown man.

"Latrans can keep a secret," she reassured him, striding toward her waterskin near the entrance. "Can't you, old man?"

"Secrets and whispers," the Fool replied with a manic glee in his eyes. "Rumors and dreams, these are the stuff of all plans and schemes."

He stood up as he spoke, arms wide as if addressing a vast unseen audience all around them. Just as he finished speaking, he leapt from the boulder, effortlessly landing in a quiet crouch in the sand next to the Princess, provoking an indulgent smile from her. With his head back and arms open in a theatrical pose, he appeared to be waiting for applause. Darienne and Kaiso exchanged glances. The little dog seemed quite distressed at suddenly being abandoned on the top of the high rock, barking and whining furiously, its little tail wagging madly. Latrans turned slightly toward the dog, at which point the scraggly beast leapt fearlessly down onto his chest. He caught the dog with one hand, then spun to a knee and somehow, during the course of the spin, he deftly had transferred the dog to his shoulder where it balanced on its hind legs. The Fool's other hand somehow produced a bright, multicolored kerchief, and again he paused in a highly theatrical pose as if awaiting the applause and thrown coins of a large audience. With a playful shove, the Princess pushed the Fool's face, forcing him into a backward tumble, which he executed adeptly and ended on his feet, fists on hips, the little dog's stubby tail wagging furiously as it ran figure eights around his feet. His smile faded as he bent down to his dog, index finger extended, whispering instructions to the animal who had apparently not executed its part of the routine correctly.

"Our secret must not be known," Kaiso said to Darienne, his hand drifting to the hilt of his dagger. Though only in his early thirties, his scar, uniform, and serious demeanor combined to suggest that he was much older.

"Relax, Captain," the Princess responded. "Latrans is fine. Our secret is safe, isn't it, Fool?"

The motley man looked up earnestly from instructing his companion, nodded, and replied innocently, "As you wish, Mistress."

Shaking his head in acquiescence, Kaiso looked down to inspect the damage to his vest. His fingers probed the cut and the missing button.

"Do you have any idea how much this will cost to repair?" He looked accusingly at her. "This is Veruvian silk and these buttons aren't easy to replace. They're only issued to officers of our unit, and can't be purchased." He looked to where the button had disappeared into the still, black waters of the lake and shook his head.

"Button!" the Fool exclaimed. "I have a button." With a running leap he dove into the air, landing in an effortless tumble on one knee before Kaiso with his arms out and the kerchief covering his right hand. With the flourish of a street magician, he whisked the cloth aside, revealing a shining silver button, which he presented to the captain with a nod.

"Yes, yes, thank you," Kaiso said dismissively, taking the button and turning it over in his hand. "But not any button will do. These are the embossed buttons... of the Blades of..." He trailed off as he examined the Fool's gift more closely. "Where did you get this?"

The Princess shook her head and began to climb the scree to the cave's narrow entrance. With a cackle of glee, Latrans scrambled after her up and out of the cavern, his little dog scampering behind.

"Wait!" Kaiso called after him. "Where did you...?"

Darienne shielded her eyes from the bright sunlight as she stepped out of the cave and around the large bushes that masked its entrance. She spotted the horses some three hundred paces distant, tied in the shade of a tree beside a fast-flowing stream. On the off chance that someone might come upon their horses and thereby discover their training sessions, they had developed the habit of tethering their mounts well distant from the cave's mouth.

Darienne had intentionally and carefully cultivated the reputation of a wastrel at court. It was Kaiso's suspicion that there were those who would object to her ascending the throne, and that the more she appeared to be the useless, self-indulgent heir, the more apt they were to underestimate her. An assassin would approach their task based on the perceived danger of the victim. So, she developed the habit of drinking routinely and indulging her Sapphic desires openly and unashamedly. She was the model of a worthless heir and absolutely no one at court took her seriously. Especially her mother, Queen Isador. Though the kingdom of Lachland was historically patrilineal, there had been exceptions over the centuries, and when Isador's father had died with no son, she had stepped forward, boldly daring anyone to deny her right to the throne. Having now ruled for over twenty years, Darienne's mother still struggled to walk the line between being a proper and courtly lady—striving to satisfy those that recoiled from the thought of a woman being too forward—and a monarch with a spine of steel. The dissonance in her own identity had perhaps informed her daughter's rebellious nature. Darienne had decided some time ago that she had no patience nor taste for corsets and ribbons, and worrying about propriety or what others might think of her behavior was dismissed entirely. Her path reflected both her mother's strength of spirit and her own iconoclastic personality.

As a part of her carefully cultivated demeanor, Darienne had taken to frequent carousing in Deep Mere and had developed a shifty cadre of underworld drinking comrades who were all too ready to join her in questionable escapades on occasion. It was through discussions with them that she had decided to seek a sword master over five years ago. The courtliness and stiff adherence to propriety of Maestro Corbin, the sword master at court, was distasteful to her, and his fighting style seemed somehow antique. So she began to inquire among her shadier friends as to where she might find just the right teacher—effective, pragmatic, and deadly. After much inquiry, and at significant expense, she had finally found the name of the perfect man. Mercenary, assassin, and personal guard, Captain Joaquin Kaiso had a somewhat sinister reputation, and a cloud of dishonor floated near his name; it was never able to firmly attach, but it always hovered close. Darienne had written to the captain, who served with the Blades of Sebastian, a storied mercenary company out of the island nation of Cantabria. After a brief correspondence in which his rather significant fee was agreed upon, Darienne pleaded with her mother that in celebration of her nineteenth birthday, she be allowed to import a personal bodyguard, as the royal guards—known as the Lake Jacks—were so "stuffy." The Queen had been perplexed by the seemingly capricious request, but knowing her daughter's restive nature and compulsion to engage in nocturnal adventures, the Queen had agreed that it would be better if the girl had a guard with her. Darienne was in the habit of slipping away from her guards—something that infuriated the proud commander of the Lake Jacks to no end—and the Queen no doubt hoped that having a bodyguard of her own choosing would keep the Princess protected more often than not.

Upon meeting him, Darienne soon learned that Kaiso was a true anomaly. A mysterious figure, he was a brilliant swordsman in his own right, though he clearly eschewed any public display of his skill. His practice was to operate in the shadows, advising, guarding, training others, and, on occasion, killing. Though not technically an assassin, his apparent lack of moral compass meant he would not hesitate to remove a threat by any means necessary. His was not the honor-bound and stuffy world of Maestro Corbin with its chivalric rules that, as he told her, got in the way of survival. Instead, his approach was focused on winning by any means necessary, and living to fight another day. He was a scarred man of mystery, with olive-toned skin, short black hair and dark, brooding eyes that led one to believe he was not to be trifled with. At the moment, however, his typical steely and grim demeanor seemed to be in disarray over a button that he continued to examine in the sunlight.

Just as Latrans caught up to Darienne, affecting an air of casual innocence, Kaiso called from behind them, "Where did you get this, Fool?"

"He gets very excited about buttons, doesn't he?" Latrans whispered to the Princess, pointing over his shoulder with his thumb. She stifled a giggle behind her gloved hand and continued walking toward the horses.

With a series of expert cartwheels and leaps, the eccentric man tumbled well ahead of her, arriving first to the shade of the willow where the horses were tethered. By the time she and the captain walked up, he was perched against the trunk of the tree, skillfully miming sitting on an invisible chair and playing a merry tune on a flute. Given the thin and scant nature of his clothing, Darienne paused to consider where the flute had come from. Kaiso attempted again to ferret out the origin of the button, but each time he opened his mouth to speak, Latrans would suddenly play with greater intensity and volume, clearly ignoring him. Darienne shook her head and again stifled a chuckle as she resaddled her horse.

Just as she was preparing to mount the speckled gelding, Latrans stopped playing and looked up at her.

"There was something else, Princess…" The Fool seemed to be searching his memory.

"Oh?" Darienne responded, absently climbing into the saddle. "And what was that, Fool?"

"Your mother… Yes, your mother wants to see you," he said, nodding. "Yes, that was it. She needs you at court right away. Quite urgent, in fact. Something about being invaded." With a shrug, he returned to his melody.

A look of alarm passed between Kaiso and Darienne. The Princess knew better than to press Latrans for important details; his thoughts led in convoluted spirals as undecipherable as the chatter of squirrels. Without another word, she spurred off at a brisk canter toward Wetheral Castle with Kaiso close behind her, leaving Latrans sitting on his invisible chair and merrily playing his melody by the side of the stream. His little dog listened with rapt, adoring attention, while a raven croaked its own song from a low branch of the tree.

Chapter 6

Despite the philosophical differences that apparently drove the Schism, those followers of the Path of the Divine Halls maintained their own martial practice independent of the martial forms of the Way of the Hand. Called *mulakima*, its seeming simplicity complements the ascetic spirituality of the devotees of the Path. A basic and straightforward art form, it is less wide ranging than the twelve fighting forms of the Way of the Hand, and does not delve into esoterica. Instead, it teaches a powerful variety of punches, kicks, grapples, holds, and throws, as well as weapons work—with the bow, staff, and spear—all taught and practiced both from the ground and mounted. While all followers of the Path are expected to be trained in mulakima, described as the third leg of the stool of the Path by 'Asasiun Bahjat at the Council of Vyashtun, its preeminence in the teachings has diminished over the generations. Now, it can be said that very few votaries become expert in the practice. But for those that do pursue mulakima with a passion, the Path still robustly supports their efforts—though my more cynical colleagues would no doubt put forward that this is largely due to the revenues generated. Tournaments and regional competitions have sprung up and become enormously popular among the lay population. Indeed, the Greening Festival in Qat Province has grown so popular—in large part due to the mulakima championship—that the regional governor recently ordered additional infrastructure, with public latrines added, broader avenues constructed, and a significantly increased constabulary presence. The festival city can now accommodate over one hundred thousand visitors. This marks the third time in three generations that the city has been enlarged to accommodate the tournament. The winners of the tournament enjoy celebrity status among the people, though their vows of humility and asceticism appropriately prevent them from being feted as the public might desire.

– Foreword to *Mulakima: its Practices and Teachings,* by Ecclesiarch Elham

574 HR - Second month of summer
Somewhere in the south of Mardin

Lupe

She paused as she cleaned her morning catch over the stream. Her teeth chattered lightly; she was unused to the morning chill in these lands. She carefully set down her scaling knife on a rock protruding from the stream, wiped her hands on her apron, and adjusted the tie on the back of the jimas around her face. The ice-cold water had numbed her fingers as she worked, and the fabric of the veil over her face kept slipping through them.

How can people live in this cold climate? To them, this is summer!

She glanced back in the direction of the campfire and was pleased to see Mama Warad sitting and drinking her morning tea. Trying to get that woman to slow down even a little was like trying to stop the desert winds from blowing in the springtime. They had been traveling now for months from their homeland in the Qat province of Asland. For the first leg of their journey, they had enjoyed the good fortune of traveling with a merchant caravan, which had provided company, protection, and shelter. But once they arrived in the port city of Tiplai and parted ways with the caravan, it seemed their good fortune had ended. The Sudlandic trading vessel upon which they had booked their passage across the Mirror Sea ran afoul of coastal pirates, and though the crew and passengers together had successfully fended off the attackers, the ship had been severely damaged in the battle. It had limped along for the rest of the trip, all hands working the pumps just to keep her afloat. What should have been a two-week journey lasted over a moon. Food and water were running critically low by the time they arrived in Cape Nihr in the south of Sudland, far south of their intended destination of Barris. Mama Warad and her three votaries, Amina, Lupe, and Yadira had been traveling north on foot in this strange, cold, green land ever since. They had been accosted four times on the journey so far: twice by bandits, which they had been able to fend off handily enough (much to the surprise of the bandits), once by a traveling priest of the Church of the Five who had cursed and spit at them, and once by a strange man driving a large covered wagon who was traveling with a group of eight immodestly dressed women. Lupe hadn't understood what the man said to Mama at the time, but from her sudden angry response—driving the man off with a sharp blow from her staff—Lupe guessed that it was indecent. Mama would not speak of the incident for days afterward, until one evening Lupe had pressed her for more details. Mama would only say, "This land has very different customs and is very dangerous. We must all show caution and be on our guard." She had then muttered a rare oath under her breath and spat into the fire.

The three votaries had nodded solemnly and let the matter drop, though Lupe was burning for more information. Of the three younger women, she knew she had the greatest challenge absorbing the sacred practices of patience and obedience. But by the Witness, she was curious about these people! *A traveling brothel… By the moon's light, how could they?* Both morally and as a matter of practicality, the concept confused Lupe and she was deeply unsettled by it. Amina, unsurprisingly, seemed unaffected by the whole affair and simply tended dutifully to her chores around camp and her studies, often reading one of the sacred texts Mama had brought by campfire light in the evenings or balancing the heavy book in her lap while eating her breakfast of spiced porridge and tea. She was the youngest of the three, having just passed her eighteenth rain, and had obviously been blessed by an angel of intelligence at her birth. She needed only read something once, and it seemed to be committed forever to memory, precisely as written. Lupe had heard Amina recite the sacred texts from beginning to end, and the girl knew all manner of scholarly esoterica—names, dates, critical opinions, the texts of holy didactica, sacred and secular poetry, and more. Her soft, monotone voice and bookish manner had originally led Lupe to assume the girl was meek and perhaps somewhat simple, but over the past three years of their dedicated service together, she had come to respect and rely on Amina's knowledge, memory, and stoic nature.

When first planning their journey, back in Asland, there had been no question but that Amina would be their navigator, guiding them through strange and hostile lands. Mama had accompanied her to the Grand Library in Tabith, where Amina had spent two full days studying the royal cartographers' maps of the far away land of Daffyd, and the various countries within its borders. Together, Mama and Amina had planned the little group's route to the cold mountains. Despite arriving in a city dozens of leagues to the southeast of their intended port of entry, Amina's flawless memory of the maps had served them well. She had guided them across this alien and wildly fecund landscape without error, steering clear of larger towns and cities when possible, guided only by the path of rivers and the topographical variations of the countryside. Sometime yesterday, Amina had notified them that as close as she could guess, they had crossed the border out of Sudland and into Mardin. They had been warned repeatedly about traveling through Mardin as the wild men—the Barbárs—were everywhere and were quite brutal, given to rapine, conquest, and the taking of slaves. But to these worries, Mama would only reply "If it is the will of the Ancestors..." and leave everything else unsaid.

Lupe dropped another cleaned fish onto a damp towel that she had set on the large rock. She paused momentarily in her labor to arch her back and wipe her cold, wet hands on her apron, then she cupped them before her mouth and puffed warm air into them to try to stave off the numbness. Glancing at the campsite, Lupe could see that the fire was ready, and Yadira had her cooking pan oiled and waiting. She was sure to be impatient for Lupe to finish cleaning the fish, and while her waspishness could be abrasive at times, Lupe couldn't fault the older votary, as the magic the woman wove with spices and herbs consistently produced mouthwatering meals that Lupe was sure would have pleased any sultan or prince. Yadira was the eldest of the three votaries by a decade, Amina having only just passed her eighteenth rain, Lupe, her twenty-second, and Yadira, her thirty-third. It was quite unusual for a votary to remain in Adherence so long. Lupe knew that Yadira had twice been offered an elevation to priesthood, and she had twice declined, for reasons of her own, choosing instead to remain in service to Mama Warad, wherever that might lead her. Lupe knew that even though Mama would be proud for Yadira to move on to her own priesthood—and Yadira was certainly knowledgeable and wise enough to have her own votaries—Mama was quietly glad to have the woman's continued company. The two had worked together now for some twenty years, and seemed to know each other's moods and needs without speaking. It was clear that they shared a deep bond of mutual respect and purpose.

Stretching her hands over her head to ease a cramp in her shoulder, Lupe mused for a moment at how very different the three votaries were in appearance and nature. Yadira was tall and angular, wiry yet strong, and indefatigable in her duties. The eldest votary slept but little, and even when Lupe rose before dawn to hunt, she would find Yadira already up, either building the campfire in preparation for breakfast or taking her *altaamuli,* a walking meditative practice. Lupe felt there was something that haunted Yadira, for the woman rarely smiled and almost never laughed. Whatever it was, Lupe had long since given up trying to be friends with the older votary. They shared a devotion and a dedicated service; in that capacity, they were sisters and would forever be there for one another. But other than Mama Warad, Lupe had never seen anyone grow close to Yadira.

In contrast, Amina was sylphlike and fragile, and seemed often to be lost in thought. Yet she too was dutiful and diligent in her childlike way. Amina had a strong aversion to human contact and would recoil at the slightest brush of skin on skin. Loud noises also seemed to affect her adversely, causing the waiflike girl to curl into a ball, cover her ears, and even weep. They had all grown accustomed to Amina's idiosyncrasies, however, and celebrated her remarkable gifts instead of discussing her shortcomings or weaknesses.

Lupe, on the other hand, was robust, with a solid build. Easily the strongest of the three, Lupe's role on this journey was that of the hunter and protector. All of the votaries of Mama Warad practiced mulakima, the Aslene martial art, as part of their devotion, but Lupe was by far the most gifted of the three. Blessed with natural strength and flexibility, she had taken to the martial practice as if born to it. Highly effective with staff, bow, knife, hands, and feet—able to kick higher than even Yadira's head—Lupe had recently found another application for the lightning-quick strikes she practiced daily: catching fish with her bare hands. She would wade into the shallows of a river or stream, braving the ice-cold waters of this northern land, and wait, internally reciting the Canon of Patience. The other women would watch as she stood still as a statue for long minutes, and then would suddenly lash out with a hand into the running water to produce a fish, still wriggling and no doubt quite confused by its sudden change of fortune. Lupe fought against the temptation to take pride in her physical skills, for pride was not an acceptable trait in a devotee of the Path of the Divine Halls. Each of the votaries had their talents, and she was happy to fill the role of hunter, provider, and protector in their small band.

"Girl, are those fish cleaned yet?" Mama Warad's voice startled Lupe from her reverie. "The fire is just right."

"Coming, sitti," Lupe answered dutifully, rinsing her hands once more in the cold stream water and wrapping the three fish in the towel. She rose from her crouch by the stream bed, stepped out of the water, and adjusted her robes to cover her ankles modestly before donning her sandals and walking back to their campsite. The smells of spiced tea and cinnamon porridge mixed with the rich smoke of the campfire and Lupe's mouth watered in anticipation. How that woman could subtly flavor such simple fare to produce culinary magic, she would never understand. Though ostensibly unfamiliar with the local flora, Yadira seemed to possess an intuitive knowledge of the wild plants of this foreign land; she had identified various medicinal or flavorful herbs, plants to be used for dying cloth should the need arise, and even some highly poisonous mushrooms—though how in the Divine Halls Yadira knew they were poisonous was a mystery. The natural world around them seemed so logical to the eldest votary, and clusters and bundles of herbs, berries, mushrooms, leaves, roots, and shoots went into Yadira's seemingly bottomless satchel, each wrapped, organized, and placed carefully within, ready to be produced at a moment's notice.

The other women gasped in appreciation when Lupe presented her morning catch. The fish were large and meaty, and she had cleaned them thoroughly for Yadira.

"Very nice," Amina said softly in her monotone voice, smiling shyly behind her jimas and nodding.

"They're quite big," Yadira said admiringly, her eyes betraying only the slightest hint of a smile. "We will eat well." The severe woman looked approvingly at Lupe.

"The stream is full of them," Lupe responded, humbly deflecting the praise. Warming her hands by the fire, she continued, "Anyone could reach in and gather them."

"I doubt that's true," Mama said, giving her a slight wink over the brim of her steaming mug, and flustering the young woman. "You bless us in providing for our needs, and we honor you."

"We honor you," the other two women intoned in unison.

Her olive skin blushing furiously, Lupe patted her tingling hands on her thighs and looked about for something that might prompt a change of subject.

"What are you reading today, Amina?" she asked brightly.

"A Doctrinal Essay on The Nine Parallels," the girl responded, without looking up.

There was a pause in which Lupe looked to Yadira for clarification. The older votary shrugged and continued shredding herbs onto the fish. After an awkward silence, Lupe busied herself breaking down the tent. Yadira and Mama shared an amused glance.

"Did you sleep well, Mama?" Yadira asked dutifully as she prepared the fish for frying, first dipping them in whipped quail's eggs, then coating them with crushed stale bread and more herbs, and placing them in her skillet, greased with goat lard. Soon the entire campsite was filled with the amazing aroma of frying fish and spices.

"I did not," Mama replied matter-of-factly. "Something stirs, and it is, as yet, opaque to me."

The three votaries paused in their various activities and looked at her with serious expressions, waiting for more. No hint of a smile softened her demeanor, and after a moment's pause—in which it became evident that she would not continue speaking—they went back to their duties, all levity gone. Though Mama Warad was only in her fifties, she looked older and carried a natural gravitas that demanded respect. Bearing only a vestige of what must have once been remarkable beauty, she was now the very image of a toughened *qariba,* an Aslene term for any middle-aged woman. Her eyes, like black holes against her dark, leathery skin, suggested a wisdom to be attended to. And her plump cheeks, ready smile, and rotund body presented an image of jollity that drew others like a lodestone. Yet she had a maternal sternness to her that brooked no disagreement. Her graying hair was worn like the other women's, in long plaits down her back, beneath a headscarf. No longer a maiden, she eschewed the jimas, choosing to present her bare face to the world—a practice that was not unheard of for qariba.

Technically, the teachings of the Path of the Divine Halls urged sobriety and a frugal existence, however Lupe had known Mama to bend those guidelines from time to time. She had a natural vivacity and enjoyed nothing more than opening a bottle of rose mead or perhaps cinnamon brandy (when the trading caravan came by) and sharing tall tales and silly songs with her protégés—only after the day's work was done, mind you, and never when anyone outside their little family might see. During their sojourn, she might suddenly break into song while hiking over the rolling hills, inspired by the green beauty of the land, or perhaps tell ribald tales around the fire at night after a few sips of her evening "tea." Never failing to tease Lupe for her furious blushes, or Yadira for the disapproving shake of her head, or Amina for her naive confusion at the subject matter. The inconsistencies in this amazing woman were part of what made her votaries love her so much. She was so much more than a teacher; she was, in all ways that mattered, their Mama.

In her youth, Lupe had heard that Mama had been the youngest mulakima master in all of Qat province, earning the grudging respect even of Grand Precept Zander before his death. And there were rumors that she had personally known Master Ashahl, considered one of the greatest practitioners of the Way of the Hand to ever live. The years and the daily privations of living on the edge of the desert had worn on her, and though still a strong and imposing figure, she now walked with a certain stiffness. Starting sometime near the end of this past rain, she had begun using an unusually tall staff that she referred to as her "cane." None of the votaries knew where she had gotten it, nor were they aware of its history, but it was clearly of a wood not native to their homeland. Taller than a man, the staff looked at first glance to be driftwood, aged and parched by the salt of the sea. There were gentle undulations in the grain of the wood up its length, and at its head, the wood curved dramatically as if it were smoke, captured and frozen just as it blew forward out of some narrow chimney. The short, rotund, and unassuming woman walking with such a tall and dramatic staff was quite an incongruous sight, and often served as a conversation starter for curious passersby. Mama took great delight in spinning new origin stories for the staff, each more outlandish than the last and delivered with complete deadpan earnestness, leaving the listeners in wonder and confusion. Over the moons that Mama had carried it, no one had seen any chip or scrape on its surface. Many times it had been struck, knocked over, and even rolled over by a heavily laden wagon, yet the staff emerged from each mischance completely unmarred. Once, it had even fallen across a very hot campfire, where it remained for several moments while an unruly goat was recaptured, and yet again it had emerged without so much as a soot stain. When Lupe would ask Mama seriously about its history, the teacher always demurred, her eyes taking on a misted and sad faraway look.

Their breakfast complete and the remaining fish packed away for the evening meal, they finished breaking down camp and prepared for another long day's walk northward, ever northward. Amina took the lead, as per usual, with Yadira and Mama following not far behind while Lupe brought up the rear with her recurved bow, so exotic for the people of these lands, slung over her shoulder. The terrain here near the coastal marshlands was rugged, muddy, and slow going. They were nearing the River Pellin, a broad, fast-flowing waterway that ran southward for several leagues before turning east to where it met the sea, somewhere in Sudland. To women accustomed to eking out their lives in the arid province of Qat, the surfeit of waterways, streams, ponds, lakes, and countless rivulets that they had to navigate daily in this land was stunning. Though after two days straight hiking over the muddy hillocks and marshes that surrounded them, Lupe would have given much for a landscape a little more like home.

Yadira

"Have you thought on my suggestion, Dira?" Mama asked the eldest protégé as they walked together.

"I have."

"And?" Mama pressed.

"It frightens me, Mama," Yadira replied.

The two women paused in their conversation to work their way through a particularly boggy area between two hillocks.

Stopping atop the second mound, Mama wiped some mud from her boots, planting the end of her staff for balance. Yadira placed a hand on the staff, adding support for her honored teacher. She swatted a biting insect and watched quietly as Mama scooped another fistful of mud out of the top of her boot. Satisfied for the moment with her right foot, Mama repeated the process with the left, still clutching her staff for balance.

"I understand the fear, my dear," Mama continued without looking up, as if the conversation had not lapsed. "But you have shown great promise in this area, and have the best chance of success in this."

Yadira weighed her words as Mama finished scooping mud from her boot and straightened, wiping her hand on the sides of her robes.

"The risk is great, is it not?" Yadira said evenly, her sea-gray eyes searching Mama's from just above her jimas.

With a nod and a smile, Mama responded, "Yes it is. But the risk is not nearly so great to your body as it is to the fences you build around your heart." With a wink and a tap of her finger on Yadira's breastbone, Mama turned and continued. Yadira stood for a moment, absorbing the implications of Mama's words. But after watching her teacher struggle onward through another bog, she sighed, her decision made, and stepped down off the mound to catch up.

Lupe

They had been hiking some two hours, Lupe appreciating the cool, loamy, and pine-scented breeze that seemed to blow steadily out of the woodlands to their west, when Amina suddenly crouched behind a nearby bush situated atop a small knoll. Mama and Yadira stopped in place, alert for danger. Lupe's bow was quickly strung and in her hand with a practiced grace, an arrow already nocked as she crouched to scan the rough land behind them, as well as the dark woods which stood not a half hour's walk to their west. After a few moments, Amina returned quietly to Mama, crouching low as she moved. Lupe crept near to hear her report.

"Smoke near the river ahead," Amina said, her monotone voice almost inaudible.

"A campfire or a settlement, do you think?" Mama asked.

"Too thick for a campfire," Amina replied simply, pointing to the northeast of their position where a steady, thick column of light brown smoke rose among the trees along the river. Lupe's eyes roved the land around them, briefly taking in the sight of the smoke, then returning to watch the woods.

The group cautiously moved to the bush atop the rise, behind which Amina had originally stopped, for a better view. After a half hour's wait in which they saw no movement, Mama decided that they could risk moving closer. If it were a settlement, they might barter for supplies, and if it were trouble, perhaps they might be of some help. Regardless, Lupe was quite pleased they would be rid of this bog.

"Let us follow this stream toward the river," Mama said. "The trees there will give us some cover as we move up closer. Be alert, my doves."

It took a little over an hour for them to carefully work their way to the river and move up the forested bank far enough to finally see the source of the smoke. A small settlement had been ravaged and burned—a farmstead of three homes and a communal barn, all of which were in smoking ruins. Bodies were strewn about in the open. From the look of the scene, the attack had happened the day before and the smoke was emanating from the charred ruins of the barn, which still smoldered.

Mama

Mama whispered to Lupe to move ahead and scout the area, while the other three waited behind. She tried to follow her progress, but within moments Lupe had vanished among the trees, silent and invisible. The teacher shook her head in quiet amazement at her student's natural gift of stealth.

Anxious moments passed. Amina had seated herself along the riverbank, her back to a gray willow, while Mama and Yadira remained a few steps away among a group of alders, scanning the area with increasing worry.

"All dead."

The whisper from behind them startled both women who spun about in surprise, Yadira snorting audibly and quickly drawing a small knife from beneath her robe. But it was only Lupe.

"Child!" Mama gasped, placing her free hand over her heart. "You'll be the death of me!"

Lupe smiled at Mama's momentary discomfiture, then became serious again, pointing at the farmstead.

"Twelve bodies," she said. "Men, women, and… children. None left alive. The raiders took the livestock apparently, and burned everything."

The three women exchanged nervous glances, and then with a nod, Mama said, "Let us tend to the dead."

While Mama and Lupe dug graves, Yadira and Amina spent the rest of the day cleaning the bodies and ritually preparing them for burial, anointing them with oils and offering prayers and incense over each one, commending them to the Halls of the Ancestors. As the sun disappeared in crimson fury over the dark forest, they laid the bodies to rest before moving away from the ruined farmstead to the river's edge. There, too exhausted to bother pitching tents, they laid out their bedrolls beneath the spreading branches and fuzzy leaves of a grand, downy birch.

Within a short time, Yadira had a small fire burning and was laying out the fish, some dried goat jerky, and a handful of wild onions she had found on their day's journey.

Just as the last glimmers of twilight were fading, a raven's hoarse call drew their attention to where it perched on one of the downy branches of the tree. The bird seemed to stare directly at Mama as it called again. A frisson washed over her and her casual interest in the bird shifted to intense scrutiny. Yadira, Lupe, and Amina exchanged curious glances as she rose slowly from her seat by the fire, her gaze locked on the raven, careful not to make a sudden move that might startle the creature. The black bird, barely visible in the flickering of their small fire, cocked its head, still staring back at her, then turned and fluttered to a perch on a branch of another tree some twenty paces further away. Once again it locked eyes with her and called, its harsh croak echoing off the far riverbank. Mama walked carefully toward the bird, her lips silently reciting the Canon of Understanding. The votaries followed her quietly as a group, a few steps behind.

Once Mama had covered half the distance to the raven's new perch, the bird repeated the process, turning and flitting to the branch of another nearby tree, then turning back to Mama and calling. She followed it, confident now that this was more than a natural interaction with a wild creature. After another half dozen repetitions, the raven stopped and allowed Mama to approach the base of the birch tree in which it perched. She stepped forward cautiously, her lips continuing her silent recitation until she had placed herself directly beneath the raven. She held the bird's gaze and opened her hands to it, inviting its message. It cawed once more, then looked to a bush nearby, then back to Mama. Frowning in confusion, Mama glanced around at the surrounding area. Unlike the area of their campsite, not twenty paces away, the ground between the trees here was completely overgrown with large, hawthorn bushes, bedecked with white flowers. Some of them were as tall as she was, with game trails weaving beneath that looked like tunnels in the dying twilight. The thick cluster of shrubbery was a barrier, and Mama could move no further. She looked quizzically at the raven, as if asking for further instruction. Yadira, Amina, and Lupe stepped up quietly beside her, all eyes on the bird, which continued to alternate looks between Mama and a place somewhere in the midst of the thick brush, cawing at her after each glance.

"Whatever does it want?" Yadira asked quietly.

Mama raised a hand to shush her, and cocked her head, listening in the growing dark. There was the slightest rustle of leaves beneath the hawthorn in the direction the bird kept looking. Mama glanced silently at her three protégés to see if they had heard it as well. Lupe and Amina nodded, while Yadira merely raised an eyebrow in silent communication.

Seeing the size of the game trails, Mama nodded at Amina and pointed at the verdant tunnel by their feet. Her tiny frame was the only one that could possibly fit through it to explore this mystery. Amina blinked in confusion for a moment, then nodded her understanding. Handing the book she was still holding to Yadira, she hiked up her robe, knelt down and began to crawl into the tunnel. Night had now fully descended, and the distant flicker of their small campfire provided no help to Amina who would have to enter blind, hoping that whatever had made the rustling sound didn't have claws and teeth. Mama, Yadira, and Lupe all squinted in the darkness to watch her disappear into the tunnel. If she got into trouble in there, they would be no help. The three women unconsciously grasped one another's hands and stood silently as they waited, reciting prayers for Amina's safety.

There was almost no sound; only the quiet burble of the river flowing nearby and the rhythmic croaking of corncrakes welcoming the night disturbed what would otherwise have been absolute silence. Against this backdrop, Mama could easily follow the rustling that marked Amina's progress through the tunnel's various twists and turns, branches and splits. But she grew increasingly tense and worried as the minutes stretched out into an hour and more. The effort of listening so intently, trying to track her young disciple's progress, as well as willing Amina's safety with all her might was wearing on her. She gripped Lupe's sweaty hand more tightly, her own also clammy and wet with worry.

Then they heard Amina's voice, muffled and distant, seeming to speak softly to something. The raven cawed in response and danced back and forth along its branch. Mama risked breaking the silence and called out softly, "Amina, dear?" No response. She looked at Yadira, though in the darkness all she could see was her dim outline against the minimal light of their distant, dwindling campfire.

"Amina!" Mama called again, a little louder this time.

They could still hear her speaking softly, her words indistinct but the tone comforting and gentle. There was a pause, then Amina spoke again, and they heard a faint rustle of movement. Soon, it became clear to Mama that Amina was attempting to work her way back through the maze of game tunnels. The raven cawed, and continued its excited dance back and forth along its branch, high overhead.

Lupe broke free of the other ladies' hands and headed back to their campsite. Within moments, she had returned with a small burning branch, which she tipped carefully downward to keep its flame alight and to provide some illumination in the utter dark within the woods. She crouched down near the tunnel's entrance, holding her small flame near the opening, and was quickly rewarded with Amina's soft response.

"This way," she said, her voice coming from a place several yards away from where they were expecting to hear it. It was now becoming evident that there were two distinct rustling movements within the bushes. They waited another quarter of an hour, listening to Amina's various soft reassurances and noting her progress as the sounds of her movement grew closer.

At last, just as Lupe's carefully tended flame flickered out, Amina's head poked out of the tunnel's entrance. With the help of Lupe's extended hand, the young woman stood and straightened her back momentarily, then crouched once more and turned back to the opening. With more soft reassurances, she beckoned to whatever or whomever had been following her. In the darkness, Mama could perceive only that there was movement at the mouth of the burrow, but she could not see more.

Amina remained crouched and spoke gently. "There you are," she said. "Let's get you over near the fire and take a look at you."

She stood once more, and in the weak, flickering light of Lupe's branch, Mama could see that it was a child that now stood next to Amina, clutching her leg.

"Let's go back to the camp," Amina said in her soft monotone, "and meet our new friend."

The bemused ladies made their way carefully back to the campfire, which was now nothing more than dully glowing embers. Yadira added the remaining branches and twigs that they had gathered earlier, stirring it back to life. In the refreshed firelight, Mama looked at Amina, who stood at the edge of the circle of light, seemingly reluctant to step forward. A tiny hand clutched at her left knee, the only visible indication of the terrified child hiding behind her. Soon, a small, dirty face with a mop of dark hair and pale skin half peeked around Amina's leg, only one eye showing.

"Lupe," Mama said quietly, "fetch some water. And Dira, see if you have something for this poor child to eat."

The women quickly busied themselves with the tasks given to them, while Amina stood patient and still, gently stroking the little boy's hair.

"Well, aren't you a brave boy?" Mama smiled her warmest maternal smile, the firelight dancing in her dark eyes.

"I don't think he understands us," Amina said quietly, being careful to not startle the child.

"Of course." Mama nodded. "Yadira, would you be so good as to speak to our young guest?"

Yadira

Yadira knelt down on the ground next to the fire. She had some goat jerky and cheese which she held up for the boy to see.

"Are you hungry, little one?" she said in heavily accented Sudlandic. The boy looked at her in surprise at the familiar tongue, his full face now appearing beside Amina, whose legs he continued to grip with both hands. His eyes sparkled like jewels in the flickering light—one eye a glacial blue like a light sapphire, and the other the golden brown of pale almonds. Yadira raised an eyebrow, and Mama leaned back in surprise at the unexpected sight.

"By the Divine Halls!" Lupe gasped quietly, returning with a full water jug just in time to notice the boy's eyes.

With a gesture Mama shushed her, then smiled warmly at the boy and opened her hands, inviting him to step closer to the fire.

"Come, eat," Yadira said quietly. "I know you're hungry and thirsty. We'll keep you safe."

The boy's eyes darted from the food and water to Mama's face and then to Yadira's, before looking up at Amina for reassurance. Then he looked over to Lupe, and back to the food. He took a hesitant step toward the fire, and then a second cautious step, then with a quick glance back at Amina, he walked to Yadira's outstretched hands and took a piece of jerky. He smelled the goat meat suspiciously, then ravenously tore into it. After stuffing nearly the entire piece into his mouth, he took the cup of water that Lupe offered him, slurping it loudly in his thirst.

"Slow down, little mouse," Mama said in her own tongue. "You'll get a cramp. Yadira tell the boy."

"Slowly, slowly," she said in the boy's language. "You're safe now. Drink the water slowly, a few sips at a time. You've been through an ordeal, haven't you?"

The boy glanced at Yadira between bites, his face showing no response as he continued to eat and drink eagerly. His torn clothing was muddy, and he smelled of his own waste. Clearly, he had hidden from the raiders among the hawthorn bushes, and had been too terrified to leave his shelter, lying in his own filth for more than a day with no food or water.

"Do you have a name, child?" Yadira asked as the boy helped himself to another strip of jerky with his left hand, a wad of cheese clutched greedily in his right.

After a moment of no response, Yadira—whose hands were now free of food—opened the satchel at her side and produced a small bundle which she carefully unwrapped. Inside were a handful of wild raspberries. The boy's jewel-like eyes opened wide and he looked to her for permission. Yadira gave him an indulgent smile from behind her veil and nodded her head. Within a moment, the berries were gone, the tart red juice staining his lips. His eating eventually slowed, and he sipped more water, which Lupe happily refilled. Catching his breath, he sat back and blinked, a huge yawn overtaking him.

"You're tired," Yadira said. "Let's get you cleaned up, and then to bed. We'll speak more in the morning."

"Amina," Mama said, "take our young guest down to the river and clean him as best you may. Yadira, assist her, please."

"Yes, *sitti*," Yadira responded and, rising, she led the sleepy boy away toward the river.

When they returned from the river's edge, Lupe had prepared a bedroll for the freshly bathed, shivering child, now wrapped in a warm robe. Yadira drove a stick she had found into the soft ground near the campfire, and hung the boy's washed trousers on it, where they would dry overnight.

Amina settled herself with her back to a large oak, and beckoned the boy to sit beside her. The exhausted child obeyed without hesitation, and as the boy cuddled against her, Mama wrapped a blanket around them both. Before laying his head down, however, the boy sat up and looked at Mama.

"Argant," he said, his high-pitched voice barely audible.

"Argant?" Mama repeated, shaking her head quizzically.

"My name," he said in Sudlandic, staring at her with those unusual and penetrating eyes. "My name is Argant and my Papa is dead."

He watched as Yadira translated for the other women. Then, seemingly satisfied, he snuggled down into Amina's lap and fell fast asleep.

The ladies exchanged glances and, with a nod, Mama told them to get some sleep, though Amina opted to remain seated against the tree so as not to disturb their young guest, whose head was in her lap. Lupe and Yadira tidied the campsite and brought out their bedrolls.

Mama

As the women settled under their blankets, Mama looked with wonder at this unexpected child, his face just visible in the dim glow of the embers. Glancing up to the distant branches of the forest, she offered a silent word of thanks to the raven for its intervention.

After a moment, she heard a flurry of wings from the branches above the hawthorn bushes as the large bird took to the air.

Chapter 7

The organization of the villages of the High Valley is unique throughout the four territories of the Green Mount, I think. In the Midlands, the White Cleft, or among the Glenfolk, the villages and towns are organized around a hierarchical structure similar in practice to the feudal systems of the rest of Daffyd—and, indeed, similar to that of my own homeland. But in the High Valley, which boasts no village larger than a thousand souls, they still cling to "na seann dòighean" or "the old ways"—a series of customs handed down through the centuries, supposedly originating with the words of Ilian himself. This unwritten collection of traditions and customs holds that no man or woman is above anyone else, unless selected and empowered by the community to be such. And even then, they hold their office only with the ongoing consent of the governed. All within the community enjoy equal status, though whenever applicable, a woman's wisdom is considered greater than a man's. It is in this that I believe the true genius and tenacity of the people of the High Valley becomes most clear. Men and women share equally in the defense of their communities, and train together as one. Indeed, over the years, it has been my distinct privilege to train those members of the fyrd, be they man or woman. A privilege that took some getting used to, given the stark separation of the sexes and their tasks and duties in Asland.

– *Diary of Yazid ben Tariq*

574 HR - Second month of summer
Dóchas, The High Valley region of the Green Mount

Corvus

"Here, Da, let me," Ligulf said, stepping in front of Corvus to retrieve the dropped belt. Corvus shook his head as he accepted the strap proffered by his younger son. In the weeks since the Day of the Seven—as it was now being called—Ligulf had been his father's almost constant companion, splitting his time each day between tending to Corvus' needs and visiting his friend Dallin. When she was attacked, Ligulf had been out of the village on a two-day hike, visiting a friend and fellow musician in a village near the falls of Glenhorn. Upon his return, he had been horrified to learn of the assault and to find his father bedridden from the injuries he had suffered in the Circle. Obviously wracked with guilt that he had not been there for either Dallin or his father during their ordeals, the earnest young man set to tending to both of his injured loved ones. Corvus assumed that Dallin was a far better patient.

"Li," Corvus said as he buckled on the belt, "I'm fine. The ribs are mostly healed and Shanna says my arm should be back to full strength in a fortnight."

Ligulf ignored his father and continued fussing about, adjusting Corvus' belt, fastening the sword to it, and then handing his father a bundle of food—a loaf of bread, some sausages, and boiled eggs, all wrapped in a clean cloth.

"Now stop, lad." Corvus batted at Li's hands in a futile effort to get him to stop, but rather than cease, the young man held up a finger as though he had just remembered something. He fetched Corvus' jacket from the coat tree and absent-mindedly draped it over his arm as he collected two or three other things and carefully packed them in his father's satchel. Corvus tempered his irritation as he watched his younger son rush about the house. *So like his mother,* Corvus thought. His two sons were, in many ways, as different as night and day. Cailean was tall, strong, and bold, earnestly practiced his martial skills daily, but never shirking his chores at home either. He was growing into a man who could face any storm, battle any enemy, and stay true to himself throughout. Ligulf on the other hand was a bit of a dreamer. Slender, with a quick wit and ready smile, he was all too sensitive; at eighteen, he still couldn't watch the culling of the herd in the fall. And, despite his devotion to his father, his musical interests commanded the largest share of his attention.

As Ligulf bustled about, Corvus mused over the differences in his sons. He drilled both boys regularly in sword, staff, and unarmed combat styles, and while Cailean took to it all equally like a fish to water, Ligulf had always struggled with most weapons work. Of all the martial forms Corvus had introduced to his sons, only Sparrow form—a lighter, almost dance-like style utilizing the puntina, a thin, needle-like sword—seemed to connect for Ligulf, though he did show some aptitude for the hand-to-hand elements of Willow form, turning your opponent's force and strength against them. The memory of a young Ligulf flashed in Corvus' mind. The lad had seen maybe four summers at the time, and wanted so badly to make his da proud. Corvus had been in the front garden training Cailean and a handful of other young boys from the village in the rudiments of swordplay when a tiny voice piped up, calling for his attention. He had turned to see the wee thing standing on the top stair by the door. He still had on his huge nightshirt—one of Cailean's old ones that the older boy had outgrown—and he was wearing a pair of Corvus' boots, which came up well past the child's knees and were massive on his tiny legs. He had found one of his father's reinforced leather fighting gauntlets too, which swallowed his little hand and reached up to the boy's shoulder, and with his other hand he was struggling to drag a great sword by its pommel. He was so proud in that moment that he had outfitted himself for training, but the pride in his little eyes had melted into tears of embarrassment as the other boys interrupted their practice and burst into raucous laughter, pointing at him. Their laughter was quickly stopped by Cailean's fists, however, as he made it clear to the boys that Ligulf was his brother and he would brook no ridicule of the child. As Cailean silenced the other boys,

Corvus had swept up young Li in his arms and taken him back inside the house. Swordplay was done for the day as he spent the next hour doing his very best to chase away the clouds from the eyes of his sweet, sensitive younger child. Corvus' eyes grew moist with the memory and he shook his head, trying for the third time to get Li to stop worrying about him.

When Li started to drape Corvus' jacket over his shoulders, inadvertently pressing painfully on his injured arm, the older man snapped.

"Dammit, boy," Corvus said sharply. "Listen to me."

Li was surprised by the tone of his father's voice and stood still, jacket held loosely in his right hand, waiting for a reprimand. Corvus looked into the eyes of his son, so like Greer. He could see the shape of her face in his. He had her coloring, nose, and eyes, and his laugh was so like hers. The way his eyes and nose wrinkled when he laughed... just like hers. Corvus' irritation dissolved, and all he could see in this young man standing before him was the wee bairn trying so hard, holding the sword and wearing his da's boots and gloves, so crushed by the ridicule of the older boys. Corvus sighed and placed his right hand on Li's cheek, just like he used to do to Greer.

"When your mother died," Corvus began, "I thought I would die as well. She was my rock and foundation, and without her I was lost with no idea how to move on. I considered taking the step off the cliffs, so desperate I was, but I had duties to you and Cai and to the fyrd. The Barbárs were at it again, but I couldn't see leaving you for weeks while I went off on campaign. You were but a wee thing, and couldn't understand what had happened and what was happening. I kept asking your mother for guidance from beyond. What should I do? How could I carry on? I wept, and I'm not ashamed to say it."

"Da, don't..." Li started to say, raising his hand to cover his father's, still on his cheek.

"No, you'll hear me," Corvus said. "I walked to the cliff's edge and stood for hours, considering my options." He paused for a moment, his eyes glistening and his thoughts far away. "They say when a man reaches his breaking point, that the spirits of the land may come to his aid. I'm not sure who came to me that night on the cliffs... Your mother, the spirits, or something else. But I had the strongest vision of *your* sweet wee face and that crooked smile, pouncing on my chest, waking me in the morning. I could hear *your* piping laughter in the wind's keening. I knew that I had no more sacred duty than to care for you and your brother. So, I marched myself right back here to the house and started to pack for all of us. I took you both on campaign with me." He laughed, shaking his head at the unlikely memory.

Ligulf nodded. "I remember."

"Against all the advice of the biddies and goodies who said a war was no place for a barra. I couldna bear to be apart from you two, and truth be told, I needed you there. With me, for me. I suppose it was purely selfish of me, and looking back I canna believe I did it, but each evening as I crawled into my tent next to you and Cai... My heart had been so filled with fighting and death all day, and your wee fingers tugging at my hair—I actually had hair back then—and Cai crawling into my lap and holding me so tight I thought his wee arms would break, well... you boys brought me back from the edge of the cliff." Corvus paused and swallowed. When he continued, his voice was thick with emotion. "You reminded me each day what was vital to me, and you've continued to do that to this very day. I swore to your mother that I'd show you all the love I could to make up for her absence, but I'd say you boys have shown me far more."

A tear ran down Li's face over his father's hand. Corvus felt a matching one tracking down his own face as he continued.

"You have *never* disappointed me. It wasna your fault that you weren't there at the Circle. It wasna your fault that you weren't there for Dallin. You couldna have known. Now stop. Please stop this constant fussing about, taking care of me, as if you've let us down. That's bollocks. I won't stand by and watch you blame yourself for something that was out of your control. You're a fine young man, and I couldna be prouder of you. Let it go, Li."

"I'm so sorry, Da." Li held his father's hand to his cheek and stifled a sob.

"Come here, ya wee dafty," Corvus said, as he pulled his son into an embrace. When they finally pulled apart, tears streaked both their faces and they each chuckled at the intensity of the moment. "Well, we're a right mess, aren't we?" Corvus said, shaking his head and clearing his throat.

Li stepped back, smiling through tears and wiping his hands on his kilt.

"Now, leave me be and go sing a song for Dallin," Corvus said over his shoulder as he busied himself with the clasp holding his sword in place. "I know she takes great solace in your visits. Her injuries are much graver than mine." He tapped his son's chest over his heart.

Li sniffed, wiped his eyes, and chuckled a bit. After fetching his cittern, he was out the door. Corvus stood for a moment watching his son walk down the dirt path toward the village, the sun highlighting his dark hair.

"You're a good father," Yazid said from somewhere inside.

"Ach, you bastard." He looked up to see the large Aslene seated on the topmost stair, drinking a mug of steaming spiced tea, watching the interaction between father and son. Corvus shook his head, flashed his friend an embarrassed smile, and walked stiffly to the door.

"You will attend the fyrd training these next two days?" Yazid asked.

"Well, they'll no' train themselves," Corvus replied, carefully tucking the food bundle that Li had prepared into his satchel and then looping it over his shoulder. "And try as you might, you're too soft on them." Glancing out the door, he decided that the day was warm enough and he needn't wear his jacket, so he draped it over his recovering left arm and started to leave. Pausing at the door, he turned back to Yazid. "Will you be joining me, Your Highness?"

"I was waiting for an invitation," Yazid said casually, standing up. "Preferably one delivered delicately by two doves." He descended the stairs, setting his mug on the short oaken table by the door, and grabbing his satchel and staff.

"I see," Corvus said, feigning thoughtfulness, as the two set out from the stone house. "Would they be lovely white doves that fly with a wee ribbon between them, or maybe in your case they'd be fat, dirty pigeons leaving their droppings everywhere? Now which would it be, I wonder?"

With a huge laugh, Yazid clapped his old friend on the back and rested his arm amiably on Corvus' shoulder as they walked to the training ground, just over a league distant. Corvus gritted his teeth and smiled through the pain.

Ligulf

Ligulf could hear Yazid's bellowing laughter across the moor on his way to the cottage where Dallin and her mother Kamdyn lived. He played his cittern as he walked, practicing a new melody that he was working on. It was a sweet song about a suitor so smitten with his love that he crosses the mountains over and again to see her and wears a path through the ferns of the woods. He liked the concept, and it seemed like a gentle enough piece for Dallin's current fragile state. He'd been worrying over the refrain for days, trying various melodic ornaments and even an elaborate bridge to the song, which he eventually discarded. Just last evening, he'd had a creative breakthrough, and now that the song was falling into place nicely, he was eager to share it with his closest friend.

Stepping up to the door of the cottage, he strummed the cittern energetically, announcing his presence without saying a word. The door opened, and Kamdyn's grateful face looked out.

"Bless you, lad," she said, worry etched into her expression. "She'll be glad you've come."

"How is she today?" Li inquired softly.

"'Twas a rough night," she said under her breath. "And a worse morning."

With a look of concern for Kamdyn, Ligulf entered the dimly lit cottage. Though it was a bright summer's day on the moor, the low earthen and stone home had few windows, and since her assault, Dallin had insisted the wooden shutters on the few it did have remain closed. Despite the warmth of the day, a fire was burning in the hearth, and Li could make out Dallin's figure sitting on the plank floor in front of it, wrapped in a blanket. There were three wooden chairs in the room that had been carefully crafted by Lundy, Dallin's father—though a sheep farmer by trade, Lundy had shown great skill at woodworking and had even built himself a lathe and started turning beautiful furniture and bannisters before his untimely death when Dallin was nine. But Dallin had clearly decided that she preferred the floor at the moment. Li strummed his cittern merrily to see if he could get any response from the young woman. None came, and she continued staring at the embers, the thumb of her right hand absent-mindedly feeling the jagged edges of the two teeth that had been broken in the assault.

"Dal?" Li said tentatively. "I've written a new song that I hope you'll like. Can I sing it for you?"

Dallin's only response was to take a long, shuddering breath, sigh, and toss something into the fire. Ligulf couldn't quite make out what it was, but it looked to be a figurine or doll of some sort. Judging by the way it flared up immediately and burned away, he assumed it had been made of dried twigs or perhaps cornstalk. He decided to ask her about it later. For now, he selected a lovely bow-back oaken chair and pulled it over next to Dallin by the fire. The chair was much heavier than it looked, and he was forced to slip his instrument around to his back and use both hands to move the heavy piece. Readjusting the cittern once more, he sat next to his friend, and began plucking a soft melody from its strings. Despite the bravado of his entrance, he was very sensitive to Dallin's needs, and felt that something soft and pleasant was what the moment called for.

They sat for a time, neither of them speaking, just allowing Ligulf's gentle melody to fill the cottage. After inviting him inside, Kamdyn had left to pick up a few items at the market. Their income had dwindled since the assault, as Kamdyn's attentions were focused on Dallin and she could not tend to her flock. Fortunately, she still had the purse earned from the shearing in the spring, and the few heads of livestock she had sold prior to the attack. Though Kamdyn was far too proud to accept charity, she was grateful when the other farmers of the village stepped in to tend her sheep voluntarily until such time as she and Dallin could resume their duties.

Li finished the tune he'd been playing, and a companionable silence fell over the two of them as they sat quietly staring at the fire. Just as he was about to begin another soft melody, Dallin broke her reverie and spoke, surprising him.

"What's your new song?" she asked, her voice little more than a hoarse whisper.

"Oh, I think you'll like it, Dal," Li answered, sitting forward in his chair and adjusting the instrument. "It's still rough, but I hope you'll enjoy it anyway." He paused for a moment and when Dallin said nothing in response, he continued. "Right, well, here goes."

The sound of Ligulf's clear tenor voice and his cleverly plucked cittern filled the cottage.

Oh, the summer sun shines on the trees and the vines,
And young Molly lives alone by the wood.
She goes out every day, milks the cows, cuts the hay,
It's a hard life, but sure, it is good. 'Tis good.
It's a hard life, but sure, it is good.

From beneath the shade of the trees in the glade,
Comes a swain with a roguish dark smile.
And he asks Molly dear if she could see clear
To let a weary man rest for a while, a while.
To let a weary man rest for a while.

And now he's wearing a path through the ferns
O'er mountain through bracken and burn.
She's a true lass and fair,
Hazel eyes, auburn hair,
And he's wearing a path through the ferns, the ferns.
He's wearing a path through the ferns.

Oh stranger, she said, with her cheeks burning red,
I would ne'er turn a traveler away.
For the mountain is high, and the evening is nigh,
And I care not what others might say, might say.
Oh, I care not what others might say.

And now he's wearing a path through the ferns
For the love within him burns.
She's a true lass and fair,
Hazel eyes, auburn hair,
And he's wearing a path through the ferns, the ferns.
He's wearing a path through the ferns.

"That's as far as I've gotten," Li said, the last tones of the cittern still ringing in the cottage. "But I know that she bears him a child, and he continues to cross the mountains to visit his Molly by the glen."

There was a long moment of silence, then Dallin said, "No man would wear a path to my door."

"Don't say that, Dal—" Li started, but she interrupted him.

"I'm not wrong, am I?" her voice rose as she turned to face him. Shanna the healer had successfully reset Dallin's broken nose, though her eyes were still bruised, and had carefully stitched the gash on her jaw. But Li knew the young woman was right; most young men would never consider her fair with broken teeth, a misshapen nose, and a pronounced scar on her face.

"Dal," he said, setting aside his instrument and placing both hands on her shoulders, "you are my dearest friend, a sweet girl with a heart ten times too big. You work hard, you have a lovely laugh, and eyes as true the goddess herself. Any man would be fortunate to have you for a wife."

"No man will ever have me!" The words exploded out of her as she stood suddenly, the blanket falling from her shoulders. She was dressed in a simple blouse and a heavy, ankle length woolen skirt, despite the warmth of the day. Her face purpled with rage as she continued to rant. "I'll grow old alone, Li! I'll be the spinster farmer who lives alone by the cliffs! They've ruined me, Ligulf. They've ruined me!"

He stood and folded her into his arms, comforting his friend as her momentary passion collapsed into sobs. This was terrain they had covered many times before during his visits, and he knew that there was nothing for it but to hold her and let her cry it out. There was no simple answer for the demons that now tormented his friend. He could only do so much. But their bond was strong—forged over many years of childhood adventure and play—and he silently vowed again that he would see her through this, no matter how long it took or how difficult the path.

He held her and stroked her red hair until her tears were spent. With a wet sniffle, she finally pushed away from him. A small, fragile smile was trying to surface, though her eyes were still flowing.

"I've ruined your shirt with me blubberin'." A self-deprecating chuckle came out as she wiped at the wet spot on Li's shoulder. She blinked back another wave of tears, her eyes looking desperately into his as once more, as the enormity of it all came over her.

Holding her shoulders with his hands so he could look at her, Ligulf shrugged off her efforts to wipe the tears and snot from his shirt. With sudden inspiration, he grabbed her hand and said, "You're coming with me!" and with that, he pulled her toward the door. She resisted with increasing urgency as he pulled it open, letting in a waft of fresh cliffside air and sunshine.

"No, Li. No. NO!" She wrenched her hand free of his, her eyes wide with terror.

"Dallin," he pressed, "you need to get out of this dark house and walk in the sunshine, girl!"

"No. I canna, Li. I canna bear it…" She shook her head fiercely, her eyes darting about in panic.

"Why, Dal?" he pleaded. "Everyone loves you and wants nothing more than for you to recover from this. We needn't walk anywhere near anyone else. We'll stay by the cliffside. You just need some light and life in you."

"Li, I canna do it." She looked into his eyes, her breathing rapid and shallow. A dribble of drool escaped her lips as she continued. "Seeing the pity in their faces, knowing that they all know what those bastards did. They'll not say it, but now they all think I'm dirty. I can see it in their eyes. And I am. I am dirty now. Soiled, ruined, filthy! That's what they'll say behind their smiles, in their warm homes at night. That's what they'll say. I canna bear it. I just canna…" Her voice dwindling to a tiny, fragile thing as she shook her head, her eyes casting about in shame and embarrassment.

Seeing her intransigence, and not wanting to agitate her further, Li slowly closed the door and darkness once more engulfed the house.

"Here," he said, gently guiding her back to her seat by the fire. "I'll make you some tea."

After serving her a warm cup, and bereft of ideas for how to be of any further help to his friend, Li simply sat with her, quietly playing his cittern as she sipped her tea and the glorious day outside passed them by.

Chapter 8

No matter how we try to ignore it, we cannot. The Lake is ever present. Her reflections shape our days, and the winds that dance across her face herald our seasons. We drink her waters and eat her fish, though we cannot guess what creatures lurk deep beneath her surface. But never doubt that she has heard and knows every secret in our hearts, for our dreams and quiet cogitations are delivered to us across her waters, be they placid or frothed with white-capped fury. She is a quiet and generous neighbor mostly, allowing our ships passage and feeding us from the bountiful larder of her depths. Though we must never forget she can be wroth and cruel, capricious and sudden in her rages. We sail upon her waters with gratitude and humility and more than a little fear.

– *Journal of Charles Dampierre, Duke of Chambrun and Royal Consort*

574 HR - *Second month of summer*
Wetheral Castle, Deep Mere, Lachland

Isador

Queen Isador IV, deep in thought, studied the view of Deep Mere from the Grand Receiving Room of her castle. Aptly named, the Grand Receiving Room was—in every way—truly grand. Its vaulted and buttressed redwood ceiling soared forty feet above her head, while the entire southern wall of the chamber held thirty large panels of glass which, together, formed the Great Viewing Window—"la Grande Fenêtre" in the neglected tongue of her forbears. Dozens of crystal chandeliers hung along the length and breadth of the hall, and at night they could be seen sparkling from across the lake. It was constructed to be a place where the monarch could address hundreds of her subjects at once. This day, however, the Queen stood alone in the vast chamber, but for the four counselors awaiting her. The blonde maple dais upon which she stood was large enough to hold a banquet table with thirty guests, but at the moment it held only her throne—an ornate chair of intricately carved mahogany with maroon velvet cushions—and a trestle table covered with maps of Lachland and the neighboring region of Mardin. Wooden tokens, painted either red or green and carved to look like soldiers running or on horseback, were clustered about the maps to indicate the location of various military units. Two of her counselors—the two generals—adjusted the tokens as they awaited the Queen's pleasure.

Queen Isador's shoulders slumped with the weight of the morning's news, and she sighed heavily as her mind processed its ramifications. Outside, the sky was a crystal blue and the sunlight sparkled on the surface of the dark lake like a thousand tiny beacon fires declaring their alarm. Despite the summer weather, she felt chilled in the cavernous hall and adjusted the rose-colored woolen shawl about her shoulders. Her regal brow furrowed as she fidgeted with the black-gold wedding ring that she still wore, spinning it on her finger. Its great ruby caught and reflecting the sunlight as it moved around her digit.

She was startled from her thoughts when one of the great, iron-banded, oaken doors at the far end of the chamber burst open.

"Sorry, I'm late!" Darienne called loudly as she walked quickly toward the other counselors while still maintaining the practiced insouciance the Queen found so very annoying. Darienne was dressed, as per usual, in men's attire: tan riding trousers, knee-high, black-leather boots which clicked and scuffed as she strode across the cold slate floor, a white, blousy poet's shirt with frills at the neck and cuff—unbuttoned to the point of being borderline scandalous—and her trademark oiled leather duster, still filthy from riding. Her flowing red hair was unbound, despite the Queen's many requests, and it spilled loosely over her shoulders. There was a wineskin in her hand, and, inappropriately, a sword buckled to her belt. As the Queen's daughter, and heir apparent, the Lake Jacks guarding the doorway would not have insisted upon her disarming, but still it was a curious choice to enter a meeting of the royal counselors with a sword at her hip. Isador made a mental note to once more remind her daughter of court etiquette and proper attire.

The Queen turned her attention back to the view out of the window as Darienne finished crossing the room and joined the four other counselors patiently awaiting the Queen's attention. Isador regretted keeping the advisors waiting, but she had hoped to have a plan formulated before the meeting, and today, her thoughts were frantic and scattered like a bevy of doves after a peregrine strikes. The dark, blue-gray lake sparkled and winked at her annoyingly, as if it understood her problems and found them humorous.

Her husband had always loved this view. *Dear Charles,* she thought, *such a dreamer.* Charles Dampierre, Duke of Chambrun and her Royal Consort, would sit at this window for hours staring at the mountain and the lake and writing in his journal. *Whatever did you write in that book of yours? I miss you, you old pirate! I could use your counsel today.* She twirled her ring in irritation. He had been an avid sailor, using his leisure time to work on his boat, and race. *How you had loved to race! You'd be out on that boat every day, even if it killed you*. And, in the end, it had. Charles had been out on the lake testing new speed clamps for his small racer when an unexpected storm had rolled in off the mountain. Despite his skills, the wind shear had capsized his craft well out in the frigid waters. By the time help arrived, he had drowned, taken by his precious lake. *So sudden. So damned unnecessary.* That was sixteen years ago now, and Isador still felt the cold pit in her stomach acutely every time she stood by this window and looked out on that beautiful, cruel lake.

Her eyes drifted up from the Mere to the majestic elevation facing her. Directly across the water from the vantage point of Wetheral stood Mallory's Peak, a richly forested mountain with a bald peak that reached well above the tree line, commanding the surrounding landscape like an angry father glowering disapprovingly at his children. In song and story, Mallory's Peak was the stern husband to Deep Mere, their moments of marital discord creating the storms and angry winds that would occasionally slice across the lake. Now, she mused, all seemed to be harmonious within their house as the surface of the lake was still. A spectacular waterfall poured down the mountain, cascading onto rocks hidden by the trees hundreds of feet below, and sending up perpetual rainbows in the mists created by the falling water.

Armel III had envisioned this castle and the vista before her. And now his great-granddaughter stood staring out of Armel's great window, mulling over this new threat from the east. She needed a plan! Her dream was to be as visionary a monarch as Armel III had been, to advance Lachland's prosperity and security. But the days of her reign, so filled with the never-ending demands and details of her kingdom, seemed to fly away from her like butterflies from a child's grasp.

And now, the Barbárs had arrived, presenting new exigencies that would define her rule and no doubt shape her legacy. They were spreading west and south from their well-established foothold in neighboring Mardin, and there seemed to be no end to their numbers. Hordes of the savage brutes had, over the past decade, virtually overrun all of Mardin and had now begun raiding into eastern Lachland. She had known this day would come, but hoped it might wait until she had reinforced the border, finished building fortifications along the roads, and taken countless other steps to prepare. The Barbárs were a tribal race that came from the vast lands of Lugo and Orense across the Mirror Sea. Originally thinking their coastal incursions were but raids, the hapless King of Mardin, Offa the Elder, had not realized the enormity of the danger until it was too late. After three years of fairly consistent and similar raiding patterns that had been painful, but sustainable, suddenly Offa had been faced with fleets of enemy vessels depositing warriors on his shores by the hundreds. Each year, new waves of invaders arrived and pushed further inland, pillaging and despoiling as they went like locusts. His armies had fought bravely against them, but his feckless approach to stemming the enemy tide had not been up to the task. A proud and ultimately foolish ruler, he had delayed sending for help from his neighbors in Sudland and Lachland too long. By the time his messengers finally arrived in their capitals requesting aid, Mardin was overrun and burning, and Offa's mangled corpse—still dressed in his robes of office—dangled from the city gates of the capital, Grado, until the crows had picked it clean.

Over the course of the intervening six years, Isador had sent multiple embassies to Serastin, the King of Sudland, as well as to Duke Rigland of Aesthir trying to develop a unified strategy against the hordes, to no avail. Rigland stood ready to commit the resources of Aesthir to their mutual defense, but in truth, Aesthir was a small mountainous nation with little military to offer. Serastin, meanwhile, sat in the richest, most populous nation in all of Daffyd, surrounded by his claque of priests and protected by his sizable army and walled towns. To his thinking, he had the most to lose by sending his troops forth, so instead, he chose to keep them on his own borders, leaving his fellow rulers to suffer the hammer blow of the invaders. Consequently the Barbár problem, virtually ignored these past years, had metastasized. And now, the blow was falling upon Lachland.

"Your Grace?" Brigadier St. Fiacre gently called the Queen's attention back to the present. She flashed an apologetic smile over her shoulder to her counselors. Brigadier Dixon, Brigadier St. Fiacre, Darienne, and Merchant Representative Bellin formed her regular council. This morning, she had also invited the visiting Archbishop Mormand of the Church of the Five to attend and offer his insights. The Church's presence in Lachland was small but growing, particularly in the south of the country nearest the border with Sudland, where the Church was well established both in the country and at court. The Queen was not sure how she felt about its growing influence—their strictures about men holding dominion over women were particularly troubling—but given its growing popularity among some of her people, she was willing to at least hear the archbishop's thoughts and proposals. The evening prior, she had welcomed him to Lachland with a state dinner, attended by some thirty members of the local nobility as well as various court officials. Accompanied by two Holy Knights of the Church as his retinue, the archbishop had arrived early, notably catching the eyes of the court and proceeding to socially float, introducing himself around and disarming any jaundiced preconceptions that might have existed in the room. Despite his clerical robes, he was a strikingly handsome man in his late fifties, with a chiseled dark beard sprinkled with gray. He possessed the gifts and natural charm of a true raconteur and diplomat, nimbly changing from lighthearted stories to serious, and making seemingly heartfelt inquiries as to the well-being of his listeners. He had been the center of attention all evening. Isador smiled at the memory of her guests laughing gustily at his mildly off-color anecdotes about members of the Sudlandic court. His ready wit and dry commentary on the various dukes, duchesses, and counts and their foibles had kept the merriment rolling throughout the meal. Indeed, she had observed that several of the women present—and a few of the men, too—seemed to take particular note of his dark-eyed good looks. Even she had to admit that he was rather handsome and charming.

Now he stood expectantly with her other advisors next to the map table. She had long dreaded this meeting and felt completely unprepared for the moment. Why could she not have been a more decisive and dynamic ruler, like her grandfather, Alain II? He had fought the great trade war against the Mardish that had secured the overland trade routes from the Claws to the sea. Then again, perhaps he too was merely responding to facts on the ground, as she was being forced to. Perhaps he had felt equally unprepared when faced with his crisis. Regardless, she wished now, more than ever, for his fortitude.

"Forgive me," she said with a wave of her hand, walking with her customary elegance to join the strategy session and flashing a perfunctory smile of welcome to Darienne.

"I'm sorry I'm late, Mother," her daughter said again, offering her a slight bow and giving a nod to the two generals and the merchant representative, while ignoring the archbishop entirely and pointedly turning her back to his outstretched hand. Raising his overlooked hand to his mouth, the cleric coughed lightly to cover the obvious slight, a wry smile playing over his lips as his eyes studied the back of the Princess' head.

"Ah, my dear!" the Queen responded, gliding to her daughter for a brief embrace, then recoiling slightly. "We would ask you to join our conference as the situation is most urgent, but perhaps you might want to freshen up first? I'm sure we can muddle through without you." The Queen's nose wrinkled in disgust at the strong smell of sweat and horse that emanated from the Princess and her filthy clothes.

"No matter," Darienne responded with a mischievous grin, weaving slightly from the wine as she positioned herself right next to Archbishop Mormand. "If I smell of horse, I'll stand next to this ass, and you'll never notice."

The room went icily quiet as the generals and merchant representative looked at one another with nervous shock, unsure how to respond to such an overt and undiplomatic insult. Even the Queen seemed nonplussed for a moment as she stared at her daughter, eyes wide. She and Darienne had argued when they had first learned of the archbishop's intended visit. Darienne resented the Church's teachings on women and its condemnation and persecution of homosexuality, and put forward that as they were a realm ruled by a woman, the Church of the Five should not be allowed within their borders. It would undermine the Queen's authority. Though she agreed with her daughter's reasoning, Isador had ultimately decided to allow the archbishop's visit. She had anticipated that there would be friction between the Princess and Mormand, but even for Darienne, such an insult to a visiting dignitary was too far. The awkward silence stretched on while the pudgy merchant representative, Bellin, sniffed loudly and found reason to suddenly be fascinated with some detail on the maps. Brigadier St. Fiacre stood impassively, his hands behind his back in his customary parade-rest stance. Brigadier Dixon scratched his short-cropped gray hair and looked out of the window, his great bushy eyebrows working furiously.

The archbishop merely gave a light chuckle to break the silence and indicated the table of maps. "We have much to accomplish today, Your Majesty," he said smoothly. "Let us not get pulled off course by the Princess, who is undeniably both *off* and *coarse*." He flashed her a disarming grin.

The tension in the room seemed to rise measurably as all awaited an explosive response from Darienne. The Queen looked at the two antagonists: the Princess, who was grinning with sudden appreciation at the visiting cleric, and the archbishop, whose expression was one of utterly charming innocence.

"Oh, well done," Darienne said to Mormand, with a nod of respect at his quick riposte. She offered him her wineskin, but with another light laugh and a slight wave of his hand, he declined it. Despite Darienne's comment, the tension in the room still hung like a thick fog on the lake until it was broken by the chuckle of Merchant Representative Bellin.

"Off and coarse," the portly man snickered in his thick, dockyard accent, shaking his balding head as if he had only just got the joke. Realizing he had spoken aloud, the meek man looked up, suddenly terrified his comment might have offended such august company. He fixed his gaze once more on the map, both hands worrying the brim of the merchant's cap he held before his significant stomach. Bellin's comic discomfiture seemed to tip the scales as both generals stirred in reaction to his outburst. Brigadier St. Fiacre wiped his nose with a white-gloved hand and sniffled to mask a grin. He was the highly starched commander of the royal cavalry. This also meant the Lake Jacks, the elite royal guard, and Major Justiniere fell under his purview. His red uniform jacket with gold trim, buttons, and epaulets was immaculate, and his polished and plumed silver helmet sat on the trestle table within arm's reach. Brigadier Dixon, on the other hand, was a hard-scrabble man who had come up through the ranks and now commanded all other military units in Lachland. Unlike his starched counterpart's controlled and minimal response, Dixon burst out in an echoing guffaw, slapping poor Bellin on the back and pointing at the archbishop to acknowledge his clever quip. The awkwardness of the moment dissipated. The Queen's eyes flashed daggers at Darienne before, with a wave of her hand, she directed the group's attention to St. Fiacre. Clearing his throat and wiping his grand mustache with the back of a gloved hand, the general began.

"The time we have long feared is upon us. We have just received reports that early last week, the Barbárs began raiding into Lachland," he reported, mostly for Darienne's benefit as she had missed the earlier reports, and sure enough, she gasped aloud. The brigadier continued, "Several villages have been razed, and the towns of Lisleux and Arras have been captured outright. We are unsure at this point whether these are tentative raids to gauge our response, capture supplies, or part of a more concerted effort at absolute conquest. However, based on recent history in Mardin, I fear we must assume the last. The facts on the ground are quite foggy, as reports are still coming in, but this much we know: this was no individual war chief acting alone as we might normally expect from the Barbárs. These attacks were coordinated over a distance of five score leagues, and all seemed to have begun together, a week ago last Tuesday."

"Our best estimate," Brigadier Dixon interjected, "is that the Barbárs committed some thirty thousand to the attacks, so whether they choose to press on for conquest or stop and consolidate their gains, this is an incursion we ignore at our peril." Dixon had a habit of wearing his uniform in a very casual, untidy manner, his blue-gray jacket unbuttoned to reveal the white shirt beneath. As he spoke, his right hand reached under his jacket to scratch some hidden itch.

"Any word from Autun?" Bellin asked.

The port city of Autun sat on the easternmost of the lakes that made up the Claws, right on the border with Mardin. A walled city, with a respectable garrison protecting it, Autun was a vital trading port for Lachland; it was the last stop in-country for goods bound overland for the Mardish ports that allowed the profitable trade across the Mirror Sea. Autun also boasted a large shipyard where all types of merchant vessels were built with rich lumber harvested in the vast forests of western Mardin. If Autun fell, it would indeed be a blow to Lachland's economy and security, as the Barbárs would then have unfettered naval access to the towns and communities along the Claws, and—through them—to the Mere Canal itself.

"No word at this time," Brigadier Dixon responded, his booming voice echoing in the cavernous chamber. "Reginald Bleiz is the knight commander of that garrison. I know him personally, and can say that he won't relinquish the town easily."

"Nonetheless," the Queen said, "Autun is critical. We must rush reinforcements and materiel to their aid immediately. If it has held out, it will have need of succor. If it has fallen, we must retake it and reinforce it at once. The enemy will be hard-pressed to continue any conquest around the Claws with Autun at their rear, holding strong. How quickly can our forces resupply it, Brigadier?"

"Sadly, Majesty," St. Fiacre said, his brow furrowed as he traced a route over the map with a finger, "given the defeats at Lisieux and Arras, our nearest response force now would be the Ninth Cuirassiers, who are positioned south of the Nail." He indicated one of the wooden horse tokens on the map. "Even then, it would take a fortnight for them to get there, and their force is insufficient to fight through enemy lines." Silence fell on the group as all present wrestled with the logistical challenges before them.

"Master Bellin." Darienne stepped forward to the table, all trace of inebriation gone. "What large ships do you have in harbor here?"

"I, uh, well," the merchant representative stammered, fidgeting with the hat in his hands and seemingly very uneasy with the sudden attention from all in the room. "We have the Sea Eagle, a brigantine, and the Lagopus, a sloop, and two timber barges have only just arrived through the locks. And there's the royal yacht, of course. Beyond that, mostly small fishing vessels at the moment."

Darienne nodded and turned to the rumpled general with the bushy eyebrows. "Brigadier Dixon, how many men at arms do we currently have here in Deep Mere?"

"Darienne," the Queen interrupted. "We appreciate your interest, but..."

Darienne raised a hand. "Please, Mother, indulge me for just a moment." Then, turning back to Dixon, she said, "Brigadier?"

The general hesitated and looked to the Queen, who sighed and nodded assent, before he answered. "Some fifteen thousand infantry," Dixon said, "and another two thousand horse, isn't that right, St. Fiacre?"

"Closer to three thousand," St. Fiacre responded, "if you include the Lake Jacks and constabulary."

Darienne nodded, taking in the information and seeming to run some quick calculations in her head. Clearly excited, she turned to her mother with fire in her eyes.

"Your Majesty," Darienne said with atypical formality, "we should *sail* to the relief of Autun."

"The brigantine can only transport roughly a hundred infantry with their kit," Dixon interjected. "And the Lagopus, maybe half that. The garrison at Autun is fully fifteen hundred strong, but when the Barbárs hit Lefevre, they attacked with some twelve thousand warriors, and there's no reason to imagine they'd hit Autun with anything less. It's too plum a prize."

"Exactly," Darienne responded, not surprised by the general's numbers. "Master Bellin, how quickly can those barges be unloaded?"

"Uh..." The merchant representative furrowed his brow. "Three days each, uh, given our current manpower." He paused in thought, scratching his belly before hurriedly adding, "Uh, Your Highness. Ma'am."

"And if you had additional workers, say a thousand men, helping?" Darienne pressed with unsuppressed urgency.

"A thousand men..." He shook his head, eyes going unfocused as he thought through the logistics of adding so many personnel to the docks. "Perhaps a day?"

"Perfect!" Darienne spun toward her mother. "Majesty, forgive me as I know this scheme is unorthodox, but when the fox is in the coop... We load troops onto the barges. Not dignified or comfortable transport, I recognize, however those ships have enormous capacity. We should be able to fit a thousand men on each, possibly even some cavalry, I would think. They could be there in days. Would a relief force of twenty-five hundred men make a difference for Autun, General?"

The Queen looked at her daughter in surprise and not a little resentment. This was a clear and daring plan, bold in conception, though quite risky. But it could work, allowing them to resupply the strategically vital city unexpectedly quickly. It was precisely the kind of thinking that Alain II had been known for. Why had such a solution not presented itself to Isador? Why did she dither and gaze out the window, wallowing in indecision, while her wastrel of a daughter could imagine it so quickly and clearly? The Queen tried to swallow against the bitterness that began to rise in her like bile.

"Significant, yes," Dixon said, perplexed. "But the men riding on barges is wholly unacceptable. Those are flat-decked ships; they're not meant for passengers. Any rough weather, and we'll have a disaster on our hands with hundreds overboard."

"I'm certainly not comfortable telling my cavalry to travel on a barge," St. Fiacre put in. "Quite dangerous, for men and horses."

Regardless of her petulant resentment for the clarity and daring of Darienne's idea, Isador saw the opportunity for decisive and effective leadership. Energized, she turned to the merchant representative. "Master Bellin, how quickly could those ships get to Autun, this time of year?"

"If winds are favorable, Your Grace, the barges can be there in a week," he responded more firmly now, seemingly warming to the idea of being a critical player in this crisis. "Both the sloop and the brigantine could arrive in three to four days time with a little luck. But the Claws can be tricky this time of year, with summer storms blowin' in unannounced, like. We could rig the decks with ropes and hand loops to protect the troops from washing overboard. Won't be comfortable, but… it could work."

The Queen was seized by the notion, her mind racing with possibilities. She had received word of the Barbár attacks in the small hours of the night and had been pacing the floors since, studying and restudying the maps, looking for any possible way to reinforce her eastern border before the barbarians devoured half her nation. Now, just such a plan seemed to be coming together. If they could just hold Autun until the snows, the Barbárs wouldn't dare press much further around the Claws and would be denied naval access to the rest of the country's interior. They would earn vital breathing room to prepare for a spring offensive against the invaders, and possibly allow time for reinforcements to arrive from Sudland or Aesthir, or both.

"Very good." The Queen nodded to the merchant representative. "See that those four ships are pressed into service immediately. General"—the Queen turned her attention to Dixon, who stood a bit taller to receive orders—"coordinate the unloading of those barges with Master Bellin. Have a thousand men, or however many he thinks appropriate, ready to unload the timber and fit them out as quickly as possible. Meanwhile, we'll need the Lagopus and the Sea Eagle stripped and prepared to carry as many men as they can. Brigadier St. Fiacre, would you be so good as to see to that?"

The cavalry general gave a crisp nod.

"Also," the Queen continued, "have the royal yacht likewise prepared. We'll need to transport every soldier possible."

The general nodded again.

"Majesty," Archbishop Mormand said humbly, "the Church would be remiss if we did not contribute to this effort to hold back the godless barbarians. Please use my personal vessel for troop transport, as well. It is of similar size to the brigantine and could add another hundred or more troops to the effort. Or perhaps you might use it to transport officers and staff."

"That is very generous, Your Grace," the Queen replied, searching his eyes for an agenda. Finding none that she could discern, she continued, "We gratefully accept your aid. Master Bellin, generals, we leave the specifics to you. But we intend to sail the day after tomorrow. See that it is done."

All eyes flashed in confusion. The generals, the merchant representative, Darienne, and the archbishop exchanged surprised looks.

"Your Majesty…" St. Fiacre began, obviously flustered.

"Mother," Darienne interrupted. "You plan to sail to Autun *personally*?"

"Of course," the Queen replied imperiously. She wondered how there could possibly be any question. "Lachland is under attack, and Autun is the lynchpin. We will sail as quickly as possible to its relief. As Queen, it is our duty and prerogative."

A sudden confusion of voices erupted in the room, all speaking over one another.

"Enough," the Queen said, raising her voice only slightly—but it was more than enough to command silence in the chamber. "It is decided. Thank you all for your counsel."

An awkward silence descended as the generals began collecting their personal effects and the merchant representative turned and began to shuffle uncertainly toward the great doors.

"Mother— Your Majesty…" Darienne's careful voice stopped everyone. "Send me instead. The people of Lachland need you here, governing and managing our defense. I can do this and be your hand to drive back the Barbárs."

"You?" Queen Isador was incredulous at the thought. "Darienne, while we appreciate your creative input this morning, you have hardly established a reputation for reliability." Irritated, she nodded to the generals, dismissing them.

"Oh, piff and waddle, Mother!" Darienne's shout shocked all present. "I could care less about the politics and gossip at court! This is important. For Lachland!" Then she added more quietly, "When will you trust me? Let me serve you in this."

"Darienne," the monarch responded with cold steel in her voice, "you will watch your tone and how you address your Queen. You do not dictate here, you advise by our invitation. We will sail to the relief of Autun two days hence. You will remain here with Brigadier St. Fiacre and manage any issues that arise. Meanwhile, Brigadiers…" The Queen turned her attention to the two officers, who had paused at Darienne's outburst. "Send ten thousand infantry and two thousand horses along the Low Road to LeGrange, and your swiftest messenger to the Ninth Cuirassiers to make for Autun at their first convenience. We must resist this invasion with all our resources. From LeGrange, those troops will be in position to respond to changing facts on the ground more quickly than from Deep Mere. We realize that it will take time for the infantry to march there, and it may mean that they winter along the route, but the sooner they begin, the sooner we can get them into the fight."

"Yes, Majesty," the two generals said in unison, waiting to see if the Queen had anything further.

Warming to her purpose, Isador added, "And summon troops up from Morvan to meet them in LeGrange. You should be able to double the number with that garrison." She crossed to the maps and paused, her jaw clenching with determination. Though she hadn't been able to imagine a solution herself, daring or otherwise, now that a plan was on the table, her mind raced with the details necessary for its fulfillment.

She looked each of her counselors in the eyes before saying firmly, "Gentlemen, understand this: it is not our intent to merely protect our borders. We must strike decisively"—she swept the red tokens from the map to emphasize her point—"so that the barbarian understands unequivocally that Lachland is not its prey. First, we shall secure Autun and blunt the enemy's advance, then, come spring, we shall once more secure the overland trading route, pushing the Barbárs back into the sea if necessary!" She looked at each of her counselors for a long moment, conveying her steely determination. Satisfied that they all understood her resolve, she said with a slight grin, "Let's get to it, then."

Dismissed once more, the two generals and Master Bellin bowed and turned briskly for the great doors, discussing the logistics of their enterprise as they departed. Darienne stood at the trestle table, her cheeks flushed with humiliation or frustration or both. She was clearly waiting for the other counselors to leave so that she and her mother might continue their argument in private. The Queen, sensing her daughter's mood and not wanting to face Darienne's obstinacy at the moment, turned to the archbishop who was midway to the doors.

"Your Grace," she said, arresting his exit.

"Yes, Majesty?" He turned back to her with an amiable grin.

"Will you walk with us?" she asked, as she glided past him toward a side door that opened onto the royal gardens.

"Of course, Your Majesty." He nodded and followed her dutifully.

Darienne

Finding herself alone, she stood fuming. Minutes passed before her temper had cooled enough for her to think clearly. To be dismissed and discarded so peremptorily, despite the fact that the plan was hers. *Hers!* Perhaps her efforts to cultivate an identity so worthless and intemperate at court had been too effective.

"That not go well?" Kaiso's voice carried from the far end of the chamber, where he stood leaning on a granite pillar near the door, cleaning his nails with a knife. He had apparently slipped in once the Queen had exited.

She sniffed derisively, not looking him in the eye. Her mother was going to war against the Barbárs, brutal and savage warriors with no honor on the battlefield. Her mind raced with the implications and dangers inherent in that decision. Who would hold the kingdom together in the Queen's absence? St. Fiacre? The nobility? No, it would fall to her to assume a greater role at court, despite the universal doubts and mistrust. That would require courting the very people she had been working so hard to disenchant these past years. Where to begin?

After standing by the trestle table in thought for another quarter hour, the toe of one boot tapping impatiently on the wooden dais, she finally shook her head and turned to her personal guard and sword trainer. "Let's go," she said abruptly as she stalked from the chamber.

Kaiso whistled a tune softly as he followed, casually sheathing his knife.

Chapter 9

But sisters, I admonish you, teach your charges. Care for them, of course. Just not too much. For that is the way of confusion and loss. It is an easy trap into which all too many fall. We, who are childless by choice, take on votaries—and they are innocent, willing, dutiful, and obedient. They look to us to teach them, to care for them. All too soon, we begin to love them as the children we never had. Discipline falls away, duty becomes secondary, our traditions and practices wither. Beware, sisters. This is the path to ruin and chaos. I tell you that your love will be your undoing. For the moment they worm their way into our hearts is the moment we stop hearing the voices of the Ancestors with clarity, and step off of the True Path. It is the moment of your spiritual peril, and the peril of those we teach. When you feel the urge to embrace your votary or indulge them in some way, spend some moments in altaamuli instead. Let the walking meditation clear your mind and bring you back to your sober duty.

– Opening remarks to the Prelacy Convocation by Effulgent One Nasira, Coadjutor for the Grand Ecclesiarch, Year of the Geminate Zephyrs

574 HR - *Second month of summer*
Somewhere in eastern Mardin

Mama

It had been a week since they had found the boy, and Mama was growing concerned about their traveling pace. Ashahl had been adamant that the staff had to reach his former student before the Equinox. At their current rate, they were still weeks, possibly even still moons, of travel away from the mountain pass that led into the Green Mount, and she had no concept of how long it might take to find this Corvus once there. Each day saw them making less progress northward. Young Argant's short legs could only walk so fast, and with him in the company, they now took care to stop more often for water and nourishment. But he was a sweet boy and a stalwart young traveler, never complaining at the long hours they spent each day hiking through the woodlands along the river. He had proven to be a willing worker too, helping with chores around the camp. Argant was not her only concern, though. The Barbár war bands were becoming much more active the further into Mardin they traveled, and avoiding them was proving increasingly difficult. Yesterday had been a particularly taxing day; three times they had been forced to make large detours to avoid groups of the savage warriors. The first two war parties they had spotted were each made up of around fifty or sixty warriors riding west, while the third numbered well over a hundred.

It had taken hours for the small group to work their way around the last war band, crouching and stealing from cover to cover. By the time Mama had finally called a halt, it was well after dark and the women did not dare light a fire for fear of discovery. Exhausted, they sat silently and ate the last of Yadira's flatbread and the remainder of a small rind of pungent goat's cheese they had bartered from a farmer days before. The group then went to their bedrolls, quietly. Mama lay on her side in a small natural depression near the river, listening to the soft sounds of her compatriots breathing and the gentle rippling of the water. The moon glistened on the line of the river like the glint of a light on a sharp, deadly blade.

Lupe had first watch, and Mama knew that the young woman would spend her shift stealthily ranging in a wide circle around their camp. Though Mama's body ached from the day's exertions and the added stress and effort of sneaking around the large encampment, sleep did not come to her immediately. Her mind was too active. She was thinking about the movements of the Barbár bands, and something important about them flitted at the edge of her thoughts. The warriors' movements seemed coordinated and urgent, as if they were trying to make some scheduled rendezvous. Clearly, these were no random raiding parties. The Barbárs were sweeping westward to go to war, and Mama's group was cutting northward directly across their path.

A stone of dread settled in her stomach as she glanced around the campsite at her sleeping charges. *How to keep these dear ones safe and still arrive in time?* Over the years, she had shepherded some thirty young women through their Adherence, and in every case she had come to love them as daughters, eschewing the official doctrine of *baed,* or emotional distance. Over the decades of her priesthood, she had come to realize many things about herself, but one thing overall: she was called to care for these young women. There simply was no other way for her to teach them. She prayed every day that her love was not in opposition to the will of the Ancestors, but there simply was no option for her. She cared for them, each and every one, like the daughters she never had. And now, she was leading these three, and Argant, into unknown danger.

She closed her eyes and willed her anxiety to pass, allowing the soft burbling of the river to guide her thoughts. Her mind settled on the child, Argant, though her reflections on the boy seemed disjointed. She knew better than to try to impose order when her spirit presented her with disordered images, and instead merely allowed her reflections to wash over her without direction. She had learned that often one's perception of a larger issue was incomplete and that the contours of the whole might only be understood by examining the fragments available and allowing the spirit to complete the picture.

Her first reflection was that of the raven leading her so directly to boy's hiding place beneath the hawthorn. She had distinctly felt the frisson of *other* when the bird had called to her. Ravens were the keepers of the bridge between the seen and the unseen worlds, and she had read that the hawthorn bush was said to hold special significance to the people of this land; many thought of the bushes as openings to other realms. *Gatekeepers and doorways,* she mused, *but what did those have to do with Argant?* She knew it was not chance that had led her to the boy, but was he here for some greater purpose? Did he have a part to play in their mission? Or were the women here to help him on some unknown journey of his own? Perhaps both.

She pictured the boy's face and those arresting jewel-like eyes—one crystal blue like the South Sea in summertime, and the other an amber brown with distinct flecks of gold. There was definitely something very special about the boy.

She reflected on how quickly the child seemed to have overcome the tragedy of witnessing the murder of his father and the razing of his village. The violent upending of all he had known. Perhaps it was the resilience of youth, or some hidden wellspring of strength, or—more likely—he was merely becoming adept at burying those horrors within. Despite all of that, however, each day found the boy opening up to them more and more.

He was Amina's constant companion, quietly walking by her side each day during their long treks, sometimes humming a soft tune to himself or swinging a stick at a butterfly, but rarely intruding on her peace with questions or comments. He seemed to understand that Amina was uncomfortable with conversation, and despite his eagerness to try out his developing—though rudimentary—understanding of their language, he chose not to bother his new friend with questions. As a rule, Amina also avoided physical contact with other people, often wearing gloves when going to the market to prevent accidental contact with someone's hand or arm. It was but one more of the girl's eccentricities that the women had come to accept as just a part of her. Mama often mused aloud that Amina must have been touched by an angel as a baby and that contact with base humans could never compare to such bliss. It was therefore quite surprising to see Amina resting her bare hand casually on Argant's shoulder as the two walked, her skin touching the boy's neck. When Mama asked about it that evening, Amina had simply replied in her inexpressive monotone, "He doesn't buzz," before returning to her campsite chores. Mama knew better than to press her for a more detailed explanation. And in any case, something about that simple contact with Amina did seem comforting to Argant, as he was quite content to walk by her side each day.

Another reflection presented itself to Mama, displacing the previous, and she allowed herself to be swept along the eddies of her thoughts without objection, trusting the wisdom of her spirit.

A few days earlier, Lupe had brought back a large hunk of honeycomb from one of her hunting excursions. Before handing it to Yadira to store in her satchel, the hardy huntress had quietly broken off a chunk and slipped it into Argant's bowl. He had glanced up in wonder at this unlooked-for treat. She simply winked at him from behind her jimas and continued over to Yadira as the boy eagerly tucked in to the sticky treasure, his crystalline eyes sparkling with delight and gratitude.

"Shukran, Lupe," the boy had said thickly through a mouth of gummy beeswax, thanking her for her gift.

"It was nothing, sweet child," she had responded in his tongue, with a dismissive gesture.

Mama smiled at the recollection. She was becoming drowsy as she lay listening to the river's bubbles and froth, but her spirit was apparently not finished presenting moments for her excogitation, as another percolated to the surface.

The day after they had found Argant, Yadira had ventured to a farm that had not yet been despoiled, and bartered for some food and other odds and ends. That evening, as they had settled in around their campfire, she had pulled out of her satchel an old pair of worn baggy trousers that she had acquired at the farm. She then proceeded to pull out the bundle of brightly colored fabric strips that she always carried. Without preamble or explanation, she produced a needle and thread and began working on the pants, taking in seams, and patching holes in the drab homespun with brightly colored silk or soft cotton. After a few days of this, she called Argant over and presented to him his gift. His eyes went wide with surprise as he looked at the motley trousers that looked to be just the right length for a boy of five summers. She had smiled and told him to try them on. When he came out from behind a tree, where he had modestly gone to dress, he was clutching the waist of the trousers in one hand. He would need a belt, but she had cleverly trimmed the pants at what had originally been the knee, and attached multicolored fringes of silk at the cuff, even taking in the diameter of the pant legs to better fit his little body. Argant was so pleased with them that he had impulsively hugged Yadira, accidentally letting go of the waist band of the pants, which promptly fell around his ankles, earning laughter from them all and a playful smack on his bare behind from Mama. Argant had blushed as he quickly pulled up the new pants, but he could not hide his delight at the colorful gift.

Mama smiled at the memory, despite their difficult and worrisome circumstances. With a sigh, she intentionally released the tension of the day, and burrowed deeper under her blanket. Within moments, she drifted off to sleep on a light breeze that arced over the burbling water.

She awoke to Amina shaking her, a gloved finger to her lips. It was still dark, though rose hues were just beginning to bruise the eastern sky. Mama sat up, blinking away the cobwebs, and looked to her young protégé, who was now waking the others. Argant rubbed his eyes and yawned as he sat up, stretching silently as the camp stirred to life. Amina had been on last watch, and though her forest sense was dull compared to Lupe's, it was keen enough to have discerned the sounds of another armed camp—this one to their north—waking and preparing to ride. Lupe gathered her bow and left immediately to investigate. Still exhausted from the stress and effort of the day before, and their paltry cold supper, Mama decided that they must eat before what would no doubt be another exhausting day. She and Yadira left Amina to watch Argant, and went foraging deeper into the narrow woodland that banded the river.

An hour or so later they returned. Mama carried a cloth bundle of chickweed, elderflower, and the blooms from a Linden tree, while Yadira's bundle was a bounty of mushrooms, wild onions, shepherd's purse, and sweet cicely. Yadira produced a small vial of oil from her satchel and poured it over the leafy mixture along with pinches of cinnamon, cardamom, and salt that she carried. Setting aside Lupe's portion, they broke their fast with the salad.

"I would have expected Lupe to have returned by now," Yadira said quietly, her voice showing only a hint of tension.

"Yes," Mama responded thoughtfully, still chewing. "Pray that all is well for her, and that we might avoid an eventful day."

Lupe

She froze, her back pressed against a tree that she hoped was large enough to conceal her. Though she'd lived her entire life in arid lands, her forest sense had become quite keen in the past weeks, allowing for superb stealth and almost preternatural hearing. That forest sense had somehow failed her this day, however. She had been so intent on following the large war band that she had missed the sound of nearby horses and stumbled upon a group of three Barbár riders, who had paused in a small valley in the wood to take a drink. Spotting her just as she crested a hill, one of them shouted and they all spurred their horses and gave chase.

The riders thundered toward her hiding place just over the crest. Her breathing was shallow and quick as she tucked in to the nominal protection of the tree, desperately searching her surroundings for an escape. The tree was just above an outcropping of mossy rocks. A dry stream bed originated at the base of the rocks and cut its way down the hill where it joined another larger and more active rivulet at the base of a shallow cleft between forested hills. In the rains, there would be a small waterfall off those stones. The shape of the rocks suggested a possible hiding place, though it would be small. She only had moments before they would be upon her. Sitting in the soft mulch of leaves, she slid partway down the hillside to the rocks, then leapt down quickly to the base of the overhang. Landing silently, she found what she was hoping for. There was a natural depression that had been carved by the water, forming a small hollow against the stones. It was barely big enough for her to lean into, and she desperately hoped it would conceal her from above. Clutching her bow before her, she tucked into the hollow, praying that she was hidden... unless they dismounted and searched. She carefully nocked an arrow and waited, her pulse racing, breathing shallow, and her body trembling.

Despite her caution, she gasped aloud as the first rider crested the hill with a shout and thundered down the slope to her left. He was followed moments later by a second, a female, right behind him. Lupe paused, expecting the last. *Where was the third rider?*

There was a scuff on the stone above her head, followed by a horse's soft nicker. A bead of sweat trickled down her neck as she struggled to control her breathing. Silently she began reciting the Canon of Stillness, striving to bring her breathing and nerves under control. Her pulse stilled almost immediately, and she leaned her body against the mossy, jagged rocks behind her, feeling the cool, moist smoothness against her head. Long moments passed as she waited for another sound from above, and several more passed before she dared to lean out cautiously from her hiding spot.

The warrior was still in position, sitting astride his mount with a practiced stillness as his eyes searched the woods around him. His mop of unruly blonde hair was adorned with small beads and feathers, tied among the unkempt strands, that rattled softly as he turned his head from side to side. He had a wiry, lean build and his bare chest and arms bore swirling tattoos. His beard, though stringy and patchy, was likewise decorated with beads and trinkets. The overall effect looked to Lupe's eyes not unlike the description her uncle would give when he told stories of the ghul, a demonic creature said to haunt the barren dunes at the edges of the Great Desert. She shivered at the thought.

He is but a man, she told herself. *Still your heart and breath.*

His eyes snapped in the direction of a distant rustle in the undergrowth. His brow furrowed in concentration at the sound, then he seemed to dismiss it as not worthy of his attention and resumed scanning the wood. She silently switched to reciting the Canon of Perception, her eyes growing more focused on the man. The smell of his sweat and that of his horse became almost overpowering. She could hear his breathing and the tinkle of the trinkets in his hair. Something about the beads disturbed her, and she stared intently at those knotted into his beard. Her enhanced focus allowed her to apprehend subtle details in the small ornaments. They didn't seem to be ceramic, the texture was too like…

Those aren't beads, she realized. *Those are knuckle bones! Human knuckle bones. The knuckle bones of children!*

Horrified at the discovery, her concentration on the Canon broke. She gasped aloud and reached out a steadying hand to the stone wall beside her, upsetting a small cluster of pebbles, which clattered noisily to the dry stream bed at her feet. She froze in terror. After a long moment, she peered cautiously out of the hollow only to find the Barbár gazing directly down at her. A grin of triumph lit his face as he pointed at her and muttered something triumphant in his alien tongue. Without thinking, she dove forward into the dry stream bed, rolled over her shoulder, and came up in a kneeling position facing the rider, arrow already knocked. The barbarian's hungry grin quickly transformed into a look of alarm and he ducked down suddenly against his horse's neck. The arrow hit him in the left shoulder, twisting him in his saddle and flinging him off his mount and onto his back atop the mossy rock outcropping. The horse startled and ran off.

Dropping her bow, she quickly vaulted off one rock, pulled herself over a second, and leapt up onto the stone next to him, landing with her long knife in her hand. With a shriek of outrage, the Barbár scrambled to his feet and drew his short sword. The arrow protruded from his shoulder, a rivulet of blood tracing a pattern down his chest that seemed somehow complementary to the design of his tattoos. He grimaced as he reached up with his sword hand and touched the arrow, then seemed to think better of disturbing the wound. He shook his head like a dog emerging from water, and looked at her venomously as the two of them began to circle one another.

"Mit csinálsz, lány?" he demanded, then lifted his chin and pointed to the ground before him. He seemed to be indicating that she should kneel and submit, though Lupe could see no reason for him to think he had the upper hand. The arrow had sunk deep and she could tell from the narrowing of his eyes that he was struggling with the pain.

As if to convince them both that the wound was no hindrance, the Barbár grinned with an open mouth, showing stained and missing teeth and a black tongue – which he waggled at her, the bones in his beard and hair tinkling as he shook his head. He crouched into a feral stance, presenting his blade before him, and began to chant some kind of battle threat, seeming to work himself into a frenzy. She had no time to dally or spar with this man. His scream may well have alerted the other riders, and his chanting was growing louder as his battle fervor grew. Ignoring his blade, she spun and kicked him across the face, staggering and silencing him with the force of the blow. Faster than he could react, she followed up with three more rapid kicks. The first sent his sword flying down the hill. The second was a powerful blow to his chest; she heard the air explode from him and felt something in him crack. The third kick destroyed his right knee and collapsed him onto his back in a patch of ferns growing around the base of a tree. Then, without pause, she stomped on the arrow in his shoulder, driving it completely through his body and into the ground beneath him. His lungs spasmed from the blow to his chest, causing his screams of agony to come out in ragged gasps and sobs, which—despite his distress—still sounded like the unholy shrieks of the dead in the otherwise silent forest. She chanced a quick look in the direction the other riders had gone to see if they were returning. No sign of them yet, but she needed to silence him quickly.

Pinioned to the ground, he couldn't move away from her as she knelt beside him. His eyes rolled in pain and his hands scrabbled desperately in the dirt at her approach. She placed the tip of her blade under his chin, and with a quick, silent prayer for his soul, drove her dagger deep into his skull until only the pommel showed beneath his bone-bedecked beard. His body arched in a rictus of pain as it voided itself loudly then grew still. Disgusted by the sudden smell, she wiped her blade on the mossy stone, returned it to her belt, then ripped the arrow from the corpse's shoulder. She heard a sound and crouched quickly behind the bole of the tree. Horses… and they were getting closer. They seemed to be over the next rise. With a heave, she rolled the body off the rock and down into the same hollow in which she had hidden. Then, glancing once more in the direction of the horses, she moved off to her left down the hill.

Mama

Having finished their breakfast, the women and Argant busied themselves refilling their waterskins and washing their bodies and clothing in the river. It would be another warm day, and the robes would air-dry quickly. Mama decided they could risk a small fire, as the wind today blew down the river from the north, and the camp Amina had heard would be upwind. She sat beside the small blaze and busied herself with her mortar and pestle, mixing herbs and some special mushrooms. Digging into her satchel, she withdrew a packet of dried berries and seeds she had brought with her from Asland. Carefully measuring and mixing the dried ingredients into the fresh, she continued grinding and adding small amounts of water to make an unappetizing, brownish-gray paste, which she rolled into a ball the size of a small river stone. She wrapped it in a clean cloth and tucked it away into her satchel.

With a sudden intake of breath, she paused in her task, closed her eyes, and turned her face up into the breeze, which had shifted and was now blowing gently from the northwest. After several long moments of focused stillness, she opened her eyes and looked to the rest of the group. Yadira had likewise paused in her efforts. Relaxing her arms so that her hands hung loosely by her sides, palms forward, she had shifted her kneeling position to face her teacher. Amina too had noted Mama's posture as she returned from the river with Argant. She had set down her freshly filled waterskin and stood facing her, hands open at her side, palms forward. Argant was looking quizzically from woman to woman for some clue as to what was happening. After a moment's confusion, he too turned to face Mama and closed his eyes, his hands hanging loose at his sides, palms forward. Though he still peeked with one eye at Amina.

Mama stood, lifted her great walking staff, and stepped away from the small fire, facing to the northwest. She held her "cane" laterally across her body with two hands, its great hooked head on her right.

"Lupe is returning," she said in a loud voice. "And danger is close behind her."

Without a further word, the other women moved into action. Amina picked up the waterskin and led Argant to a hiding place behind a tree near the edge of their camp, where she left the skin and told him to guard it. The boy nodded earnestly, his eyes—one a crystal sky and one a field of ripening wheat—glimmering as he accepted this important duty, his round cheeks flushed. Yadira, meanwhile, reached into her bag and located two small sachets—which she tucked into the waistband of her robe—before quickly closing the bag and placing it in the rotted hollow of a nearby tree stump. She then drew two respectable cooking knives and took up her place two paces behind Mama, offset to the left. Amina arrived a moment later and took her place behind Mama, offset to the right, with a thin walking stick clutched in her hands. All three faced northwest and began quietly chanting the Canon of Readiness.

"There she is!" Amina proclaimed, pointing.

Following Amina's gesture, Mama saw Lupe cresting a nearby rise, sprinting madly for their camp, with her bow in her left hand and her *jimas* askew, allowing her to gulp air in ragged gasps. Moments later, two Barbár riders appeared over the rise in pursuit. Mama's brow furrowed.

"It will be close," she said over her shoulder to her votaries. "Dira, I'll take right, you left. Mina take the center, and be ready."

"Yes, sitti," the women intoned in unison.

"And hear me, atfali," she said, using the Aslene term of endearment for her protégés, "if these riders escape, they'll return with many more and we'll be captured or killed."

Yadira and Amina both nodded grimly in response.

Mama grimaced as the riders gained on Lupe—a man and a woman, both bare-chested, their pale skin tattooed in swirling patterns and their white-blonde hair flowing madly in the wind. Both had drawn their weapons and were leaning over the necks of their horses, mouths agape with black tongues waggling. The Barbár to Mama's left brandished an axe in his right hand, while the female rider to the right wielded a sword with a curved, broad blade. Despite her impressive speed, they were almost upon Lupe, her powerful legs driving her toward an overgrown thicket of bramble between their camp and the open grassland to their west. With their focus solely on their quarry, the riders had not yet spotted the others in the camp.

"The thicket! Quick!" Mama called, and ran to the right of the bushes, crouching down while Yadira mirrored her to the left, readying one of her sachets. Amina dashed forward into the middle of the bushes, ducking down and using the thicket for cover. Anticipating what was to come, Mama swore a silent oath. It was a brutal reality that when faced with an attacking rider, the only real option, more often than not, was to kill or cripple the horse. The beast did not deserve to die, but there was no choice; unless they could dismount the riders, Mama and her charges would be killed or captured. They could not afford to allow either rider to escape and report their presence to the Barbár camp. She offered a prayer, asking forgiveness of the horse's spirit, and tightening her grip on the staff.

Finally within reach, the rider with the sword swung at the back of Lupe's head just as the votary dropped into a leg-first slide into the base of the bushes. The blade missed her by a finger's breadth as she slid on the dew-damp grass, her legs crashing and tangling into the base of the overgrown thicket. Her momentum carried her deep into the cover of the dense leaves and branches. The two riders sawed their reins and veered to either side of the brush, the horses barely turning in time before rounding the obstacle.

Too late, the female rider spotted Mama crouched behind the hedge. With a grunt of effort, the priestess swung her staff and struck the charging horse full in the face. There was an audible crack and deep thrum that seemed to emanate from the weapon as the beast's skull shattered. The horse toppled, dead in an instant. The rider pitched violently forward, crashing and tumbling through their campsite and smacking roughly into the trunk of a tree on the far side, where she lay dazed.

Simultaneously, as the other rider cleared the thicket on Yadira's side, she threw a cloud of white powder from her extended hand. The fast-acting dust coated the rider's face, blinding him as he rode past. Seemingly unaware of how many opponents he faced, the blinded Barbár rider reined in and began turning his horse in defensive circles as he desperately wiped at his now streaming eyes, blinking furiously and loudly swearing oaths and challenges in his own tongue.

Amina charged the lathered and circling beast, shoving the rider with her thin walking stick and almost succeeding in dismounting him. The Barbár clung to his saddle with his left hand as her attack pitched him far off-balance to his right. That's where Yadira stepped in, expertly slicing the inside of his upper arm with her knife. With a howl, he dropped his axe, but the still-circling horse's hindquarters smashed violently into Yadira, pitching her face-down in the grass. Clutching his injured arm to his side, the desperate rider regained his seat and stilled his mount, trying to peer through streaming eyes that were beginning to swell shut. His horse reared and struck out at the women with its hooves, its stamping feet dangerously close to Yadira's prone body.

"Peace!" Mama's voice commanded the animal with authority as she stepped forward, her word carrying an echo. Instantly, the panicked animal stilled like a chastened child in the midst of a tantrum, its eyes rolling with barely contained panic as it snorted and seemed to resist the strangely enforced stillness. The moment the animal's physical fury was quenched, Amina dashed in once more and struck the blinded rider with a sound blow across the back of his skull, shattering her small staff and toppling him from his saddle to lie face down next to Yadira, who had risen to her knees and was shaking her head woozily.

Argant

From his hiding place, Argant had a clear view of the first fallen rider, who lay crumpled against the tree trunk. Despite an obviously broken arm and multiple cuts and gashes, she was starting to rise, not five paces away from him. The bare-chested wild woman looked furious and savage as she cast about for her lost weapon. He looked around for help, but Mama and the others were still completely engaged with the mounted rider and his terrifying horse. He heard a noise and looked back to the rising Barbár nearest him.

With an audible gasp of pain, the injured warrior rose to her feet, clutching her broken arm to her side. Finally spotting her dropped sword, she staggered over to collect it. As she stooped to pick up the blade, she glanced up and her eyes met the boy's. A feral, triumphant grin spread over her face, and with a shout, she lunged at him. Argant tried to scramble away into a patch of deep ferns, his hands slipping desperately on the moist blanket of dead leaves. Luckily, her injuries seemed to throw her off and she stumbled as she charged, colliding again with the tree. She gasped in agony and folded around her injured arm. Quickly, Argant dashed toward her and grabbed the heavy waterskin that Amina had charged him with protecting. Before the warrior could shake off her pain, he slipped around the bole of the tree, dashed across the campsite and made a mad run for the thicket. He slipped unseen behind Mama's legs and dove into a narrow game trail at the base of the brush, pushing the waterskin ahead of him. His tiny body just fit into the hole, and he crawled deep within the thicket.

Mama

Mama approached the horse with her staff in her left hand and placed the palm of her right on the nose of the still-panicked animal. With an audible sigh, the horse calmed and stood obediently. Amina, meanwhile, had dashed to Yadira's side and was helping her to collect herself. Now the horse was still, Mama approached the prone Barbár cautiously, and—holding her staff with two hands—she prodded his body with the tip of her weapon.

Chaos erupted.

The still blind male rider surged up to his knees, grabbing her staff with both hands and wrestling for control of it, while the female Barbár leapt at Amina's unguarded back, sword raised, with a shrill and startling war cry. Yadira shoved Amina out of harm's way and flung her knife inexpertly at the charging warrior's face. The spinning weapon's handle struck the woman's cheek, momentarily disrupting her charge. Amina regained her balance and foolishly rushed at the much larger woman, wrapping her slender arms around the muscular warrior's waist in an ineffectual attempt to tackle her. The Barbár snarled down at Amina as she scrabbled and struggled. The warrior had just raised her sword for a killing blow when Amina clutched at the woman's broken arm. With a howl of pain, her knees buckled, and Amina was able to push her off-balance. The two of them landed in a heap, Amina on top of the warrior's injured arm. The Barbár's eyes rolled in agony as Amina desperately scrambled into a sitting position on top of her, her fingers pressing into the flesh of the broken limb. Still, despite her injuries, the Barbár was a skilled warrior and outweighed the sylph-like votary by several stone. Though she had dropped her weapon when she fell, the brutish woman seized Amina by the throat with her good hand, and threw her disdainfully into the dirt. Amina hit the ground hard, the side of her head bouncing off a root.

Meanwhile, Mama struggled over her staff with the blinded Barbár. He had surged to his feet and maintained a vice-like grip on the staff as the two danced in a circle, pulling and pushing on the weapon for dominance. Having seen Amina hit the ground hard and knowing time was short—and her patience wearing thin with the brute—Mama opted for a desperate maneuver. She pulled the Barbár firmly toward her, and suddenly fell back onto the ground, keeping a tight grip on the staff. The warrior was pulled off-balance by the unexpected move. With powerful legs trained for decades in the art of mulakima, she kicked upward into his chest as he staggered forward, propelling him into a flip. He landed hard some five feet behind her. Scrambling to her feet, she spun toward her foe, who was momentarily dazed and slowly struggling to his knees. Raising the staff with both hands, she struck his face with a shout. As with the blow to the horse, there was an audible crack and a deep thrum from the staff as the Barbár's head snapped to the side, where it remained at an impossible angle. His lifeless body flopped to the ground.

Yadira stood protectively over Amina's prone form and faced the fierce female Barbár, who had regained her feet and collected her weapon. The warrior advanced shakily on the two of them, her broken arm clutched tightly to her side. Yadira held her one remaining cooking knife, though it would be no match against the warrior's sword. The Barbár smiled her feral grin and spat a bolus of phlegm at Yadira's feet as she stepped toward them. Yadira crouched, ready to defend her sister votary with nothing more than a cooking knife. But with a shrill, piping scream, Argant suddenly appeared on the warrior's left and rushed at her, wildly swinging the waterskin at her wounded arm. The Barbár stepped back in surprise, instinctively avoiding the blow to protect her broken limb. In an instant, her mouth filled with the fletchings of an arrow as her head snapped back violently. Her eyes glazed and drifted upward, her sword fell from her limp hand, and she collapsed.

As one, Mama, Yadira, and Argant looked beyond the thicket to find Lupe standing there, bow in hand.

"I wondered if you were going to join the fight," Yadira said waspishly as she retrieved her thrown knife.

"I am sorry for the delay," Lupe said as she hurried around the hedge to rejoin the group. "The string on my bow broke when I slid into the bushes, and I was all fumble-fingers trying to restring it. Is Amina alright?"

"I'm fine," Amina answered in her characteristic monotone as she rose slowly into a sitting position. "Just bumped my head."

Argant was immediately by her side, offering her the waterskin, which she accepted with a wan smile.

"Let me see to that," Yadira said. She collected her satchel from the hollow stump and began rummaging for bandages and ointments.

Mama stretched and grimaced as she rubbed one of her new bruises. Looking around at their ruined campsite, she said, "We must leave this area before more riders discover us. Lupe, what did you find?"

"The war band that had camped to our north rode out this morning," she reported, as she began to unstrap the saddle from the fallen horse. "At least two hundred warriors. I followed them westward into the forest, but I was discovered by three riders."

"Three?" Mama clarified.

"I dispatched one in the forest," she said. "Then these two gave chase."

Mama took a moment to absorb the information thoughtfully.

"Quite an eventful day, after all," she said as she watched Yadira clean Amina's injury. Then she added over her shoulder, "Lupe, butcher what meat you can off of that poor dead horse, and then we need to be off." She turned to Amina. "Does the river continue northward from here?"

"For a time, sitti," Amina replied softly, wincing at Yadira's ministrations. "Though within a few leagues it will cut to the northwest as the land becomes more hilly."

"We'll need to find a way across the river," Mama said. "Better we do so before the river cuts across our path. Can you walk?"

"With Argant's help," Amina replied, placing a hand on the boy's shoulder, "I'll manage."

"Yes," Mama said with a wink to the boy. "Our young one was quite brave today."

Argant didn't seem to understand everything that was being said, but he smiled and put a protective hand on Amina's arm.

A sudden cold breeze blew in from the north, chilling them all. Mama turned her face into it, closed her eyes, and whispered a prayer of protection and guidance. Then, with a sigh and a huff, she turned and busied herself preparing to depart. She hoped no one heard the muttered imprecations she heaped on Ashahl and this Ancestors-forsaken quest he'd sent her on as she packed her bag and collected her things.

Chapter 10

The lands of the Green Mount are bordered by impassable, majestic mountains to their south, north, and east, and the great cliffs and dramatic fjords on the western coast that rise hundreds of feet over the coastline below. The River Gomul cuts a mostly diagonal path across the great valley, finding its headwaters in Lach Stár at the base of the great peak An Teallach in the northwest. From there, it flows southeastward through the Midlands and through the lands of the Glenfolk. The mighty river passes the town of Esper, the royal seat of the Glenfolk, before turning southward just past Eagle's Gate, where it descends into a series of dramatic waterfalls that cut through the impassable Fearchom Spur. At the center of the great valley, situated at the border of the Glenfolk, the Midlands, and the White Cleft, stands the Tor. Over the generations, it became a symbol of the common beliefs and traditions of all who lived in the Green Mount. It was said that Ilian of the Golden Hand himself had shaped and built the Tor, which towered some two hundred feet above the surrounding farmlands. The purpose and intent of the mysterious ruins that stood atop the unusual pillar-like hill were lost to antiquity. But legend held that Ilian had placed the Tor in the center of his sacred lands as an ongoing blessing to his people, and a reminder that internecine warfare should never be tolerated in the Green Mount. Regardless of whether one lived among the Glenfolk or in the

Midlands, the White Cleft or the High Valley, all were considered Highlanders and were the people of the Green Mount.

Given the topographical challenges of reaching these lands from Mardin and the rest of the Lowlands, the Highlanders were largely denied social intercourse with the other nations of Daffyd, though limited trade did exist. Consequently, they became a fiercely self-reliant people, making, growing, brewing, and crafting all they needed to live. The Green Mount was, in many ways, idyllic in its bucolic and simple traditions, but it would be a grave error for anyone to assume that its people were therefore soft or might prove easy to conquer. The Mardish spent generations trying to forcefully exert hegemony over the Green Mount, only to finally be expelled by the proud Highlanders. The people of the Green Mount were a stout, strong, and proud folk, fierce and disciplined in battle.

– *Encyclopedia Daffydia,* Third Edition

574 HR - *Second month of summer*
High Valley region of the Green Mount

Corvus

"Feargal!" Corvus called over the noise of weapons clashing. "Hold your place, lad. Don't let him push you out of position." Then turning to Cailean, Corvus instructed, "Work with the lad, Cai. He's going to be a weak point if he can't hold his place."

"Aye, Da," Cailean responded, and moved—sword and shield in hand—into the group of trainees, reinforcing Feargal's left side and giving instruction and encouragement to the boy as together they pushed back against the opposing wall of trainees.

Feargal, the son of a butcher from the village of Ben Auchen, was a good lad, hard-working and earnest, but smaller of stature than the beefy boy from Crodh he was struggling against. A fyrd, traditionally, was an amateur militia of local farmers, shepherds, ranchers, and the like—common folk who would grab whatever implements might be handy and answer the call to defend their lands. It was typically just a mass of bodies to soak up an enemy attack and take pressure off of the professional military units fighting alongside them. Long ago, however, Corvus had envisioned a different kind of fyrd. One with training, that would fight with sword, shield, and spear just like the infantry. Twice a month, for two days each time, he would gather two hundred young men and women from surrounding villages and train them in swordplay, how to hold a shield against an attacker, how to stand in the shield wall reliably, and general soldier skills. They were given the weapons to continue training in their villages with local veterans of the fyrd. The trainees were expected to have improved each time they arrived for further sessions with Corvus and Yazid, and somehow, over the years—perhaps by setting high expectations, perhaps by being a patient but demanding instructor, or perhaps simply by holding the reputation of the Raven—Corvus had managed to foster a culture of excellence within the villages and towns of the High Valley. He had paid for the weapons and supplies at first out of his own pocket with some of the treasure he had captured on his adventures across the Mirror Sea, employing multiple smiths and wheelwrights throughout the High Valley in the gainful tasks of building wains and shields, and forging swords and spear heads. His generosity had gained him both notoriety and popularity within the villages as the infusion of significant wealth had spread through the communities, creating if not affluence, comfort, and a willingness to listen to his radical ideas. Now, decades later, the culture of the fyrd had taken hold across the High Valley and each village proudly purchased new weapons for their young men out of the common purse. Ceremonies were held when lads came of age to join the fyrd training, and young women even jockeyed for inclusion—which Corvus welcomed, believing that the more people that were trained and skilled, regardless of gender, the better. By and large, his young charges took the training seriously and strove diligently to improve, wanting nothing more than to earn the approbation of the Raven himself. They took pride in the reputation of the black banner they fought beneath, and worked hard to be worthy of standing in the shield wall.

Corvus looked out over the training ground, his practiced eye noting skill levels and progress, individual weaknesses that needed to be addressed, and spotting those who might not have the heart or fortitude to be relied upon. His skilled veteran trainers roved among the recruits, shouting words of encouragement and instruction over the clamor of the weapons work. He now had dozens of veteran trainers upon whom he could rely; on any given training day, he would have twenty squad leaders present, each responsible for ten recruits. Corvus had worked closely with a number of armies in his youth, fighting alongside their men, helping to train them, even standing in their ranks on occasion. He knew their common practices: demeaning recruits, treating soldiers as less than a person, demanding blind loyalty and obedience. But from the beginning, he and Yazid had taken a different approach. They knew these people, lived with them, worked with them, shared meals with them. They would not bark orders and belittle friends and neighbors. Instead, they treated them fairly, with respect, encouraging and instructing them. Their shared belief was that if the defense of their homeland became a point of pride, if they could experience victory and establish a culture of excellence, they wouldn't need to batter them into some semblance of an army; they would become one of their own choosing. Each man or woman taking pride and ownership of the fyrd and demanding the betterment of themselves and their fellows. It had worked spectacularly. The fyrd under the Raven banner was renowned for its effectiveness in combat throughout the lands of the Green Mount, and Corvus was the heart and soul of it.

"She does well, I think," Yazid said, after stepping away from working with a small group of trainees from the woodlands in the hills. The object of his comment, a strong, determined young woman named Adaira, had taken a bash on the lip from the edge of her own shield when the large young man opposite her had surged forward. Yazid had stepped in to check on the injury and to show her how to reinforce the shield with her shoulder to prevent that from happening again in the future. A trainee's first injury was often a telling moment. Some would lose heart and quit, others might be fearful of further injuries and become timid or tentative in their efforts, which could prove disastrous in combat. But there were those who learned from the injury like young Adaira, who had laughed it off and chalked it up to experience, listening intently to Yazid's instruction, nodding respectfully, and diving right back into the work.

"Aye, she has heart," Corvus responded. "And she's devilish clever with her sword tip."

"Yes, yes," Yazid agreed. "She has been well trained by her mother, I think."

"Who's her mum?" Corvus asked, not recalling.

"You remember Ailsa," Yazid responded, "with the flowing black hair and the bracers…"

"The bracers she had decorated with buttons, aye." Corvus nodded. "You were sweet on Ailsa, weren't you?"

Yazid nodded, embarrassed, and looked around to see if anyone was listening.

"I still am," he responded confidentially. "But she has a husband and a life in Coillhallan, I think."

The two stood for a moment in silence observing the field of trainees. After a time, Yazid continued.

"Life gives us many opportunities, I find. In this one, my chance has passed. I tarried too long, trying to find the courage to speak my heart. Victory to the bold, eh?" He smiled ruefully at his friend.

Corvus returned the smile and put a hand on Yazid's shoulder. He was about to say something encouraging when he spotted a figure on the hillside, sitting with his back against a tree, watching the training. He was dressed in motley trousers that came to his mid-calf, and a matching motley vest over a bare chest. He had a great mop of unruly hair and a scraggly little dog that ranged the grassy hillside near him.

"Take over a for a wee spell," Corvus said. "I need to speak to someone."

Following his gaze, Yazid looked to the strange man resting against the tree. "You know this man?"

"You could say that..." Corvus nodded, not taking his eyes from the distant figure. "Perhaps more a ghost from the past." With that, he strode away, leaving Yazid to oversee the training.

"It's been a wee while, Fool," Corvus said as he approached Latrans, who looked up with curiosity in his eyes. "Last I saw you was before the massacre of Cairgean."

"Was it?" Latrans responded laconically. "I don't recall." He carelessly tossed a small treat to his dog, who jumped high and snatched the treat from the air, then turned, wagging his nub of a tail, expecting more.

"I didna heed your warning then," Corvus said meaningfully. "I wish I had."

"Secrets and whispers, rumors and dreams, these are the stuff of all plans and schemes," the Fool responded quietly, tossing another treat to his dog—who caught this one with an even greater acrobatic maneuver.

"What brings you back to the High Valley?" Corvus asked.

"What?" Latrans looked up, the model of nonchalance. "Just wandering about, as I do. Thought I'd peek in on your training session here."

Corvus was confused. When he had last seen the Fool, some eight years prior, Latrans had spoken in riddles and behaved like a gleeful madman, but now he seemed thoughtful, his speech and behavior less eccentric, more measured.

Corvus had dismissed the Fool's warning last time, thinking him mad, and it had resulted in the massacre of an entire village at the hands of a contingent of Räubers, the elite shock troops of the Barbárs, who specialized in terrorizing the civilian populace. They hit fast and left no living thing behind. If it hadn't been for an early snowfall that blocked the passes, the Räubers would have cut through much of the High Valley, and Corvus would have been to blame.

"What news from the Lowlands, Fool?" he asked, sitting next to Latrans and leaning back on the tree trunk.

"Oh..." Latrans considered his response. "Much that's good, and very much that's not, leaving far too many to fall and rot."

He tossed another treat to his dog, who executed a perfect backflip to snatch the treat in mid-air.

"Does danger approach the Green Mount?" Corvus pressed, at which point the Fool turned to look him directly in the eyes, all merriment gone from his expression.

"You will be tested, Corvus the Raven," he said. "Your sons, as well."

Corvus stiffened, not taking his eyes from Latrans. Something about his words resonated as truth, though he could not put his finger on exactly why.

"What comes?" Corvus croaked, an inexplicable frisson of apprehension stealing over him.

"Many, and One," Latrans said, slowly and clearly. "Danger is at the Gate, and you must gather your band—and *introduce* yourself." He smiled.

Corvus' mind swam trying to follow the Fool's words. "Introduce… What mean you?" he stammered.

"Your eldest has a task, and you have allies to gain if you are to prevent the conquest of the One."

"Cailean?" Corvus demanded. "What are you saying, Fool? Spit it out, man."

Latrans stood and brushed off his pants. "Look to the place of Eagles, Raven. Soon, or all is lost." And with a casual wave of his hand, he turned and strode away up the hill.

Corvus watched him leave, mulling his uncharacteristically sober words. Surely this was the nonsense of a madman, but… something bade him listen. To *hear* this warning. What if the Barbárs were returning? What other warning would he have? Images of the burned bodies at Cairgean flashed in his mind. Could he risk ignoring Latrans again and risk the enemy plundering the Green Mount before he could stop them? And yet… what if he summoned the armies, roused the fyrd, and no enemy arrived? Who would listen to his warnings ever again? He played over Latrans' words again. *Danger is at the Gate, and you must gather your band… if you are to prevent the conquest of the One.*

There were parts of this puzzle that he simply could not understand, but his inner voice, that part of his intuition he had learned to trust on battlefields long ago, told him to heed the Fool's words.

"This was very good," Yazid called to the trainees gathered before him. They were dripping with sweat from the morning's exertions, but the Aslene's compliment seemed to breathe new life into the recruits. "You will all make fine additions to the fyrd. Let us pause now, refresh and rest. Your afternoon will not be so easy, I think."

Corvus stepped up next to his friend just as the troops were dismissed to find shade, water, and to eat the midday meal that each had packed from home. "Who was that on the hillside?" Yazid asked amiably.

"A harbinger…"

"Ominous." The Aslene looked at his commander for deeper meaning.

"I think it is," Corvus said softly. "Gather the officers."

Yazid nodded and moved off, calling to the various instructors present. Within a few minutes, a small knot of veterans stood around Corvus, well away from the trainees' hearing.

"Alright, lads… and lass," he said, acknowledging Bradana, the one female trainer he had in attendance today. "I'm afraid plans have changed. We need to sound the horn, gather the fyrd in full. Here in two days' time. Select the best of the trainees to join us, and dismiss the rest back to their homes. This is not an exercise."

There were shocked gasps from the instructors as they exchanged concerned glances. Corvus held up a hand to quiet them before continuing.

"We march for Eagle's Gate," he said solemnly. "Tell the fyrd to prepare for war. Tell the villages to supply food for a month's march immediately, med'cines and weapons too. Bradana will command and lead the fyrd to the Gate. Cailean, you're riding with me. We leave tomorrow."

There was an instant clamor of questions and worries, which Corvus interrupted without raising his voice.

"You have your orders," he said firmly. "Now, let's move, we have much to prepare."

Turning to Yazid, Corvus said quietly, "Send riders to the White Cleft. Tell them to meet us at Eagle's Gate in a fortnight, and pray to Ilian we aren't too late. Cai and I will alert the Glenfolk on our way."

"A fortnight will be difficult, I think," Yazid responded, rubbing his chin.

Corvus placed a hand on his friend's shoulder. "I know it will."

"What should I do?" Yazid asked.

"You've got to ride to the Midlands and convince Donella to send her troops. Take Ligulf with you; the lad has a persuasive gift."

Yazid sighed. "You might ask me to convince the mountains themselves to join us. It would be easier, no?"

"I know, but if you two leave at first light, you can be at the lady's court in four days' hard ride. Plead our case. Tell her the Barbárs are returning to the Gate and we must stop them and push them back, or all is lost. Remind her of the ancient agreement."

Yazid's eyebrows shot up at this news, his mouth wide in surprise. After a moment, he simply nodded and moved off quickly to gather his things.

Corvus watched as the officers made their selections and spoke with the trainees. Within a matter of minutes the training field was clear as everyone made their way back to their villages somberly but with purpose. He looked at Cailean, who stood by his side, his hand resting casually on the hilt of his sword. His son met his eyes and nodded meaningfully.

War had returned to the lands of the Green Mount.

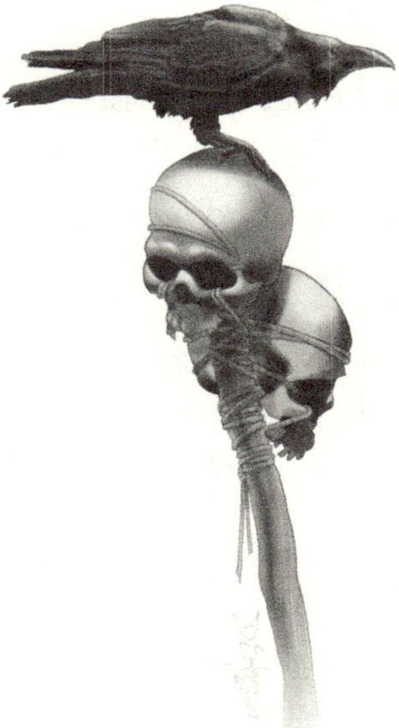

Chapter 11

The Barbárs were a brutal, tribal people from the lands of Orense and Lugo across the sea. Over many generations, their raiding parties had regularly attacked along the coastline of Daffyd—striking the villages of Mardin and Sudland. Historically, the raids were small, with war bands of fewer than a hundred, savaging fishing villages or small towns and carrying off valuables and prisoners to be enslaved. In the year 554 HR, however, for reasons unknown, they began to send what proved to be but the first wave of a mass migration across the water. Their forces ravaged the coastal towns and fishing communities of Mardin and then, uncharacteristically, began to settle there, carving out fiefdoms of their own in the beleaguered country. The invaders continued sending wave upon wave over the subsequent years—each constituted of hundreds of warriors arriving in their dreaded longships—eventually overrunning all of Mardin, burning the capital city, and hanging the flayed corpse of King Offa from the city gates. In 567 HR, the Barbárs completed their conquest of Mardin entirely by capturing the last fortification of the kingdom, Eagle's Gate, located in the far north of the kingdom at the mouth of the Green Mount. Then, in 569 HR, they made the fatal error of pressing forward into the Highlands. It was then that the allied forces of the Green Mount rallied under the leadership of Corvus Corax, the untitled Warden of the Highlands, and expelled the Barbárs after a series of fierce, running battles. Five years later, the Barbárs returned.

– *Encyclopedia Daffydia*, Second Edition

574 HR - Second month of summer
(38 days before the Equinox)
Western forests of Mardin

Bone-Eye

The Barbár camp was a bustle of activity after the day's hard ride. Bone-Eye watched as the massive Räubers built tents and campfires, scuffles and arguments erupting periodically between them. The horses were groomed, fed. and hobbled for the night. While Barbár warriors were generally large to begin with, the Räubers—their elite shock troops—were all well over six feet tall, and towered over the slender Bone-Eye. To be considered a Räuber, a Barbár must first be of appropriate size, then distinguish themselves upon the battlefield, killing at least a dozen enemies and demonstrating a savagery beyond the norm. The Räubers enjoyed a greater share of any loot pillaged, got first pick of the women—on the rare occasions that women became Räubers, many of them partook in the ravishing of female captives right alongside their male counterparts—and served themselves first at any feast. It was an honor to be admitted into their fearsome number, and long-standing tradition placed them in the highest stratum of the Barbár people. Only a Räuber could ever hope to be a stone-bearer to the Great Hadvezér, and only the tribes of the stone-bearers were worthy to offer women to his tent, thus binding them to his tribe through marriage.

Though not a Barbár himself, Bone-Eye had accompanied their ships years earlier, landing on the green coast of Mardin—the land that the Barbárs referred to as *Új Otthon*, or "New Home." He had traveled and fought alongside their troops on multiple occasions, including the sack of Grado, bringing his special expertise to bear both during the battles and afterward, when he was given prisoners. He had fond memories of that day in Grado, flaying the skin from the Mardish King while his defeated subjects watched. Oh, how he had screamed! Like an injured rabbit, gibbering and drooling, tears streaming from his eyes… at least, until Bone-Eye removed them. The memory still sent a thrill through him. The king, the prisoners… a memorable day.

It had been quite surprising when the Great Hadvezér himself, Lord Vajk, sent a personal messenger to Bone-Eye with the news he had been awaiting! Bone-Eye had lobbied the Great Hadvezér for years, begging him to understand the importance of the Tor and the need to capture the lands of the Green Mount before the Equinox of this year. But Vajk had been slow to trust an outlander, an Angor shaman, like Bone-Eye. Vajk himself had invited the council of shamans to work with him years before, valuing their unique talents, and Bone-Eye, along with six of his brethren, had agreed. But the Barbárs were notoriously contemptuous of outsiders, especially those of smaller stature. The people of the jungles of Angor were a diminutive race, few reaching as tall as five and a half feet, and though the arcane practices of the shamans extended their lifespans to be almost immortal, they also shriveled and wasted their physical forms until they more resembled walking corpses than men. Consequently, the Barbárs tended to look upon the shamans with barely disguised disgust, despite their unique talents. Finally, however, after years of battle and torture that had earned Bone-Eye notoriety and a certain grudging respect among various Barbár war chiefs, word had come this past spring. Lord Vajk was forming an unprecedented expeditionary force of ten thousand Räubers to seize the Highlands, and Bone-Eye would accompany the Räuber commander, Gaszi, Third Stone-Bearer to the Great Hadvezér.

Throughout all of the various campaigns and skirmishes in which he had participated with the Barbárs, he had never seen the Great Hadvezér commit a sizable force of all Räubers like this. The shock troops were normally scattered amongst the regular warriors, adding their bulk, skill, and the undeniable inspiration they provided to the common Barbárs. Which was just as well, as the brutes each behaved like the lead dog of a hunting pack. When grouped together, they were prone to fighting amongst themselves, striving for dominance. Unless they were kept on the march or attacking an enemy, the Räubers would tear themselves apart. It was what they knew. They were bullies and brutes, bred and trained from birth to dominate and brutalize. Bone-Eye valued that, to a point. The creatures had their uses. But Vajk had delayed too long and the shamans had collectively fretted that time was short. Sangine, the leader of their faction, had personally ordered Bone-Eye to accompany this force and urge haste. They would be pressed to arrive and fight their way through before the Equinox, but with this unprecedented force of giant, savage brutes, it might just be possible. However, trying to get that fool, Gaszi, to understand the urgency of his deadline was like trying to coax snow from a summer's day. Assuredly, the man had his hands full, trying to command this many Räubers all grouped together; he struggled daily to keep them from killing each other or killing him. But the man was arrogant and contemptuous of Bone-Eye as an outlander, and—the shaman suspected—more than a little unnerved by his unique talents.

With a sigh, the Angor knelt and reached into his bag to prepare his various implements.

Gaszi has not yet seen one tenth of what I can do.

The shaman grinned a small, twitching smile. Satisfied that all was in readiness, he stood and paused to take in the view. The sky was bleeding with a portentous sunset, its dimming light casting sanguinary shades of rust on the camp just as an evening mist rose, virtually swallowing the gargantuan Räubers. Bone-Eye watched it from the top of a small hill near the encampment, absorbing the sights, sounds, and—most importantly—scents of the warriors. Holding his staff, which was topped with a bleached ram's skull, decorated with various feathers and bones, and wrapped in the dried sinews of enemies, he sniffed the air. He couldn't smell significant fear among the Räuber force. Not that he expected to yet. They claimed to be fearless. A boast that had proved true, more often than not. However, they had yet to see his true work, and observe his talents. Fear would come. It would come to them all.

He turned to the task at hand. Two of the brutish warriors held down a naked, squirming farmer they had abducted along their ride. He was an older man with blackened teeth and a long, scraggly, gray beard. He was lean, but the muscles of his arms and legs looked strong in a wiry way. His belly was slightly distended, probably more from diet than malnourishment, Bone-Eye thought. The man kept jabbering and begging, spittle flying from his lips and sticking in his beard. He lay on a sturdy folding table that the shaman traveled with for just this purpose. One of the Räubers held the man's arms and the other his legs. The man thrashed and struggled, but despite his best efforts, he might as well have been shackled to the table. Bone-Eye examined the man's face, touching his cheek, then tracing a line along his jaw almost absent-mindedly. The man stared into his eyes and stilled like a trapped fawn, trembling but no longer struggling. Bone-Eye pulled a curved dagger from his bag, and examined the blade closely. He closed his eyes, and sniffed it. Dried blood from multiple victims still encrusted the well-used blade. His hands trembled with anticipation as he reached up to scratch his scalp, his hand coming away with one of the last remaining clumps of greasy black hair that still clung to his head. He opened his eyes to examine the hair and the small patch of bloody skin attached to it.

It is past time.

Chanting quietly to himself, Bone-Eye breathed in his victim's nascent fear, the shaman's eyelids fluttering as the first rush of energy suffused him. He felt his muscles tighten with newfound strength, his body tense with unused power, as the familiar fugue overtook him. Breathing a euphoric sigh and unable to suppress a twitching grin, he looked at the farmer adoringly.

"Thank you," he whispered. "Oh... *Thank* you."

He then placed the blade at the base of the farmer's belly. *Just here, a shallow cut,* he thought. *Prolong the agony and the blessed fear.*

Leaning into the cut, he nearly swooned as waves of the man's terror washed over him. The screams of agony only registered distantly in the Angor's perception.

Räubers

The warriors in camp were busy preparing their evening meals when the blood-hued mist enveloped them. Most sat around individual fires in groups of three to five, talking, drinking, swearing oaths, bragging of their conquests, and loudly boasting of their intended actions. They had stopped their march early enough to erect their tents and establish their pickets before dark. They knew the days ahead would be filled with more of the same. Wake, eat, break camp, saddle up, ride for long tiresome hours, then stop, pitch tents, light fires, eat, drink, argue, sleep. It might be weeks before they saw any action. They were sullen and bitter, waspish with their fellows. Here they were, the cream of the forces serving the Great Vajk, and yet they had been pulled from the fighting to go on this fool's errand. Denied the rapine, conquest, and glory to be had in the rich Lowlands, they had been sent to conquer the meager farms of the Highlands. Grumbles around the campfires grew each day: Why send ten thousand Räubers to kill goat-fucking farmers? And who was this shifty little outlander shaman that had Gaszi's ear, with his flaccid, scabby skin and his goat-turd eyes? There was definitely something wrong with that one.

Then the screaming began—an inhuman sound that echoed through the mist-covered camp, seeming to come from all directions at once. The trees of the wood that flanked their northern edge seemed to sigh in response as a breeze stirred them without touching the fog. More shrieks of agony, soul-deep wails as if someone's spirit were being rent from their body piecemeal.

Whatever was happening and to whom, the torturer knew his business. None among the fearsome warriors acknowledged the baying openly, but their conversations became more muted, and as one, they sat a little closer to their fires, absently fingering the charms and trinkets they wore for protection.

Bone-Eye

Time passed. The sun set and twilight began, and still the man's agony continued. Bone-Eye was an expert at prolonging and increasing the torment and the terror, and long before he was ready to stop, the two veteran troops standing watch began shifting uneasily. They were no longer needed to restrain the prisoner, as he was well beyond escaping. Struggling to focus through the waves of euphoria, Bone-Eye examined the farmer's twitching body beneath him. The belly was open, exposing his organs: a long coil of intestine had been pulled out and draped on the ground: the tendons of each limb had been severed: much of the skin from the chest had been flayed off: and one of the farmer's eyes was now a gory ruin of jelly. Bone-Eye's blade moved toward the man's other eye, hungry to milk every last ounce of terror from his victim.

The shaman glanced at the warriors, and noted their barely masked nausea and unease. He smiled to himself. *Good. Word will spread. Unease will lead to fear. Even among these brutes.* He noted that the sun had long set now, and looking back at his victim, he saw with disappointment that the farmer had slipped into unconsciousness. With a sigh, Bone-Eye slit the man's throat and straightened, the strength and sense of power still washing over him. It wouldn't last more than an hour, but fear like this gave him the strength of ten men and the speed of a viper's strike. His body trembled with the unused potential as he looked up into the darkening sky and laughed. He had been careful, so very careful, never to show the Barbárs this power. He would reveal his secret in time, but not yet. *Not yet.* He closed his eyes and reveled in it silently.

"What omens, wizard?" Gaszi demanded roughly, climbing the hill behind Bone-Eye, the two Räuber warriors raising their heads at the arrival of their leader. "We can hear your efforts all through camp."

"The mists bleed," the shaman responded. "The coming days will yield peril."

He did not bother to look up at the imposing commander, who towered over him; he had an irritating habit of standing too close to people, intimidating them with his formidable size. Instead, Bone-Eye looked down at the eviscerated corpse on the table. Reaching down, he roughly wiped his blade on a small towel and slipped it back into his leather bag.

"Hunh," the commander grunted. He clearly didn't trust omens, though Bone-Eye suspected he was not fool enough to ever say so aloud. The gods tended to punish those who scoffed. Gaszi touched the iron necklace at his throat and looked at the bloody mess on the table. "Nothing more from this one's entrails?"

"Oh, a great deal," the shaman answered with a quivering smile, but still not meeting the commander's gaze. "A great deal, indeed. I will need to consider the meanings."

The spirits spoke to Bone-Eye only in riddles and half-truths, but night after night he awoke from his fevered dreams certain of one thing: the secret was in the mysterious Tor, and time was short. His brethren knew the balance point drew near, and they were drawn toward it. Nothing would stop them. Bone-Eye bared his teeth in a feral grin, knowing that of all the shamans, he would be first to the Tor. He *must* be the first. Not the hungry Blood Tooth, nor Singer, nor even Sangine, himself. No, it must be Bone-Eye. He would unlock its mysteries, then all would kneel to him—all his fellow shamans, so smug in their deathless and endless machinations. But time pressed on. They were ten days from the ruins of Eagle's Gate, and less than a month after that was the Equinox. So much to do in so short a time. He looked once more at his handiwork and suppressed a grin, savoring the still-strong euphoria. But there would be more of this… so much more.

"We must not tarry at the pass," the shaman said finally. "We must push through the Highlanders and storm the Tor."

"We will do as I think best," Gaszi said, grabbing Bone-Eye's shoulder and turning the wizard to face him. He leaned down into the shaman's face, his cheeks reddening above his shaggy white beard. "You do not command here, sorcerer." His massive index finger poked Bone-Eye in the chest forcefully. "Forget that at your peril."

Bone-Eye glanced down at the commander's finger, the power still coursing through his veins. How easy it would be to seize and mangle that hand, to break the bones of this goliath's arm, to rip out his heart. *Not yet,* he mused. *In time.* He smiled a faint, twitching smile up at the commander, who seemed somehow unnerved by the expression.

"Gah!" Gaszi exclaimed in disgust, before gesturing to the two warriors to follow him. He then turned and strode from the hilltop back toward camp, the two warriors behind him, seemingly all too eager to leave Bone-Eye alone with the corpse as the last glimmers of twilight faded. The Angor shaman rubbed his chest resentfully, staring silent venom at the commander's departing back.

"In time," he said, under his breath. "In time."

Chapter 12

'Tis true I bear no poniard twixt my legs.
Wouldst thou think me less fierce?
My blades can reach unto your breast.
My poisons stop your mouth.

Man's duty is but one once seed is set:
Protect the wife and babe.
Yet I defend and nurture from my breast.
So what need of you have I?

– "Lady Gwynara's Reply,"
Courts of Love, Second Collection,

574 HR - *Second month of summer*
Deep Mere, Lachland

Darienne

"Do you have to go?" Lila asked, her voice drowsy with drink and spent passion.

"They'll be worried," Darienne responded, pulling on her boots. She paused for a moment to look at Lila, naked and lying in a tangle of sheets, her olive skin, slender body, and long legs so very tempting. Darienne bent down to smell the floral oils she had used in her long, black tresses and kiss her bare shoulder. *So beautiful,* Darienne thought, stroking Lila's cheek.

She debated changing her mind and crawling back into bed, but a glance out the window showed that dawn was approaching. Soon, her servants would be knocking on her bedroom door back at Wetheral, bringing breakfast and preparing to straighten her room. If they found her missing, the alarm would go up, soldiers would be dispatched to search for her, and gossip and complications would follow. As a rule, the princess didn't mind being the source of scandal, but with her mother on campaign, the Lake Jacks and, indeed, the entire capital, seemed more jittery than usual. This was not a time to stir things up further. Brigadier St. Fiacre had come close to insisting on a curfew for Darienne, strongly suggesting that she not leave the castle. Major Justiniere, St. Fiacre's second, had even dared to clutch Darienne's bridle as if he would prevent her departing by force! They had had words, and she had left the two men fuming in the courtyard as she rode out into the night, Kaiso not far behind.

With a playful slap on Lila's bare rump, she stood and drew on her duster and broad-brimmed hat. Lastly, she buckled on her sword belt, tucking her dagger into the back of the waistband, hidden by the long, brown coat. With a wink and a blown kiss, she slipped out of Lila's room at the Salty Mermaid and stole quietly through the whorehouse, the sounds of snoring coming from doors she passed. *Quite different from the sounds coming from those rooms just a few hours ago,* she mused. She carefully avoided a creaky stair as she descended, pushed aside the red velvet curtain, and passed through the parlor to the front door, noting the disarray of the room. Wine mugs and tankards were overturned and strewn about from the night's excesses. It would all be cleaned up by the servants before noon, when the doors would once again open to welcome guests. With a quick glance back over her shoulder to see if she'd been observed, she slipped out of the door and into the pre-dawn streets of Deep Mere.

The Salty Mermaid, though a brothel, was in a nicer area of town. Merchants' shops, taverns, and even a jeweler also made their home on that cobbled street, though all were quiet now, and the only person Darienne could see was a lamplighter making his morning rounds, extinguishing the lanterns along the row of shops. Taking a quick glance at the sky, she gauged the time and swore under her breath. She needed to hurry. She shook her head to try to clear it of the lingering effects of the night's wine. She'd had too much, even for her, but she'd needed the release. The tensions of the past few days, and the worry about her mother, had built up. With a deep, cleansing breath of brisk morning air, she turned to her left, and headed toward the stable where she had left her horse for the night.

I wonder where Kaiso is, she thought, then dismissed the worry. He was probably sleeping in the bed of one of the other whores at the Mermaid. *The man deserves a little recreation. He'll report back to the castle once he's up.*

The early morning streets were dim and empty as the sky was just beginning to pale. She pulled her coat around her more tightly in reaction to the morning chill. The sound of a boot scuffing on a cobblestone somewhere behind her made her instantly alert, the wine's residual effects evaporating as a shiver of danger suffused her. Without turning to look, she quickened her step slightly, still taking care to purposely stagger her gait—affecting more drunkenness than she felt. The footsteps seemed to be keeping pace with her as she turned the corner onto Canal Street and began walking up the hill. The empty street was lined with well-tended stone town houses, each with a fenced front garden behind locked gates. Though an upscale neighborhood, it was still in the heart of town, an area where you kept your doors locked at night.

Another scuff of a boot sounded behind her, this time closer. She was only a quarter of the way up the hill. At the top was the intersection with High Street, where she would turn right for two blocks before arriving at the Whale's Tail. The tavern had a stable out back, and she knew the innkeeper well. His sons took good care of her gelding each time she enjoyed one of her jaunts into town. Her generous tips made sure they treated him to an extra portion of oats and brushed him down thoroughly. Scanning the street for a possible way to hide from whomever was following her, she noted a narrow alley between two homes on the right, thirty paces ahead. Quickening her step, she put a hand to her head, pretending to be woozy and looking for a place to vomit out the night's wine. She staggered around the corner into the alley and made retching sounds to continue her ruse, while silently drawing her sword and dagger, and facing the street.

Moments later, a large man turned the corner and stopped, facing her. He was a dock worker, by the look of his clothes. A beefy man with a pock-marked face and a small knit cap on his head. The sleeves of his jacket were partially rolled up revealing thick, tattooed forearms, large hands, and fingers that resembled plump sausages. Seeing Darienne standing there with weapons drawn, the man grinned a gap-toothed smile. His meaty face was covered in graying stubble and he looked to weigh some fifteen stone, mostly muscle, which meant that she dared not let him close with her.

"Looking for something?" Darienne asked.

"Found it, thanks," he growled.

"I see."

Her eyes quickly scanned the alley for terrain, obstacles, levels, and possible escape as Kaiso had trained her. Behind her, the alley ended in a brick wall that would be difficult to scale, though there was a slanted doorway to a root cellar near it that could be used as a vault, in a pinch. She hoped, should she need it, that it would be sturdy enough and that the frame wasn't rotten. Last resort. *Well, nothing for it then,* she thought, turning back to the man approaching her.

"Pretty princess playin' with swords," the man chuckled as he sauntered closer. Reaching behind him, he drew out a long knife with a bone handle that looked well tended. It had a full, thick blade with a slight curve to the true edge. The false edge had a sharpened cut out along one third of the length. This was no workman's knife; this was a blade for killing. And judging by the way he casually flipped the blade and tossed it from hand to hand, he was skilled in its use.

He smiled confidently, shaking his head with disdain at her weapons. Clearly, he assumed her unskilled in their use—that the Princess just wore the weapons as part of her swaggering persona, and didn't know how to use them. *Good. Let him think that,* she thought, adopting an awkward guard stance and purposely holding her sword with tension in her arm, feigning nervousness and a lack of skill. *Just a few more steps.*

Just as he came within her measure, he cocked his head playfully to the side, his eyebrows shooting up and his mouth making an "O" shape like he was playing "catch me" with a child. He rushed forward, his knife in his right hand coming across to trap her saber as his massive shoulder slammed her off her feet. At least, that had been his plan. Things didn't quite work out that way. Reading his body's movements, Darienne dropped into a deep, defensive lunge while her sword easily deceived his blade and the tip of her saber slipped expertly under the handle of his knife and into his belly. The momentum of his charge skewered him. Darienne's deep lunge put her shoulder right at the level of his thighs. As their bodies collided, she surged forward, catching his legs on her shoulder, and—with a heave—flipped his significant bulk over her onto the cobbled alleyway. It was a grappling maneuver she had spent many painful hours perfecting, getting kicked and thrown repeatedly by Kaiso until she eventually learned to see the opponent's center of gravity and how to use his own momentum against him.

Her assailant landed with a bone-crunching crash, his knife skittered away on the cobbles. She turned to look at him. Momentarily horrified by the sight of her blade still protruding from his belly, she nonetheless allowed herself a moment of pride in her victory. Her training was working. She retrieved her hat, which had been knocked off in the assault. The man was grimacing and groaning loudly. She pulled the saber free, which only increased the volume of his cries. Bending down to his face, she placed the tip of her dagger just under his left eye, at which point he gasped and became silent, his breathing shallow and ragged.

"Who sent you?" she demanded.

"Bugger off, bitch," he growled.

She pressed down with the tip of her dagger, drawing blood from the top of his cheek, a finger's width from his eye.

"Who hired you to kill me?" she demanded in a quiet voice that belied the trembling in her muscles.

With a roar, he suddenly rolled over, his hand batting her dagger aside, the tip dragging a long gash across his cheek. From his knees, he surged forward, tackling her and slamming her against the stone wall of the alley. She dropped her sword as the air exploded from her lungs and her head snapped back against the wall painfully. Stars flashed before her eyes as she felt his massive hand close on her left wrist, trapping her dagger hand. He stepped back, released her throat, and grabbed the lapel of her duster with his left hand, lifting her off of her feet. Then he slammed her into the wall again, this time disarming her. She could feel a warm trickle of blood down the back of her neck from the impact to her head. Her feet were still several inches off the ground as the massive man reared back to slam her once more into the wall.

"Say goodbye, bitch," he said with a snarl, sweat dripping from his nose and chin.

Darienne's hand clawed desperately at his massive arm, seeking leverage. Black spots began to swim in her vision as her hand struggled in vain against the meaty limb. Just before he could smash her once more into the wall, she brought up her left knee sharply into his face. She felt a crunch as blood exploded from his mouth and nose. He released her, staggering back, hands instinctively covering his face. Bracing herself against the wall, she raised her right foot and kicked him squarely in the chest with everything she had, slamming him into the bricks on the opposite side. She scooped up her dagger in her right hand and just as he managed to blink away the pain and snarl a murderous growl, she sprung forward, slamming her blade into his chest. His face purpled as he looked down at the dagger hilt protruding from him, and he gurgled several half words, bloody spittle flying from his lips and spattering her face. With a groan, he collapsed. His eyes rolled up into his head as a death rattle escaped his lips.

Panting and trembling, Darienne knelt by the man's body to stave off a wave of nausea. Despite all the hours training with Kaiso, she had never actually killed a man before. She stared, morbidly fascinated as his skin grayed suddenly, the life gone. She put a shaking hand to the back of her head to check her injury. It wasn't too bad, but like all head wounds, it bled profusely.

"Well done, Princess," Kaiso said approvingly from the opening of the alley.

Darienne looked up sharply. "How long have you been there?"

"The whole time," he replied laconically as he stepped past her further into the alley to retrieve the weapons. "Nice job with the Soto Defense," he said, indicating the bloody stain on the cobbles where she had first flipped her assailant.

"You're supposed to be my bodyguard," Darienne panted, trying desperately to control her shaking.

"You had things under control." Kaiso examined the attacker's bone-handled knife, then slipped it into his own belt.

"What?!" she exploded. "He could have killed me!"

"But he didn't," the mercenary replied with a rare wink, his piercing dark eyes glinting from beneath his black brow. "Your training kept you alive. That's what you hired me for, Princess. And besides, all the training in the world is no good until it's put to use and you kill a man. Now you have. Congratulations. I was ready, though, in case you didn't remember that you had knees available for attacking."

"Thanks," she said, shaking her head—a bad choice as a fresh round of stars flashed in her vision, causing her to bend over and place both hands on her legs for stability.

"Let's get you back to the castle and have that looked at," Kaiso said, wiping off her saber and handing it back to her. He then reached a hand under her arm to help her stand, and together they continued the walk to the stables.

"Who… who did this?" she stammered, leaning on his shoulder as they walked out of the alley. "Who would want me dead?"

"That," he said, lifting his index finger, "is an excellent question, and one to which we must find an answer quickly before more attempts are made."

She stopped and looked at him. "You think this will happen again?"

"Undoubtedly," he replied, and nodded. "They underestimated you this time. Whoever they are, they won't make that mistake again."

Chapter 13

Four women from a far-off land and a child of Mardin struggled 'gainst the dangers of the wild, fought off roving bands of cruel Barbárs, traveled weary leagues northward, ever northward as summer waned and the storms beset them. Fording rivers, crossing bogs, climbing mountains, hiding in caves and crofter's cabins, the weary travelers pressed on—all in their single-minded journey to deliver the Key to a man they had never met and hoped they could trust. For Fate had put it in their hands, made it their quest. If they failed, untold evils would befall humanity. If they succeeded, they might turn the sharp blade from the breast of Manu's children. Perhaps. But some chance was better than none, and so they struggled onward.

– *The Saga of the Key* as told by Rhona the Bard

574 HR - *Second month of summer*
Somewhere in eastern Mardin

Mama

The next morning found Mama slow to rise. Her body ached from the battle with the Barbár riders the day before, and she was sure the others suffered similar pains as well. She had checked on Yadira twice before turning in last night, but the tall, stoic woman had assured her she was fully recovered from the collision with the horse and would be fine, despite the scrapes and bruises on her arms. Fine or not, Mama knew they would make slow progress this day.

Lupe had patrolled in a wider-than-usual circuit during the night and assured them that they were safe to build a fire and cook a morning meal before continuing their journey. As usual, Argant positioned himself beside Mama where she sat beside the fire ring. Despite her aching muscles, she leaned forward and reached her hand into the kindling. As was her custom, she closed her eyes and emptied her mind. She envisioned the same bright, white light that was her internal meditation point; the Hall of the Ancestors, her teachers had termed it. As a youth, she had struggled for weeks to perceive any actual warmth, at first only holding the image in her mind as an aoristic concept, not as an actual place or thing. Her teacher, dear fragile Zilpah, had been patient with her, guiding her meditations day after day until her experience shifted. She still remembered the sense of wonder she felt the first time her mind finally relaxed into the image and she felt actual heat from the light. Her sense of wonder then multiplied as she realized the light had changed from the static model she had created in her mind as a meditative focal point; it transformed into a living, blazing incandescence, sparkling with its own iridescence that seemed to warm her very soul. After that, it had been but a simple matter of learning to translate the warmth from that illimitable source through her hands and onto kindling. Not all devotees were able to summon the fire. Amina and Lupe still struggled to find that internal shift that would allow them to perceive the actual light and its warmth, though Yadira had long ago mastered the bringing of the flame.

Mama heard Argant stir restlessly beside her and she paused to look at the child before summoning the blaze. He sat cross-legged in the grass, eyes pressed closed, hands palm up on his knees, just as she had taught him for meditation. A flying insect landed on the boy's ear as he concentrated, but he seemed so focused on his meditative efforts that he didn't react to shoo the bug away.

Impressive concentration for one so young. I wonder…

Reaching out, she took his hand in hers, and guided it to the kindling. Then she sat back to observe. His sparkling eyes opened and he looked at her questioningly.

"You try," Mama said, encouraging him.

He started to shake his head, but stopped himself. Instead, he closed his eyes and furrowed his brow, seeming to concentrate with all his might on the pile of twigs and leaves before him. Moments passed and nothing happened. He scrunched his brow still further, obviously redoubling his efforts. She knew he was working too hard, but withheld any comment. Something about the boy suggested to her that he could, in time, achieve this. But for now, still nothing. After a moment, Mama patted him on the knee and said, "We'll try again tomorrow."

She then covered his hand with hers, closed her eyes, touched the twigs, and summoned the fire. As always, his eyebrows shot up in surprise at the moment of ignition, and he turned to her, a quizzical smile on his face.

"What wrong?" he asked in a broken sentence, gesturing to his own hand.

"Oh," she replied, speaking slowly, "I suspect that you're trying too hard. Don't worry, it will come. You can feel it, and that's the first step." She chucked his chin and shooed him off to help with camp chores.

Amina returned from scouting the riverbank north of them. She knelt gracefully across the fire ring from Mama, not making a sound, her sylph-like form going from standing to kneeling as suddenly as a delicate bird might alight upon a branch.

"There is a ford ahead," she said in her soft monotone. "Half a league."

"We can cross?" Mama asked, leaning back and adjusting her legs.

Amina nodded.

Yadira was preparing the horse meat they had cut from the fallen beast yesterday, while Lupe busied herself packing their bedrolls and tying their bundles.

"Lupe," Mama said, interrupting her work. "A word."

"Yes, sitti," Lupe dutifully replied, rising and wiping her hands on a dirty rag as she crossed to join them beside the small fire.

"Amina tells of a ford some half a league north," Mama said. "Perhaps you should scout ahead and see if the other bank of the river there looks clear and safe for us to cross. Never mind the packs, I'll finish."

"Yes, sitti."

With that, Lupe scooped up her bow and quiver and set off into the woods along the riverbank, her footsteps making no more sound than the soft passing of a small woodland beast. Mama reflected on the previous day's attack and the two vicious riders, seemingly so hungry for slaughter. The little group had taken the time to hide the bodies in the forest before pressing on. Lupe had captured the remaining horse, with no small amount of difficulty. The riders' saddlebags had contained little of value beyond a handful of silver trinkets, some dried jerky of questionable origin, and two waterskins. The skins smelled rank and Mama had chosen to discard them, not trusting the Barbárs to have properly tanned them. Yadira had inspected the jerky closely before tossing it aside in disgust as well. The silver could be useful to trade for food or shelter in the days ahead, should they be fortunate enough to encounter any farmsteads not yet ravaged. The real treasure, though, was the horse. While it was obviously a trained war mount, routinely snapping at the women and kicking at anyone foolish enough to walk behind it, the horse could carry a lot. And perhaps they would be able to calm the beast enough to allow Argant to safely ride it, which would speed their progress.

Mid-morning found the small party wading across the ford in hip-deep water, their arms held high. Though the river was not fast moving here, it was broad, and the constant pull of the current was tiring to struggle against. Lupe led the way, holding

Amina's hand to steady the slight votary as they struggled to find secure footing on the shifting river rocks below. Yadira followed next, leading the horse with Argant on it, clutching tightly to the beast's mane. Their satchels and camp gear were securely tied to the beast's saddle. Mama brought up the rear, walking with her "cane," probing the river ahead with the great staff for unseen obstacles beneath the surface.

Lupe climbed out of the river on its eastern bank, pulling Amina past sucking mud and up onto a grassy patch between two overhanging oaks. Yadira, Mama, and Argant were still midstream when Lupe whistled an alert. Mama and Yadira looked up in alarm. Lupe was pointing urgently across the river just as a shout went up from the far woods. Looking behind her, Mama saw movement in the trees. Yet another small band of Barbárs had spotted them and was making its way toward the ford.

Yadira urged the truculent horse to greater haste, while Mama fought against the current. She was not a tall woman, and the water here was mid-chest for her now. Yadira asked if she needed help, but Mama urged her onward. "Just get across, Dira!" she called. "I'll be fine." Behind her, she heard the riders entering the river in pursuit. From their approaching shouts and the splashing footsteps of their horses, she knew they would likely overtake her before she could gain the eastern bank. Not wasting time to look back, she pushed on urgently, her hip and back aching from the effort.

Something streaked past her head in the direction of the riders, and she heard a cry of pain followed by the sound of a body hitting the water. Lupe, half-hidden behind a tree on the bank, quickly nocked another arrow as Mama gave her a thankful and encouraging nod. She quietly muttered a prayer of thanks for the girl's skill with the bow.

Yadira reached the far side, turning to use both hands to pull the horse's bridle, urging it forward up the muddy bank. With a surge, the beast rushed past her, knocking her into the muck. Amina jumped forward and grabbed the horse's reins, before it could bolt off, carrying Argant with it. With soothing words and a firm hand, she calmed the beast and guided it further into the woods, out of sight. Lupe released three more arrows in rapid succession, and another rider fell with a cry. Mama head the Barbárs cursing from behind her as she reached the far bank and with great effort, and Yadira's muddy help, hauled herself out of the sucking water and up onto the shore, where she turned to finally look at their pursuers.

Three riders remained on their mounts midstream, while two riderless horses milled about ahead of them, blocking their progress; two bodies floated downstream, feathered arrows sticking up out of the water. The three remaining riders had pulled out short bows and were nocking arrows. Lupe shot again, missing the lead Barbár's face by inches. In ducking to avoid the arrow, he aborted his own shot, but the other two fired into the woods, one arrow striking the trunk of an oak not three feet from Mama's head. Yadira helped her scramble past the mud and onto the slippery grass, where she crouched behind a thick bush to watch the archery exchange. Lupe reached back to her quiver to grab another arrow, only to find it empty. Casting a resigned glance at Mama, she set down her bow and drew her long hunting knife.

"Mina," Mama called over her shoulder, "take the boy and the horse and wait for us further north!"

"But Mama—" Amina began.

"Go, child!" Mama snapped. "Take Argant to safety and hide. We'll find you."

Before Amina could lead the horse further away, Yadira fetched her satchel from its saddle and quickly located one of her sachets and one of her cooking knives. Now it was just the three women in the small clearing near the water's edge. Mama positioned herself behind the tree closest to the path out of the river. She closed her eyes and once more muttered a silent prayer of forgiveness for what was to come. Yadira stood at the far edge of the clearing. She would be in clear sight of the riders once they left the river and she would, hopefully, draw their attention. Lupe quickly scampered up one of the oak trees, positioning herself on a thick, low branch at a rider's head height.

Having apparently lost sight of their quarry, the three Barbárs shouldered their bows and pushed their mounts past the riderless horses still milling in the river. With a whoop of anticipation, the lead rider burst from the water, up the muddy bank. With another whispered prayer of forgiveness, Mama stepped out to meet the oncoming mount and swung her staff into the horse's face, just as she had done the day before. Again, there was a loud crack and thrum that echoed through the hillside, and the beast fell to the ground, blocking the path out of the ford. Its rider leapt from its back, cleared the mud entirely, and landed in a crouch on the grass directly across from her. The wild man shook his shaggy white-blonde mane, snarled, and waggled his black tongue at her.

The other two riders, stalled by the dead horse blocking their exit, dismounted and waded the rest of the way across. The Barbár facing Mama drew a short sword in one hand and a wicked-looking, barbed dagger in the other. Apparently wary of the stout woman with the staff that had somehow felled his mount, he began circling toward Yadira, not spotting Lupe on the branch above his head. With a shout, the young woman leapt from the tree, kicking the rider in the face as she dropped, the momentum of her leap adding to the power of the kick. Stunned by the blow, the wiry rider staggered several steps, dropping his dagger. Before he could recover his wits, she was upon him and sliced his throat with her knife. He looked at Lupe in stupefaction as he grasped at his neck, blood sluicing through his fingers and down his bare, tattooed chest. He stumbled about, impossibly striving to remain standing, then collapsed suddenly in a heap. Lupe then turned to face the other two warriors, who were now working their way around the dead horse and up the muddy bank.

The two male Barbárs advanced cautiously. One carried a great axe and the other a broadsword, which he held lightly in one hand. They whispered admonishments to one another in their own tongue as they spread apart to engage the women. Lupe and Mama backed away, careful to stay out of reach of the warriors' weapons. The Barbár carrying the sword glanced at his fallen comrade, then locked eyes with Lupe, his face a mask of rage and vengeance. Just then, Yadira stepped forward almost calmly, holding a small tree branch. With a word, it burst into flame and she thrust the flaming brand directly into the Barbár's face. He screamed and covered his face, staggering away quickly. He bumped into the other Barbár fouling an intended swing at Mama from the great axe. In a coordinated movement, Mama and Lupe both struck at once. The older woman brought her staff down onto the axeman, while Lupe grabbed a branch above her head and used it to swing a powerful two-legged kick at the blinded warrior's head. Both fell to the ground, instantly dead. Lupe's kick had snapped the neck of the blinded Barbár, and Mama's staff had struck the axeman's chest and collarbone with the force of a falling boulder, shattering his chest and crushing lungs and heart.

The danger past, the women sat for a moment in the grass to collect themselves. After a time, Mama said, "Well, at least now we have more horses."

Chapter 14

What are we to say, when the finger of Destiny points to us?
Shall we say, "I am not ready"?
Or shall we say, "Unworthy though I may be, I go"?
– Saltyr aphorism

574 HR - *Second month of summer*
The Claws, Lachland

Zach

Zach was going to throw up. He was cold and miserable, soaked to the bone, and the barge had been pitching dramatically for the past three hours as they rounded the southern tip of Great Claw. His hand was numb where he clutched one of the rope loops that had been tied all over the deck to help keep the soldiers from washing overboard. Despite that, they'd lost over thirty men during the night and nearly that many the day before. The sheer mass of soldiers made clinging on difficult when the barge shifted and the weight of all those bodies moved. Several men had made the mistake of tying their hands into the loops—thinking that they might be able to catch a few hours of fitful sleep if they were tied in—but that had only resulted in agonizing injuries to those hands and arms, as the weight of bodies shifting crushed those unable to release themselves. Like the rest of the troops, Zach had discovered that crouching as low to the deck as possible minimized being pitched about in the rough passage, but they'd been crouched here for days, their knees screaming in agony. They were soaked too by the splashes of icy water and frozen by the merciless, glacial winds coming off Mount Xeno.

Zach blinked away the water from the last wave and looked around for a place to vomit. The soldiers were packed shoulder to shoulder with only a narrow strip of deck visible between rows. He'd at least try to not hit the uniform of anyone nearby. After all, these were the men of his company and he was their captain.

Some captain, he thought bitterly. *What kind of captain plans to kill the Queen?*

It wasn't something he ever would have imagined himself doing. He'd always been a loyal and faithful soldier. He took his oath of duty seriously and tried his best to serve with honor. He came from humble origins and had risen through the ranks, earning his commission through excellence and diligence, rather than patronage. Last year he had been promoted to captain, and now was responsible for over a hundred soldiers. With this promotion, he and his wife had started to be invited to officer's parties and dinners. He routinely interacted with senior officers and minor nobility. He was proud of his service to Lachland, proud of his achievements, proud of his newfound and rising position in society. He and Loeiza were planning to start a family. His future was bright. But all of that came crashing down the day his wife was taken.

The orders for this expedition had come five days earlier, with very little warning. Those soldiers not ordered to work at the docks had less than a full day to prepare to ship out. As a company commander, he had passed the orders to his men and seen to the necessary exigencies of imminent departure before hurrying home to his wife to tell her the news. When he had arrived, he found the front door of his walk-up broken and hanging by the hinges. Still in uniform and armed, having come directly from the muster yard, Zach drew his saber and entered the house cautiously. He searched the downstairs first, and saw signs of a struggle; a table had been tipped over and a clay pitcher lay shattered near the hearth. Zach paused to listen at the base of the stairs. There was a muffled thump from the bedroom above, followed by a whimper.

He bounded up the stairs two at a time, bursting through the bedroom door to find his wife, Loeiza, strapped to a chair, a gag in her mouth. Her cheek was red and puffy where she'd obviously been hit, and tears streaked her terrified face. A large man wearing the clothing of a dock worker stood directly behind the chair, his hands resting on her shoulders. His sleeves were partially rolled up, revealing heavily tattooed and muscular arms. He wore a small knit cap and his pock-marked face was covered in graying stubble.

Sitting on the bed near his wife's chair was a slender, beautiful woman with a dark complexion. She was dressed in black trousers, riding boots, and a dark-gray shirt, open at the top. She was leaning back on one arm, and in her other hand she held a long, needle-like knife before her, examining the blade as if it fascinated her. She had straight black hair that draped over her shoulders and full lips that were twisted into a mocking smile.

"Captain Zachar ben Zachar," she said in a deep, husky voice.

"Who are you?" Zach demanded. "If you hurt her..."

The threat remained unfinished as the beefy man slipped his massive hands around Loeiza's neck, producing a terrified whimper.

"What do you want?" Zach implored the woman with the knife.

"Sit down, Captain," the woman said, indicating the empty chair by the door. "We have much to discuss. Place your sword on the floor and kick it over there," she said, pointing to the corner of the room by the foot of the bed.

"Yes, but… Please, don't hurt her." Zach complied and perching on the edge of the chair, his breathing quick and shallow.

"If you do as you're told," the woman replied, "I assure you no harm will come to your lovely wife, and… you will be paid handsomely." She smiled alluringly.

"What do you mean?" Zach asked, his eyes fixed on the burly man holding Loeiza. He could see no way to rush him quickly enough to prevent harm to her.

"You are descended from Aslene merchants, are you not?" she asked.

He frowned, confused by the question and what bearing it had on the situation. Nodding his head dumbly, he responded, "Yes, my grandfather came here long ago. What does that have to do with—"

"Never mind," she said, with a knowing smile. "You are about to ship out with your unit, am I correct?"

"Yes, how did you know that? We only just got the orders…" Zach was perplexed. *How in the world could she know that?*

Something about the woman's confidence and the unknown source of her information made him feel helpless, as though he were trapped in a web with tendrils and anchors that were beyond his meager resources to grasp and untie.

"The mission is to rush support to Autun, yes?" she pressed.

"Yes," Zach responded quietly.

"Filo." The woman turned her attention to the dock worker. "You've been to Autun, yes?"

"'S'right," he grunted.

"Small city," she mused. "Isn't it?"

The large man shrugged and nodded.

"Well," she said, leaning forward to place her elbows on her knees and point the tip of her blade at Zach. "Here it is then… The Queen will be leading this expedition, for whatever foolish reason she's come up with. You and all of the soldiers being shipped by barge will be crammed within the city walls, cheek by jowl. There will be much fighting, as I'm sure the Barbárs are quite determined to take it." She paused. "Does everything I'm saying make sense so far?"

"Yes," Zach responded, his eyes darting to his wife who had started to struggle again, only to have one of Filo's meaty hands once more placed around her throat. *He could crush her neck like ripe fruit,* Zach thought.

"There will be much confusion, I suspect," the dark woman continued. "What with multiple assaults on the walls, the injured being rushed about, men dying… Quite a bit of chaos, wouldn't you think?"

Zach nodded, his eyes pleading with the grizzled man to not hurt Loeiza. "That sounds right."

"During the hubbub, you will find an opportunity to kill the Queen," the woman said matter-of-factly. She then tipped her head to the side in an almost coquettish manner, an anticipatory grin on her face.

"What?!" Zach jumped to his feet, but Filo held up a cautioning finger with one hand while applying just enough pressure to Loeiza's throat to elicit a choked gurgle. Chastened, Zach immediately held up placating hands and sat down again.

"You will kill the Queen," the woman repeated with authority. "Ideally you will do it in a manner that does not implicate you, but I leave that to your discretion. Should you live through this adventure, your wife will be released to you, unharmed. Upon your return you will be paid the princely sum of ten thousand scepters. And, should you want, we will help you and your wife leave the city and relocate somewhere of your choosing."

Zach nodded, his eyes searching the floor as he took in the scope of his predicament. After a moment of thought, he asked, "What if I die on campaign? Or am hanged for treason?"

"Your wife will be released and paid on your behalf," the woman assured him, "provided you succeed in the assassination. Should you fail, for whatever reason, your wife will have her legs broken, stones tied to her ankles, and will be cast into the Mere in the dead of night. Do I make myself clear?"

He searched the woman's merciless eyes for a long moment, glancing once more at Filo, then at his wife. His mind raced as he cast about frantically for any way out of the situation.

"Decide quickly, Captain," the woman said, standing and slipping her blade into a hidden sheath in her bosom. "If you say no, we'll have to kill you and your wife and move on to another candidate. And time is short, so if you don't mind..."

The woman stood and crossed the room to Loeiza as she spoke, placing the tip of her needle-like blade on his wife's throat. Zach's mind was spinning. All thoughts of honor, patriotism, or duty to his military oath fled his tortured brain. All he could see was that stiletto tip beneath Loeiza's delicate chin.

"Yes!" Zach said loudly. "Yes, I'll do it. Just, please, don't hurt her."

"Excellent," the woman said, lowering the blade and crossing to look out of the window at the darkening streets. "I'll leave the details to you. Filo, please assist Mrs. Zachar to our carriage, and be gentle."

With a nod, the brute untied the ropes, reached under Loeiza's arms, and lifted her to standing, her feet coming momentarily off the floor. The woman meanwhile handed Zach a card on which was printed an address in the warehouse district.

"This will be where to contact us upon your return. And don't waste time trying to follow us before then, Captain," the woman said calmly. "Now, be a good boy and stay right there until you hear our carriage depart. Good?"

"Good," Zach said, nodding. "Yes." He rose and reached out to touch Loeiza's hand as his wife was led from the room, hands tied and mouth gagged, with terror in her eyes.

Five days had passed since then, and his despair had only deepened. Again, he closed his eyes against the relentless pitching of the ship, and the bitter cold of the constant waves splashing over the soldiers. He could hold it in no longer. Leaning as close to the deck as he could, he vomited until his stomach was empty, then retched again and again, not sure if it was seasickness or simply the horror of his situation.

Chapter 15

The people of the High Valley, more so than any of the other territories of the Green Mount, possess a communal sense of responsibility. If one in their village is sick or suffering, the community comes together to lend support, even if they don't know exactly how to do so.

– *Diary of Yazid ben Tariq*

For who can truly know the deep mysteries of the woods? What secrets lie hidden in vale and glade? Only those willing to leave behind the comfort of their towns and villages to tread upon the rich loam beneath the soaring arches of branch and bough. Only those who understand the silent beckoning of wild places upon their heart. Who is to say what mysteries they uncover?

– Foreword to *For the Wild Places,* a collection of nature poetry by Ansel Hawkins

574 HR - *Second month of summer*
High Valley region of the Green Mount

Dallin

It was late afternoon, and Ligulf was in his customary position beside the hearth, playing soft melodies on his cittern. Dallin sat staring into the small fire, a forgotten mug of tea on the small table beside her. Into the darkened calm came a soft tap on the door. She assumed Li would answer it, but instead the young man stood and excused himself to the privy, moving through the kitchen toward the back of the house. The knock sounded again, this time more insistent.

Dallin looked around to see if her mum was near, but saw no sign of her. With an exasperated sigh, she stood and moved to the door. From the color of the light coming in around the shutters, she could tell that sunset was approaching. She opened the door a tiny crack and peered out to see a number of people standing outside in a large semicircle. Her mother stood by the door; apparently she was the one who had knocked. Dallin opened the door a little wider, confused.

"Ma," she whispered. "What are you doing?"

She glanced around at the crowd. It looked to be most of the village, and they had ribbons, flowers, and bundles in their hands.

"Dal," her mother said, stepping back from the door. "These people have something for you. Can you step out, please?"

Dallin immediately shook her head in panic and started to close the door again, but her mother stepped forward and forced it open wider. Reaching inside, she took Dallin's wrist, and despite the girl's protestations, pulled her outside to stand in the light of a golden sunset for the first time in weeks. Dallin blinked her eyes against the brightness, then she raised her hands—her right hand shading her eyes against the unaccustomed light and her left covering her mouth and nose. Stepping out of the door beside her was a smiling Ligulf.

"Dallin," he said in a loud voice, "the people of Dóchas have some things to give you and some things to say to you." With that, he nodded to a woman standing near the front of the crowd. It was Aine, the miller's wife. She held a bunch of wildflowers in her hand, and on Ligulf's cue, she walked forward and gave them to Dallin.

"You're one of us," she said, looking Dallin in the eyes. Then she embraced her in a long hug and kissed the girl's forehead before stepping aside. Right behind her was Deirdre, a weaver she had known for years. Deirdre stepped forward and wrapped a lovely, delicate shawl over Dallin's shoulders and said, "Let this wrap you in comfort as we wrap you in love. You belong here and are one of us." Another embrace, and Dallin realized the entire village was gathered to bring her gifts. Women at first, but the men as well. Each, in turn, gave her a heartfelt gift and words of encouragement, one after another, until the gifts overflowed her arms and her mother was enlisted to hold some. She too was soon overloaded and a pile of gifts began to form on the ground near their feet. There was a pot of honey from the beekeeper, a freshly butchered chicken, baskets of herbs and flowers, sweaters, soft blankets, a large tub of butter, a necklace with the symbol of Nuada on it, and so much more. Dallin stood dumbfounded, tears streaming down her cheeks as the people of her village, apparently organized by Ligulf and her mother, surrounded her in love and acceptance.

The final gift was given by Nan the baker—a fresh shortcake topped with gooseberry jam—and the villagers departed into the brilliant glow of the sunset, each waving and wishing her well as they went back to their homes and shops.

Dallin stood in the doorway and cried, sobbing openly and clutching the gifts to her breast, rubbing her cheek on the soft wool of the shawl. Eventually looking up at her mother and at Li, both of whom were grinning from ear to ear, she shook her head and said, "Oh my. Who would have ever imagined?"

"C'mon," Li said, bending down to pick up an armload of gifts. "We'll help you get these inside. That shortbread is calling."

Dallin stopped him. "Li, did you...?" Her words died away.

"We all love you, Dallin," Li said, smiling and shaking his head. "Everyone was heartsick and didn't know how to tell you they cared. Your mother and I just suggested a time. They did the rest." He gestured at the bounty of gifts. "Grand folk they are, wouldn't you say?"

"Aye," she replied, as new tears formed in her eyes. "They are indeed."

With a sniffle and the first smile anyone had seen on her face since the attack, she led them back into the house.

Ligulf

It was well after dark by the time Li climbed the front steps to the stone house, humming a tune. The door was already ajar and just inside, he found Yazid packing his saddlebags.

"Heya," Li said, by way of greeting. "What's doing?"

"Oh, Li," Yazid said, pausing in his activity and flashing a wide toothy grin. "I am glad you are back. The fyrd has been called up, and will march the day after tomorrow, I think."

Ligulf set down his cittern on the low table by the door. He could only imagine one threat that might demand the mobilization of the fyrd. His blood ran cold. "The Barbárs have returned, I take it?"

"They have," Yazid answered. "And your father has a special task for the two of us."

"Aye, and what's that?" Li asked.

"You and I are to ride for the Midlands," Yazid said, indicating his saddlebags.

"The Midlands? Why?"

"The threat is dire, and it is critical that Lady Donella commit her troops to the Eagle's Gate," Yazid replied, continuing to pack while he spoke.

"I see," Li responded calmly. "And Da thinks you and I can convince her? Is that it?"

"It is. We are to speak with Donella then ride to join the fyrd."

"So, it's war then," Li said softly, absorbing the news.

"It is," Yazid said again, "and we leave at first light."

Li looked him in the eyes for a moment, then said, "Alright then. Let's get to it." With that, he headed upstairs to gather his things.

Shanna

The next morning, Dóchas bustled with activity. Word had spread that the fyrd was being called up, and wagons were being loaded with supplies, while men and women collected food and weapons and prepared for a long absence. Shanna had already loaded her "battle bags"—as she called them—onto her cart. They were filled with med'cines, bandages, ointments, and her surgical instruments. Now she was busy instructing her apprentice, Liana—who would be staying behind to care for the villagers—on the locations of various implements and ointments.

"And here's my calendar showing when to harvest the medicinals," she said, pointing to a large piece of parchment she had stuck on the wall of her kitchen.

"Yes, thank you," Liana responded dutifully.

"Don't forget to look in on Aelswith," the healer continued. "She'll be coming due before the Harvest Moon. Och, and here are the drops for Maclan's eyes, twice a week… and dinna forget to lance old man Graeme's boils and wipe them with this." She handed Liana a small vial. "Use a clean cloth, and—"

"Shanna, I ken," the girl interrupted. "I'll be fine, I've watched closely."

With a sigh, Shanna stopped and looked at her young apprentice. Barely sixteen summers old, and now responsible for so much. "I know child," she said with a reassuring smile.

A knock sounded on the door. Shanna opened it to find Corvus standing there.

"May I come in?" he asked.

"Please do," the healer responded amiably. "Liana, would you mind finishing loading the wagon?"

The girl nodded and excused herself out the back of the cottage.

Shanna turned back to Corvus, who was standing near her hearth with his arms folded. "Please, sit, Corvus. Would you like some tea?"

"Thanks, but no," he responded softly. "I know you have much to do, and I apologize for this interruption."

"It's fine," she said, though her mind was still full with all that yet needed to be done before their departure. "How can I help you, Corvus?"

"I wonder if you have any ground white willow bark," he asked hesitantly. "I realize you probably need all you have for the wounded."

"Are you in pain?" she asked.

"Still lingering from the events in the Circle," he said. "And I have hard days ahead. I'd rather not be slowed by aches and pains."

"I see," she said. "You do realize you're not a young man any more?"

"We're none of us as young as we once were," he said with a slight twinkle in his eye.

She chuckled and went over to her workbench, which was covered in jars, bottles, and vials of all manner of tinctures, ointments, and potions. "You're right that I will need all of the willow bark I have for the wounded, but I think this may work better." She picked out a large, bulbous root and held it out to him.

"What's this?" he asked, taking it and weighing it in his hands.

"'Tis called the Angel's Root," she replied. "Shave a wee bit into a cup of tea and allow it to steep for a quarter hour 'fore drinking. It'll ease your discomfort."

He nodded his understanding of the instructions.

"Careful, though," she added. "If you take too much, you're liable to fall out o' your saddle. It's quite pungent and will have a parching effect on your mouth. You'll be thirsty as a demon."

He laughed and tucked the root away in a pocket. "I thank you," he said, standing. "How much do I owe you for it?"

She waved her hand dismissively. "Not a whit," she said flatly. "You are the heart and soul of the fyrd, and we all have to do our part to keep you healthy and sound. Now, if you dinna mind, I have much to do."

With a nod of thanks, he turned to leave, just as another knock sounded on the door.

"Busy morning," Shanna said with a sigh, and she opened the door to reveal the tall form of Toren the hunt master.

"Good morning, Toren," Shanna said. "Do you need something?"

Without a word, the taciturn hunt master indicated Corvus, and stepped back from the door to make room for the other man to join him.

"Right," Corvus said. "Duty calls. Thank you, Shanna."

With a wave, he stepped out into the bright morning sun and Shanna watched as the two men walked down the hill toward the center of the village.

Corvus

"How many archers have we trained?" Corvus asked, before Toren could speak.

"You should have two hundred bows standing with the fyrd," the tall man responded quietly.

"That's a help," Corvus replied. "I wish it was two thousand, but I'll take what I can get."

"I'm not marching with the fyrd," Toren said abruptly.

Corvus stopped and looked at his old friend. The tall man's perpetual scowl was half-hidden behind his shoulder-length hair but Corvus noted that his friend hadn't shaved in a few days, suggesting he'd just returned from one of his longer sojourns into the mountains.

"There's something I must see to first," the hunt master continued. "I should be able to join you at the Gate in a week's time."

"You'll be sorely missed," Corvus told him. "I trust it's something important?"

"It is," Toren assured him.

"Right." Corvus decided not to press further. "Join us as soon as you're able."

With a curt nod, Toren turned and strode purposefully away. Corvus sighed and continued into the bustling market for his next stop. He knew this would be difficult, but it had to be done. He worked his way through the various stalls, stopping at the side of the smithy and waiting for John to pause in his work. The smith was busy hammering out the edge on a glowing axe head that he held with his great tongs. Seeing Corvus arrive, John struck a few final blows, then doused the head in water sending up a plume of steam. Then he set down his implements, wiped his hands on his leather apron, grabbed a rag from a line and wiped his brow, and turned to face the war chief.

"John," Corvus greeted him.

A grunt and a small nod was the only reply.

"I've come to check on the list of arms I sent you," Corvus said in a businesslike fashion.

"You'll have your weapons," the smith replied sharply. "Is that all? I have work to finish."

"John, I—" Corvus began, but the smith raised a hand, interrupting him.

"Don't," he said firmly. "Just don't."

Recognizing the futility of trying to heal the gaping wound that now existed between them, Corvus clenched his jaw, turned, and started to leave.

"You killed my boy!" the smith called after him. "I'll not forget that!"

Corvus stopped for a moment and considered arguing the point. John's son had participated in a horrible crime and had deserved his punishment. Corvus had been within his rights to invoke the Law of the Circle, and virtually the entire village agreed with his actions. Now he was going to ride into battle still nursing the injuries that John's son had given him; he walked with a limp now, and still didn't have full strength back in his left arm. A jumble of other arguments ran through his head, justifying his actions and putting him in the right. But none of that mattered. *John's son died that day, pleading for his life, at my hands. Nothing will change that.* He supposed if he were in the smith's position, he'd feel much the same way. He couldn't imagine the pain and shame the big man felt.

Without looking back, Corvus bowed his head and continued on his way.

Dallin

There was a knock at the door of Dallin's cottage. Her mother was out tending the flock, and Ligulf —her near constant companion—had left the village early, riding out with Yazid. The window shutters were open, and a warm breeze flowed through the house. Dallin was still chewing the last mouthful of shortcake as she opened the door, and looked up into the eyes of Toren.

"Toren?" she said, a question in her voice.

"Dallin," he said, by way of greeting. "Are you well?"

"I don't know if I'd say 'well,' but much improved." A shy smile formed on her lips. "Thanks, for asking."

The tall man reached down, grabbing the handle of a woven wicker basket that had been on the ground behind him. The basket was stuffed with muted plaid wool that seemed to move on its own.

"You need to care for this," he said, handing it to her. Confused, she pulled aside the blanket, revealing a badger cub snuffling about the basket's lining.

Dallin stared at it, amazed. "What would you have me do?"

"Its clan ran afoul of some wolves in the hills," Toren explained. "He was the only survivor, and without his ma to feed him, he'll die."

"I suppose I could…" Dallin started, but she wasn't sure what she could do. She had hand-nursed lambs when their mother had rejected them, and as a child, she had nursed an eider drake back to health after some mischance had broken its wing, but never something like this.

"Well, there you go," Toren said abruptly, and turned to leave.

"Toren, wait," Dallin called. "What am I to do with it?"

"*It* is a he," Toren said over his shoulder. "Care for him, train him. I'll be back in a few days with something for you. Then I'm off to join the fyrd. Meanwhile, you practice your pull. Your arm's getting soft."

Toren instructed the village youth in the art of the longbow, and Dallin had always been near the top of her group when it came to aim, though she struggled with pulling the string of a full longbow. She was as strong or stronger than most of the young men her age, but to fully draw the bowstring of a longbow required still more. The bowmen of the fyrd had each worked with the bow for at least fifteen years, strengthening their arm and back muscles until the arrows they fired had the power to blast through armor or shield. Dallin was doubtful she could ever develop that kind of strength.

She watched the tall man's back as he crossed the moor away from her cottage. He and Davonna, the village matriarch, had always been kind to her, but this gift left her flummoxed. A badger cub? She lifted the basket to inspect its contents once more. The cub stuck his head up out of the soft blanket and looked around. Coming eye to eye with Dallin for the first time, the cub sniffed, sneezed, rubbed its nose, then looked at her and sniffed once more. She couldn't help but grin as she reached in with a finger to stroke the cub's head.

"Ach," she cooed, "you're just a wee thing, aren't you?" In response, the cub began to suckle her finger. "You're hungry, eh?" she asked him with a smile. "Well, let's see about getting you a bit of milk." She turned and carried the basket inside, closing the cottage door behind her.

Chapter 16

The Royal Guard of the Kingdom of Lachland, colloquially known as the Lake Jacks, are quite possibly the most highly trained and effective cavalry force on all of Daffyd. Their impressive destriers, known as Castellans, are bred of the finest stock from the legendary horse lords of Lachland. Blessed with long, luxuriant manes and tales, a powerful stride and incomparable strength, these fearsome mounts, which stand at a minimum of sixteen hands, provide shock value to any charge of the Lake Jacks, unparalleled in rival kingdoms. Indeed, so important is the power and maneuverability of these mighty steeds to the security of Lachland that since the days of King Alain II it has been a crime to sell prime breeding stock from the Castellans or in any way allow the bloodlines to spread outside of Lachland— punishable by death.

– *Encyclopedia Daffydia,* Third Edition

574 HR – *Second month of summer*
Wetheral Castle, Deep Mere, Lachland

Darienne

Darienne laid her head back, luxuriating in the steaming, aromatic bath that eased the aches and bruises from her encounter in Deep Mere. The afternoon sun flooded her room through the row of windows along the western wall. Dust motes sparkled in the aromatic steam rising from her bath. Her chamber maid, Maddie, had scented the water with a complex and interesting mix of herbs; rosemary, mint, and sage were three she could discern. She'd have to ask Maddie what the orange petals were. She closed her eyes and tried to relax, but her mind was active, playing and replaying the events of the morning. Her attacker had clearly known who she was and where to find her. Judging by his clothing and speech, he was a rough laborer from town, hardly the type to concoct a plan on his own to kill the heir apparent. *No, he was sent by someone,* she thought. *But who?*

She and Kaiso had discussed the topic at length on the ride back to the castle, and she felt no closer to any insights. Her thoughts played over the faces and names of the nobles at court, trying to imagine some motive that any of them might have to sponsor such an attack. The Viscount Lavigne and the Comtessa du Chatelain were both fiercely loyal to her mother, and Isador counted them among her closest friends. The comtessa served as something of a direct conduit of court gossip, alerting Isador to any grumbling or discontent among the other nobles, as well as keeping the Queen up to date on the constantly shifting alliances within the court. It was unimaginable that either of them would be a party to something like this. There was, of course, the faction of minor nobles that called themselves the Collines. They were a group of perpetual malcontents from the south of Lachland, whose ancestral holdings had lost value and cachet when the capital was moved to Deep Mere by her great-grandfather. Foremost among them was the Duke de Phélypeaux, a conniving sort, constantly maneuvering to enhance the former capital of Morvan. Among his various petitions was a proposed royal college, to be built in Morvan and funded by a tax increase on Claws shipping. Isador had dismissed the notion out of hand.

Then there was his request to enhance the judicial keep in Morvan, broadening its royal charter, and thereby its influence and sway. Never mind that his cousin, the Duke du Fontaine, served as senior justice there, and that such an enlargement of the royal charter would have made him second only to the Queen in power and wealth. Darienne's mother had seen no value to such an elevation. Particularly since du Fontaine was a frequent critic of her taxation policies, which offered no dispensation or special consideration for the nobility. Phélypeaux's most recent efforts had been to suggest the Queen pay the city a royal visit, to coincide with the arrival of a high-level trade mission from Sudland. Isador had considered this and had expressed to her daughter that it had indeed been too long since she had visited the south. But the Barbár invasion had quashed that notion.

Darienne's mind flashed through others of the nobility: Duke Comtois, Viscountess Abadie of Lagrange, the Comte de Rennes. Comtois was like a beloved uncle, while Abadie and Rennes tended to keep well out of political intrigue. Both seemed quite content with their riches. Abadie was preoccupied with finding another husband, while Rennes was far too old and senile to be involved. There were so many others. Her head swam.

Frustrated, she opened her eyes and took a deep breath, hoping the sharpness of the mint and rosemary in the steam would clear her head. Instead, she found herself lulled by the warm water and soothing scents. Clearly, the day's events had exhausted her more than she realized. Her eyelids began to flutter. Faces, names, relationships all merged together as she drifted off.

Kaiso

After seeing Darienne to her chambers, Kaiso had alerted Major Justiniere, the second-in-command of the Lake Jacks, that there had been an attack on the Princess that morning, and requested that the guard on her room be doubled.

"No danger will pass these walls," the major had replied archly. "And I would add, *Captain*, that had the Princess stayed within the castle as requested, no harm would have come to her."

Kaiso knew that the major took his duty to protect the royal family very seriously, and clearly saw the Princess' willfulness and libertine ways as making his job more difficult. On more than one occasion, the major had made quite clear that he saw Kaiso's role as Darienne's personal bodyguard as an encouragement to the Princess to make risky choices.

"I understand, Major," Kaiso replied professionally. "I am just keeping you apprised of a new development that suggests the Princess is at increased risk. I will exert what small influence I have to try to curtail her wanderings, but she is a strong-willed woman."

Somewhat assuaged, the major seemed to relax a bit. "Very good," he said, summoning an aide to his side. "I'll see to it." With that, the major turned to his subordinate and began issuing a flurry of orders.

Dismissed, Kaiso made his way to his own chambers. He mused on the events of the past hours as he turned from the vaulted stone corridor into the open colonnade that edged a sunlit atrium on one side, ringed with eight fountains that surrounded a marble statue of Armel III. The interior doors that lined the colonnade accessed the bustling kitchens, and the entire area was filled with the scent of roasting pork and bread, fresh from the ovens. He hadn't eaten since last night and it was past noon. He stopped a serving man carrying a tray of dishes, and requested that a meal be sent to his chambers. The serving man nodded curtly and headed into the kitchens.

It had been a long night, and Kaiso had spent much of it on a rooftop adjacent to the Salty Mermaid, scanning the street and surrounding area for dangers. An hour or so before dawn, he had spotted a large dockworker coming out of a modest town house a few doors down from the brothel. Stepping onto the stoop, the man had looked right and left, before descending the three steps to the street. The captain had noted the man's caution and repeated surreptitious glances up and down the lane. The man's very presence there was suspicious; even a modest town house in that neighborhood would be far too dear for a dockworker to afford. Within a few steps, the man paused, examined the darkened windows of the whorehouse closely, then crossed the street and slipped into the darkened recess of an alley. Kaiso watched quietly for thirty minutes or so to see if other threats might appear, then, shortly before he assumed Darienne would make her appearance, he quietly descended the side of the building—climbing down the same ornate, iron trellis he had ascended earlier and out of sight of the alley. He crept around the side of the building, crouching behind an ostentatious marble plinth holding a massive planter overflowing with blooms. From this vantage, he had a clear line of sight to where the man lurked in the alley. As Darienne stepped out and began walking down the hill, he had watched the burly laborer emerge and follow her. Kaiso waited a few moments before he too stepped out to become the third in the skulking procession.

He noted the moment Darienne became aware of the man trailing her and picked up her pace, though not enough to alert her stalker. He also noted approvingly that she began to affect a more drunken gait, staggering slightly. *Good. Lower expectations.* He watched her duck into the alley, ostensibly to expel the night's wine. *Excellent. Choose your battlefield. Somewhere private to prevent interruption or ambush.* The dockworker, unaware of Kaiso, shook his head slightly and chuckled as he followed her into the alley. *You have no idea what awaits you, oaf.* Kaiso turned the corner into the narrow, dead-end lane, just in time to see Darienne run the man through with her sword and flip him violently to the bricks. *Well done, girl,* he thought. *The Soto Defense. Use the man's size and momentum against him.* He watched as the man rallied, pinning the Princess to the wall. The captain almost intervened when the brute lifted Darienne and began slamming her into the bricks, but something told him to trust the Princess' instincts and training. *She is ready,* he thought. *Let her finish this. She needs the confidence it will yield.* Still, he readied a throwing dagger and crept into position, just in case she wasn't yet quite up to this challenge. Moments later, as a staggered Darienne plunged her dagger into the chest of her assailant, Kaiso relaxed, affecting an insouciant posture and leaning against the wall at the alley's entrance. Not a care in the world.

He fought to keep the pride for his Princess from showing on his face. *It would do no good to let her see that.* Despite her efforts and accomplishments, Darienne had a softness to her that wanted to yield, all too readily, to praise. Raised in the comfort and security of the palace, the Princess had never been pushed—nor had she ever truly pushed herself—to achieve something truly difficult. *"Good enough,"* he thought. *Poisonous words.* He saw it in her in a thousand details. The moment she felt she had reached a goal, her tendency was to relent in her training. "There, I did it!" her face seemed to say, the first time he had made the mistake of complimenting her progress, shortly after their work together had begun. "That's good enough, isn't it?" *She has no idea what's out there,* he thought acidly, *and just how far she has yet to go to face it. Never "good enough."* Consequently, Kaiso had adopted a near-constant air of disapproval, even going so far as to suggest his disbelief that she, a soft princess, would ever be capable of handling herself with the necessary grit when things got bloody. This had spurred the proud young woman to redouble her efforts, working relentlessly to break through the icy demeanor of her teacher and earn his approbation. He looked again at the dagger protruding from the burly assailant's chest. A slight smile tugged at his scar. *She's coming along. Still much to learn, but now she is blooded and we can progress to the real training.*

Swept up in his remembrance of the early morning's events, Kaiso was surprised to find himself suddenly standing before his chamber door. *Lost in thoughts, Captain,* he silently upbraided himself. *Unaware of your surroundings. A raw recruit's mistake.* He opened the door and immediately felt an almost gravitational pull toward the comfortable bed and down duvet. He sighed, gritted his teeth, and turned away from comfort toward duty, opening his wardrobe. There would be no rest in the coming hours. He needed more information about the assassin, and he knew where to start: I town house. He had to move quickly or the trail would be cold. He quickly changed clothes, choosing the attire of a modestly successful merchant rather than his accustomed uniform, though he did take care to ensure both his boot dagger and the hidden knife he wore beneath his vest were in place. A soft knock at the door announced the arrival of his requested meal. Thanking the servant, he took the food to his small desk and sat and ate. Braised pork, seasoned with rosemary and thyme, and crusted with salt and sugar, on a bed of steamed turnips and potatoes. He honestly could not remember anything ever tasting so good in his life. He washed it all down with a small measure of wine, then as he stepped out of his chamber, he paused to cast a last, longing look at the bed. With a quiet groan, he closed the door behind him. Pulling an unremarkable, broad-brimmed hat down low on his brow, he headed to the stables for a fresh mount.

It was mid-morning by the time he arrived back at the site of the attack. The body had been found in the alley, and there was a cluster of people gathered around it. Four constables in their short-waisted, royal-blue tunics were examining the scene and keeping the curious at bay. Kaiso ducked his head, letting the brim of the hat obscure his face as he walked past the scene. Turning on Haverstrom Place, he walked slowly up the cobbled lane, past the Salty Mermaid. Removing his hat, he stepped up to the door of the town house from which he had seen the assassin emerge and knocked loudly. There was no answer, nor could he hear any movement within. He knocked again with the same result. The street was busy with the morning's usual rush of passersby, clutching cloaks against the cool morning air. Slipping his hat back on, he descended the stairs and continued up the lane past the house. At the top of the hill, the street emptied into

Adrianu Circle, a large, round, cobbled confluence of six broad thoroughfares with a carved marble fountain in the center. He skirted the Circle on the right until he came upon an alleyway that ran all the way back down the hill, behind the homes and businesses on Haverstrom. Walking with purpose, he turned down the alley, silently counting the doors he passed until he arrived at the rear of the town house. He reached into his pocket and withdrew a small leather wallet, which contained a set of well-crafted lockpicks. Seeing no one else in the alley or at any of the nearby windows, he moved quickly to the back door. Within a few moments, he was letting himself in to the pantry of the home.

Despite the residence looking unoccupied from the front windows, he could smell breakfast cooking. He cracked open the door that led from the pantry into what seemed to be a scullery, and saw a robust woman busy at work in the next room, dishing up a steaming plate of sausage, boiled eggs, and fried pike. The plate rested on a sterling service tray, the setting was of fine silver and the tea service was Cantabrian porcelain—ridiculously expensive in Lachland. The cook finished dishing up, using a clean towel to wipe up a small smear of sausage grease from the plate before covering the meal with a domed metal lid. She then lifted the entire tray expertly in one hand and proceeded up the back stairs. Kaiso quietly drew his boot knife and followed, taking care to ascend slowly, in case the stairs should creak. He stopped just high enough to spy the short upstairs hallway and observe the cook, tray in hand, as she knocked gently on a bedroom door.

"Mistress," she called. "Your breakfast, ma'am."

There was a murmured response that obviously satisfied the cook, as she opened the door and went inside. The brief glimpse that Kaiso got through the opened door was of a well-lit bedroom, with cheery yellow walls. He spotted the corner of a four-poster bed and a carved, oaken dresser against the far wall. Then the door closed.

Quickly ascending the rest of the way, he silently moved down the corridor, past the bedroom, to a door across the hall.

Quietly, he checked to see if it was locked. The knob turned. Glancing over his shoulder one last time to make sure he was not observed, he stepped quickly into a darkened room. He paused for a time, listening for any movement. Satisfied that he was alone, he found his way to the shuttered windows, and quietly opened the blinds. Daylight poured in, revealing a modest-sized bedroom with a thick feather bed, the covers in disarray. The room smelled of a man's sweat. Moving to the tall, narrow dresser situated between the windows, he eased the drawers open. All empty. In fact, the room had no personal effects in it whatsoever, apart from a small purse of coins on top of the dresser. Kaiso sorted through and weighed the coins, estimating there to be around thirty scepters in it. That would be six months' wages for a common dockworker. *He won't be needing this,* he thought with a grim smile, and pocketed the pouch before returning to the door to listen.

"Yes, ma'am," The cook's voice echoed in the hallway as she exited the other room, closing the door behind her. "I'll have it ready."

She moved down the hall back toward the staircase and a moment later, Kaiso could hear her steps descending to the kitchen. He glanced once more around the darkened room. *Nothing more to learn here,* he thought. *But I'll wager that whoever is in that room across the hall knows something.* He waited until he was sure the cook was not returning, then pulled the brim of his hat low over his eyes, walked across the hall, and knocked twice.

"Enter," a woman's voice called from within.

Kaiso opened the door, slipped inside, and closed it quickly behind him, his knife pointing directly at the dark-haired woman sitting at a small table by the window, tucking into her breakfast. She paused, her laden fork— which he noted she held tines down, in the manner of the gentry—midway to her mouth.

She had a dark complexion and full, red lips and was wearing black trousers beneath a bright turquoise blouse, not yet tucked in. The collar of the shirt was open at the top. Not quite revealing, but daring and unusual.

"May I help you?" she asked in a calm voice, placing her silverware on the plate and slowly putting her slender hands in her lap with a grace that again suggested breeding— *or at least,* Kaiso thought, *training.*

"Oh, I think you can." Kaiso moved quietly around the room, checking to see that they were alone. The woman looked as if she were about to call for help, and so Kaiso lunged forward suddenly, stabbing his dagger firmly into her breakfast table. She leaned back sharply in her chair, hands raised. Though she seemed alarmed, he noted that her hands were not trembling, her breathing steady and slow. *Careful, Kaiso,* he thought. *She's a fighter.*

"Raise an alarm," he said softly, his dark eyes peering out beneath the brim of the hat, "and I'll slit your throat."

"Who are you?" she asked. Her voice was calm, showing no hint of panic or fear.

"Doesn't matter," he answered brusquely. "Who is the man who stayed in that room last night?"

"What man?" She feigned innocence poorly, cocking an eyebrow in a mocking smile.

Kaiso freed his knife from the tabletop and pointed it directly at her face. "Don't toy with me," he said softly. "Who are you, and what's your business in Deep Mere?"

Her eyes sparkled with delight, and despite the proximity of his knife to her face, she leaned forward, placing her elbows on the breakfast table until her eyes were mere inches from the tip of his blade.

"What fun!" she marveled. Then, her eyes lingered on the scar that connected the edge of his mouth to his left ear. "I know you. Aren't you her personal guard?"

With a quick lean in, he placed the knife's edge to her throat and said, "I ask the questions here. And I say again, who are you and what is your business in Deep Mere?"

"Easy now," she said, holding her open hands up before her. "There's much to explain, and it is challenging to hold a conversation in this position. If you wouldn't mind stepping back, I'll answer all your questions." A small drop of blood appeared along the edge of the knife.

Wary of a trick, Kaiso moved back only one step, his blade leveled with her eyes. Wincing, the woman rubbed at the small cut before placing both hands on the table and standing slowly. Kaiso backed off another step. She had a statuesque figure and stood a good four inches taller than he. Her dark hair fell in gentle waves, cascading over the collar of her blouse. She was broad of shoulder, and her form-fitting trousers revealed muscular, though not unfeminine, legs. She took a step away from the table, one hand still rubbing her neck as she turned to glance out the window.

"My name is Lady Ormond, of the Westhaven," she said. Suddenly, the hand that was on her neck slipped down the front of her blouse and she spun, hurling a long, needle-like poniard. The blade pierced his shoulder. He staggered back just as she upended the breakfast table toward him, the platter and plates making an incredible din. Kaiso heard shouts and movement from below.

With a growl, he ripped the dagger from his shoulder and faced her, a blade now in each hand. The woman quickly grabbed the metal dome from her upset food service and the silverware knife, and faced him in a fighter's crouch, left foot forward. He recognized the stance immediately as a standard blade and buckler defensive stance, confirming his suspicion that she was a trained fighter. The captain circled a few steps to his left, forcing her back toward the corner of the room. Pain lanced from his shoulder and his eyes swam as he adjusted his own stance to favor the wound. With a sudden lunge, he slashed his dagger at her left knee, which she deftly avoided, riposting with the cutlery blade in a quick thrust toward his face. With a sweep of the poniard, he batted away her attack and recovered his stance just as the door burst open and two large men dressed as dockworkers rushed in, each armed with a cudgel.

Without a pause, Kaiso spun and lashed out, stabbing the closest man in the base of the throat with the poniard. The surprised man staggered back into the hallway, clutching his throat to stanch the flow of blood, the dagger still protruding from the wound. The second man swung his club at Kaiso's head, but the captain ducked beneath it and buried his knife in the man's knee. With a howl, the attacker collapsed into the doorway, dropping his club and clutching his leg with both hands. Kaiso scooped up the fallen cudgel and, with two savage blows to the man's head, finished him. His shoulder wound protested sharply and he winced as he turned to face Lady Ormond once more, only to discover that she was gone, the sash of the window open. More booted feet thundered up the stairs.

He took a moment to retrieve the lady's dagger from the neck of the gurgling man in the hallway just as two more bravos hit the landing at the top of the stairs. Kaiso spun back into the room and with a dash, tumbled out of the open window, his wound making the maneuver clumsy and awkward. He rolled off the eaves and dropped into the front garden, landing roughly. The two men shouted at him from the window as he staggered to his feet, ungracefully vaulted the garden fence and dashed down the cobbled street, clutching his bleeding wound as curious passersby pointed at him in confusion and alarm.

An hour later, he rode up into the courtyard of Wetheral Castle. Carelessly handing the reins of his horse to an attendant, he crossed the cobbled stones and approached the guards at the entrance, who looked to bar his approach, apparently not recognizing him. The guards relaxed as he removed his hat. "I need to speak with the major, right away," he said in a strained voice.

The senior guard's eyebrows raised as he noted the blood dripping from Kaiso's hand. "Very good, sir," he said, stepping aside. "You head to the kitchen to get that tended to and I'll send him right in."

Major Justiniere found him a few minutes later, while he was sitting barechested by the great hearth in the castle's kitchen, with the cook fussing and cleaning his wound.

"Here now, sir," the portly cook reassured him as he dabbed at his shoulder with a wet towel. "We've sent for the chirurgeon. It don't look too bad. He'll fix you up right as rain."

"What's this?" the major demanded sharply.

Kaiso described his morning's excursion to the town house in Deep Mere, sheepishly admitting that the woman had gotten the better of him and escaped. "We need to gather your men, ride into town, seize that town house, and find out who this Lady Ormond really is—and what interest she may have in trying to harm the Princess."

The major bristled and was about to speak when Darienne rushed in, the white-haired chirurgeon huffing behind her, his bushy eyebrows flashing up and down furiously in confusion.

"Captain?" she asked. "What happened?"

As Kaiso prepared to repeat his story, Justiniere excused himself to ready a platoon to ride, glaring at the captain as he departed.

Kaiso paced the cobbled street behind Darienne in an effort to stave off his fatigue, as Lake Jacks, fully bedecked in sparkling steel cuirasses, ransacked the town house looking for any clues or hidden compartments. Justiniere approached the Princess, bowed, and nodded curtly to Kaiso before reporting.

"House is empty, ma'am," he said curtly. "They've cleared off and left nothing behind. They were thorough. Even extinguished the cookfires."

"We should get the records of this house," Kaiso told him. "Who owns it, and who has rented it recently."

The major looked at him for a moment before saying, "While that sounds like a reasonable next step, I would remind the *captain* that the Lake Jacks do not take orders from a mercenary."

"Then take the order from me, Major," the Princess said, stepping between Justiniere and the captain. "Send some of your men to the records office for this quarter, and find the information the captain has sensibly requested."

Unaccustomed to the Princess issuing orders, the major stiffened and blinked in surprise at her peremptory tone before responding. "Yes, ma'am," he said diffidently. Then he offered a slight bow, turned sharply on his heel, and began barking commands.

Kaiso moved to stand next to Darienne, searching the faces in the gathered crowd of onlookers suspiciously.

"Lady Ormond of Westhaven, did you say?" Darienne asked quietly, as she scanned the buildings thoughtfully.

"That's what she said," Kaiso responded, his right hand clutching the freshly stitched wound in his shoulder.

"I've never heard of her." The Princess' eyes flitted back and forth as she worked to recall all of the families of the Westhaven nobility.

"Well, she's heard of you," the captain said ominously.

Chapter 17

It is in the crucible of battle that the true heart is revealed. A man may think he knows himself, his strengths, weaknesses, fortes, and foibles, but until he has stood in the line and chaos of battle, smelled the blood and fear, heard the screams of his comrades, and measured his response, he cannot say he knows himself.

– General Joachim Salazar, address to the graduating class of the Pfister Military Academy, Aesthir

574 HR - Last month of summer
Autun, eastern edge of the Claws, Lachland

Zach

The barges crammed with troops had arrived in the night and taken hours to unload. The docks were jammed with soldiers, heavily laden wagons, dockworkers, mule teams, and materiel. After being shown to a warehouse that had been hastily converted to a barracks, Zach had seen to his company's arrangements, then made his way to the small office that he had claimed as his chamber. Word has spread among the men that they would attack at first light, so the soldiers were told to get a few hours of sleep if at all possible. His mind would not stop racing with worries. Frantic for his wife's well-being, as well as not having any notion how he could possibly affect the task that had been assigned to him by her kidnappers, he tossed and turned for hours, finally dozing off a short time before the knock on his door alerted him to rise and prepare for the day's assault.

He didn't think of himself as a particularly brave man. He was no coward, but neither was he one to charge forward and inspire others. When his company rushed out of the city gates that day, screaming into the teeth of the enemy, he held back and gravitated toward the Queen's banner. Perhaps some unforeseen opportunity would present itself and his dilemma would be solved.

The first Barbár he encountered came rushing forward out of the chaos, casually dashing past battling pairs and vaulting over two struggling bodies locked in a deadly embrace. His eyes seemed inexplicably fixed on Zach as he wove his way through the frenzy. Zach had never seen a Barbár up close, and though they had discussed them constantly when training—their dress, weapons, tattoos, fighting styles—he found the reality of the brutish warrior terrifying and could only stand transfixed as the wild man rushed at him. A fellow soldier apparently sensed his frozen indecision and shoved him out of harm's way at the last moment, engaging the warrior himself. Shaking his head to regain focus, Zach watched as his unknown savior was spitted on the Barbár's spear. While the Barbár struggled to extricate his pole arm from Zach's fallen comrade, the captain seized the moment and lashed out with his sword, taking the Barbár's right eye and a chunk of his skull. After that, everything was a blur.

He lost his sword at one point, then was tackled to the ground by a monstrous brute, who outweighed him by several stone. He struggled ineffectually against the much larger warrior, whose huge hands had closed on his throat. Frantic and desperate, Zach had writhed, punching and kicking at his opponent in a last-ditch attempt to get the huge man off of him before he blacked out. Nothing was working. Gasping for breath, his vision going dark,

Zach's scrambling hands finally found the handle of a large, hooked knife in the Barbár's belt. Seizing the blade, Zach buried it in his attacker's ribs repeatedly until the brute fell off of him, vomiting blood. Blinking back stars and coughing, he rose shakily to his feet just in time to see the bearer of the royal banner fall, his head smashed by a mighty hammer blow. Not thinking any further than wanting to get close to the Queen, he slipped the Barbár dagger into his belt and rushed over to grab the faltering flag before realizing that the massive brute that had killed the previous banner carrier was right there. Zach saw his death before him, as certain as the rising of the sun. An image of Loeiza, terrified, bound, and gagged, flashed in his mind. He was going to fail in his task because of this hulking barbarian, and she would be tortured and drowned because of his failure. Too many failures. He had *failed* to win promotion to major as his humble origins had not been to the liking of the colonel, he had *failed* to protect his wife, he had *failed* to keep the respect of his men by vomiting in close quarters during the rough passage through the Claws. He would fail no more! With a roar of defiance against an unfair world, he charged his giant foe, burying the flag staff in the monster's gut and changing his life's trajectory forever.

Sir Reginald

"Your Majesty!" Sir Reginald Bleiz shouted to be heard over the din of battle. "You must retire to the city. The risk is too great!"

Rather than respond, Queen Isador stood up again, ignoring the blood flowing freely from her scalp where a Barbár axe had clipped her helmet, removing it. Her two personal guards, Jean Pierre and Jean Francois, flanked her on the battlefield to protect her. Sir Reginald had fought his way to the Queen's side after they had gotten separated in the fighting. *Damned woman is going to get herself killed,* he thought with frustration. *Then where will we be?*

The Barbárs had arrayed close to twenty thousand warriors against Autun with the clear intent of overrunning the city defenses and taking a quick victory. The city's walls had held through three brutal days of continual assaults, but Bleiz's beleaguered men had been exhausted and attrition was high. He had confided to his aides that he did not expect the city's defenses to hold out another day. Then, like a miracle, the ships packed with troops, food, and medical supplies had arrived in the dark of night, and by the next morning the Barbárs had found Autun to be a city with a fresh defense and a fighting chance, though still horribly outnumbered. He noted the renewed spirit in his men's eyes at the sight of their Queen's arrival. *Bless her, but she's given us a fresh chance.*

Conventional wisdom would have dictated that the defenders hold within the walls and continue making the Barbárs pay a very high price for every assault. However, the Queen had insisted that her fresh troops attack out of the city the next day and bloody the enemy. What was worse, she had insisted on leading the charge herself. Bleiz, Brigadier Dixon, and some archbishop that Bleiz didn't recognize had pleaded with her not to make such a foolhardy move, but Isador was not to be dissuaded, and the next morning at dawn, the Queen led three thousand men in a charge out of the city gates against a Barbár force of roughly five or six times that number.

The attack had apparently caught the barbarians unawares. The enemy was not yet formed up for the day's attack, and the charging Lachlanders had penetrated well into the Barbár camp, destroying baggage trains and killing or capturing several of the enemy war chiefs. But the numbers were against her forces and the Barbárs had eventually rallied. Bleiz's practiced eye scanned the battlefield. Despite the surprise, their forward progress had stalled, and they were being pushed back toward the city walls. If they didn't pull back behind the gates soon, they would be crushed by the superior numbers of the enemy.

"Majesty," he pleaded, "we must sound the retreat and retire behind the walls. We've gained what we can for the day."

The Queen looked sharply at him, then rushed forward and struck the back of a nearby Barbár engaged against one of her troops. Her blow was well placed and her longsword nearly decapitated the man. In response, a massive Räuber came charging through the lines, pitching two Lachland soldiers onto their backs and smashing his war hammer down into the helm of the Queen's banner carrier, pulping his skull instantly. The rose-colored banner faltered for a moment and began to fall. Just then, a young officer with dark skin that suggested Aslene heritage ran forward and seized the banner before the golden emblem of the stallion rampant could touch the ground. Waving the banner above his head, the young captain screamed defiance and remarkably charged the huge Räuber who was momentarily engaged with the Queen's guards. Thrusting the pointed tip of the banner staff like a spear, the enraged captain crashed into the massive Barbár, impaling him through the heart. The momentum knocked the Räuber onto his back. The captain released the flag staff and grabbed a discarded hand axe. He decapitated the corpse, and with a shout of triumph, hurled the gory trophy into the Barbár lines.

A roar went up among the Lachlanders. Inspired by the captain's feat, they rallied around their Queen, surging against the Barbár line and driving it back for a time. Just then, Isador swooned, holding a hand to her head wound. Seeing that the captain's actions had created a window of possibility, she called to Sir Reginald to sound the retreat. Within minutes, they began a fighting withdrawal back behind their gates, as the Lachland archers on the walls sent out waves of death against the Barbár horde to cover their retreat.

"Despite my misgivings, it was well done, Your Majesty," Sir Reginald said grudgingly. He, the Queen, Brigadier Dixon, and the archbishop—who Bleiz now knew was called Mormand—all stood in the stone watchtower on the north side of the gates. The Queen was seated on a short stool, her jaw clenched. Only the slight wince in her eyes belied her discomfort as the chirurgeon attended to her head injury. The enemy forces were gathered across the field, but were making no move at the moment. Archers crowded the ramparts directly over the gates and harried the few small bands of Barbárs that ventured too close to the city. Bleiz had been against the idea of a frontal assault, but seeing the damage wrought on the enemy, he had to agree that to attack while her troops were fresh and had the advantage of surprise had indeed been the right strategy. The damage to the enemy baggage train alone was worth the cost.

"Thank you, Sir Reginald," the Queen said, wincing again as the chirurgeon stitched her scalp. "We've bloodied them, and now they'll be more cautious in their assaults."

"You've certainly bought time, Majesty," the archbishop said in his cultured, baritone voice.

"That you have!" Brigadier Dixon boomed, slapping his knee with a bloody hand. "By the horns of Ceremon, that was a sight! The Queen of Lachland in shining armor wading into the enemy by the golden light of dawn, her banner proudly advancing against the foe! By Feryn! Songs will be sung of it!"

"I didn't realize you had such a poetic heart, Brigadier," the Queen said with a smile, holding still as the chirurgeon applied a sticky ointment to the fresh stitches.

Suddenly embarrassed at his outburst, Dixon blushed, then turned and pointed at an archer on the far wall, harrumphing under his breath about the man's poor aim.

"Sir Reginald," Isador said, turning to Bleiz. "We suspect any further action from the enemy today will be desultory, at best. Would you agree?"

"Yes, Majesty," Sir Reginald responded. "I imagine they'll take the day to count their dead, reorganize a bit and most likely attack fresh in the morning."

"They'll come on strong when they do," Dixon added loudly. "You've tweaked their pride and my guess is they'll hit us with everything they've got come tomorrow's dawn. Try to wipe us out in one mass attack."

"How many troops do you imagine the enemy still has at his command?" The Queen asked Sir Reginald.

"I'll have the official scouting report this afternoon, Majesty," Bleiz replied, "but my guess is they can field no more than twelve thousand, give or take. Would you agree, General?" He turned to Dixon.

"Provided they don't resupply with fresh troops," the brigadier said, absent-mindedly rubbing his chin with a bloody hand, leaving a gory smear on his face.

The Queen looked to the chirurgeon and quietly gestured for him to see to the general's arm. The brigadier, at first, resisted the man's prodding, apparently unaware of his injury. After a moment, he relented and carefully removed his jacket to reveal a long gash down his left arm, from shoulder to elbow.

"Huh." Dixon's bushy eyebrows raised upon seeing the injury. "Bastard got me after all."

"Twelve thousand," the Queen said. "Well, we shall certainly have our work cut out for us then, gentlemen." With a gesture to her two attendants, she moved toward the stairs leading down to the courtyard before pausing and turning back to the group. "See that you locate that brave captain before the day is out. Rewarding such valor will hearten the troops." With a slight smile, the Queen turned and descended, Archbishop Mormand close behind her. Sir Reginald turned to survey the battlefield before the city gates as Brigadier Dixon began to swear loudly at the chirurgeon's ministrations.

Twelve thousand... The knight commander frowned as he gazed out at the massed, ragged enemy before them. *Even with the reinforcements, how will we ever hold?*

Sir Reginald had commandeered a luxurious manor house to serve as the Queen's residence, displacing Tomás St. Luc, his wife, and their seven children. St. Luc was a wealthy fur merchant who had been visibly upset when Sir Reginald had informed him two days ago of the Queen's imminent arrival and the need to appropriate his home and grounds as her temporary residence. He had been a constant thorn in Sir Reginald's side throughout the defense of the city, repeatedly making calls for Bleiz to treat with the enemy, to surrender the city if the Barbárs would guarantee their lives. The man was a coward. Clever with money, but possessed of the garish taste so common among merchants who had climbed the social ladder by the purse, rather than through breeding. St. Luc had seemed outwardly flattered and gracious that Bleiz had chosen his home for the Queen's stay, however he had complained repeatedly that it was no small expense and bother to uproot his entire family and their movables to suitable housing elsewhere in town. Sir Reginald had waved off the man's complaints, since the St. Luc family would be well compensated for the inconvenience.

Despite the man's uncultured taste, his manor was a palatial affair, filled with marble and the finest carved mahogany, sitting high on Armel's Seat, a large plateau that overlooked the city's High Street and wealthiest neighborhoods. It was originally built as the home of a count distantly related to the royal family and, despite its current occupant, was the most dignified residence Bleiz could imagine to house the Queen during her stay. He was aware of her love of her gardens at Wetheral, and felt that St. Luc's rose maze would be of some comfort to her.

He watched as the Queen strolled through the manor, acquainting herself with the layout of the building, while Tomás St. Luc nattered on about the various architectural and decorative elements of which he was so proud. Sir Reginald worried that the morning's exertions might have overtaxed her but, despite her injury, she smiled graciously and nodded in appreciation at the various minutiae St. Luc discussed. But she seemed to be paying only partial attention to him as he showed her the house and rambled in exhaustive detail about the history of various pieces of furniture and decoration. Isador dragged her fingers over the texture of the upholstery, gazing distractedly out the window that overlooked the town, while St. Luc droned on.

"It is all quite lovely," the Queen said, interrupting the merchant's latest explication of the history and origin of a particularly bright and poorly crafted painting in a carved frame coated inexpertly with gold leaf. "With your indulgence, Monsieur St. Luc, we are weary from the morning's exertions and would cherish some time to rest."

"Of course. Of course, Your Majesty," the flustered merchant replied, looking nervously to his wife, a stern woman with upswept hair piled atop her head in a frontier imitation of the latest fashion from the Sudlandic court. "Per-perhaps Your Majesty would care to at least see the upstairs rooms?"

From his earlier walk-through with the merchant, Sir Reginald knew that the marbled bathing chambers on the second floor were a treasure of the house's layout, and that the merchant had so far held off directing the Queen's attention there, no doubt hoping to finish the tour on the highest note. But now the St. Lucs were being dismissed without the enjoyment of seeing the anticipated royal envy when the Queen beheld such splendor. Sir Reginald placed a hand on the shoulder of the stammering merchant and gently ushered him and his wife toward the door.

"Her Majesty will no doubt marvel at the beauty of the rest of the manor and share with you her compliments at a later date," he said courteously. "Your generosity is noted, and the Queen thanks you and your family for your temporary discomfiture."

"N-no bother at all," the merchant responded, taking his hat and coat from the hands of a servant and stepping out the door to join his wife on the generous landing outside. "All good wishes to Your Majesty, and bless you for saving our town," the merchant added over Bleiz's shoulder as he closed the door.

"Finally," the Queen sighed once the corpulent merchant had exited and the door closed behind him. "What a truly tiresome man."

"My thoughts, as well, Majesty," he replied, finding himself uncomfortable with her candor.

"Francine," Isador said, addressing her personal attendant, "be a dear and run a bath. And please have some food and wine brought up."

The attendant, an attractive and quietly elegant woman of middle-years, curtsied and moved toward the stairs.

"White wine," the Queen clarified. "Nothing heavy, the day is yet young."

"Yes, ma'am," Francine said, and signaled to two of the merchant's house servants to relay the message to the cook and to begin fetching hot water for the Queen's bath. Then she climbed the sweeping staircase to go and discover the rooms above.

The Queen herself stood in the comfortable sitting room, surrounded by its plush, over-cushioned furniture. She stared for a moment out of the lead-lined, segmented window at the rose maze and the terraced gardens beyond. She ran her fingers across a triangular section of glass that was rippled and bubbled. Sir Reginald moved to stand closer. The Queen's fatigue was becoming evident in her posture, and he didn't want her to have to raise her voice to be heard.

"Sir Reginald," she said. "We are quite certain you have many details to attend to in town. You needn't concern yourself with our comfort."

"Of course," he replied. "With your leave, Majesty."

"Barring some intervening surprise from the enemy," she added, "attend to us at the evening meal, where we might discuss the defense moving forward."

"It will be an honor, Your Majesty," he answered with a bow, and exited. Though the Queen had her own retinue and a sizable contingent of the royal guard, he nonetheless took the precaution of posting additional units around the perimeter of the manor grounds. Now that the enemy was aware the Queen was present, they had to be vigilant. The Barbárs were known to utilize a variety of assassins, kidnappers, arsonists, and other underhanded means to undermine the morale of the cities they assaulted. No target could possibly be as tempting as the Queen herself. He walked the perimeter once more, checking on his men. Content with his precautions, he mounted his horse and departed.

Isador

Once she was finally alone with only two female attendants present, the Queen placed a hand on the marble banister of the staircase and sagged. *A fifty-three-year-old woman has no place on a battlefield,* she chided herself. Her legs and shoulders ached from the fighting, and she grimaced at an unfamiliar ache in her right hip that seemed to be blossoming into something almost debilitating. She stifled an involuntary gasp as her leg protested at the first stair.

Isador, you're growing old, she thought. *You're lucky you weren't killed! Then where would the country be?*

She shook her head, gripped the banister firmly, and began to slowly climb the stairs, imagining her wastrel of a daughter trying to assume the throne in the midst of an invasion.

It would be chaos, she thought. *Utter chaos.*

Zach

That evening, Captain Zachar ben Zachar found himself at a sumptuous feast served at the Queen's table: roasted pheasant stuffed with chestnuts, apples, and onions with a steaming reduction of cherry brandy poured over top, piping hot loaves of bread next to tubs of butter, poached quail's eggs, soft pungent cheeses, and jams. Servants filled the wine goblets before everyone was seated and then a large, silver tureen was brought out, filled with a mushroom and leek soup. Zach had never seen such bounty at one meal, and he fidgeted with his dress uniform nervously, unsure how to behave in such august company. Sir Reginald, Brigadier Dixon, and the unfamiliar priest Mormand—whom everyone referred to as an "archbishop," whatever that was—all mingled comfortably with the other guests. Zach was painfully aware that his dress uniform had not been pressed, and the wrinkles made him feel paltry. He noted the crisp uniforms on the other officers, the rose-colored, tailored suit—*Is that silk?*—worn by a portly gentleman he didn't recognize with a colorful blue and gold sash, who seemed somewhat nervous, despite his immaculate attire. Zach tried again to smooth the wrinkles from his jacket.

"Relax, lad," Sir Reginald said kindly, walking over and laying a reassuring hand on Zach's shoulder. "You'll be fine. Just enjoy the meal. Don't say much." The knight commander offered an encouraging smile that Zach found somehow condescending, then moved around the table to his designated place and stood behind his chair.

Zach smiled and nodded his thanks. He looked around the table at the various guests waiting for the Queen to arrive and be seated before taking their own seats. The enigmatic Archbishop Mormand stood behind the chair directly to the right of the Queen's place at the head of the rectangular table. Zach failed to understand why the foreign cleric was being afforded such honor, but was careful not to show any surprise or discomfiture at the man's presence. Mormand was not wearing ecclesiastical robes this evening, instead having selected a sharply tailored black tunic with silver buttons up the front and a high collar. Of course, it was immaculately pressed, and the buttons shone like mirrors. Next to him stood Brigadier Dixon, whose dress uniform looked rumpled and ill-fitting. Zach took some comfort from this. Though Dixon was not wearing a sling, Zach noted that he kept his left thumb hooked in his belt—an old soldier's trick to immobilize an arm without the indignity of wearing a visible bandage or brace. To Dixon's right stood Sir Reginald's wife, Londine, a respectable and somewhat austere noblewoman whose perpetual grimace seemed to convey an expression of distaste at everything and everyone. To her right, at the foot of the table, stood her husband, his hands resting easily on the back of his chair as he began a conversation with the man in the silk suit—who stood to his right. Zach listened for a moment before realizing this was the Lord Mayor of Autun. He was a man in his late sixties with a sizable belly and a carefully groomed white beard that left his chin shaved clean. He had a red, bulbous nose which he wiped nervously as he made small talk and waited for the Queen's arrival. The mayor's wife, an unfortunate-looking woman—as wide as she was tall with a ruddy and pocked complexion—but with a nonetheless cheery disposition, stood to Zach's left and chattered on to no one in particular, in a never-ending stream of conversation about the weather, the look of the meal, the flowers in the rose garden and whatever else entered her head. The only break in her nonstop patter was for brief nervous titters that seemed to have no bearing on the words flowing out. Zach smiled politely at her, and once more smoothed his jacket.

Conversation stopped as the Queen made her entrance, dressed in an elegant, yet practical rose-colored gown with gold trim along the collar and sleeves. The colors of her banner. Zach's breath caught in his throat, and his knees felt suddenly watery. This woman had been Queen of Lachland for his entire life, passing edicts, giving speeches, issuing commands that affected the lives of all within her lands. She existed, in his mind, in an exalted place. Almost unreal, but ever present. Of course, he had seen her before, but always from a distance as the troops paraded past her viewing stand, her hand raised in acknowledgement of their bravery. He had never been close enough to notice her breathtaking beauty, the almost ephemeral elegance that seemed to emanate from her. She glided into the room with the type of grace typically attributed to angelic beings from children's stories. With a gentle smile and nod to all present, she was seated, allowing the rest of the gathered company to resume their conversations as they sat and the food service began.

The general hubbub at the table died down as people began to eat. Just as Zach was preparing to slice into a succulent piece of pheasant, a hand appeared on the wrinkled forearm of his uniform. The Queen's hand. He froze, staring at it. Slowly, he looked up into the eyes of the elegant monarch as she graced him with a broad smile and said, "So, Captain Zachar, tell us, wherever did you get the courage to attack a crazed Räuber head-on with nothing but a banner in your hands?"

Chapter 18

To dance among the spirits is a gift unbounded
To know such joy as a babe newborn
To laugh with the innocent abandon of a child
To see and learn the mysteries of the stars
I tell you, it is a gift unbounded

– *A Traveler's Verses,* Sarilla

574 HR - *Last month of summer*
Somewhere in the wildlands of northern Mardin

Mama

Mama Warad and her small band made much better time after crossing the river. Barbár patrols seemed to be fewer on the eastern bank, though they did still encounter the occasional war band of fifty to sixty men rushing west or southwest, and had to lose precious hours skirting around them. This was made much easier, however, by the addition of the horses. Now that the group was mounted, they pressed onward toward Monarch's

Pass, which was apparently the only route to the Highlands of the Green Mount.

Traveling into the unknown and unsure how they might ever hope to locate Ashahl's former student in time, Mama felt great urgency and drove her group hard, pressing each day for an early start and a long day's travel. Just as Amina had described, the river had veered away to the northwest shortly after they had crossed it, and now they found the land becoming increasingly rugged the further north they traveled. Worried that they might be seen, Mama had opted for the group to stay in the foothills east of the road as long as possible, but as the valley of Devil's Hoof narrowed, they were relegated to navigating increasingly steep foothills and narrow basins. At some point soon, they would need to come out of the hills and follow the road, but Mama wanted to wait as long as possible before accepting that level of exposure.

"Lupe," Mama called back over her shoulder just as the group topped a rise—a small mountain, really—only to face a sharp descent into a narrow defile, followed by another, steeper rise beyond.

"Yes, sitti," her votary answered, riding up to Mama and pausing on the hilltop to rest her horse for a moment.

Pointing ahead and to her right, Mama indicated a scree-covered area near the bottom of the narrow valley ahead. "Somewhere there we will camp tonight. I'd like you to scout ahead and find a suitable spot. We are likely not moving tomorrow, so find a site where we can remain hidden throughout the day."

"Yes, sitti," Lupe said, her sharp eyes scanning the terrain. "We will need to be somewhere on the slope and not in the crook of the valley in case of a storm."

"Good thinking," Mama agreed. "Argant needs a short rest, but we'll be behind you. You ride ahead and select a spot for us. We'll be there before the veil of night falls."

"Yes, sitti," Lupe repeated dutifully and rode off, cutting across the slope of the hill eastward.

Yadira directed her horse to walk beside Mama's. "Tonight then?" she asked her teacher.

"We can't wait any longer," Mama replied. "And this looks to be as safe a place as any we've traveled through. Have you reviewed the Canon of Wisdom?"

"Yes," she answered, eyes downcast in embarrassment, "though I still struggle with the phrasing of the fifth strophe."

"Dira, Dira, Dira." Mama clucked her tongue. "How many years has it been, and still you struggle with the Canons? Well, you have some hours yet to review. Look to it."

Yadira nodded acceptance, though her eyes looked troubled over her jimas and her bony shoulders slumped forward as if carrying a burden.

Mama studied her for a long moment before adding, "You needn't worry, Dira. I'll be right with you the whole time."

Yadira's looked out over the horizon, and the tension in her eyes told Mama that her reassurance was of small comfort.

There was a long pause before Yadira responded, "Yes, sitti."

Corvus

Corvus and Cailean reined in their horses as the sun began to set behind them. They had been riding hard all day, and Corvus' leg was cramping from his still-healing wound. It had been over a month since the Day of the Seven, yet Corvus still walked with a limp and couldn't put his full weight on his leg. He worried that it may never fully heal. As it was, he worried he would be little use in a fight.

"That looks like a good spot," Cailean offered, pointing to a relatively level copse of trees low on the mountainside they had been skirting for the past three hours. Corvus agreed and within a short time, they had dismounted, fed and brushed their horses, and tethered them for the night. As Cailean gathered wood for a fire, Corvus opened his saddle bag and pulled out some food that Ligulf had packed for them.

"Looks like venison jerky," Corvus called to his son. "Potatoes, if you don't mind fetching some water, and... parsnips. Where did he get parsnips?"

"He probably picked them up on his recent jaunt o'er the mountain," Cai suggested.

"Huh." Corvus shrugged. "He's a good lad."

"Aye," Cailean responded as he dropped a load of branches and twigs next to his father. "I'll fetch the water."

Corvus produced his flint and started the fire. Once the blaze was reliably going, he grabbed his stewpot from where it hung on the side of his saddle, fished out his small supply of salt and other spices, and within a short time had a respectable stew bubbling merrily over the fire as the twilight faded.

"Any idea what we'll face at the gate?" Cai asked.

"Well," Corvus said, rubbing his brow, "we trounced them soundly at Esper, five years ago. That time they came with just under three thousand men, a light raiding force. Years before, when we beat them at Eagle's Gate, they had over seven thousand... and the fort."

"So they'll likely bring more this time," Cailean concluded.

"Aye," he said darkly. "I expect no less than ten thousand."

Cailean whistled softly and poked at the fire with a stick. "How many can we field with the fyrd?"

"Just shy of two thousand," Corvus responded grimly.

"The White Cleft should be back to full strength by now, eh?"

Corvus nodded. "I would hope so. I expect Fergus to bring at least twenty-five hundred men."

"And Mannon?" Cai pressed.

"About the same, I reckon," he replied, stirring the bubbling pot.

"Even wi' the castle destroyed," Cai mused, "they'll still have a strong defensive position and superior numbers if they reach the Gate before our forces arrive."

"Aye, that they will."

Cailean broke a stick and added it to the fire. "If Donella sends her forces, we may have a chance."

"It'll be a struggle," Corvus said, dishing up two heaping bowls of stew and handing one to his son. "Tomorrow, we'll talk to Mannon and see exactly how many he can bring to the ceilidh."

"Ceilidh?" Cai laughed softly. "More of a full-on donnybrook, I'd say.

"'Twill be," Corvus agreed with a chuckle. "'Twill be, indeed."

They finished their meal in silence and laid out bedrolls for the night. Corvus was glad for the woolen warmth of his great kilt, for the mountain air was chilly, even with the fire. Shortly after lying down, Corvus judged by the sound of Cai's breathing that he'd drifted off. *Lucky lad,* he thought. *Able to dismiss tomorrow's worries and sleep.* He envisioned the ruins of Eagle's Gate and imagined various ways the enemy might array themselves, planning counter strategies for each possibility. Sitting up, he traced various rough battle plans in the dirt with his finger by the light of the dying fire. Eventually, satisfied that he had worked through as much as he could with the information he had, he once more settled himself, wrapping himself in his woolen kilt and closed his eyes.

Still, sleep eluded him. As had become his habit over the years when his mind was troubled, he silently spoke to his dead wife. Though he often laughed at himself for the practice, it somehow brought him comfort, and more often than not, answers did seem to come to him—whether they came from Greer, or his own mind.

What am I to do, love? he asked, concern for his many charges coloring his tone. *How am I to protect them?*

He heard the distant croak of a raven as unbidden memories suddenly washed over him.

He saw himself, years earlier, leading his men at the first battle of Eagle's Gate. They had been outnumbered then, and the enemy occupied the as-yet-undamaged fort. Conventional wisdom suggested that the Highlanders had no hope, but Corvus had managed to fool the Barbárs into committing their troops outside the walls, where he had confronted them while the archers of the Green Mount had peppered the enemy from the forested mountainside.

Next, he saw the battle at Esper and how he and a youthful Cailean had pulled victory from imminent defeat when the White Cleft line had crumbled. They had annihilated the Barbárs to a man. He remembered Cai's beaming face after the battle. He had only been fifteen then, young to be even among the fyrd at all, much less commanding the reserves.

Then, with a dizzying swirl, he was back in the desert in Asland, his starving and whipped men stooped from weeks of malnutrition and abuse from their erstwhile masters. But despite their weakness, his plan had given them hope and a wild ferocity in their sunken eyes. He saw himself standing before the ragtag company of misfits he had commanded. He shook his head in amazement. He had been only twenty and slender as a whip, and he'd had a full head of dark hair then. Yet it was the same dark, calculating eyes that surveyed that battlefield. The cruel enemy troops, the infamous Blades of Sebastian, were furious at his betrayal. He had captured much of their baggage train and destroyed the rest before switching sides. It had been a mortal blow to the Blades' plans of conquest and had handed victory to the beleaguered Aslene forces making their last stand.

More memories flashed through his mind as he dozed on the edge of sleep, each reminding him of some clever stratagem, stolen march, or victory through sheer dogged determination. Somehow the aggregate of the images reassured him, calmed him, and familiar sense of warmth and comfort washed over him as a raven's croak once more broke the still of the night.

An image of Greer's face came to him, as he had last seen her. She was propped up in her bed, wrapped with blankets against the chill morning air. Her long dark hair had developed streaks of gray, and the lines of pain around her eyes had become more pronounced. He remembered stroking her cheek softly. She had gripped his calloused hand with hers, which somehow had remained soft despite her years of hard work. Turning her face into his hand, she had kissed his palm. Then she had looked up at him with those eyes full of wisdom and love, and smiled. She had smiled at him, despite the agony of the disease eating her. Despite the worries he knew she felt at leaving her boys and her husband behind. It was a smile of warmth and of a love that he knew would last beyond death, and it had warmed and reassured him then, as it reassured him now beside the smoldering campfire. With a sigh that released his many concerns, Corvus drifted into a restful slumber, wrapped in his great kilt and the lasting love of his departed wife.

Mama

Her small band sat around a fire together. They had eaten well this night. Lupe had managed to spot, track, and kill a wild goat late in the day, and the shoulder they had roasted over their small fire was savory, gamy, and aromatic. Yadira had skillfully coated the haunch with a sharp curry, stuffing it with ample chunks of precious goat cheese. She carefully turned the spit, ensuring that the melting cheese would coat the meat, adding its butteriness to the crusted curry and cinnamon. Mama wiped the last vestige of grease from her chin with a cotton kerchief before reaching into her satchel and unwrapping the pasty, gray ball of ground mushrooms and spices that she had prepared days ago.

"Amina," Mama said softly, "please fetch more wood and build up the fire a little. We need it to last through the night."

Amina silently rose and wandered into the dark to find more fuel for the fire. Argant, still engrossed in devouring his dinner, looked up a moment later and, realizing she was gone, set down his bowl and dashed after her.

Yadira was meditating, her legs crossed, eyes closed, hands on top of her knees, palms up. Her lips moved and her brow furrowed in concentration as she silently recited the Canon. Mama gestured to Lupe, silently dismissing her to begin her ranging watch. It would be a long night, and the spirit journey would take much out of Yadira—and Mama, who would tend her. It would be up to Lupe and Amina to cover the watch shifts for the night.

Mama poured a steaming mug of hot water, crumbling the ball of ground mushrooms into it and stirring with her spoon. She let the mixture steep while Yadira continued meditating. Before long, Amina and Argant returned with more wood for the fire.

"You two should rest now," Mama told them. "Lupe has first watch."

A slight wince creased Amina's eyes. Mama recognized her worry and smiled reassuringly. Amina nodded and, placing her hand casually on Argant's head, led the child off to their bedroll. Mama had told them to sleep well away from the fire tonight, as Yadira's experience may involve speaking, and Mama didn't want her to disturb their sleep any more than necessary.

"Dira," Mama said softly once they were alone.

Yadira's eyes popped open and she looked at Mama expectantly.

"It's time."

Her eldest protégé offered a resigned sigh and nodded grimly, a frown of worry creasing her brow. Mama handed the mug of tea to her. Yadira reached a trembling hand forward to take it. She grimaced at the smell but drank deeply, the draught having cooled as she had meditated. After the first gulp, she gasped, and her mouth worked at the unpleasant flavor behind her jimas. "That's awful," she said.

"Finish it," Mama insisted.

"Must I?"

"Drink." Mama pushed up on the base of the cup, urging it to Yadira's mouth. With another grimace, Yadira drank the cup dry, fighting back bile as she chewed and swallowed the slimy dregs. Despite being in her thirties, the resentful glare she gave Mama looked for all the world like a recalcitrant child being forced to finish her meal. Mama chuckled and shook her head.

"Now, resume the Canon," Mama said with resumed solemnity.

Setting down the cup, Yadira once more placed her hands on her knees, closed her eyes, and began her silent recitation.

It was a clear, moonless night, and the stars were in full glory. Mama noted the passing of time by watching the movement of the heavens. Though the surrounding mountains obscured much of the sky, she could just make out the edge of the Lion and the Bull as they crawled along the jagged horizon to the south, locked in their perpetual battle. The Archer was clearly visible to the north, rotating slowly, yet forever sighting his target—Najm Shamal, the polestar. An hour passed and still Yadira sat muttering the Canon, waiting for the spirits to speak. A cool breeze came down from the mountain and Mama wrapped her shawl more tightly around her shoulders. The night would be cold. She placed another branch on the fire and continued watching her votary closely.

Suddenly, Yadira's lips stopped moving, her brow furrowed more deeply, and her head tilted to the right as if she was seeking to understand something. After a moment, she muttered something under her breath and her brow relaxed.

"Of course," she said, then groaned in awe at something only she could see. "Of course."

"Spirits of the Ancestors," Mama said to the night, "we ask for guidance and clarity. We ask you to aid Yadira in this journey. Guide her, keep her safe."

Yadira nodded and her brow furrowed once again. She remained like that for several minutes before another groan escaped her and she lay back on the soft grass of the hillside, opening her eyes to the stars.

Mama knew she would remain like this for some time and chose not to disturb her. The fugue of the drug would overwhelm her at first, but Mama was patient and would wait until after the crest of the effect to ask more questions. She quietly added more wood to the fire, noting that the pile that Amina and Argant had brought was already dwindling. But knowing that Amina and Lupe would both be pulling double watch shifts this night, she was loath to disturb the sleeping votary to ask for more. The area immediately around their camp was devoid of trees, and it was clear to Mama that she would need to venture away to gather wood. Her brow creased as she considered her options. She hated the thought of leaving Yadira alone on her journey, even for a short time, but she must keep the fire burning through the night. The beneficial spirits would be drawn by the flames, while those of a more malign nature would be kept at bay by its light and warmth.

Perhaps Lupe is nearby? Mama's eyes scanned the dark hillside, but saw no sign of the stealthy votary.

The sound of a soft footfall roused Mama from her indecision. She stood, hefting her crooked staff, and searched into the darkness for the origin of the sound. Another footfall, closer this time. Mama took a step toward the sound, moving further from the light of the fire in the hopes that her eyes might adjust and reveal the intruder. Slowly, a figure emerged from the gloom. A man, walking carefully toward her, his hands open before him. The light of the fire reflected in his eyes and in the eyes of some creature near his feet.

"You're not welcome here," Mama said with authority.

"Oh, but I think I am, Honored One," the man's lilting voice replied in flawless Aslene from the dark as he took another step forward. As he moved closer, Mama saw he was dressed strangely, wearing motley trousers that reached to his mid-calf, and a matching motley vest over a bare chest despite the chill. His skin was pale, and he had a mop of unruly hair of a color somewhere between the bright flaxen of the Barbárs and the chestnut of the Mardish. He was accompanied by a small, scraggly dog, with a stubby tail that bobbed furiously. The dog snuffled at the ground by the man's feet as he advanced.

Mama was about to call out the alarm when the man produced a long wooden flute from somewhere within his vest. He stopped his forward movement, and with a calming gesture began to play the instrument softly. Mama heard Yadira respond with an immediate sigh of seeming joy. She looked back at her and saw that Yadira's hands were clasped to her mouth; she seemed to be in the throes of some wordless euphoria. The stranger continued playing. He stepped into the light of the fire, and with a wry wink to Mama, sat cross-legged, his little dog hopping into his lap contentedly. The music was deeply soothing and obviously affected Yadira profoundly. Mama relaxed her guarded stance and sat studying this bizarre visitor. His melody changed from the soft pleasant tune he had begun to one with a haunting and foreboding refrain. Despite herself, Mama was transfixed by his playing, his presence. She felt her own spirit being carried aloft by the doleful tune and dreamlike images began to dance at the edge of her perception. She closed her eyes and tried to summon the half-seen images in greater detail, but the vision danced away from her the more she tried to see it directly. She opened her eyes as the stranger's melody changed yet again. The fire had been built up and was now a sizable blaze, giving both warmth and light. There was a large pile of firewood that she was sure hadn't been there moments before. Mama was warm, content, and comfortable despite the steady, chill mountain breeze. She dropped her shawl from her shoulders and again closed her eyes, following this new melody.

The tune stopped abruptly soon after, jarring Mama's eyes open. Yadira had said something and was sitting up, her eyes on the fire.

Mama looked around for the stranger, but she and Yadira were alone.

"The One," Yadira said again.

"Yes, Dira?" Mama asked softly.

"He seeks the Tor," Yadira said, her eyes glazed and unseeing. "It is the first Gate. He wants them all."

"Yes?" Mama said encouragingly.

"A Man of Iron will oppose him," she continued. "He is our hope, our… The eyes… I saw the eyes…"

"Whose eyes, Dira?" Mama urged gently, trying to follow the votary's disjointed recollections.

"A song, a bow, the Man of Iron wrapped in black… The eyes bind them all together. The eyes! Of course, the eyes."

"Whose eyes, Dira?"

"Argant," she replied, as if explaining the obvious. Then she suddenly blinked as if in clear recollection, adding, "The breath of the mountain. We must not forget it!"

"Alright," Mama agreed, confused.

Yadira suddenly focused on Mama with an urgency that startled the older woman. "He must not gain the Tor!"

"Who, Argant?"

"What?" Yadira shook her head in frustration. "No. The One. The One! His servants must not gain the Tor!"

Cailean

His father seemed to have slept much of the night on that cold hillside, in the kind of deep, restful slumber that he usually only enjoyed in the depths of winter, snug in his bed wrapped in a thick, down comforter. Cailean had woken in the night, and since he'd been watching, Corvus' sleep had become increasingly restive. He tossed and muttered on his bedroll. When his father suddenly thrashed about, Cailean sat up quickly, gripping his sword's handle and looking for danger. Finding none, his eyes fell back on his father's disturbed sleep. He was about to wake him when Corvus spoke, his eyes still closed.

"The Tor," he muttered. "Not the Tor."

Cailean waited see if his father would speak again. But after a moment, he sighed and once more fell into a deep sleep. Cailean jerked his head at a sound coming down the mountain. Or perhaps it was nothing. For a moment, he thought he had heard haunting music... A flute perhaps. He was sure he must have imagined it, though the sound left him unsettled, uneasy. Unable to sleep now, Cai stirred the fire back to life and sat, watching over his father, as the sky began to gray with the first hints of the approaching dawn.

Mama

"I was surprised you let that man approach us," Mama chided Lupe as they prepared their morning tea . "You knew how delicate Yadira's trance would be. Did you not see him?"

"A man?" Lupe asked, alarm in her voice. "Where? when? I watched you both the whole time from high on this rise. I saw no man."

"Surely you heard his flute?" Mama asked, though from the frisson that stole over her, she already knew the answer.

"Flute? No, Mama," Lupe insisted. "I found an elevated vantage from which I could sit and see this whole valley. I could see you plainly, and I saw no man approach and heard no music." Then after a moment she added tentatively, "Perhaps you slept and dreamt it?"

"Child," Mama responded firmly, "I am not so old that I cannot tell the difference between sleep and awake." Her eyes drifted westward as she added, wistfully, "Nor am I so young as to not recognize the hand of the Ancestors at work."

"Mama?" Lupe asked softly.

"I dreamt flute," Argant offered with a yawn as he stumbled toward the fire, wiping the sleep from his eyes. Amina had the watch now, and had quietly slipped off to relieve Lupe hours earlier, leaving Argant wrapped in his blankets. Mama and Lupe both looked at the boy who nodded his head, firmly.

"Of course you did, eazizi," Mama responded warmly, despite the spider-like chills crawling up her spine.

The group fell into an awkward silence that was broken when Lupe stood and crossed around the fire, crouching down to examine the grass just to Mama's right. It had clearly been pressed down, as if by someone sitting there. After a moment, she straightened, holding something in her hand. It glittered in the morning light.

"What did you find, child?" Mama asked.

"It looks like a little bell," Lupe answered.

"A bell?" Mama asked, confused.

"Yes, sitti." Lupe held the trinket up to the morning light. "You know, the kind worn by jugglers and acrobats." She handed it to Mama, shaking her head in confusion.

Mama turned the little jingle over and over in her hand in awe, and mouthed a silent prayer of thanks.

"What does it mean, Mama?" Lupe asked as she studied the small bell.

"It is a marvel, dear," the teacher responded, a slight smile tugging at her cheeks. "A true wonder, and a sign that we must press on."

Yadira's voice interrupted their conversation. "What would you like for breakfast?"

Mama looked at her typically dour protégé to see a relaxed, almost joyful smile light up her face behind the jimas. The weight, burden, and worries that always seemed to follow Yadira throughout her life had apparently lifted. To Mama's eyes, the woman almost glowed with a quiet contentment.

"Good morning, Mama," Yadira said softly. "And… thank you."

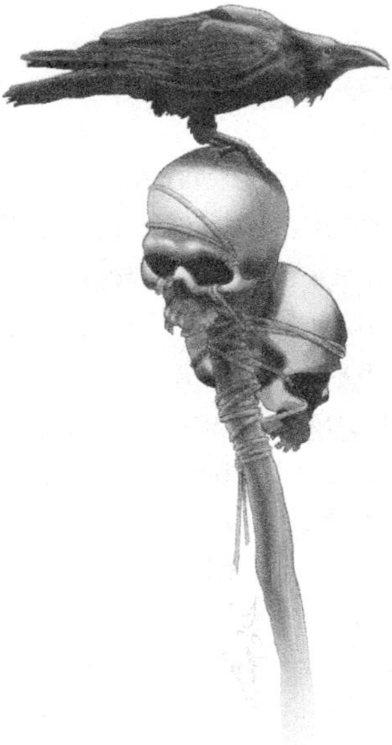

Chapter 19

A summons in the night— so soft, it was like the breath from the flutter of the wing of a moth—but its reverberations echoed in the hearts of the twelve. Twelve men clustered in the fetid swamps of Angor. Twelve hearts leeched of vitality by their foul blood practices. A conclave of practitioners of esoteric and stygian mysteries, uncaring that the voice they followed—those whispers softer than the scrape of an eyelid over their jaundiced orbs—was the voice of Fel himself, trapped in an eternal dreamscape, able only to insinuate through the susurrous murmurations of the mephitic swamps. Yet they heard. And these men's hearts, putrid and shriveled though they were, turned toward the summons. Their lips quivered, shaking their pallid, sagging skin as rheumy, enlarged eyes looked with undimmed hope toward this whispered beckoning.

– "The Creation of the Angor Shamans"
from *The Tales of Pellium,* as translated by
Cyrus of Visivia

574 HR - *Last month of summer*
Isle of Vas, off the northwest coast of Orense

Zsoka

Empress Zsoka glared at the outlander sitting across the fire from her. The cold emanating from the walls and floor of the black cavern that acted as her audience chamber seemed to bother the Angor shaman, who clutched his shaggy woolen cloak tighter about his shoulders and edged closer to the fire. *If this idiot inches any closer, that cloak will be ablaze,* she thought, a wry smile playing over her lips as she imagined the lanolin catching.

It had taken seven months for the Barbár war chief, the Great Hadvezér, to receive and respond to the urgent missive she had sent suggesting an alliance and hinting at the powerful information she held. After the archbishop's intriguing visit in the dead of winter, she had wasted no time reaching out to her old adversary—and lover—Lord Vajk. She knew he would be suspicious of her motives and more than reticent to become entangled with her again, but this was an opportunity that could not be wasted. She hoped that he would at least afford her the dignity of sending an ambassador from his inner circle, someone with whom she might have confidence that they actually held the ear of her old love. But Vajk had sent this sniveling, sickly outlander alone to represent him. The man's unctuous greetings somehow managed to be both pompous and obsequious at the same time, his yellow eyes taking her in hungrily. And now, the frail thing sat shivering by her fire, reeking of sheep's grease and staring at her from his sunken, red-rimmed, and rheumy eyes. She noted with disgust the few strands of greasy black hair that failed to cover the pallid skin of his mostly bald head, and the steady stream of drips coming from his hooked nose, which he wiped repeatedly with the back of his hand. He sat, trembling and staring at her not unlike a trapped and diseased animal awaiting its death.

Vajk sent this to me? she thought incredulously. *Have I fallen so far in his estimation that this creature is all the dignity he can spare me?*

She remembered the flaring torches of the Barbár encampment that night so many years earlier when she and Vajk had met to sign the treaty that would limit his people's incursions across the Nagyapa mountains. She had been barely twenty summers old, and already had more than doubled her lands and honors since assuming the throne, rising from the title she had inherited from her father—"Úrasszony" of the Orensian people—to become the Empress of the Steppes. *And beyond,* she thought, *were it not for treachery.*

Oh, how Vajk had reacted upon seeing her! Her retinue and guard had preceded her into his great pavilion, where the Hadvezér awaited her. A notorious bully, the gargantuan man had no doubt imagined it would be easy to intimidate a mere girl, and that he would overwhelm her with his size, bellicosity, and the thinly veiled threats that were the hallmark of Barbár "diplomacy." Instead, he had been dazzled and clearly rattled by her beauty as she had glided elegantly into his pavilion, her dark hair and its now-famous silver streak lifted by an elaborate green and jet feathered headdress into a breathtaking mane of black and silver curls that cascaded over her bare shoulders. Her personal attendant had urged her not to wear the green satin gown with its plunging neckline, lest it get muddied and ruined as she walked from her carriage through the foul Barbár camp. But Zsoka had insisted. She remembered clearly the hunger in the amber eyes of Lord Vajk as he drank in the sight of her. Standing upon a dais, the tall man had seemed a giant in her eyes, his muscular and tattooed chest only partially covered by a woolen vest, crudely ornamented with beadwork. Her entrance had interrupted him in mid-boast in his guttural tongue, and he had openly stared at her, his eyes wide. She smiled at the memory of the sheer wonder, awe, and unabashed lust that had played over that savage ruler's visage at the sight of her. The ubiquitous Barbár mop of flaxen hair, so ridiculed by those in her court, somehow looked regal on him—like the mane of a fierce white lion. Though his jawline was obscured by his full, braided beard, the strong lines beneath the hair were unmistakable. He had high cheekbones and piercing blue eyes that conveyed a shrewd intelligence. A horizontal scar beneath his left eye, somehow enhanced his power and raw magnetism. Here was a god among men, rife with confidence, skill, and cunning. Here was a man upon whom women would throw themselves. A man used to being in control of every situation. And yet, seeing the unabashed lust and almost youthful confusion that her presence had caused in him, she had known exactly how the negotiations would progress, and that she was the one who held the power here.

There had been ceremonial toasts and occasional bursts of warlike pugnacity from the man as he strained to maintain some semblance of dignity and dominance in her presence, but to each demand or threat, she had responded with silky, clever counters, each time disarming him with the intense gaze of her violet eyes, and the implacable, iron fact of her army's might. By the end of the evening, she had won every concession from him she had demanded. The Barbárs would cross the Mirror Sea in search of new plunder and leave her people unmolested. They would no longer demand access to the Saltin Sea through her southern demesnes, and her merchants would not be accosted as they traveled into Lugo. The one concession she had made to him had been one she, herself, had desired. She had stayed the night with him, much to the chagrin and horror of her advisors. Perhaps in the long run it had been folly, as the son she had borne as a result—her beloved Talon—had provided the fuel for her cousin to overthrow her to prevent a barbarian bastard from eventually ascending the throne. But truth be told, she could not regret her decision that night, despite all the sorrow it had brought. Never mind that the outcome had given her a darling, towheaded boy with a wild, untamed streak, larger and fiercer than his peers, and with an incisive mind. She had desired Vajk as strongly as he had obviously hungered for her. Here was a conqueror of kings, a ruler of nations, and a man who could plunder entire dominions. If anyone were worthy of her bed, it was he. The two had spent a sweaty, athletic night tangled in each other's arms. A night of legend that both would forever remember. Or so she had thought.

Her face pulled into a disgusted sneer as she now contemplated the feeble, infirm, and seemingly diseased outlander that Vajk had sent in response to her message. Neither Orensian nor Barbár, this so-called "shaman" from the pestilential lands of Angor, was a slap in the face. It was all she could do to maintain a somewhat civil tone as she felt her hopes for escape and reinstatement plummet to dash upon the rocks that surrounded this island prison.

"Empress?" the shaman asked querulously.

"What is it?" She strove unsuccessfully to keep the resentment from her tone.

"You did not answer my question," he said with a slight grin, his purpled lips trembling in a half smile.

"What question?" she demanded.

"I asked," he ventured timidly, "if you were familiar with the Angor shamans and our unique… gifts."

"No. Why would I be? Until this moment, I can assure you, I have thought but little of the territories of Angor, and I am sure I am the better for it." She impatiently waved off a servant holding a tea service.

"I see," he said, the slight grin blooming into a broader smile, revealing yellowed, uneven teeth.

"What do you see, you tiresome man?"

"Tiresome, Majesty?" He leaned forward suddenly, pouncing on the word with a feral energy that surprised her.

"Yes," she responded, struggling to maintain her composure in the face of his sudden intensity. "I had expected your master to respond to my missive with… someone different."

"Someone of more visible power or influence, perhaps?" His rheumy eyes bored into hers as his grin broadened still further. She could imagine him breaking into cackling glee at any moment. The four guards standing nearby were clearly disturbed by his manic demeanor and stepped toward him in response, placing their hands on their hilts. The shaman did not seem to notice their presence, maintaining an almost hypnotic stare into Zsoka's eyes.

Unsettled, the Empress broke off her gaze and signaled for the tea to be served after all. As the servants settled a small table beside the shaman and began pouring the steaming beverage, she calmed her thoughts, taking a few deep breaths to compose herself before continuing.

"Was your master not intrigued by my note?" she asked diffidently, her eyes focused purposely on her cup.

"Master? You mean Vajk?" the strange man responded between sips. "Yes. So intrigued, in fact, that he sent the one man that might allow him to learn the meaning of your missive in a timely fashion."

She looked up, incredulously. "How so?"

The shaman chuckled, as if at a private joke, as he reached into a ragged pouch at his belt. The nearest guard took another step toward him, menacingly.

"Tell your dog to be at ease," the pallid man said with a nervous chuckle. His attention stayed on the contents of his pouch as he rooted about within it, apparently searching for some particular item.

"Watch your tone, wretch," the guard growled. "You are blessed to be in the presence of the Empress, and you will speak to her with respect."

Despite the tension in the chamber, Zsoka found herself mesmerized by the man's search, and was unable to gesture to the guard or even respond to the shaman.

With a small cry of triumph, the unsettling shaman proudly held up a small, fleshy nub, which he displayed before the fire, staring adoringly at it as though it were some long-sought treasure. Zsoka's stomach roiled as she realized what he held. The flesh was withered and foul with rot, the nail yellowed and ragged, but it was nonetheless unmistakably a man's finger, severed at the last knuckle.

"What a ghastly thing—" the Empress began.

"You dare!" The guard said at the same time, and grabbed the shaman's shoulder roughly.

As quick as a viper, the shaman's empty hand lashed out and gripped the face of the guard, who immediately began screaming as though boiling oil coursed over his skin. Zsoka stood in alarm as the other guards drew their weapons and rushed forward.

"Hold them back, Empress!" the shaman shouted over the stricken soldier's shrieks. "I need something this man can give me in order to fulfill your wish."

The confused guards paused and looked to Zsoka, who held up a hand to stay their advance. The screaming man collapsed limply to his knees as his skin began to boil and smoke, black blisters rising and bursting on his face, bloody pus streaming over the shaman's fingers. The Angor seemed somehow taller, stronger, more vital as he gripped the guard's head in his hand like a child's ball, staring into his suffering, horrified eyes with a feral hunger.

Without releasing the smoking guard, the shaman turned suddenly to the Empress and with a brief cackle of delight, he popped the rotted fingertip into his mouth and began to chew. The sight caused Zsoka's gorge to rise, which was made all the worse by the smell of blistered and roasting human flesh wafting from the suffering guard—whose screams had now diminished to no more than a pathetic mewling. Her vision swam and she struggled to focus.

"Empress!" another guard shouted, trying to break through her enthrallment. Zsoka could only stare in mute and fascinated disgust at the sight before her, shaking her head in a silent denial of the horror.

As the dying guard's whimpers finally faded to nothing, the previously withered and frail shaman, now standing as strong and robust as any warrior she had ever seen, tossed the corpse onto the fire like a doll, sending up a shower of sparks as the fire began to hiss and snap. The remaining three guards could apparently abide this horror no longer and rushed to attack him. Somehow trapped by the sight of the horrors unfolding, Zsoka stared in a stupor at the blistered and sizzling face of the corpse in the fire pit, only vaguely noting the sounds of struggle about her. After a moment, she became aware that the chamber had fallen silent, but for the hissing and popping of the body in the flames. With a sharp intake of breath, she came back to herself and glanced around to find only the shaman remaining. The three guards lay dead and broken, pools of blood spreading slowly around them. Her servants had apparently fled the chamber, leaving her alone with this monster. She brought a trembling hand to her mouth and sank back heavily into the fur-lined cushions of her throne.

The shaman grinned at her with his yellow teeth, still chewing the dismembered finger.

"Am I next, then?" she asked, her voice husky and soft.

"Whatever do you mean, Empress?" the crazed man said between chews.

"You're here to kill me, are you not?"

A slow grin spread across the Angor's face as the engorged muscles of his jaw clenched and flexed, his yellowed teeth—now almost fangs—appearing and disappearing behind mucous-covered lips. "Not today, I'm not,"

"Then what is this?"

Faster than she could react, the shaman's hand lashed out and seized her wrist. Immediately, the dark, cold stone chamber disappeared and Zsoka found herself standing alone in the warm afternoon sunshine outside a familiar pavilion. Crude banners fluttered in the summer breeze, and there was a bustle of activity around the front of the tent; Barbár warriors, messengers, and attendants entered and exited in a chaotic stream.

"Where am I?" Zsoka whispered in awe.

"Enter the tent, Empress," the shaman's disembodied voice whispered.

Obediently, Zsoka moved forward, drifting in a dreamlike haze, her feet floating inches above the ground. The brilliance of the summer's day quickly gave way to the muted colors of sunlight through canvas. The bustle of activity seemed like a beehive, with scribes at tables along the perimeter of the tent scribbling messages furiously then handing them off to messengers as fast as they could arrive. No one seemed to notice her as men and women rushed about purposefully, passing her on all sides. At the center of the tent stood Vajk, like a sturdy oaken beam supporting not just the tent, but somehow holding his entire nation on those broad shoulders. He was taking reports from breathless warriors fresh from a hard ride, then barking instructions to his scribes who would begin scratching them down to be carried off by sweating, overworked messengers.

She floated toward him, remembering the hard lines of his chest, the firm jaw beneath his white-blonde braided beard, the sharp-blue decisive eyes. Assuming this to be some sort of dream-like trance, she reached out a hand to touch his face, not really expecting to feel his skin under her fingers. To her surprise, he immediately recoiled from her touch as though it burned, and spun around to see her before him for the first time. His eyes widened in shock, then in a booming voice he shouted over the hubbub.

"Everyone out, now!"

All activity in the tent paused as everyone looked at him.

"I said, out!" he screamed, in a voice of command that brooked no question.

In a flurry of parchment and overturned writing desks, the pavilion emptied until only Zsoka and Vajk remained. Apparently satisfied that they were alone, the Great Hadvezér sighed, poured himself a horn of mead, and dropped into his sturdy wooden chair near the back wall of the tent.

"So, my man found you, eh?" he said after a long drink.

"Is this a dream?" Zsoka asked softly.

"It is no dream, Zsoka," he replied with a distant smile. "The Angor shamans have rare talents, unique to each. Blood-Tooth's special gift allows us to speak from afar, though at a steep cost." With a wry grin, he held up his left hand, which was missing the tip of its smallest finger. Zsoka gasped at the sight, the memory of the shaman chewing the ghastly digit causing her bile to rise again.

"I have seven of the shamans in my service," he continued. "I find their talents quite useful. Blood-Tooth told me that he cannot maintain this spell for long, so you will forgive me if we cut to the chase. As pleasant as it is to see you again, this has cost me. So, what is your information and what do you propose, Zsoka?"

"*Empress*, Grand Hadvezér," she protested. "Let us not—"

"Let us not waste time on *former* titles," he snapped. "As you no doubt can tell, I am very busy at the moment. What do you have to tell me?"

Seeing no point in arguing over honorifics, Zsoka swallowed her annoyance—and the feeling of disempowerment that had become a constant companion these many years—and plunged right in.

"Are you familiar with the legend of the Great Wheel and the Lost Keys?"

"I am," he replied. "Have you found one?"

"You seem unsurprised by my question," she said, nonplussed.

"There are many things in motion at the moment," Vajk replied evasively. "I have seen and learned much in recent years. Nothing surprises me anymore."

The image of Vajk suddenly flickered as though she were seeing him through the heat of a fire.

"Be quick, Empress," the voice of the shaman whispered. "The spell fades."

"I know the location of one of the Gates," she said bluntly.

"So do I," Vajk replied with a dismissive wave. "In fact, I know the locations of three of them. Tell me what you know. If it has value, I'll listen to your offer."

"You know of the Tor in the Green Mount?" she prodded.

"My forces are on the way there as we speak," the Grand Hadvezér responded. "It is central to my plans. We'll have the Tor before the Equinox."

"I doubt that," she said, with more confidence than she felt. "The Highlanders have defeated you twice before, and they are, no doubt, prepared to stop you again."

"Not this time," he said, draining the last of the mead from the horn. "I know what I face, and how to overcome it. Do you have something to propose, or are you merely wasting my time and costing me a finger?" His image flickered again, this time taking a moment longer to settle once more.

"Hurry, Empress," the shaman whispered.

"I know a way into the Green Mount," she said. "A secret path through the mountains."

"The Long Stair?" he asked incredulously. "That's a myth. My men have searched for it for years. How do *you* know of it?"

"You forget that though my father was a king, my mother's kin came from less regal issue. I come from a long line of smugglers and pirates. Perhaps another day, I'll tell you the full story of how I come by this knowledge. For now, rescue me from this prison and give me your oath that you will lend your aid to see me regain my throne, and I will show your men the way."

"Bah!" Vajk shouted, casting his empty horn aside. "My Räubers will overrun the Highlanders. Your assistance is not needed."

"And what if they don't?" she countered. "No doubt, you're right and your warriors will prevail. But what if, against all odds, the clever Highlanders once more outwit your commander with their stratagems? What if they manage to stall you just long enough, so that the window of opportunity slips past and you don't reach the Tor by the Equinox?" Warming to her argument, Zsoka pressed on. "What if, Great Vajk, the unthinkable happens and your frontal assault on the Green Mount fails? Shouldn't you have a secondary plan in place? Can you afford to lose this moment? If the Gates are not opened at the Equinox, when will you have another opportunity to seize one of the Gates? Months? Years? Decades? What then? What will happen to your great plans if suddenly you lose your planned access to the Tor? The momentum of your invasion will stall, and winter will trap your men far from home. How many of your forces will die as a consequence? Your secret alliance with the Church will fail. They will turn against you and all will be lost."

Throughout her speech, he seemed to be considering her words, his brow furrowed and his eyes flicking from side to side with each thought. At her mention of the Church, however, his brows shot up in shock and he looked at her questioningly.

The image of Vajk flickered again and took on a smoky haze as his voice began to dwindle into the distance. "You fade away," he said, rising from his seat. "Very well, we'll free you."

"Swear you'll see me returned to my throne!" she demanded as his image dimmed. "Swear it, Vajk!"

"Very well, damn you!" he shouted, as from a great distance. "I'll see it done. Blood-Tooth, see her free and accompany her to the Tor. Whatever must be done, see to it!"

Zsoka's eyes swam as the image of the tent blurred and seemed to shift to the interior of her audience chamber. She could feel, once more, the biting cold of the mountain, as the sunlit pavilion faded away.

"Do you hear me?" Vajk's shouting echoed, but from a great distance now. "Blood-Tooth, see it done!"

Zsoka's vision went black and she collapsed forward, only to be caught and held up by a pair of hands that guided her gently back into her seat. The stench of burning flesh once more assaulted her senses, causing her to gag as her audience chamber swam slowly back into view.

The shaman stood before her solicitously, his shoulders stooped, all signs of vitality gone from his emaciated and sickly form. She arched back from his repugnance reflexively, holding her hands up to ward him away. With a low chuckle, the pallid man cast his watery eyes about the chamber, taking in the sight of the dead guards. His head bobbed with a slight swagger. Turning back to her, he leaned in, his hands on the arms of her throne and his fetid breath foul with rot and mucus.

"Well, Empress," he said thickly, his grinning face close enough to see the veins in his eyes. "Sounds like you and I are about to set off on an adventure."

Chapter 20

Little Johnny Corncrake
Running from the knight.
Leap and dodge
From the sword in your flight.
Whoosh and swoop!
The blade nearly bites,
But Little Johnny Corncrake
Ne'er does he fight!
Higgle, piggle, jump, and scoot!
Down comes the mighty man
Toot, toot, toot!
Wiggle, tiggle, curl, and plop!
Little Johnny Corncrake
Hop, hop, hop!

— Sudlandic nursery rhyme

574 HR - Last month of Summer
Autun, Lachland

Zach

Zach was dressed for battle, wearing a heavy coat of chain mail under his new tabard. In his new role as official bannerman to the Queen, he was no longer attached to his company, but instead wore the Queen's emblem: a golden horse rampant on a rose-colored field. He nervously stood at attention, against the wall of a ballroom that had been converted into the army's headquarters for the duration of the defense. Despite the early hour, the air was thick with smoke from the dozen or so lanterns spaced around the room, five of which sat on the map table, surrounded by the commanders. Zach's eyes stung from the smoke and his lack of sleep. He wanted nothing more than to rub them, but as the new bannerman, he dared not break his stance. The Queen, Brigadier Dixon, and Knight Commander Sir Reginald Bleiz were discussing the city's defenses in detail, while several other officers listened intently. Dixon reminded the group of the different types of Barbár warrior they would encounter that day: common warriors, mounted archers who would ride close to the wall in squadrons and harry the Lachland defenders, and, of course, the dreaded Räubers. Based on previous encounters, Dixon told the group, one could expect a ratio of around one to ten Räubers to common warriors. The big brutes generally would mix in with the assault force, providing extra muscle to help the massed warriors break through a defensive line. However, in city assaults, the Barbárs had been known to mass their Räubers and—under cover of their mounted archers—send the brutes ahead as shock troops, letting them gain an opening through which the horde could follow en masse.

"But according to our scouts, this army looks to have a smaller percentage of Räubers," Dixon reported. "It is almost as if they have committed their shock troops elsewhere."

The Queen had remained silent for much of the morning's briefing, absorbing the information and studying a charcoal drawing of the city's walls that had been laid out on the central table. As was her habit, she wore a white and rose tabard beneath chain mail, which had clearly been fitted to her. Over this she wore a sparkling breastplate with the sigil of Lachland's stamping horse engraved in its center and inlaid with white enamel. She wore the chain cowl bunched around her neck for the time being, framing her elegant, graying hair, which was pulled up in a tight bun. Instead of a crown, she wore a delicate circlet with graceful waves that perfectly suited her features, and a teardrop-shaped amethyst the size of Zach's thumb in the center. Though it was still well before dawn, she looked bright and focused; no sign of early morning fog marred her elegant features, though he knew the struggles of the past days must be wearing on her. She was every inch the monarch, showing neither frailty nor indecision.

"Do we know who their commander is?" she finally asked, once Dixon had finished.

"No, Majesty," he responded, rubbing the stubble on his chin. "Sadly, our intelligence on the Barbár commanders is thin, and the tall banner we saw yesterday with the vertical black stripes and the three human skulls is not one known to us."

"Why did we leave Kermadec at Wetheral?" the Queen muttered. "He would know."

"No doubt, Majesty," Dixon replied, his lip curling in distaste at the mention of the shadowy spymaster.

Zach's eyebrow rose at this. Among the rank and file, Francois Kermadec had a dark, sinister reputation, but Zach had assumed that to be barracks nonsense. Dixon's reaction seemed to imply that the man's notoriety had been earned. The conversation continued before he had a chance to ponder the question further.

"Sir Reginald," the Queen said, pivoting to the knight commander. "How are our supplies of arrows?"

The knight commander glanced over his shoulder to a female captain standing just behind him; Zach thought he remembered her name as Captain Maurice. While the two conferred and all attention was momentarily focused on them, Zach slipped his left hand off the banner and rubbed his tearing eyes with his thumb and forefinger.

"With the addition of the supplies Your Majesty brought," Sir Reginald said, and then paused, making mental calculations, "we should have barrels containing roughly thirty thousand arrows."

Maurice nodded agreement with his assessment.

"We'll spend most of those today," the Queen mused, "will we not?"

"I would imagine, Your Majesty," he replied, staring at the rough drawing of the city before them.

"Dispatch a vessel to the capital," the Queen said, turning to an aide. "Request additional arrows, food and medical supplies at once."

"Which brings up a question, Your Majesty," Dixon interjected. "The two barges that brought the relief troops here still lie at anchor. Shall we send them back for more troops?"

The Queen mulled this for a moment, then replied, "Should the defense of this city be successful, it is entirely possible that a relief force or counterattack may be needed quickly elsewhere along the Claws. If we send both barges back, our infantry will be stranded here in Autun."

There was a general murmur of agreement around the briefing room.

"However," the Queen continued, "it would seem prudent to send one back for more troops. They can be loaded and return within a fortnight. See that it is done."

"At once, Majesty," Dixon replied.

"If there is nothing else?" the Queen asked the group.

"There is one minor detail..." Archbishop Mormand spoke up from his place behind the Queen. He was dressed for battle, with black knee-high boots, black trousers, and a long-sleeve black shirt with a hooded chain mail coat that reached to his knees. Over this, he wore a long muslin tabard with the symbol of the five diamonds of the Church emblazoned on the chest. He had a longsword strapped to his waist and wore black gauntlets, the cuffs of which reached almost to his elbows.

"Yes, Archbishop?" the Queen turned to the priest, surprised at his interjection.

"The Church feels strongly that the defense of Lachland against these barbarians is critical." He spoke loudly, obviously accustomed to inspirational public speaking, his rich, smooth baritone carrying easily in the room. "In my retinue is a small contingent of Holy Knights of the Church. With Your Majesty's approval, I should like to add them to the city's defense."

There were murmurs of approval among the arrayed commanders.

"With Sir Reginald's permission," the cleric continued, with a magnanimous sweep of his hand over the map, "I would suggest holding my knights in reserve in the central courtyard. They are particularly adept at countering Räuber assaults. They will be at your disposal to respond to any focused attempts to breach the walls by the enemy's shock troops."

"Very good," Sir Reginald replied. "How many knights did you say?"

"A small contingent," the archbishop responded smoothly. "Thirty knights."

Sir Reginald nodded, absorbing the information and adding it to his plans for the day.

"The generosity and friendship of the Church is duly noted," the Queen said, smiling to the archbishop. "We thank you."

"I only wish I had known in advance, Majesty," the priest responded. "I would have brought entire companies of Holy Knights to this worthy cause."

"Yes," the Queen replied. "If only we had anticipated this invasion, much would be different." She held the archbishop's eyes for a moment, and Zach thought he sensed a fractional glimmer of challenge, as though something unsaid was being communicated.

The cleric lowered his head with a gracious smile. Then, speaking to the assembly, the Queen said, "Gentlemen, if there is nothing else?"

She looked around the room at her commanders, meeting each set of eyes for a moment with her own steely gaze: Sir

Reginald, Brigadier Dixon, Archbishop Mormand, Colonel Reeve—the commander of the archers, Major D'Asgoyne—commander of the medical battalion, Captain Maurice. Each met their monarch's eyes with determination.

"Then we wish you all good fortune!" Isador said, raising her voice in dismissal.

The briefing concluded, the room broke up into a buzz of smaller conversations, various hands gesturing to different points on the map. Within a few moments, the hall had emptied, leaving only the Queen, the archbishop, and Zach, who was still standing at attention behind the monarch with her banner.

"It is still an hour until dawn," the Queen said offhandedly. "Captain, go and find yourself a morning meal. We shall meet in the watchtower on the north side of the gate soon."

Snapping the flag back to its vertical position, Zach clicked his heels, pivoted sharply, and exited the building, leaving the Queen and the archbishop in quiet conference.

Stepping out into the pre-dawn chill, he broke into a light jog. He had a task to complete and time was short. The streets, alleys, and thoroughfares of Autun were all jammed with troops moving to their various posts. Zach pushed his way against the tide, heading back toward the docks and the warehouse in which his company had been quartered. He dared not be late to the Queen's side, and even at a run, it would take twenty minutes or more to reach his gear—and the particular item he sought—especially against the flow of troops headed to the city's walls.

Pushing free of a crush of soldiers, Zach found himself momentarily confused. He had crossed the city three or four times the day before, but that had been in the light of day. Now, in the pre-dawn dark, surrounded by thousands of soldiers, mules, wagons, and archers rushing to their stations, he searched the buildings and landscape for a familiar landmark. Spotting the fountain at the center of the square, he suddenly realized where he was. He had taken a wrong turn and now found himself several blocks further east than he needed to be. Taking off at a sprint, he dashed across the square, momentarily running along the edge of the fountain to avoid a laden wagon that blocked his path. Once across the square, he set off down the hill, past a row of merchants' shops. He turned left at the first intersection only to find the road completely blocked by what looked like a full battalion marching his way. Backtracking up the hill, he turned and cut through a narrow alley that ran parallel to the blocked road. The north side of the alley was lined with the backs of shops, though their service entrances were closed and their windows still dark. Along the south side were the manicured, narrow gardens of a row of modest, but well-tended homes. A large dog in one of the gardens suddenly barked at his passing, startling him. Swearing under his breath at the hound, he pressed on faster.

He emerged from the alley at a run and crashed headlong into a young messenger rushing up the hill, sending the boy sprawling. Zach helped the lad back to his feet and then scanned the area to get his bearings. The narrow road was crowded with shops offering him no vantage or familiar landmarks. Trusting his instincts, he turned right, heading downhill to an intersection, only to have to pause while a procession of three laden wagons—each pulled by two mules—trundled past. He looked at the sky, painfully aware of the precious minutes slipping past. Finally, the last wagon entered the crossing, allowing Zach to squeeze behind it and turn left onto the broad boulevard. With a quick glance, he spotted the docks off to his right and knew that his warehouse was across the street from them. Holding the banner staff vertically in his left hand, he took off running once more. It would be close. His dash across town had taken too long, and given the crush of soldiers and personnel, his return would be likewise slowed. He might just have time to get back before the Queen noted his tardiness.

He dashed along the boulevard, across another large intersection, and past the large stone building on his left that he knew was next door to the warehouse he sought. Slipping on the slick cobbles as he rounded the corner, he rushed through the building's entrance. He ran past the rows of cots to the stairs at the rear of the cavernous building, which he took two at a time, and burst breathlessly into his quarters. He tossed the banner onto his bed and quickly pulled out the chest containing his personal effects from beneath his cot. Glancing once over his shoulder to make sure he was alone, he popped the chest open. There, on top of his clothing and other personal items, lay the wicked, barbed Barbár dagger that he had collected on the battlefield the day before. He tucked it into his belt, hidden beneath the tabard he now wore, closed the chest, and turned to begin his long sprint back to the city wall. He didn't get far before he stopped suddenly at the top of the stairs, realizing that he had left the banner behind. He quickly collected it and dashed back down the stairs, across the warehouse floor, and out the door. As he rounded the corner, he spared a quick glance to the docks on his left. He had taken several steps up the hill before he paused again, his mind finally catching up with what he thought he had seen in the early morning light. Looking back over his shoulder to the end of the docks, he could just make out a group of large, shaggy figures emerging from the water and gathering at the end of the pier. Still breathing heavily, he took a few steps back down the hill to get a better view. It took several moments before his frantic mind was able to understand what he was seeing. The figures were huge, muscular, and bare-chested. Their sodden hair was much too long and shaggy for Lachlander dockworkers. Like a thunderbolt the realization hit him: *Räubers on the docks!*

He stood staring for a moment, trying to get a rough count of the enemy, then realized he was the only soldier in the area—possibly the only one for several blocks. *I have to sound an alarm somehow!* He knew it would take far too long for him to push his way through the chaos of the streets, find a commander, and communicate the danger. He stood in momentary indecision, staring at the growing mass of enemies gathering at the end of the pier. There were dozens of them, and should they move away from the docks, they could cause untold mayhem at the unprotected city's rear. *Now, Zach! Do something!*

One of the Räubers near the front of the group peeled off from the mass, and headed toward him, carrying something in his hands. As he neared the first warehouse, he tossed whatever it was through a window on the front of the building, then he pulled down a city lantern and tossed it casually through the window as well. With a massive *WHOOM*, the fire caught and quickly engulfed the downstairs of the warehouse.

Oil, Zach realized. *They're carrying kegs of oil! They plan to burn the city, starting with the docks!*

The fire solved his dilemma for him. Heedless of his own safety, Zach ran back to the warehouse in which his company was quartered. Each building near the docks was fitted with an alarm bell near its entrance, in case of fire. Since ships, docks, warehouses, and supplies were all highly flammable, every town with a dock took the danger of fire very seriously. Zach spotted the bell hanging a good ten feet high outside the door with a small set of stairs beside it, where a short hammer hung by a chain. Zach dashed up the stairs to the landing, grabbed the hammer and began laying into the bell, hoping its shrill peal might be heard over the hubbub and din of all of the soldiers in town.

As he hit the bell in rapid, hard strokes, Zach glanced over his shoulder and saw windows fly open in nearby buildings. He thought he could hear shouts of alarm being taken up too, though he couldn't be sure as his ears were filled with the harsh clangor of the bell. Catching movement over his left shoulder, he looked back to see several Räubers rushing into the street, seeking the source of the alarm. Realizing again how alone he was, he stopped hammering and cast about frantically for an escape. There were seven of the brutes running straight toward him, their shaggy hair dripping menacingly. Imagining a mad dash back into town, he gauged the distance to the corner and realized he wouldn't make it before they caught him.

The Räubers had their weapons out—axes and swords—and would be upon him in mere moments. Dashing down from the alarm landing, he turned into the warehouse, slamming the door shut and barring it behind him just as the brutes arrived. They crashed against it with enough force to bring a shower of dust down from the doorframe. *That door won't hold long,* he thought as he backed away. Frantically his mind raced through escape options. *No ground-floor windows, no back door.* He was trapped!

He searched about desperately for any weapons that might have been left behind by the troops, but saw only orderly cots, uniforms neatly folded, and chests of personal belongings tucked beneath each bed.

There was another slam on the door, and Zach was sure he had heard something crack this time. He found himself instinctively moving toward the stairs to his quarters. At least if he fought them from the top of the stairs, he could encounter them one at a time and they wouldn't be able to surround him. Turning to rush the remaining distance to the bottom of the staircase, he drew up short when one of his boots hit the telltale hollow sound of a trap door.

A cellar? It may have another way out!

And without a moment's pause, he grabbed the inset iron ring and heaved the heavy wooden door up. Tossing the banner in first, he quickly lowered himself down a ladder and closed the trap just as he heard the Räubers burst through the front door. Backing away from the ladder cautiously, he felt about in the darkened cellar, careful to not make a sound. To the left of the ladder, he felt a stack of small barrels—perhaps a dozen of them—next to a workbench. He thought he could just make out a sliver of light behind the workbench. Reaching toward it, he found a wide, rectangular shuttered window that he could just reach. Footsteps thundered about above him as the Räubers rushed to search the warehouse. He knew he only had moments before they found the trap door. As quietly as possible, he eased open the shutter, allowing the faint morning light to pour in. The window was situated just under the landing where the alarm bell was, and allowed a worm's view of the street outside the warehouse. He could see more Räubers rounding the corner, scattering and heading in all directions into the city.

The footsteps above him seemed to still for a moment and he could hear them conferring in their guttural language. He moved back beneath the ladder and listened carefully, though he could not understand their tongue. He was startled by a drip of water on his shoulder. It was followed by several drips coming in from all sides of the trap door. *They're soaking wet from swimming the lake,* he realized. *They must be standing right on top of the hatch.*

Zach looked around again, desperate for an escape. The window was too narrow for him to squeeze through and the rest of the room seemed to be storage: barrels of cooking oil, various tools and implements, and several burlap sacks piled in the far corner. After a moment, he heard the Räubers move back to the front door. Then there was the sound of something crashing. Looking out the window, he saw several pairs of booted feet exit the building and take off running in various directions. After a moment, he heard another crash, followed by the distinctive *WHOOM* of oil igniting above him, then one more Räuber hit the cobbles outside the window and took off running to his right. Despite the spreading blaze above him, Zach paused to listen for a moment at the base of the ladder to be sure they were gone. Hearing nothing but the sounds of fire, he grabbed the banner staff, climbed the ladder, and eased the hatch open, peering around the deserted warehouse.

The fire was centered by the stairs leading up to his quarters. The Räubers had apparently opted to set the blaze at the back of the building, since this warehouse abutted several other structures just behind it. From there, the fire would spread up the hill into the adjoining merchant district.

Zach pushed his way out of the cellar and immediately doubled over as searing smoke swirled around him, blinding him and producing a violent coughing fit. Falling to his hands and knees, he managed to get beneath the noxious fumes and gasp in a lungful of fresh air. He wiped his streaming eyes in an attempt to clear them and get his bearings. A loud *crack* came from the rear of the warehouse, and he knew time was short. Blinking madly, he thought he could make out the light from the front door. Staying low, he scrambled madly across the floor, dragging the banner with him, until he found himself at the broken entryway. He crouched and peeked around the doorframe cautiously. More than twenty Räubers filled the cobbled street directly in front of him. He could hear shouts and screaming down the block to his right as various buildings turned into infernos. The fire behind him was growing rapidly, its tongues already licking the top of the stairs. He could already feel the heat like a baker's oven. *The roof will catch soon,* he thought. He wouldn't have long before the whole building was ablaze and he would be forced to flee right into the waiting arms of the enemy.

A handful of civilians came hurrying down the street to try to fight the fires. Most of the Räubers in front of him turned and rushed forward to gleefully slaughter them, leaving only three of the brutes still standing in the street before the warehouse. Something massive collapsed behind him, suffusing him in a plume of scalding smoke. He blinked through the haze as his eyes filled with fresh tears. Through his suddenly distorted vision, the shape of the three Räubers seemed to shift, taking on the appearance of burly dockworkers, one holding a woman by the throat... *Loeiza!* Zach's stomach dropped, and despite the encroaching blaze and blistering air, chills ran the length of his body. With a sob, he clutched the banner staff like a spear and rushed out the door of the burning building, screaming defiance. As he leapt, the image of the men resolved back into fearsome Räubers and Loeiza's form faded into mist. The nearest barbarian looked up in surprise as the pointed tip of the banner staff ran through his neck. He fell with a gurgle. With a surprised shout, the two that remained moved toward Zach. Wrenching the staff from the body of the fallen man, Zach slashed about wildly, backing to his right and trying to keep his assailants at bay. The closest Räuber was armed with a hand axe in his left hand and a barbed short sword in his right. His eyes gleamed with a feral hunger, and Zach recoiled as the man waggled a black tongue tauntingly at him. This was made all the more horrifying by the fact that half of the brute's nose was missing, the scarred nub purple and misshapen. The massive warrior sneered at Zach's staff, the beautiful rose-colored banner now streaked with the blood of his comrade. The other man, taller and more slender than the first with an intricate tattoo that covered most of his face, circled to Zach's right, trying to cut off his escape.

Zach lashed out at the first brute's mangled nose with the tip of the staff, causing the man to lean back and bat the weapon away with a quick rise of the hand axe. Seeing an opening, the second brute rushed at him from behind. Without thinking, Zach jabbed at the tattooed face with the butt of the staff, catching his attacker in the right cheek with a solid and unexpected hit. Panicked, Zach thrust back again at the first Räuber with the pointed tip. The brute deftly brushed aside the attack with his sword and stepped forward, chopping down with the axe. Pivoting to his right, Zach managed to barely block the incoming blow with the middle of the staff, the hook of the axe head momentarily locking onto the pole. With a chopping motion, he bound the enemy's weapon to his right, despite the fearsome strength of his attacker. He spun to strike the man with the mangled nose in the back of the head with the butt end of the staff. But as he did, the spear tip happened to cross the face of the tattooed Räuber behind him, slashing a painful gash across the center of the tattoo and claiming some teeth. With a howl of pain and rage, the tattooed Räuber staggered back, his mouth a ruin of blood and his upper lip half severed and dangling to the side of his face like some grisly new beard decoration. Zach finished his spinning attack against the man with the mangled nose. A satisfying crack resounded as the butt end of the staff connected with his skull, dropping the man forward onto his face. Having purchased himself a moment to think, Zach scanned the area desperately for a possible escape. Both barbarians were shaking off their injuries and moving to stand together, staring death at him. He backed away, brandishing the spear tip as the men pressed forward, more wary of him now. Zach stumbled as his heel hit the bottom stair to the bell platform. Severed Lip lunged forward in response, but Zach flashed the spear tip at his face, almost claiming an eye. Mangled Nose circled left, pressing Zach backward up the stairs. He could feel the intense heat as flames licked the front of the building, directly behind him.

Just then, a platoon of cavalry led by Sir Reginald himself—his breastplate and helmet glistening in the morning light—burst into the intersection. The two brutes facing Zach both looked over their shoulders at the new threat. Zach could feel the skin on his neck beginning to blister, and seizing on the momentary distraction, he leapt once again from the landing, ramming the spear point into the chest of Mangled Nose. The Räuber collapsed, his mass wrenching the staff out of Zach's hands. Severed Lip screamed an inchoate response and tackled Zach to the ground. Stars exploded in his eyes as he slammed into the cobbles, the massive warrior landing on top of him. The Räuber locked a hand around Zach's throat as he raised his sword. The captain tried feebly to grab the muscled sword arm, but the Barbár simply sneered, blood dripping from the torn lip, which dangled pendulously over Zach's face. While his left hand reached for his enemy's sword arm, Zach's right slipped to his belt and drew the barbed dagger he had hidden there. With a vicious stab, he buried the hooked blade in the bicep of the brute's left arm. The Räuber recoiled his arm reflexively with a howl of pain, freeing Zach's throat and allowing him to roll his head to the right just as the sword stroke fell. Sparks flew when the blade struck the cobbles and Zach ripped the dagger free, producing another roar from the warrior. Before the man could recover, Zach plunged the dagger into his exposed ribs and twisted violently. The brute arched to his side in agony, his eyes rolling in pain. Zach stabbed again and again. With a groan, the huge warrior collapsed onto his back, freeing him.

He climbed shakily to his feet. His face felt like it might blister from the heat of the burning warehouse just feet away, but the clangor of battle sounded close on his other side.

"Captain!" a voice shouted. Zach pulled the dagger free of the body and quickly tucked it once more into his belt.

"Captain!" This time the shout was more insistent. Blinking against the smoke, Zach glanced around and saw that it was Sir Reginald that was calling to him. He raised a hand weakly in acknowledgement.

"Get out of there, man!" Bleiz shouted. "The building is going to collapse!"

Still struggling to get air through his bruised throat, Zach wrenched the banner free of Mangled Nose's corpse and staggered over to where the knight commander sat astride his horse. Still more troops were streaming into the intersection, a portion of them engaging the enemy while the rest moved to begin fighting the various fires the Räubers had started.

Sir Reginald glanced up at the alarm bell behind Zach and asked, "Was it you that sounded the alarm?"

Coughing roughly and wiping his still-streaming eyes, Zach nodded in the affirmative.

"That was well done, Captain," Bleiz said. Then, as if taking it in for the first time, the knight commander noticed the three massive enemy corpses behind Zach. His brow furrowed in disbelief as he took in the scene. Turning to his left, he gestured to a nearby lieutenant sitting astride a striking chestnut mare with flaxen mane and tail.

"Jean," Sir Reginald called. "Kindly give the captain your horse. He needs to get to the city gates quickly, and he's already had a busy morning."

Minutes later, Zach found himself clutching desperately to the horn of his saddle as he rode at a quick trot through the fountain plaza, the Queen's bloody banner aloft, shouting for soldiers to make way. Once past the plaza, he spurred his mount into a canter down the broad boulevard that led to the gates. He could hear horns blasting from the walls, and the shouts and screams of a battle already underway as he drew up behind the base of the watchtower on the north side of the gate.

Taking the stairs two at a time, he burst out of the doorway at the top to find the Queen, Brigadier Dixon, the archbishop, and two Holy Knights crowded into the small tower. All eyes turned to him, the Queen immediately taking in his ragged appearance and the blood staining the banner.

The captain snapped to attention as Dixon said only, "Report."

"Räubers at the docks, sir," he panted. "Dozens of them. They've lit fires."

The listeners all immediately looked westward out over the town to see the columns of smoke rising from the warehouses.

"Sir Reginald is dealing with it, sir," Zach finished.

A string of curses issued from the general and he slammed his fist into the stone wall.

"You are unhurt, Captain?" the Queen asked archly.

"Yes, Majesty," Zach replied, rolling his head to ease the lingering pain in his throat.

"Good," she responded, turning toward the battlefield before the city gates. "Then perhaps you would like to take your place and present our banner. The enemy should know that a monarch opposes them."

"At once, Your Majesty," Zach said, chagrined, and stepped to the forward wall. All of a sudden, the excitement and exhaustion caught up with him and his knees buckled. He steadied himself with his left hand on the parapet wall for a moment and took a deep breath, blinking away the dizziness. The Queen did not notice his stumble, but Brigadier Dixon did, looking at him with concern. With a slight reassuring grin, Zach snapped to attention and presented the bloody banner out over the walls. A cheer immediately went up from the Lachland troops when they saw the flag.

Zach felt conflicted. As a proud Lachlander, his heart soared with pride that he bore the Queen's banner. But it could not banish the dark cloud of guilt and anxiety that hovered over him as the Queen stepped up next to him—so near as to brush his arm as she waved to her soldiers, acknowledging their cheers.

Chapter 21

I follow your words, my teacher, my sitti.
I kneel with gratitude at your feet.
And there, I drink the wisdom you share
Like honeyed tea.

– Anonymous

574 HR - *Last month of summer*
Somewhere in the wildlands of northern Mardin

Yadira

Yadira and Mama were walking alone along the eastern side of the small valley in which they had camped for the night. While Yadira trusted her fellow votaries completely, she needed to process the night's vision privately with her mentor.

Still a little unstable and quite exhausted after the experience, she walked carefully, stepping over the stones shed by the hills around them.

"The overwhelming beauty…" she said, shaking her head.

"Yes, my dear," Mama agreed. "The spirit realm is filled with wonder."

"Wonder," Yadira said, latching onto the word. "Yes, that's it exactly. There was such wonder. Everywhere I looked and with each new revelation."

Mama nodded in understanding, the creases at the edge of her eyes soft this day.

"Tell me, sitti," Yadira began, "why did you not choose to drink the mixture yourself?"

Mama paused and took a deep breath before answering.

"I have sought wisdom in this way several times," she said. "And with familiarity, came confidence. I learned, as you will learn, how to penetrate deeper into the mysteries, to seek out and even speak with allies and guides, whether they were spirit or flesh."

Yadira's eyes opened wide with wonder, but she remained silent, allowing Mama to continue.

Her reaction prompted a low chuckle from the teacher. "Yes, Dira," she continued. "You will learn to farspeak. With this gift, you can enter the dreams of another, regardless of distance, and commune with them."

Yadira paused in her progress as a lesson learned in the vision bubbled up from the recesses of her mind. A chill suddenly washed over her as she grasped at the profundity of it. Her hands began to shake and she busied them by untying the braid in her hair, shaking it out and plaiting it once more.

"Oh," Mama said, sensing the change in her. "You experienced this already?"

"I saw so much," she began quietly. "At one point, I traveled northward, flying to ruins in a high mountain pass. In the great distance, I saw a pillar of green and white light. It was too bright for me to look at, but it seemed… healthy?" She looked at her teacher, confused by her own description.

"Go on," Mama encouraged her.

"I saw two men sleeping on a hillside." The words came slowly, as she sifted through the images of a dream that wanted to slip away. "One was younger, pure and good. I don't know how I could tell this, but I *felt* it. The older man..." She paused in her retelling as her brow relaxed in realization. "The Man of Iron. I saw him, Mama."

"Corvus?" Mama asked urgently. "You saw Corvus?"

"I think I did," Yadira responded hesitantly. "There was a raven on a nearby branch that saw me. Its croak directed my thoughts to the sleeping man." She shook her head to try to focus her thoughts.

"What happened next, Dira?"

"I reached out and touched him," Yadira continued, "and suddenly I was speaking with him... in his dream, perhaps?"
"What did you say? Did he speak?"

"I don't recall." She rubbed her brow, trying to ease the slight headache brought on by the memories. "I remember leaving him, his dream, and he was nodding as if he understood. Then I was back here with you at the fire... So much, too much to recall and understand."

"Yes, Dira," Mama agreed, her eyes dropping momentarily. Then with an encouraging smile that didn't quite reach her eyes, she added, "I know."

Blinking, Yadira shook her head once again and looked to her mentor. "But you still haven't answered my question," she said softly.

"No, I didn't," Mama responded, and puffed out her cheeks, seemingly wondering how to proceed. She offered Yadira a wry smile filled with the limitations a teacher feels when their student takes a huge leap. After a moment's reflection, she said in an even voice, "The spirit realm is a wondrous place, and it is filled with love and acceptance. But there *are* some malicious spirits who lurk within it, slinking amidst the shadows at the edges of perception. And malicious men who traverse that realm much as you did last night."

"Oh?" Yadira's eyes widened.

"I encountered such a man during a spirit journey, years ago," Mama said with a faraway look in her eyes. "He nearly killed me. And he set within my heart a poison that blocks me from experiencing the bliss of the spirit realm. The two times I have attempted the journey since then, the realm—once so glorious and joyful to me—has been dark, cold, and malignant. I was fortunate to return with my sanity. I fear my journeys there are at an end."

"Mama," Yadira said, after taking a moment to absorb her teacher's words. "I cannot help but feel like the sleepwalker who has crossed a great chasm on a narrow beam and only realizes the danger she faced upon waking."

"Very apt," Mama agreed with a chuckle.

"Why did you not tell me of the dangers before I journeyed?" Yadira pressed.

"In that realm," Mama replied, "to think of a thing or a place is to go there. Had I told you of the dangers, some part of your mind may have called them up, summoned them, traveled to them. By keeping you ignorant of the hazard, I protected you in the only way I could."

Yadira stood for a moment, mulling over Mama's answer. Eventually, she nodded and smiled briefly at her mentor, satisfied with her answer's simplicity and honesty. Mama responded to the rare grin with a warm embrace, and pulled the tall votary down to kiss her cheek.

"You were so brave, my dear," she whispered. "Thank you."

Then their conversation was interrupted by the sound of Argant screaming from the direction of their camp. Looking up with alarm, they saw Lupe running toward them, carrying the wailing child.

Lupe did not wait to arrive to begin shouting. "They've taken her! Riders captured Amina!"

Chapter 22

The Church of the Five, measured in the grand sweep of history, is a relative newcomer compared to the countless denominations and sects that populate Daffyd and the lands across the Mirror Sea. It was founded a mere three hundred and twenty years ago (as of this writing) by Pietist Carver Ransford, the so-called prophet of Mumsford Hollow. Though of Sudlandic origin, Ransford was captured and enslaved by a corsair raiding party as a young man, then sold to a wealthy wine merchant in Cantabria. It was there in the misery of his cell, beaten, starving, and shivering from the cold, that the first of his "visitations" was said to happen. For five nights in succession, each of the Five supposedly came to him to speak of their plans and his destiny. They intended for him to found their new Church and organize his first followers, whom he labeled "heralds." In time the Church grew in influence and political might, driven largely by the conquests of the Pentalpha Order of Brothers Militant—also called the Holy Knights—a highly trained cadre of men, deathly loyal to the Church and its hierarchy, steeped in mystery and myth.

– *Encyclopedia Daffydia,* Third Edition

Suffer not women to speak in your gathering hall, for their humors are unbalanced. Though they may at times seem wise, to heed their counsel is to venture away from the Divine Plan of the Five. Indeed, even the Blessed Mother and the Sacred Sister held silent in the presence of the Father, the Warrior, or the Master.

– "Epistle IV to the Brethren of Halstadt,"
Herald Mattias

574 HR - *Last month of summer*
Autun, Lachland

Zach

From his vantage on the north watchtower, squinting into the morning sun directly before him, Zach could survey the battlefield before the thick wooden gates. It was largely a bowman's battle at the moment. Teams of mounted Barbár archers galloped along the length of the city's walls, firing with remarkable accuracy up at the Lachland bowmen, who returned fire to nominal effect. Hitting a moving target was challenging. Hitting one at full gallop directly beneath you while remaining conscious of incoming arrows, even more so.

Massed to the city's east, outside the range of the Lachland archers were thousands of barbarians. They waited under a tall banner featuring three vertical black stripes, roughly painted. Zach could just make out the three skulls at the top of the flag. Near the banner lay the massive trunk of a felled tree, with handles affixed along it: a battering ram.

"They'll come soon," Dixon muttered, rubbing his stubbled chin, "and they'll come hard."

Just then, a deep horn sounded from somewhere in the midst of the enemy throng and, as predicted, they came. The roar of thousands of voices rose from the field, as the tall banner tilted and begin lumbering forward. Countless Barbárs swarmed past and around it, their black tongues extended, the whorls of their dark tattoos standing out against their pale skin.

As the mass of the enemy rushed toward them, the Queen stepped forward to lean against the parapet beside him, her hands clenching the stone wall with white-knuckled intensity. Brigadier Dixon suddenly grabbed the monarch by the shoulder and hauled her back into the shadows of the tower. An arrow whooshed by, narrowly missing Isador and thrumming as it stuck into the wooden ceiling of the watchtower.

"Apologies, Majesty," the general muttered.

"None required, General," the Queen replied, obviously shaken.

The enemy crashed against the walls, arrows flew in both directions, and scaling ladders—single poles studded with rungs jutting out either side—were hastily thrown up. Zach was amazed to see how quickly the massive Räuber shock troops could fly up the studded single beams. From his vantage, he counted no less than seven breaches where the elite warriors gained the wall, pitching defenders to their deaths below. The first such breach was near the watchtower on the south side of the gate. A massive brute gained the top, an arrow sticking out of his left shoulder, and proceeded to carve a path for those behind. He had killed three defenders by the time another Räuber had joined him. Within a matter of seconds, that section of wall was in chaos and more troops rapidly swelled the enemy's foothold.

With a quick command to the two Holy Knights by his side, Archbishop Mormand drew his blade and charged out of the north watchtower, across the wall atop the city gate, and rushed toward the mess at the south tower. Zach stepped to the Queen's right, positioning himself between the monarch and the crenellated wall atop the gate. Should the enemy win the south tower and fight their way across the gate wall, he and Dixon would be the last barrier protecting her. He watched as Mormand paused in the center of the wall over the gate, and whistled shrilly, catching the attention of the thirty Holy Knights in the courtyard below. With a series of quick gestures, he instructed five of them to move at once to the south tower, then he crouched down beneath the lip of the wall to bar access to the Queen's tower. The two Holy Knights he had sent ahead raced into the contested tower, as the five from below rushed toward the stairs to the right of the gate, swords drawn. Zach watched in amazement as two flashes of brilliant light emanated from the south tower in rapid succession, and soon the two knights emerged from the enclosure onto the far wall, swords flashing.

Mormand's men held their own against the Räubers, though three more of the massive brutes soon gained the wall, swelling their number to ten. The wall-top walkway was not wide enough for the Räubers to press their numerical advantage against the knights, who fought bravely side by side, holding off the enemy but not able to advance against them. Just as the five additional knights arrived in the south tower, a massive Räuber—easily the largest man Zach had ever seen—shoved aside one of his comrades and rushed the knights, sweeping one from the wall with a backhand stroke of his great axe. The remaining knight plunged his sword into the belly of the giant Barbár, who ignored the wound, grabbed the knight's head with his massive left hand, and—with a grunt—tossed the man screaming over the wall into the frothing horde below. Two of the five knights from the courtyard rushed forward to engage the brute, their swords scoring multiple hits on him. A mighty swing of his axe struck one of Mormand's men in the neck with enough force to fell a small tree in one blow. There was another blinding flash of light, and when Zach's eyes cleared, the knight was somehow unharmed and had thrust his blade to the hilt into the chest of the massive barbarian. With a defiant roar, the brute twisted his body. The knight, who still had a firm grip on the handle of his weapon, was tossed off the wall back into the city and crashed through the roof of a stable below. The brute was slowing now, and sustained several more wounds before finally succumbing to the falling blades of the Holy Knights.

On the far side of the Räubers, a small clutch of archers had rallied and were peppering them with arrows. In time, the defenders were able to reclaim the section of wall. One of the knights reached over the edge with his sword and, with an almost casual stroke, shattered the ladder, dropping two climbing barbarians back among their fellows. Seeing the breach closed and the wall regained, the archbishop sheathed his sword and rejoined the Queen in the north tower just as a massive crash sounded from below. The enemy had brought up their battering ram, some two dozen men lifting it while another score stood beside them, holding up their shields to protect the ram-bearers.

"Oil!" Dixon shouted to the soldiers on the wall above the gate, and the soldiers responded by cracking open several small barrels tucked along the inside of the wall. They waited until the ram had struck a second time, and in the pause before the attackers could change direction and back off for another stroke, the soldiers rained barrels of lamp oil and pitch down onto them. Dixon grabbed an unlit torch, stuffed it into a small brazier until it blazed, then tossed it down on their heads. For the third time that day, Zach heard the telltale *WHOOM* of oil igniting, followed by screams of agony as the smell of roasting flesh and burning hair was carried aloft in a whorl of acrid smoke.

Zach noted that the flaming oil luckily had not splashed onto the wooden gate itself. Had that happened, the day would be lost. With no ladders remaining upright and their battering ram engulfed in flame, the enemy withdrew across the field, allowing the Lachlanders to collect their wounded, restock arrows, and rotate troops, bringing up fresh men from the reserves. The Barbár wounded were left where they lay, to either crawl their way from the battlefield, or die as the archers on the walls dispatched them.

The Queen turned as Sir Reginald limped into the north tower, his armor dented in half a dozen places and covered in blood and soot. He was favoring his left leg and appeared to have a deep wound in his thigh.

"Sir Reginald!" the Queen called in alarm. "Here. Sit at once, take water." The Queen herself pulled over a camp stool for the knight commander, which he gratefully accepted and eased himself onto with a groan. Archbishop Mormand handed him a waterskin, which Bleiz accepted gratefully.

After allowing him a moment to catch his breath, Dixon said, "Report."

"Your Majesty, Brigadier," the knight commander began in a stronger voice than his weary and beaten body would have suggested him capable of, "the enemy sent some five score men to swim the lake during the night. They set fire to the docks and warehouses and sewed chaos in our rear."

"Five score!" the Queen exclaimed.

"We've seen the smoke," Dixon replied. "The young captain here told us what they had done and that you were attending to it. Were you successful in rooting them out?"

"Well," Bleiz said with a nod toward Zach, "thanks to the quick thinking of Captain Zachar, we were alerted in time and were able to engage the enemy before more damage could be done. However, the fires have spread well into the merchant quarter and now threaten the hilltops. We've roused the populace to fight the blazes, and we have put all of the saboteurs to the sword. Big bastards— Uh, I beg pardon, Your Majesty… Räubers, all. I've instructed my men to bring their bodies to the wall, where we might drop them for the enemy to see that his stratagem failed."

"We are confused," the Queen said. "How exactly did Captain Zachar alert you and your men?"

The knight commander reached a weary hand out and patted Zach's shoulder as he laughed. "He rang the damned fire bell! He was alone on the docks, surrounded by the enemy and knew he had to alert us all to the danger. Rather than hide and try to save his own skin, our valiant bannerman sounded the alarm, then proceeded to fight and kill no less than three Räubers single-handedly."

Zach blushed furiously and looked straight ahead, out over the battlefield. He had rushed back to retrieve the dagger, and it was pure ill-luck that had placed him at the docks. He was no hero, not like Bleiz or those valiant knights lying dead at the base of the wall. Fortune had smiled on him by placing Sir Reginald near enough to hear the alarm and bring a platoon of cavalry to bear. His eyes moistened at the thought of the dark deed he was considering.

"Captain," the Queen said, turning toward him. He snapped to attention and pivoted crisply to face her. "You said nothing of these heroics upon your arrival here."

"Not heroics, Majesty," he responded with a professional soldier's demeanor. "I foolishly left something in the barracks, and had dashed back to fetch it when I happened to see the enemy emerge from the lake and begin to set the fires. Ringing the bell seemed to be the logical thing to do. Sir Reginald arrived moments later with a platoon of cavalry and bravely engaged the enemy."

"We will speak more of this, Captain," the Queen said slowly, a new appreciation for Zach seeming to dawn in her eyes. She turned to Dixon. "Brigadier, what do you estimate the enemy's casualties to be from the morning's exercise?"

"Hard to say with any certainty, Your Majesty," the general said, looking out over the smoldering wreckage of the battlefield. "A significant number, to be sure. I would estimate that the enemy has lost another thousand fighting men, dead and wounded. If not a thousand, at least several hundred."

"Not enough to break his will," the Queen commented. "He will return for more?"

"Undoubtedly, Majesty," the general said, and exchanged a dour glance with Sir Reginald. "Though I imagine we will have a bit of a lull in the fighting for the next hour or more, while their leader plots this afternoon's effort."

"Very good. We shall retire from the wall for a brief rest," the Queen announced. "Please alert us the moment the enemy begins to gather for another assault. And Sir Reginald, get those wounds looked at, at once."

"Yes, Majesty," the knight commander responded wearily.

As the Queen left, Zach retired her banner, propping it against the interior wall and flexing his hands to ease their cramps. Sir Reginald stood with a grimace. Though still an energetic man in his prime, the knight commander's exhaustion and pain made him suddenly look ancient. Clutching Zach's arm for support as he walked past, he then patted the captain's shoulder in a friendly manner before making his own way gingerly toward the stairs.

"You're certainly full of surprises, aren't you, Captain?"

Zach hadn't realized that he was now alone with the archbishop until that moment. With a sigh, he relaxed for the first time in hours and collapsed onto the now-vacant camp stool.

"We all do our part," Zach replied wearily, not sure what honorific to use for the cleric. The Church of the Five did not have a strong presence in Lachland as yet, though its influence was growing. He really didn't know much about its teachings either, other than in broad strokes.

"What was it?" the archbishop asked after a moment.

"I'm sorry?" Zach asked, confused.

"What was it that you forgot in the barracks that was so important?"

"Oh." Zach rubbed his face wearily with his hand while thinking quickly. "My wife gave me a charm before we shipped out. It was supposed to bring me luck and protection."

"A pagan trifle?" The cleric grinned in disbelief. "You were nearly killed fetching a pagan trifle?"

"That's one way to look at it," Zach said with a defiant tone, standing and collecting the banner. He leaned close to the cleric. "Or, you could say that it worked, and that I was lucky to spot the enemy early in their efforts. I'd say that was luck and protection. After all, isn't Feryn's hand evident in all examples of good fortune?"

The archbishop's eyes glinted with suppressed outrage at his effrontery, but Zach didn't care. It was not yet midday and he was already spent.

"As we know from the early epistolaries," Mormand responded with well-practiced ease, "the blessings and lessons of Feryn are often misconstrued by the simple and unlearned as luck. Any educated explication yields the inarguable conclusion that Feryn's teachings are rather on obedience and humility."

"And that," Zach said, raising a hand in exasperation to forestall any further discussion, "is precisely why I consider myself a simple man. Five protect me from such convoluted reasoning that can turn a blue sky red!" He knew he should be more diplomatic, but didn't care. He was exhausted, and the last thing in the world he had energy for was entering into a theological dispute with this arrogant and unsettling churchman. He turned and descended the stairs, leaving the archbishop alone atop the tower.

Chapter 22

The Glenfolk see themselves as the "Defenders of the Green Mount." It is, after all, their capital city and population center that is closest to the entrance to the lands of the Green Mount at Eagle's Gate. The White Cleft think of themselves as "The Miners," delving deeply into the northern and eastern border mountains and providing all of the Green Mount with quality ores and quarried stone, as well as finished ironworks of high quality. Indeed, it is said that the smiths of the White Cleft are as clever and skilled as the dwarven metalworkers of myth. The inhabitants of the High Valley provide unparalleled woolen textiles, dairy and farm goods, and the highest quality wooden furniture. They are widely viewed as the "keepers of the old ways." But it is to the Midlands that one must look for a clear image of prosperous, cosmopolitan Highlanders. Stilling, the capital, is the largest city in all the Green Mount, and its citizens enjoy a degree of abundance unrivaled anywhere else in the Highlands.

– *Encyclopedia Daffydia,* Third Edition

574 HR - *Last month of summer*
Stilling, Midlands region of the Green Mount

Ligulf

Yazid and Ligulf had ridden hard for four days. As the sun took on the red tint of dusk on the fourth, they finally crested the rise that overlooked the picturesque town of Stilling, the lake town that was the seat of Lady Donella, Matriarch of the Midlands. Situated at the confluence of two rivers, the Duine and the Bhean, Stilling boasted the largest population of any town or village in all of the Green Mount, and it was easy to see why. Sheltered to the northwest by the rocky peak of An Teallach, the walled town was situated on the banks of Lach Stár, and was surrounded by miles of arable land, plenty of fresh water, and a relatively central location for trade with the rest of Green Mount. From their position on the hill, Ligulf could see the deep cut in the land where the great Gomul River rushed southeast from Lach Stár to the Glenfolk town of Esper, where his father and brother had fought the Barbárs five years earlier. He paused to marvel at the vast fields planted with green feathery barley that pulsed and waved with the winds of the imminent storm. They had been racing against the approaching clouds since spotting them on the horizon earlier that morning, hoping to reach their destination before the rain.

"We've just made it in time, I think," Yazid said, pointing to the gray curtains of rain fast approaching from the northwest.

Li agreed and spurred his mount down the final hill toward the rough timber gate on the western edge of town. Stilling's wooden wall rose out of a steep earthen palisade that surrounded the settlement, though the prosperity of the town had caused it to long ago outgrow its boundaries, and now hundreds of homes, farms, and shops clustered around the outside perimeter too. To Ligulf's eye, the busy settlement outside just the western gate had several times the population of Dóchas.

They passed farmhouses, craft workshops, and two graveyards filled with carved stone markers as they approached the Westside Market. A gaggle of children dashed around their horses, shrieking in delight and answering outrage as they chased one another. Merchants hawked their wares loudly, holding up examples from their various stalls. He and Yazid were forced to pause in their progress as a farmer led a herd of some two dozen shaggy cattle through the lane, their bells and lowing adding to the aural chaos of the busy exchange. Ligulf chuckled to himself as an unwary customer of one of the shops turned blindly from concluding his purchase and came face-to-face with one of the brown, scraggly beasts. While the man was in no real danger of being gored by the cow's long horns, it clearly gave him a start and he scrambled away from the creature, his feet slipping in the muddy lane and causing him to drop the bundle he had just purchased. Before he could react, the slow-moving, docile beast pushed on, stepping on the bundle and grinding it into the mud. There was much angry shouting as the man berated the farmer and tried to demand a replacement for his purchase from the befuddled shopkeeper.

As they continued guiding their horses slowly through the throngs massed in the narrow lane, Ligulf noted the approaching cloud front with some anxiety. They soon reached a broad intersection near the city wall, and the breadth of the avenue there meant that the density of the crowd thinned significantly, allowing them to move at a less guarded pace. Finally free of the congestion in the Westside Market, the two rode through the unguarded gate and into the town of Stilling proper just as the first drops of icy rain started to sting their cheeks. Donella's great house was the largest building in town and was easily spotted from any vantage as it was perched atop a hill on Stilling's northern edge, right against the wall and overlooking the lach. It was a long rectangular log structure with a deep, thatched roof and a generous wooden balcony that stretched around the entire building. From the outside, one might think it a two-story structure, but in reality, it was a large communal hall with a high vaulted ceiling and a clerestory of windows around the top, tucked just under the thatch. Smoke could be seen escaping the central vent in the roof ,and as they rode nearer, they could see dozens of men and women arriving and entering through its ornate wooden doors.

They settled their horses in a nearby stable just as the storm hit in earnest, immediately transforming the packed dirt lanes into rivers of mud, and washing away the gathered refuse and waste. Passersby still doggedly ran their errands, dashing past the stable doors and leaping the flowing streams, their heads bowed beneath the rain. Li carefully wrapped his cittern in an oiled canvas, slung his saddle bags over his shoulder, pulled his traveling cap lower on his head, and—with a quick nod to his companion—dashed up the hill to the great house. Yazid was not a small man, standing a full head taller than Li and several stone heavier. Yet, despite that, he quickly crossed the distance from the stable to the great house, nimbly hopping over quick-forming streams, leaping a bench in an outdoor seating area, and somehow arriving at the door before Li. They paused under the overhanging eaves to shake off the water and straighten their apparel before pushing open the heavy doors and entering the dim, smoky interior.

It seemed that some celebration was about to start, as rows of trestle tables had been set up all along the length of the hall, and clusters of attendees were talking and laughing with full cups already in hand. The men were attired in formal great kilts and ruffled shirts with bloused sleeves that were open at the neck, decorative clan pins fastening the plaid tossed over their shoulders. The women were wearing floor-length gowns of brocade or plaid, open at the neck to reveal jewelry of wrought silver and gold. Their hair fell in cascading ringlets about their shoulders in what Li assumed was the local fashion. Looking at his own humble attire, and the Aslene robe Yazid wore, Li couldn't help but feel woefully underdressed. Huge, shaggy wolfhounds circulated among the guests, sniffing in vain among the rushes on the floor for any dropped morsels of food. A dais stretched the width of the building on the far side of the hall, and on it sat two empty curule chairs with deep-green upholstery and a small table between them.

The two travelers stepped off to the side as more guests pushed past them, rushing in out of the rain. A shout of welcome resounded from those gathered as a woman dressed entirely in buff leathers entered, removed a broad-brimmed hat with a long pheasant feather stuck in it, and shook out her long hair. She was a fit and attractive woman that Li guessed was nearing forty as her flowing dark locks showed silver streaks. The wrinkles around her eyes suggested a merry spirit. Her frontier clothing was in stark contrast to the rural finery on display in the rest of the hall, but no one seemed to notice or care as she reached into her large duffle and produced a tabor and pipe which she held triumphantly over her head, earning another cheer from the guests. The woman laughed and pointed at someone in the crowd, then jogged toward a four-foot-wide square platform, some three feet tall, on the left side of the hall. With an athletic leap, she mounted it and turned to face the crowd, who were gathering around expectantly.

"Now, now, mates!" she called out in a strong voice, low-pitched for a woman. "Who has a song they'd like to hear before the lord and lady arrive?"

Li looked questioningly at Yazid. "*Lord* and lady?" he asked. "Did Donella take a husband after all these years a widow?"

Yazid lifted his hands in a shrug, as the noise in the hall suddenly made speaking impossible. Guests were calling out their song requests, shouting over one another to be heard. The woman lifted her hands in a placating gesture to calm them, as she chuckled to herself and readied to play her drum.

"Sounds like you want 'Luce the Lovely,' do you?" she asked the crowd, and it responded with a roar, as cups were refilled and people pressed closer to the stage to hear their singer. Li slowly unwrapped his cittern from its waterproof covering as the woman began the bawdy tune. He was amazed at the her command of the room, the ease and charm she exuded as she paced the stage, gracing one audience member with a wink, another with a shared smile, and still another with an encouraging nod as she launched into the song.

See silly old Domnhall, his head shaped quite conal,
The sleepy-eyed man from G'dair;
But these were the days when his half-lidded gaze

Had fallen on one that was fair, so fair,
He gazed upon one that was fair.

Oh, she was the one, though she tipped twenty stone
Yet her boils were lancéd and clean.
And in his dull eyes, she was just the right size,
Though she stood with a one-legged lean, a lean,
She stood with a one-legged lean.
O Luce, Luce, she's brazen and loose,
She's scarred, she's dirty, and dresses in puce.
With unusual allure, she seems bright and pure,
To the sleepy-eyed man from G'Dair, G'Dair,
The sleepy-eyed man from G'Dair.
By gum and by gavver he swore he would have her,
Determined to be her man.
For Luce was a find, slightly out of her mind
Yet her smell weren't too bad with a fan, a fan,
Her smell weren't too bad with a fan!

For hours and hours, he picked out flowers,
From bramble, cornstalk, and hay.
He arranged them just so, for his pure, lovely doe,
He knew today was the day, the day,
He knew that today was the day.
O Luce, Luce, she's brazen and loose,
She's scarred, she's dirty, and dresses in puce.
With unusual allure, she seems bright and pure,
To the sleepy-eyed man from G'Dair, G'Dair,
The sleepy-eyed man from G'Dair.
He had eaten his porridge, for to gather his courage,
and straightened his doublet and trews.
With a roguish stare, he tidied his hair,
And gamboled along to see Luce, his Luce,
He gamboled along to see Luce.

Approaching her door, he waved to a whore
Who worked from the rooms that they shared.

For Luce was a strumpet but played on the trumpet
Of the heart of this man from G'dair, G'dair,
On the heart of this man from G'dair.
O Luce, Luce, she's brazen and loose,
She's scarred, she's dirty, and dresses in puce.
With unusual allure, she seems bright and pure,
To the sleepy-eyed man from G'Dair, G'Dair,
The sleepy-eyed man from G'Dair.
She laughed at his callin', not kenning he's falling
In love with a girl who's no looker.
With a drunken laugh, she accepted the chaff,
A bouquet from a fool to a hooker, O Ho!
A bouquet from a fool to a hooker!

But Domnhall was certain he'd pull back the curtain
That blocked her from seeing his love.
He pulled out a ring, thinking it was the thing,
To melt ice from the heart of his dove, his dove,
To melt ice from the heart of his dove!
O Luce, Luce, she's brazen and loose,
She's scarred, she's dirty, and dresses in puce.
With unusual allure, she seems bright and pure,
To the sleepy-eyed man from G'Dair, G'Dair,
The sleepy-eyed man from G'Dair.
Amazed by the trinket, she started and thinkéd,
Of married life, honest and fair,
To this cone-headed swain, from over the plain,
The sleepy-eyed man from G'Dair, G'Dair,
The sleepy-eyed man from G'Dair.

With cuddling and coo-age, tho her breath smelled of sewage,
They were wed, and made an odd pair.
The garish old strumpet, who played on the trumpet
Of the heart of the man from G'Dair, G'Dair,
Of the heart of the man from G'Dair!

Ligulf watched the performance with a mixture of feelings. He was shocked at the bawdy words of the song in this well-dressed gathering, but at the same time he was amazed at the singer's obvious popularity with the crowd and her command of the audience. They sang along loudly with each refrain, pounding the tables in rhythm and laughing raucously at each humorous verse, dancing along and spilling their drinks. This was the way crowds in taverns acted once they had drunk enough to become carefree and rowdy, not at all what he expected in the great hall of the ruler of the Midlands—especially before drink and a meal had loosened them up. Li watched as ring-bedecked hands refilled goblets and loud laughter resounded as readily as might happen in any humble inn after a festival day.

He stared at the singer, and marveled at her energy—her charm and the rich quality of her voice—and at the adoration heaped upon her by the assemblage. As the song reached its final high note, the crowd erupted in laughter and cheers, and coins were tossed onto the stage. From somewhere in the crowd, the singer was handed a full horn of ale, which she drained on the spot, earning more appreciative cheers. Wiping her mouth with her sleeve, she glanced around the hall, smiling at the crowd, and spotted him at the back of the audience, clutching his cittern. Her eyebrows shot up in surprise and she beckoned him to join her on stage, waving at the crowd to part.

"We have one on the hook!" she shouted to the crowd, pointing at Li. "Come up, come up!"

The familiar flush of anticipation colored his cheeks. No matter how often he performed, or in what setting, he always felt the flutter in his stomach just before he began. Li nodded sheepishly and the crowd parted, hands clapping him on the back, urging him forward. The woman reached a hand down to help Li up onto the platform, which he took. Still holding his hand, even after he had reached the stage, the woman shook it with a welcoming smile.

"Rhona," she said.

"Ligulf," he said with a shy grin.

"What brings you to Stilling, Master Ligulf?" she asked, leaning in close to be heard over the din of the crowd.

"We're here to see Lady Donella," he answered.

"Right," she said with a nod. "She'll not arrive for a time. She and Aengus were out hunting and got caught in the storm."

"Aengus?"

"Her husband," Rhona responded with an indulgent smile. "The new Lord of the Midlands."

"Oh, right." Li nodded, looking around at the audience who were beginning to chant and bang on the tables, demanding more music.

"Looks like you're up, Ligulf," she said, and gestured theatrically for him to take the stage.

He stepped to the front of the platform, tuning his cittern as Rhona gestured to the crowd to settle down. Then he gave his instrument a strum and, satisfied with the sound, launched into a well-known and stirring song about the beauty of the Highlands. With a nod of recognition, Rhona pulled her pipe from her belt and began playing a soaring descant as Li sang, his clear tenor voice echoing in the great hall. The audience fell silent as Li's performance swept them up rocky slopes, over raging rivers, through forested glens, and to bold promontories bravely facing the cruel northern seas. As the last notes of his cittern rang in the quieted hall, Rhona lowered her pipe and gave him an appreciative smile. The crowd erupted in cheers, hammering the trestle tables almost to the point of collapse in fierce approbation. Some even had tears in their eyes. Li smiled, accepting their applause humbly. While he had regularly been the featured performer at the festivals in and around Dóchas, this was by far the grandest assemblage he had ever sung for. He caught Yazid's eye. The burly man smiled and gave him an encouraging wink.

Li turned to Rhona. "Your turn, I guess," he said with a grin.

"Let's do one together!" Rhona shouted over the noise. "Do you know 'The Stony Road'?"

He nodded and strummed a few chords in practice. Before long, the two were performing together like old mates, giving and taking cues seamlessly for solos, leads, harmonies, and tempo changes. Li's clever fingers alternated between strumming his instrument and picking out intricate melodies, while Rhona energetically accompanied their efforts on her drum or pipe. They played song after song, carrying their rapt audience with them as they moved from playful tavern songs to sensitive love songs, and from soaring, heroic ballads to more bawdy content and clever instrumental melodies. They had just finished a beautiful love song—Li improvising a heartbreaking tenor harmony to Rhona's sultry alto lead—when the sharp tattoo of two drums from behind the dais interrupted the crowd's applause. All eyes turned to the end of the hall to see the lord and lady make their entrance and sit in the matching chairs on the platform. Lady Donella was an elegant middle-aged woman with curly silvered hair piled atop her head and pinned in place with a golden brooch. She was dressed in a flowing gown of forest green, trimmed in yellow and brown. At the open neck of her gown, she wore a stunning necklace of swirling gold, with minute triskeles cleverly worked into the swirls; in the center was an emerald the size of Li's thumbnail. She bore a beneficent smile that only enhanced her elegance. Lord Aengus, her husband, was shorter than her by several inches. He had a neatly trimmed black beard, silver on the chin, which framed a ruddy complexion under thick, black brows. He seemed to scowl as he scanned the room, as though silently counting just how much this festivity was costing him. His hands were bedecked with jeweled rings and he wore a long, fur-trimmed cloak over his kilt, boots, and a doublet of rich brocade. His graying hair was carefully coifed, despite the fact that the couple had just returned from a hunt.

Li felt a hand on his shoulder as Rhona whispered in his ear, "I guess we're finished here."

He turned to her and shook her hand. "That was great! What fun! You're amazing!" he said, in a rush.

She laughed and patted his shoulder, then beckoned for him to follow as she hopped down off the stage, crossed to the center of the hall, and walked directly to the edge of the dais on which sat the Lord and Lady of the Midlands—both wearing pleasant smiles at her approach.

"Cousin," Lady Donella remarked. "As always, our people love you and your talents."

"My lady, my lord," Rhona said with a formality that seemed uncharacteristic, "please allow me to present Ligulf of the High Valley."

Ligulf stepped forward, clutching his cittern, and bowed formally.

"Ligulf," the lady said, her brow furrowing. "That name is familiar to me. Are you kin to Corvus Corax?"

"I am, Lady," Li responded. "I am his son."

Aengus' brow furrowed, his forced smile melting away as his chin lowered toward his chest. Donella's eyebrows shot up and her mouth formed a smiling "O" before she said, "Welcome, Ligulf! Twice welcome to our fire! What brings you to the Midlands?"

Looking over his shoulder, Ligulf gestured to Yazid to join him. There were whispers in the crowd as the burly, robed Aslene stepped up beside him.

"My lady, my lord," Yazid said in his richly accented baritone, "I am afraid we bring sad tidings. Corvus has sent us to seek your aid."

The lady and lord exchanged a glance, then with a smile for the sake of those gathered, she said, "Let us speak of this over food. You must both be hungry after your journey, yes?"

"It would be churlish of us to not share meat and drink at your table," Li responded with a slight inclination of his head.

"Excellent," Donella responded. Then, raising her voice for all in the room, she called, "Let the feast begin at once!"

Chapter 23

The River Gomul flowed directly between Stilling and Esper, and though commerce on the river was difficult due to the quick current, trade between the towns was robust. Shipments from Stilling flowed rapidly downriver on lightweight river barges, which were then hooked to teams of mules by long ropes on well-worn paths that paralleled the Gomul on either side, and towed back upriver laden with trade goods. This strong trading relationship was one of the keystones for the Peace of the Valley accord. Agricultural goods, textiles, and craftwork flowed downriver, while timber, fish, and artisan goods were shipped upriver. The accord had been forged generations past between the four regions of the Green Mount: the Glenfolk, the White Cleft, the Midlands, and the High Valley. It was this accord that provided for open trade, movement, and mutual defense among all the communities of the Highlands.

– *Encyclopedia Daffydia,* Third Edition

574 HR - *Last month of summer*
Glenfolk region of the Green Mount

Corvus

It was late afternoon as Cailean and Corvus reined in at the turnoff to the walled town of Esper, royal seat of King Mannon of the Glenfolk. Perched on a long, narrow island near a bend in the River Gomul, Esper was highly defensible. The river was fast running on the north side and wide and deep on the south. The island was tear-drop shaped, with the wide, round end facing northwest and its narrow tip pointing downstream to the southeast. The town filled the entire island and, over the years, its timber fortifications had been replaced with a tall stone wall. A narrow causeway crossed the south fork of the Gomul and connected the town to the main road, which ran along the base of the foothills on the southern edge of the great valley. Two stone towers framed the town gate, which boasted a massive iron portcullis with thick oaken gates behind it. Another tower stood on the southeastern tip of the town, and a fourth—the tallest—was on the northernmost edge of town, looking over the fast-flowing rapids.

Corvus paused at the edge of the causeway to take a small bite of the bitter root that Shanna had given him. It dried his mouth like cotton batting, but eased the ache in his leg. It made him somewhat woozy, though, as if he'd had a few tankards of ale—not drunk, just a little unsteady. He wouldn't be able to eat any before battle. He took a long draught from his waterskin as his practiced eye scanned the fortifications of Esper, as well as the banks of the river around the town, looking for any faults or weaknesses that an enemy might exploit. It had been five years since he had last visited and it looked like improvements had been made to the walls and towers in that time. The towers, which had always been open topped, were now enclosed with pointed wooden roofs—from which the green and gold banners of the Glenfolk flapped frantically in the swelling wind. In addition to the tower enclosures, it looked to Corvus as if the battlements had been widened along the town walls facing the causeway. The timber walls had been replaced with stone fortifications with a crenellated top. Corvus nodded approvingly.

Though much of the stonework was granite that had been quarried nearby, he noted several areas where the gray walls were dotted with black basalt stonework from the ruins of Eagle's Mount. King Mannon had wisely made use of the tumbled stonework from that fortress when improving his town's fortifications.

During the last Barbár attack, Esper's already formidable timber defenses and inaccessibility had proven too challenging for the fast-moving barbarians, whose light raiding force was not equipped for a siege. The enemy had simply bypassed the town, pillaging the smaller villages and settlements in the hills to the south, before being brought to bear by Corvus' fyrd and the armies of the White Cleft and the Glenfolk. Now he feared that enemy would return again in greater numbers to the Green Mount, and if Corvus was unsuccessful at stopping them at Eagle's Gate, Esper's defenses would be tested as they hadn't been since the days of the Mardish invasion. These wider stone battlements would allow more archers to line the walls and pepper any invaders on the causeway, while the tower enclosures would allow guards to remain vigilant regardless of the weather. *Good,* thought Corvus. *Mannon has not been idle these five years.*

He nodded to his son as the first drops of rain fell, and spurred his mount across the narrow stone bridge. Two guards stepped forward casually from the gate as the riders approached. A broad smile broke across the face of the older of the two as he recognized Corvus. The guard's face bore pox scars from childhood, and was covered with a short, stubbly beard that had at one time been red, but was now mostly gone to gray.

"Well, now," he said with hands on his hips, "if it isn't the Raven himself!"

"Alasdair," Corvus responded, his grin matching the guard's. "What, they have you on gate duty? Who did you insult?"

"Ach, now," the older guard replied with a chuckle. "It's me nephew's handfast day, and I said I'd cover his shift for him." Pointing over his shoulder with his thumb, he continued, "You've arrived just ahead of the storm, I see."

"In more ways than one," Cailean interjected with a meaningful expression. The light tone between them shifted, and Alasdair's brow creased in concern. He looked from Cailean to Corvus. Seeing confirmation in the Raven's eyes, he stepped back to clear their path.

"Right," he said. "Sounds like ye've important fish to fry. But be warned," he said, placing a hand lightly on Corvus' stirrup as he passed. "The King is not well, and the line's in doubt."

A swirl of wet wind prevented any further discussion, so Corvus nodded his thanks for the warning and the two rode into town to find shelter.

Within a half an hour, they were climbing the steps of the long house, King Mannon's residence and seat of power. Corvus climbed the stairs slowly, as the aches and pains of six long days in the saddle made themselves known, and combined with the dread of what he feared he would find within. The root was dampening the discomfort, but regardless, he was feeling his fifty-two years. Two guards, one male and one female, with features so similar that they had to be siblings, were sheltering from the rain under the eaves. With matching ginger hair and dark eyes, they each looked to be no more than eighteen or nineteen summers, though they carried themselves well. The female one raised a hand to stop Cailean, who had rushed ahead to open the door for his father.

"Corvus and Cailean from the High Valley to see His Majesty," Cailean said.

"He's takin' nae visitors today," she said curtly.

"He'll see us," Corvus said with authority, stepping onto the landing. "And right away."

"Sorry," the young man interjected, stepping forward. "Nae visitors today, d'ye ken?"

"You'll open that door, lad," Corvus said, his voice growing quiet with menace, "without another word. There's an enemy army approaching, and I've ridden six long days from the High Valley to speak to the King."

"Look, old man," the female guard said with a saucy attitude and a thick Glenfolk accent. "We have strict orders—"

"Do you no' know who this is?" Cailean interrupted her, adopting the thick dialect common among the Glenfolk. Corvus smiled inwardly. His son's childhood among the rank and file of the soldiers had taught him more than swordplay. "This is the Raven himself! Now, we dinna ride all the way here for a pleasure trip and a friendly bandy. You're aboot to be attacked, and if we canna see the King, then the baw's on the slates. Now move oot th'way, before ye find yerself in a muckle o' woe!"

The two guards exchanged glances, seemingly as much perplexed by Cailean's command of the vernacular as by the fact that the older man before them was the legendary Raven. With a slight bow, they stepped back as one. Each pulled one of the great doors open, revealing the dim interior of the building.

The two travelers stepped in out of the growing storm and removed their wet cloaks and hats.

"That was effective," Corvus said, nodding in appreciation to Cailean. "Good blether, that."

Cailean's blue eyes sparkled at his father's uncustomary use of slang. "Aye, good blether," he responded with a chuckle before dropping his voice to a whisper. "Speakin' of blether, what did the gate guard mean by 'the line is in doubt'?"

"I suspect," Corvus said quietly, "there's some question as to the succession, should Mannon's health fail. He has no children."

"Timing is poor for that," Cai said.

"Aye 'tis," his father responded gravely.

"Who is it there by the door?" called an old woman's voice from the shadows at the far end of the long hall.

"Corvus, the Raven," Cailean responded in a clear voice, "and his son, Cailean."

Murmurs and discussion followed the announcement. Corvus thought he could make out three voices, but was unable to discern what was said. There seemed to be some disagreement prompted by their arrival, but after a few moments, the woman's voice spoke once again.

"My lord the King will see you."

Corvus exchanged a glance with his son, then the two of them walked the length of the hall together. He could hear the sound of a harp being tuned, and soft conversation somewhere. As their eyes adjusted to the dim light, he could see the others in the hall. He spotted the harpist by the wall, and, across from her, two scribes huddled in quiet discussion near a small table strewn with parchments. The far end of the hall was partitioned off from the rest of the building by an ornately carved wooden screen with a door on the right-hand side. An old woman, presumably the King's physician and the one who had spoken, was standing in the doorway holding a bowl of incense. The air was thick with smoke and her eyes were moist and red from it. As they approached, she raised a hand to stop their progress.

"The King is dying," she said in a quiet, flat tone. "His nephew Kevin is attending him, despite my urging to the contrary. You mustn't agitate him."

"Kevin…" Corvus searched his memory. "From the Cleft?"

"Aye," she answered in a conspiratorial tone, rolling her eyes. "The King has no heir, and suddenly Kevin shows up after seven years to show his *devotion*." The last word was whispered with obvious sarcasm.

"Well," Corvus said, acknowledging the information. "Sadly, I dinna bring good news, but His Majesty has to hear it, nonetheless."

With an air of resignation, the old woman stepped out of the doorway and gestured for them to enter.

The chamber beyond the screen was a large bedroom, lit by a handful of candles and a small oil lamp by the bedside. The bed was a grand four-poster with linen drapes hung on all sides. There was a lit brazier near the foot of the bed fighting the unseasonable chill. A figure that Corvus assumed to be Kevin sat hunched by the bedside, holding a cup solicitously. The air was thick with incense and the pungency of sweat, soiled sheets, and the unmistakable sweetness of rot, which combined to make the spacious room feel claustrophobic. The smells swept Corvus back to his last days caring for Greer, knowing that her end was fast approaching. He instinctively placed a hand on Cailean's shoulder as the memory washed over him and he could once again see her dear face, smiling weakly.

"Is that Corvus?" a frail voice called from the bed, though its owner was hidden by the linen drapes.

"Aye, my friend," Corvus responded, coming out of his reverie.

Kevin looked up sharply at the surprising familiarity with which the King was being addressed, though he said nothing. The man had a sharp face, narrow nose, and small, black eyes that flashed from Corvus to Cailean and back.

"Come closer," the King commanded feebly.

Kevin stood at Corvus' approach, inclining his head slightly as he stepped aside. Cailean noted that the young man did not leave the room to give them privacy, instead choosing to tend to the coals in the brazier at the foot of the bed. Mannon's once proud eyes were sunken and weary, and the pallor of his skin spoke of the gravity of his illness. His breathing was quick and shallow and his eyes winced with intermittent moments of pain. There was a blood stain on the pillow near his mouth. Corvus' heart sank at the sight of the once robust monarch, now so reduced.

"Mannon, you old warhorse," Corvus said affectionately as he took the King's hand and sat in Kevin's chair. "I have to say, you've looked better."

The King wheezed a laugh at that, which grew into a fit of wet coughs that wracked his frail frame. The two of them helped Mannon sit up during his fit, and Cailean dutifully fetched the cup from Kevin, offering it to the stricken monarch. His fit passed and the King sipped gratefully, leaving a trace of blood on the lip of the cup. After he handed it back to Cailean, he sank, exhausted, back into his pillows.

"What news, Raven?" he said, his lips barely moving.

"I'm afraid I bring ill tidings, old friend," Corvus said softly. "The Barbárs are returning to the Gate."

The dying man's eyes filled with alarm and he struggled vainly to sit up, but Corvus placed a restraining hand on his shoulder.

"We'll rally the troops…" the King began, but was interrupted by another coughing fit.

"Aye, we will," Corvus reassured him. "Though it will be a grave blow to our cause not to have the stalwart Mannon on the field, we'll muddle through if you'll give the order to raise the army."

Mannon grasped his friend's hand urgently. "Will you command?"

"I will," Corvus said thoughtfully.

"Good, good," the King said, sinking back deeper into his pillows with a tear of exhaustion in his eye.

"Mannon…" Corvus leaned forward to whisper in his friend's ear. "Who will lead the troops of the Glenfolk? I need to know who I'll be dealing with. Is it Kevin, then?"

"Kevin?!" the King barked in a surprisingly loud voice. "By Ilian's Teeth, I wouldna trust him to empty my bed pan!"

Cailean spared a quick glance over his shoulder to see Kevin's lips purse in suppressed rage. The hatchet-faced man bowed and made an ungraceful exit, pushing roughly past the woman at the door.

"No, no," the King continued agitatedly. "You must command, Corvus. I'll trust no man to lead the Glenfolk army but you." Mannon brought his trembling hands together and fumbled with a ring. He struggled for a moment before finally getting it past his swollen knuckle with a grimace. He handed the ring to Corvus meaningfully. Corvus bowed his head, acknowledging the honor being afforded him.

"I will command our overall efforts, my friend," Corvus said in a placating tone. "But I need a point of contact for the Glenfolk troops. I'll have my hands full overseeing all the armies. Someone's got to command your lot."

"Fair point," the King said, nodding slightly and closing his eyes.

"Would Murray be up to it, d'ye think?" Corvus asked.

"Nae, not Murray," Mannon replied without opening his eyes. "Too vain… Impulsive."

"What of Harris, or Willoughby?" Corvus pressed, squeezing the King's hand with urgency.

The King's lips moved slightly but no words came out. His eyelids fluttered as he drifted suddenly into a deep sleep.

Corvus lowered his head and sighed in resignation. *It canna be Harris,* he thought. *Too slow of mind, though stout of heart. And Willoughby has the gout, something fierce. Nae, it must be someone young and inspiring. These people need a hero to follow.*

The storm howled against the shuttered windows of the long house, and the two Highlanders remained by the bedside of the stricken monarch as the shadows lengthened. Finally, with a deep breath that seemed to acknowledge a great weight, Corvus stood, looked to his son, and gestured for them to retire from the chamber. As he passed the old woman at the doorway, he placed a reassuring hand on her shoulder and thanked her for her efforts. Once clear of the King's room, Corvus ushered Cailean to the side of the hall for a private conference.

"We have to act quickly, lad," he said. "Follow my lead."

"Always, Da," Cailean replied with a firm nod.

Corvus smiled proudly, patted his son on the shoulder, and strode purposefully down the length of the hall to the table around which the scribes huddled. He flashed the ring and gestured for them to follow him. Opening the great doors, Corvus commanded the two guards to summon the King's council at once and meet in the covered pavilion by the town square.

"Go fetch Alasdair," Corvus directed Cailean. "Tell him to bring a squad of trusted men."

"Aye, Da," Cailean responded, unspoken curiosity playing across his brow. But Corvus knew Cai wouldn't waste time asking for an explanation now; the lad trusted him and knew he'd unfold his plan in time.

"And Cai," Corvus said, momentarily stopping his son's exit. "Make sure they're armed."

With a nod, Cailean dashed off into the storm. Gesturing for the two scribes to follow him, Corvus made his way down the stairs and set off quickly for the center of town.

The feeble remnants of daylight faded further as he made his way through the muddy lanes and stepped under the nominal shelter of the roof of the pavilion. The octagonal structure had no walls, just a roofed area with bleacher seating on four of the eight sides. Stepping into the center of the space, furthest from the reach of the blustering winds and spattering rain, he directed the two scribes to prepare to take formal notes of the proceedings. With questioning looks, the two sat obediently on the lowest bleacher bench, placed their lap desks, and pulled out ink, quills, and parchment. Corvus then flagged down a passing servant and instructed her to bring lanterns at once. By the time the wet, bedraggled, and curious councilors began to arrive, the pavilion was well lit and Alasdair's squad of troops was standing at attention by Corvus' side.

"You stand next to Alasdair," he directed Cailean, "and lad" —he leaned forward and locked eyes with his son meaningfully—"follow my lead."

Cai nodded, confused.

Corvus knew would have to walk a delicate balance here. The citizens of Esper were in a time of crisis, with their beloved King dying, and the succession unsettled. The urgency of the Barbár advance meant he simply had no time for a diplomatic approach, which might take days to resolve. *Best to move quickly and decisively,* he thought. *Sort everything after the dust settles.*

He stood patiently with his hands behind his back, and waited for the council to assemble. Formed of town elders and the few nobles that made their home in or near Esper proper, the eight men and four women of the council stood in a cluster near the bleachers, conferring with one another and waiting for the last stragglers to arrive. He noted with irritation that Kevin stood near the back of the group, whispering to three well-dressed men who shot suspicious glances at Corvus and the assembled squad of soldiers.

The last to arrive was the Countess Derwhillie, a stately old woman accompanied by two servants holding an oiled fabric between them to shelter her from the downpour. Corvus watched as she stepped meticulously over a muddy patch and strode with grace to the cluster of councilors, nodding a greeting to various members before turning her attention to him.

The council now fully assembled, Corvus waited a moment longer, looking at each face and noting their varying moods—which ranged from open curiosity, to irritation at the untimely interruption of their evening, to only very thinly veiled hostility at being summoned by an outsider. He took the measure of these men and women before beginning. Two women of middle age seemed by their clothing to be merchants, as did a portly gentleman with a bushy brown beard. The three standing with Kevin looked more like wealthy landowners, judging by the rich fabric of the robes they wore over their kilts, and the fine leather of their boots. He recognized the clan chiefs for the houses Comyn and Pitgilly standing with a young woman that he didn't know, but who bore a resemblance to Old Stuart and was probably his daughter and heir. Near the countess stood the Lords Willoughby and Murray.

Before Corvus could speak, the countess stepped forward and addressed the gathering.

"For those of you that do not know this gentleman," she said, her clear, strong voice conveying elegance and education. "This is Corvus Corax of the High Valley, known colloquially as 'The Raven.'" Murmurs and whispers followed her introduction; some were clearly anxious at his presence, while others expressed a mixture of awe and surprise. "As you all know," she continued, "he commanded the Green Mount's effort against the Barbár menace five years ago." Then turning to Corvus, she said, "We can only assume that your arrival here presages some imminent danger, am I correct?"

"Thank you, Countess." Corvus took a step forward to address the assembly. "In ancient legend, the raven was ever the harbinger of death, and I fear I must now fulfill that role. You are correct. The Barbár is returning to Eagle's Gate, in great numbers."

There was a rush of questions and frantic statements from the councilors, but Corvus waited patiently for it to subside. He had years of experience commanding and reassuring groups: soldiers, townsfolk, and the like. Their agitation would still in a moment, and they would turn to him for more information. One by one, the chatter subsided and each face turned back to him.

He looked intently at each of the councilors as he spoke again. "As you know, your King stands on the brink, and is in no condition to answer the peril of the time."

He raised his hand to silence an objection from Lord Murray, a big bellied man leaning heavily on an ornate cane.

"He has instructed me to see to the defense of the Glenfolk," Corvus said clearly and with authority. Anticipating objections, he held up the King's signet ring. The faces of most of the councilors registered a mixture of shock and surprise, but Corvus couldn't help but note the triumphant glance the Countess shot at Kevin.

Clearing his throat, Corvus continued. "As most of you know, I will be commanding the fyrd of the High Valley and I have decided to place my son, Cailean, in command of your forces. Though young, he is experienced, tested, and has effectively led men against the Barbárs." Corvus spared a glance at Cailean, whose only reaction to this move was to raise his eyebrows briefly in surprise. Then, catching his father's eyes, he gave the smallest of nods before resuming the practiced thousand-yard-stare of the soldier.

"Hold on, there!" Kevin spoke up in a reedy voice, interrupting Corvus. "Just who do you think you are to step in and tell us how to arrange ourselves? I am the nearest in blood to the King, and should rightfully command." The three landowners nearest the King's nephew voiced their agreement with him, each shouting objections in turn.

Corvus took a step forward. His piercing eyes fell on Kevin, silencing his cohort. He took a long moment, just staring at the sharp-faced young man and breathing steadily. He knew the force of his gaze was intimidating,; over his years dealing with warriors, he had stared down drunken brawlers, belligerent soldiers, and enemy commanders. Intimidating this weasel was child's play. After a defiant moment, Kevin began shifting under the uncomfortable gaze, glancing at the ground, while the three landowners stepped away, distancing themselves from the unfortunate man.

"Kevin McKay, is it?" Corvus asked quietly. "You live in the White Cleft, do you not?"

"Aye, but what does that—"

"And you have only returned upon hearing of the King falling ill without an heir, am I correct?"

"How dare you!"

"Listen, boy." Corvus' voice suddenly took on a dangerous edge that silenced everyone assembled around the pavilion. "I don't have time for political maneuvering. The wolves are at the gate, and we have to mount an effective defense quickly and efficiently. My fyrd is already marching and should arrive at the Gate within three days, where they *will be* met by the armies of the Glenfolk." He paused for a moment, looking around, daring anyone to contradict him. "Not only have you never commanded an army, but your uncle expressed to me grave doubts about your character. Now, I don't know you, lad, but when my friend King Mannon says to me that he'd not trust you, I take him at his word."

There was a mixture of gasps and chortles from those assembled.

"I don't play politics, lad," he continued. "The King and I have a friendship that stretches back long before you were born, and I have worked closely with him for decades to keep the lands of the Green Mount safe. We've shed blood and lost good friends doing so. And I'll not see that safety jeopardized by a festering bawjaws with illusions of royalty. Once all the hurly-burly's past, if the good people of the Glenfolk decide that you should be their king, then you can speak to me—and harshly, if you like. But in the meanwhile, it would be best if you just sit yourself down, and think of ways to be helpful, for I'll not argue this… And if you get in my way, lad, I'll kill you, simple as that. We dinna have time for your nonsense."

Shocked at the bald-faced threat, Kevin looked to Alasdair to see if the soldiers would stand for this. The hardened veteran returned the look, then nodded his unspoken support for Corvus' words. Kevin's face blanched and he took an involuntary step backward, where his heel bumped the bottom bleacher and he suddenly sat, quite unceremoniously, looking not unlike a chastened schoolboy.

Corvus turned and flashed a grateful wink at Alasdair before returning his fiercely determined gaze to each of the gathered councilors in turn. This was the crux of it. No one here could doubt his resolve, nor his authority. He sensed acquiescence from the three landowners, and bitter resentment from Kevin, though the man's eyes were downcast. Beyond that, every face was open and ready to receive instructions. "Now, we'll follow the wishes of your King. That means I'm in command, and I'm placing my son in charge of the Glenfolk forces. Are there any objections from the King's council?"

Various councilors exchanged glances. Most were reassured and comforted knowing that Corvus was taking charge, and those who might have taken issue with it dared not speak. After an awkward pause, the countess stepped forward and spoke on behalf of the council.

"Thank you, Corvus and Cailean of the High Valley," she said smoothly, "for the continued friendship you have shown to the people of the Glenfolk. We, the members of the Royal Council, stand ready to offer any assistance you may require in these dark days. We are at your disposal."

Corvus inclined his head in acknowledgement of her words, then turned to his son. "Cailean, do you have anything to add?"

Corvus knew Cai all too well and he was certain the lad had been silently preparing what he would say when he was inevitably put on the spot. His son smiled and stepped forward. Corvus wondered how much of the confidence his son was showing right then was feigned, but Cai had an easy, natural charisma to him that showed as he smiled gratefully to his father and then extended that smile to the assembled worthies. Though Corvus' face remained the stoic, dark visage of the Raven, he felt a surge of pride.

"Friends," Cai said, putting as much meaning into that word as possible, "we have much to do in a very short time. Food and med'cine must be gathered, troops assembled, horses and carts loaded, and…" He paused, gesturing to the torrential downpour all around the pavilion. "I'm afraid it may rain a bit." He flashed a winning smile. There was nervous laughter at the jest, but his calm self-assurance and grasp of the logistics and challenges seemed to reassure them that this young man had things well in hand, and that they could trust their fortunes to him and his storied father.

With a few closing words, the meeting was adjourned and those gathered quickly broke up into small discussion groups and cliques. Kevin and his faction slipped out without a word, while the countess cornered Corvus, peppering him with intelligent and insightful questions before once more pledging her support.

Cailean answered questions from several present, reassuring and impressing them with his grasp of logistics. After a time, the councilors started to drift away into the night to tend to their Preparations.

Cailean

Seeing the group breaking up, Cailean turned to the soldiers, thanked them for their time, then dismissed them to begin spreading the word and preparing for war. He was surprised by the light touch of a hand on his arm. Turning, he saw a woman looking up into his eyes. She seemed to be no more than thirty, though the piercing intelligence behind those eyes could well have come from the wisest elder he had known. She had curly hair that was somewhere between blonde and ginger, unbraided and flowing about her shoulders. Her luminous light brown eyes were set in a round face that was sprinkled with freckles that he only noticed now that they stood so close. Her open expression seemed guileless and honest, and he found himself smiling involuntarily as he looked at her.

"My lord?" she asked after an awkward pause. Clearly she had said something that he had missed. He searched vainly to recall it.

"I'm sorry," Cai said shaking himself with a grin. "Did you say something?"

"I asked what we should call you?" she said, a slight smile playing at her lips. "Cailean seems too familiar. Do you have a title or an office that we should use?"

"No, I..." Cai stammered, the question catching him unprepared.

"For the duration of the conflict," Corvus interrupted, noting his son's discomfiture, "he will be referred to as the Lord Commander of the Glenfolk."

"Oh." Cailean looked at his father with surprise, before looking back to the young woman. "There you have it," he said with a disarming grin. "But what do I call you, my lady?"

"I'm the Lady Stuart, Lord Commander," she said with a mock curtsy, "but please, call me Brigit." Then, with a wry look and a small wave, she turned and walked into the dark.

Corvus watched his son stare after her for a moment, then with a slap on Cai's shoulder, he said, "Keep your head in the game, lad. Head in the game."

Cai stood staring after her, only distantly noting his father's words.

Chapter 24

The sharpest knife is truth.

— Anonymous

574 HR - *Last month of summer*
Stilling, Midlands region of the Green Mount

Ligulf

He was seated to the right of Lady Donella, with Rhona beside him to his right. Yazid sat directly across from him, on the left hand side of a glowering Aengus. The feast was spectacular, and the spirit in the hall was light and joyful, despite the lord's darkening mood. The game pies were rich and delicious and featured a mixture of wild boar, venison, and hare in a rich, dark gravy sealed in a flaky crust. Plates of mushy peas, boiled potatoes, seasoned fried cabbage, and fresh baked soda bread heaped the tables. Cups of ale or mead were constantly refilled.

"This is amazing," Ligulf commented to Rhona between mouthfuls, making her laugh. "Lady Donella certainly knows how to celebrate the First Harvest! We had our festival last week, but it was nothing as grand as this!"

"The Midlands are prosperous," Rhona said with a grin as she slathered butter on another slice of bread.

They continued eating and fell into light conversation about performance technique, alternate tunings for the cittern, grips for the drum's tipper, and other topics of interest to two musicians. Rhona wanted to visit more of the communities of the Green Mount, while Li expressed an interest in returning to Stilling, perhaps to perform with her again.

The meal wound down, and confident that he could not possibly eat another bite, Li pushed his mostly empty plate away and leaned back, feeling the days of travel in his seat and legs. A young serving man in a cream-colored, sleeveless linen shirt leaned over his shoulder to remove his plate. His arms were well muscled and Li looked up to see that he had long, braided dark hair. He smelled of rosemary and cedar wood. Li's glance up at him was rewarded with a sparkling smile that made him blush suddenly. *Too much ale, Li,* he told himself. *Best slow down. Remember, lad, you're spoken for.* An image of Piper's laughing face flashed in his mind.

Some ten years his senior, Piper lived in a village called Mallaig near the falls of Glenhorn, a day's hike over the mountain from Dóchas. Piper played a variety of instruments, was well traveled, and seemed to know everything about the legends, history, and lore of the people of the Green Mount. Li had met him just over a year earlier at the Midsummer Festival, and they had spent a glorious day and a half sharing songs, playing music together, drinking, and laughing. The highlight for Li was performing with Piper as the great bonfire was lit. The two had sung "The Turning of the Wheel," with Li strumming along as his comrade drummed a stirring tattoo. At the song's climax, the crowd had cheered and hoisted the two upon their shoulders. Li could still remember that moment, Piper laughing as several lads lifted him up, the single earring he wore sparkling in the firelight, and that wicked, mischievous smile that had urged Li beyond merely making music with this man. Later, the two had found a private place in a grassy meadow, where they fell into each other's arms beneath a smiling, slivered moon. Afterward, panting and sweat-soaked from their labors, they had pledged their troth.

Besides their shared love of music, the two may have seemed an unlikely pair. Piper had a rich, deep voice which was a perfect counterpoint to Li's pure tenor, and where Ligulf's skin was pale and fair, Piper's was tanned and rough. The older minstrel took a charming delight in embracing the thickest mountain dialect in his speech, in contrast to Li's erudite clarity which had been drummed into him at an early age by his mother. Everything about the man brought a warmth and fervor to Li, and soon he found himself making the trek over the mountain to Piper's secluded cabin in the woods outside Mallaig. There, they would enjoy a day or two of singing songs and comparing notes between athletic bouts of passionate lovemaking. He knew Piper would appreciate Rhona's skill on the stage and considered how grand it would be for the two of them to travel together back to Stilling and perform here.

Let's not get carried away, Li. You have a task here, and it's urgent. You canna let your da down.

He was about to turn to Donella and begin the serious discussion of troops when a steaming bowl of bread pudding in treacle sauce was set before him. He turned to decline the dessert, but the server had already moved on down the line, placing bowls before the other guests. It smelled divine. And before long, Li somehow found himself tucking in yet again.

"That's Sigurd for you," Rhona said, ruefully examining a forkful of the heavenly dessert. Apparently she, too, was eating well past her capacity.

"What?" Li was confused.

"He's the cook for today's feast," she clarified. "And anytime he's in the kitchen, you can be sure the meal will have delicious pastries and breads. He's a baker at heart, though the man knows what to do with a hunk of meat, as well."

"Really?" Li asked, perhaps encouraged by the ale.

The twinkle in his eye surprised Rhona as she realized her unintended double entendre and shook her head, laughing and playfully slapping his arm. "Whisht now, young Ligulf," she said, dropping her fork back into her bowl with a grin. "You know that's not what I meant."

"Do I?" Ligulf asked innocently.

A burst of laughter from across the table drew their attention before Rhona could respond. Yazid had been telling a story of some humorous misadventure he and Corvus had experienced long ago, and the punchline elicited howls of delight from the listeners, and a scowl of disbelief from Aengus—who hid his frown by raising his cup and taking a long draught, but then slammed it down noisily on the table. The laughter quickly tapered off then died.

"Why exactly have you come?" he asked abruptly, staring at Yazid, who exchanged a glance with Ligulf before speaking on behalf of the two of them.

"The Barbárs are returning to Eagle's Gate," he said simply. "Corvus has called up the fyrd and is marching to meet them even now, I think."

Aengus leaned back in his chair and tossed his napkin over his plate in disgust. Donella put a hand on his arm, restraining him from some outburst, and leaned toward Yazid.

"Are Mannon and Fergus sending troops?" She asked.

"I would hope so, my lady," the big man responded, turning his attention from the lord's scowl to her more open expression. "They have ever honored the sacred pact," he added, with a meaningful glance back at Aengus before continuing. "Corvus believes that we will face the largest invading force yet, and fears that even all our combined resources may not be sufficient to keep the wolves from the gate."

"And you would have us martial our forces and march off to help, eh, *Aslene*?" Aengus spat.

"My Lord," Li interjected, "if the Barbár horde is not stopped at the Gate, no one in the Green Mount is safe."

"Don't lecture me on safety, whelp," Aengus snapped, his voice rising sufficiently to cause more heads to turn. The merriment in the hall stilled.

"Aengus, don't," Donella whispered to her husband as she squeezed his arm with urgency.

"So the great Corvus," Aengus started, shaking off her hand to stand up and turning his vitriol back on Yazid, "sends his filthy foreign slave and his minstrel-boy son to issue commands to the Lord and Lady of the Midlands, eh? To summon us like vassals to do his great bidding?"

Ligulf watched as the huge Aslene stood to tower above Aengus, his round face calm but resolute.

"My *friend,* Corvus," Yazid began firmly, "asks that the you might join the mutual defense for the good of all, as has been promised and sanctified by tradition. To that end, he sent his son and his comrade in arms to make the request, I think."

"My Lord," Aengus said quietly, staring into Yazid's dark eyes.

"Pardon?"

"You will address me as 'My lord,' foreigner," Aengus said disdainfully.

"My Lord Aengus—" Li began, trying to defuse the situation.

"Quiet, boy!" the drunken lord spat, not breaking eye contact with Yazid. "Go play your harp while the *men* talk."

Yazid was a patient man with a huge laugh and a ready smile. Over the years he had learned to deal with the often-xenophobic Highlanders, choosing to charm rather than confront them. As a result, he had become a trusted and beloved member of his community—a raconteur sharing stories of exotic lands and derring-do. When Corvus' wife had died, Yazid had moved into the stone house to help care for the boys and look after his friend through those dark days. He had grown to love Cailean and Ligulf as an uncle and was, like Corvus, fiercely protective of them both. He had been there the day when a caravan guard had callously ridiculed a young Ligulf, calling him "girlish." He had watched Corvus beat the guard nearly to death, forcing the man to kneel and mutter an agonized apology to his son through a broken jaw. After the incident, Yazid had commented, with storms in his eyes, that the guard had been lucky Corvus got to him before he did. The Aslene way was not so gentle, he had explained.

"I know you did not intend disrespect to the Raven's son," Yazid said in a steady voice, his dark gaze not breaking contact with Aengus. "Call me what you will, but you will not insult my friend's son, I think."

"I'll insult whomever I please! I am the Lord of the Midlands, slave! Am I to be spoken to thus in my own house?" the lord exploded. "And by a filthy Aslene, no less!"

"Uncle!" Rhona called out, horrified.

"Aengus, stop," Donella pleaded weakly, burying her face in her hands.

"No, I'll not be silent!" The man's face had purpled with rage and flecks of spittle flew from his lips as he screamed. The partygoers had fallen silent and were watching the spectacle with horror.

With a casual move of his left hand, Yazid shoved Aengus back into his chair. The lord's eyes flew wide in surprise both at the shocking strength of the shove and at the fact that someone dared lay hands on him in his hall. Two guards standing at the rear of the dais started to rush forward, while a handful of other attendees stood up in alarm. Yazid raised a warning finger to the guards, momentarily arresting their progress as neither was eager to engage the burly man. He scanned the guests with a dark look before leaning over the lord menacingly, his hands on the arms of Aengus' chair.

"Your famed hospitality does not live up to its reputation, Aengus," he said, his smooth, deep voice loud enough to be heard throughout the hall. "We will depart, at once, but know this..." He stood and turned to face the gathered guests before continuing. "While you enjoy your prosperity here in your beautiful town, your brothers and sisters of the Green Mount will be fighting and dying to preserve your tranquility. Not a man or woman from the Midlands will be there to share the burden."

"Guards, get this—" Aengus started, but his outburst was interrupted by Yazid's meaty hand clamping hard over his throat, choking off any further comment.

"And should we fail in our defense," Yazid continued, "your safety here may be numbered in days, I think." He looked around the hall, his intense gaze meeting the eyes of the guests, whom he then addressed. "You are led by a small man"—he shook his head piteously at Aengus—"who has never once raised sword to protect hearth and home. A man who never loved anything enough to be willing to die for it. Instead he sits and festers in his jealousy of the bravery of those who have. I am not from your land, true. But in two days' time, I will be standing in the shield wall beside the Raven—the man who defended the Green Mount five years past *without* the Midlands' help—and I will be fighting to protect *your* homes. Fighting for people like this dung beetle here, who view me only as a slave and dirty." Turning back to Aengus, whose purple, gasping face was a mixture of hatred and outrage, he added, "I am neither, I assure you."

With another casual shove of his hand, he tipped Aengus backward in his chair, causing him to fall with a great crash, his kilt flying up as his naked legs splayed in the air. There were muffled snickers among the guests, and those few that had stood indignantly earlier now sat back down with their eyes averted as Yazid turned casually to leave.

"My Lady," Ligulf said in his clear performer's voice that penetrated the hubbub in the room. "It was a delight to see you again after so many years and to enjoy such a bounteous feast at your table. I will pass your greetings on to my father, who will be disheartened to hear that the people of the Midlands are unwilling to honor the age-old pledge of joint defense of the Green Mount."

Turning to Rhona, Li added quietly, "I hope to play music with you again someday. And, if we've gained nothing else from our visit, it has inspired a new song." Then, with a strum of his cittern, he began to sing extemporaneously.

O Aengus the callow, his spine soft and yellow,
The cockwomble Lord of the Midlands…

Still gasping for breath, Aengus struggled to roar and scrambled to his feet, croaking for his sword. Donella rushed to placate him, and the two guards looked unsure as to whether they should engage the large Aslene or just let him depart. Yazid and Ligulf exited the hall before they made up their minds. Once more shielding themselves from the beating rain, the two of them dashed across the muddy street and into the stable to fetch their tired horses.

"It will be a miserable ride, I think," Yazid said as he saddled his weary mount.

Just then, Rhona rushed into the stable, clutching her duffle, her broad-brimmed hat already dripping wet just from crossing the short distance from the great hall.

"Well, he's in a towering rage," she said as she began to prepare a mount for riding. "He ordered the guards to arrest you both at once, though Donnella was able to belay that order for the time being."

"You're leaving the feast too?" Ligulf asked, cinching the strap of his saddle tightly.

"A singer must always know when a party sours and its best to depart," she responded with a wink. "Besides, I thought I might show you two to a safe, warm place outside the town where you can rest the night and wait out the storm. You must be knackered from your ride today."

"You don't stay with your aunt and uncle?" Li asked, confused.

"He's only my uncle by marriage," Rhona said lightly, tossing her saddlebags onto her mount. "And since he's been around, my aunt's home is... decidedly less merry, shall we say? Now, are you two with me? It's a bloody long ride to Eagle's Gate."

Yazid and Li accepted gratefully, and before long, the three of them rode through the south gate of the town. The icy rain was brutal, stinging their hands and faces, and the weary horses' heads hung low as they trudged along, enduring the punishing weather after an already long, hard day of riding. Fortunately, their destination was but a short distance. They veered off the road shortly after passing out of the south settlement and came upon a farmhouse with a generous barn. Rhona waved briefly to the farmer, who had peeked out of her door at their arrival, then led them into the structure and out of the rain. Once inside the barn, she doled out a generous portion of oats for each of the soaked mounts. After they had brushed and tended to the horses, Rhona directed them to a wide loft, where they were able to settle themselves quite comfortably for the night.

Exhausted from the eventful day, they spent only a little time in conversation before the rafters reverberated with Yazid's bold snoring. Just as sleep was overtaking Li, he heard a muffled snicker from Rhona.

"Cockwomble!" she chortled.

It had been a satisfying insult to hurl in the moment—and well deserved—but Li worried that in doing so, he and Yazid had damned his father and the armies of the Green Mount. Aengus would never send his soldiers now. And without the Midlands' troops, could the rest even stand against the Barbár horde? With a sigh, he closed his eyes and drifted off, fearful of what the next days would bring.

Chapter 26

I am the face of the forest,
I am the laughter of the leaves,
I am the hare and the stag and the wolf,
Come dance, dance with me.

I am the whisper in the trees,
The health within the loam,
I am the green and the gold and the barren branch,
You dance within my home.

— Traditional song of the Greening Festival

574 *HR - Last month of summer*
Dóchas, High Valley region of the Green Mount

Dallin

She sat back on her haunches and stretched her sore back. She had spent most of the day in the garden, weeding and pruning, and now she paused to assess her progress. She had made good headway among the vegetables, tying and reinforcing the strings for the beans to climb, weeding out the garlic and onion patch, and picking out the grubs that found their way into the kale. Her little badger cub, Brochy, was happily rooting around in a patch of upturned earth by her side, seeking out juicy earthworms. The little creature seemed to have an insatiable appetite, constantly searching for grubs and berries when outdoors, and snuffling for goat's milk when inside.

The setting sun cast a rose hue on the cliffs to her left, and a stiff wind was whipping up from a storm approaching from the northeast. Though their home was only a modest cottage, Dallin and her mother took great pride in their garden. They had it neatly divided into quadrants, with sawdust-lined paths leading throughout. The herb section boasted healthy patches of borage, feverfew, sage, mint, chives, and fennel. Dallin had carefully planted a boundary of marigolds around the vegetables to keep out the rabbits, but—though lovely—the flowers had proven ineffective at deterring the pesky little beasts.

"What d'ye say, Brochy?" she said with a smile for the cub. "Shall we look to the apples next?"

The little cub looked up at her and sneezed the dirt from its snout.

"Exactly what I was thinking," she answered, and offered the badger a juicy grub. "We'll need apples for tonight's lamb. Oh, and some fresh mint and fennel too." She plucked generous sprigs of each and put them in her basket. Gathering the squirming cub into her arms, she walked along the sawdust path to the fruit trees, pausing to note a large raven that had alighted atop the hawthorn tree in the corner nearest the house. The bird seemed to be staring at Dallin intently.

"And what is't that you're wanting, Mr. Black Feather?" she asked lightly, amused at the bird's insistent stare.

The raven answered with a croak and a flutter of its wings.

"You don't say," she responded, and turned back toward the apple trees.

The bird croaked again, louder this time. Dallin turned once more to the bird just as a gust of wet wind swirled around her. In a flurry of black feathers, the raven lifted off and flew low across the moor. As Dallin's eyes followed the bird, they fell upon a tall figure crossing toward her house from the village. From the elegant height and graceful stride, she could tell it was Toren walking with a staff of some sort. She set her basket on the fence at the edge of the garden and stepped out to meet the taciturn hunt master.

"Dallin," Toren said by way of greeting.

"Come to visit your wee friend?" she said, holding up the cub.

The edge of Toren's mouth flickered with the slightest hint of a smile. "I'm leaving in the morning to join the fyrd," the man said.

She glanced up at the approaching storm. "'Twill be a rough day to travel, will it not?"

"Aye," he said with a slight nod, "but it canna be helped." There was an awkward pause as he seemed like he wanted to say something but wasn't sure quite how, then he abruptly handed her the staff in his left hand. "I fetched this for you. 'Tis a longbow."

"Ach, Toren," she said, examining the unstrung bow. The weapon was covered in intricate carvings, runes, and symbols that she didn't recognize. The yew wood had been stained a deep hickory color, and the carvings around the handgrip were well worn. This was no new bow. No, this had seen long years of use and careful handling. It was, despite its age and wear, the most beautiful bow she had ever seen—or imagined, for that matter. She was breathless. "Fetched it? I—I dinna know what to say."

"You'll need to hunt for the village while I'm away."

"Why me?" she asked.

"Donella and I have discussed it," he explained. "You've got the strength of shoulder to draw the string, though you'll need to work on that. You've got a natural forest sense about you, and your wee friend there will enjoy the trips to the wood."

"I'm not sure if I…"

"It's what's needed," he said flatly, then turned and strode back toward the village. Toren was known to be a man of few words, often awkward in conversation unless the topic was hunting or something to do with archery. But this abrupt end to their talk seemed strange, even for him.

"Well, what do you make of that, Brochy?" Dallin asked, turning the long, beautiful bow over in her free hand.

With a disinterested grunt, the cub tried to climb down to hunt for more worms.

"You're no help at all," she said with a shake of her head, lowering the cub to the ground. After a moment's further consideration, she leaned the bow stave carefully against the cottage, shrugged at the wonder of it all, and headed back to collect her basket and finish picking the apples.

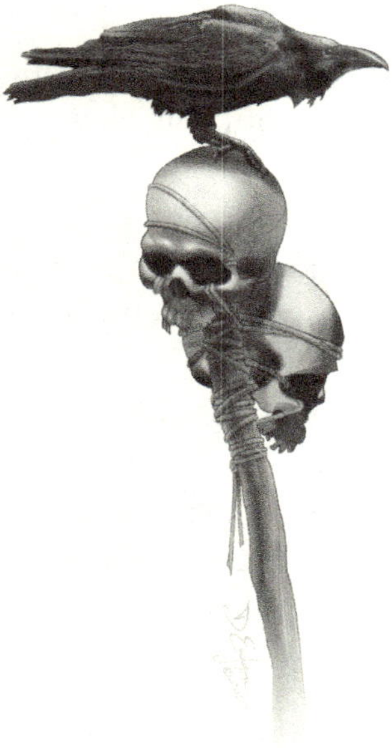

Chapter 27

The Canons bring peace and balance to our hearts. The Canons settle us and calm our agitations. But more than that, the Canons are a source of great and varied power on the lips of the truly faithful. Sadly, the discipline of practicing the Canons has declined, of late. There are those of the younger generations who deny their importance, saying the recitations waste time that might otherwise be spent feeding the hungry or tending the sick. But I say what my teacher said, and hers before that: the heartfelt recitation of the Canons opens doors in our souls to the deeper mysteries, and with that, a closer relationship with the Ancestors. Indeed, there is no greater calling in our sisterhood. Quite simply, the Canons are the Path. I urge you to not neglect them, but instead to keep them as the centerpiece of your daily practice, and that of your votaries.

— From *Missives to the faithful of Saraj Al'iimbiratur*,
by Effulgent One Iesha, Keeper of the Sacred Scrolls

574 HR – Last month of summer
Somewhere in the wildlands of northern Mardin

Barbár warrior

The storm had dimmed the late afternoon to better resemble night, lit only occasionally by flashes of angry lightning. Wind whipped around the shoulders of a lone Barbár warrior, who rode with his shoulders slumped and head dipped low as his mount slowly made its way southward along the road toward the horde's camp. The warrior was bare-chested, tattooed, and, as was their custom, wore bone fragments as ornaments in his hair. To all outward appearances, there was nothing unusual about him—save perhaps for the tall staff of what looked to be driftwood strapped to the side of his saddle, its dramatic hooked top pointing downward. An unkindness of ravens, some two dozen of the birds, seemed to take particular interest in the rider, and swarmed about him, ignoring the icy, driving rain pelting down on them. The birds took turns alighting on the grass of the valley to either side of the road, then in a swirl of black feathers, they flew up to rejoin their fellows, croaking and swooping about the rider's head, before repeating the process. The rain ran in steady rivulets from the warrior's shaggy blonde mop of hair, dancing over the beads and trinkets knotted therein. His right hand rested on the horn of the saddle, fingers twitching subtly in a pattern that repeated, lips moving to chant some silent recitation as he passed the camp's outlying pickets. Those on guard nodded to him, then returned their attention to their uncomfortable watch.

With disgruntled croaks, the ravens dispersed into the gloom as he rode into the camp. He surveyed the tents, their flaps lowered against the storm. Campfires steamed as the glowing embers struggled in a losing battle against the pelting rain. Almost no one stirred in the huge cantonment, as the ten thousand Barbár warriors had been forced to stall their advance toward Monarch's Pass. In this weather, an army's movement up the road of the Devil's Hoof would turn the ground into a churned muddy mess, and the final stretch up the narrow switchbacks to the pass would be treacherous and slow going.

The Barbár commander had instead opted to wait out the storm here.

The rider stopped on his mount and closed his eyes, focusing his attention on the sounds of the camp. Somehow he was able to pierce the roar of the rain and discern details: laughter and drinking from a group of tents to his right, an argument and the sounds of a scuffle breaking out behind him to the left, pots clanking somewhere ahead, the nicker of horses tied among the trees, a weapon being filed nearby, the low murmur of various conversations in tents, and… there. The rider opened his eyes and looked deeper into the encampment. A pavilion tent, larger than most, stood on a small rise near a wooded stream that was swollen with the rain. As the man focused his attention, he could now hear screams of agony emanating from it, despite the distance and the storm. Someone—a man—was being tortured there. The rider spurred his mount forward, careful to maintain a slow desultory pace and not draw attention, his right hand still gesturing subtly and his lips still moving as he recited something beneath his breath.

He drew up on the road where a path between campsites led off to his right. The pathway was too congested and serpentine to take his horse, so he dismounted and tied off the beast to a heavy iron tripod mounted over a washed-out fire pit. He then pulled the strange staff free of its bindings and proceeded to pick his way toward the pavilion, careful to not disturb the occupants of the tents he passed.

As he got closer, he saw two large, muscular guards enduring the weather outside the front flap. One of them flashed a glance in his direction, but evidently saw nothing amiss: just a Barbár warrior moving among the tents, seeking his own canvas hut. Still, to avoid further attention from the guards, the man swung wide around a cluster of nearby tents to work his way toward the stream, and the back of the pavilion. There were more screams from within, screams of prolonged agony and terror. Whoever was torturing the man inside was drawing it out intentionally. This wasn't excruciation to elicit information, this was sadistic torment—and judging by the ragged quality of the man's shrieks, it had been going on for some time. The victim was nearing the end of his endurance.

The rider continued to work his way behind the pavilion until he saw the slaver's wagon. It was packed with filthy and shivering, miserable men, women, and children, their dirty faces pressed against the bars despite the pelting rain. Listless eyes stared into the growing gloom as the sounds of agony, like the icy storm, washed over them. One child caught handfuls of rain, drinking it with a desperation that bespoke privation. The rider edged closer to the caged wagon, checking for other guards. Seeing none, he slipped silently to the cage door, his lips still muttering soundlessly and his right hand still weaving unseen symbols by his side.

The hopeless prisoners ignored his approach, assuming him to be another of their keepers come to check the security of their enclosure. Despite the failing light, he searched the faces within with increasing urgency until he spotted the one he was looking for. She sat huddled in a corner of the wagon, her back to the other prisoners. The thin, sylph-like young woman with the jimas stared despondently at the back of the large tent, wincing at each new scream as if feeling the pain herself.

The man moved along the wagon until he stood directly in front of the young prisoner, catching her eye. Blinking to refocus, the captive woman examined the face of the Barbár before her, noting something familiar in the eyes. She cocked her head to the side and examined the warrior more closely. She noticed his lips moving in his silent recitation, and his fingers twitching in their repeating pattern.

She spoke to the Barbár in her soft monotone. "Hello, Mama."

~~Barbár warrior~~ Mama

The warrior raised a finger to his lips, then with a sigh and a shudder, the features of the warrior melted and fell away from Mama Warad, washing away with the rain like sand. Despite her fatigue, the older woman quickly moved to the back of the slave wagon and tapped the lock with the hooked end of her staff. With a loud snap, the lock broke open and fell to the ground. Mama glanced around to see if anyone had heard and reacted to the sound, but saw no movement. Quickly, she opened the door to the cage, gesturing to the shocked prisoners to be quiet and get out.

A moment later, she and Amina were behind the wagon in the pouring rain, with a cluster of some fifteen confused, weak, and filthy captives. Without speaking, Mama indicated to them that they should follow the stream south and escape the camp as quickly as possible. The captives nodded their understanding, and took turns clasping Mama's hands in thanks before heading off quietly into the stormy night. As the last one slipped away, Amina moved to follow, but was stopped by Mama's hand on her shoulder. Mama pointed to the north, then lifted the hem of her robes and waded into the knee-deep water of the stream, hissing quietly at the bitter cold of the water. Amina followed silently.

A prolonged scream came from the pavilion, ending in what Mama could only assume was a death rattle. The sound stopped both women, and they instinctively cowered behind a cluster of ferns on the bank. They watched as a slender, bare-chested, and blood-streaked man pushed his way out of the large tent, holding a torch and peering at the now empty prisoner cage in surprise and growing outrage. He shouted something and within moments, two guards burst from the pavilion behind him, while the two Mama had seen at the front of the tent rounded the pavilion to answer his call. The two women watched as the guards held up torches that sputtered in the rain, trying to see footprints in the mud around the wagon. A guard knelt by the cage and inspected the ground more closely. After a moment, he stood and gestured downstream after the other escapees. Mama watched, a knot of anxiety in her stomach, as the four guards stepped silently into the stream, turned away from her and gradually faded into the blackness—their bobbing torches soon the only remaining sign of them. She muttered a silent prayer of protection for the escapees, and touched Amina's shoulder before moving upstream. A frisson of danger stopped her, and she once more crouched, looking back toward the pavilion.

The blood-streaked torturer still stood beside it, his black eyes scanning the stream as the pounding rain washed the gore from his chest and arms. He seemed to focus directly on the patch of darkness where Mama and Amina hid. Amina gave a low moan and Mama felt the telltale sensation of hostile magic, not unlike hundreds of needles pricking her skin at once. She sank lower into the stream; her every instinct was to make herself as small as possible. Sensing the nature of the danger he represented, she began to silently chant the Canon of Awareness, heightening her physical senses as well as opening her mind's eye to the spiritual plane. Fighting off the dizziness that always accompanied the opening of the mind's eye, Mama could now perceive a nimbus of black energy that suffused the man, orange-black flames dancing on his skin. This was no mundane warrior or torturer. This was blood magic, perhaps even an Angor shaman. She had heard tell of their dark mysteries and how each possessed unique abilities, but all were steeped in and triggered by blood. Long ago, she had faced one of them in the spiritual plane and had barely survived the encounter. Now, she shivered as the familiar, blood-soaked evil washed over her.

He stepped closer to them, sniffing the air like a dog, then once more settling his eyes directly on their hiding place with a feral grin, the flames around him seeming to grow more powerful. Too terrified to move, Mama gently searched the stream bed with her left hand until she found a fist-sized stone, which she carefully tossed downriver to produce a sudden splash. The shaman turned to the sound, taking several steps toward the stream's edge in that direction. Seeing an opportunity, Mama tapped Amina's shoulder gently, and they began to edge their way upstream through the swollen current as quietly as possible.

"Comee dojdam za tebe vešterka!" The man's shout once more arrested their progress, as both women spun toward him and crouched, trying to overcome their shivering. "Comee dojdam za tebe vešterka!" he repeated, seemingly staring directly at Mama.

She focused on the words, once more reciting the Canon of Awareness, which could also allow her to penetrate a foreign tongue. A wave of vertigo washed over her and she clutched Amina's shoulder to keep from falling over. She could hear his shout echoing in her mind as a secondary echo began to reverberate contrapuntally in her interior landscape. The second layer was softer than the first, but that echo was in Aslene.

I will come for you, Witch!

Staring into those feral eyes, a cold dread washed over her and she couldn't stop her body from trembling. In the light of the guttering torch, she saw a grin suddenly spread across his pallid face, and knew it was in direct reaction to her terror. *He feeds on fear,* she realized. She didn't have the strength to try to affect another illusion, so they would have to escape the camp through conventional means.

"Recite the Canon of Stillness, child," she whispered in Amina's ear.

Amina shook her head to clear it, then obediently began reciting the desired Canon. Mama was grateful in a way that it was Amina that had been captured. The girl's memory for the Canons was flawless. Both women took a deep breath, closing their eyes against the menace of the shaman and allowing the frigid water of the stream to flow around them. Within a heartbeat, the familiar Canon stilled their terror, slowed the frantic beating of their hearts, and calmed their trembling bodies.

Mama did not stop, even when she heard the shaman sniffing the air, urgently trying to recapture the scent of their fear—of his prey. Nor when she sensed him stepping to the edge of the stream to search for them, trying to pierce the gloom and the driving rain. Eventually, he snarled with irritation, and stalked back to the pavilion, throwing the heavy, wet flap open with anger.

Still, Mama and Amina waited over a hundred heartbeats, calmly continuing their meditation in the shadows of the stream bed. Finally, Mama opened her eyes, stood, and began picking her way upstream, murmuring to Amina to move. Her votary followed behind her, clutching the end of Mama's robe. No longer under the effect of the Canon of Stillness, Amina's shivering resumed, her teeth chattering so loudly Mama feared for their discovery.

She remembered the rough layout of the cantonment from her arrival and she guided Amina to a cluster of about fifteen horses, tied within a copse of trees by the stream. They were hobbled with short ropes tied between their legs to prevent them wandering, and Mama could see no sign of bridle, tack, or saddles. The horses stirred at their approach, and more than one neighed as Mama stepped out of the stream, making her way carefully up the slippery bank. She raised a hand and spoke a phrase from the Canon of Beasts, and the horses quieted immediately. She directed Amina to begin untying the hobbles and tethers for all of the creatures, as she stepped up to a large, dappled stallion.

"You will carry us to safety," she said softly, rubbing the destrier's neck, reinforcing her words with phrases from the Canon. "Despite the rain, the dark, and the lightning that may affright you, you will take us with speed to rejoin our friends."

The mount lifted its head in acknowledgement of her charge. As Amina worked quickly and quietly to untie the horses, Mama took a moment to explore a small, unoccupied tent near the beasts and was rewarded with bridles and blankets for riding. Within a few minutes, she and Amina were both mounted on the stallion as it shuffled in anticipation. With a yell and a wave, she scattered the other horses into the night, then—clutching tightly to Amina's waist—she spurred their mount forward along the trail that led between the tents to the main road.

The commotion brought three Barbárs out of their tents. Seeing the freed horses, they at first seemed to assume the beasts had been frightened in the storm and somehow escaped. Two of the Barbárs scrambled after the fleeing mounts, shouting to rouse their comrades to help recapture them. The third heard the approach of the stallion and turned toward them, his arms up to capture the horse. Mama watched the surprise suddenly register on his face as he spotted the women.

She had hoped they might slip out of the camp unseen, but now there was nothing for it. She kicked the startled horse forward, crashing into the warrior, then struck down with the head of her staff, crushing his skull in an instant. The powerful beast shot forward into the night, storming its way over tents and around drowned campfires, stepping deftly despite the multiple obstacles. There were shouts of pain, shock and alarm, and the night quickly became a confusion of rain, lightning, mud, and fear as the stallion crashed its way to the road. Fortune somehow smiled on them, and the horse's legs did not tangle in the tent ropes and canvas it trampled over. At one point, Mama thought she saw a spear fly over her shoulder. Gaining the road, she turned the mount to the north, and spurred it onward. The storm and dark meant that the beast was galloping blindly into a slippery night, but Mama remembered from her journey here that the road was relatively level and straight for the first few miles out of camp. Trusting to the Divinities, she put her head down against Amina's back and prayed that the pickets might be slow to pursue them.

After several moments of blind terror, she heard the shouts of the guards as she flew past, and despite the exhaustion of her spirit, she closed her eyes once more and began the Canon of Perception. The pounding of the rain and the wind's howling suddenly receded, and she could distinctly hear two sets of horses' hooves in pursuit.

With a sigh, she pressed her forehead into Amina's back in frustration. Gritting her teeth, she urged the stallion to greater, more reckless speed, desperately trying to take glimpses of the road through the occasional flashes of lightning. Her right hand clutched the staff, while her left reached around Amina's waist and managed the reins. Peering over Amina's shoulder, she blinked furiously through the sheets of rain.

She was surprised when Amina's hand suddenly covered the one of hers that held the reins, and made a quick adjustment to their direction. After a moment, Amina made another adjustment, guiding their mount deftly in the blackness. Mama realized the young woman was also chanting the Canon of Perception as they rode, allowing her to see in the darkness before them as Mama used its powers to perceive the sounds of their pursuit. Accepting this as a blessing, Mama released the reins, allowing Amina full guidance of the madly galloping stallion. Instead, she wrapped her left arm firmly around the young votary's waist and concentrated on the guards chasing them. The Barbárs were not gaining on the powerful destrier, but also were not slowing down—and Mama knew that bearing two riders, their horse could not keep ahead of them for long, however powerful he was. The icy rain continued to fall in sheets, and Mama hugged Amina more tightly to try vainly to combat their shivering. They rounded a curve in the road, and Mama felt her votary urge the stallion to greater speed. She could vaguely recall that bend in the road, and seemed to remember that the road north of that bend would traverse a series of low, rocky hills, weaving between great boulders. Amina slowed their mount to navigate between the first of the huge rocks. Mama gestured for her to stop the horse, then slid from the back of the stallion, her numb feet stumbling on the uneven ground.

"Mama?" Amina asked, "What are you doing?"

"Wait for me up ahead," Mama told her, "just past the rocks."

Teeth chattering and lips pulled tight against them, Amina nodded uncertainly, and urged the horse forward in a walk. Through a flash of lightning, the image—Amina's frail form slumped on the back of the mighty beast, great clouds of steam billowing from its nostrils and hide—burned into Mama's eyes. Gripping her staff tightly with fingers made clumsy by the cold, Mama Warad slipped and fumbled her way behind the larger of the two boulders framing the road. She placed a hand on the stone, closed her eyes and concentrated. After a moment, she opened her eyes and shook her head to clear it of the fog of fatigue and cold.

"Come on, old woman," she scolded herself. "You must do this. For Amina… Ancestors, I ask your aid."

Closing her eyes again, she began to recite the Canon of Stillness to calm herself and help her slip past the agonies of cold and exhaustion. After a moment's effort, she sagged against the stone, tears of defeat mixing with the rain. She stood for a time sobbing against the back of the great boulder, lacking even the strength to walk back to Amina.

"They're almost here."

Amina's soft voice surprised her. She hadn't heard the girl approach. Despite the young woman's aversion to touching anyone's skin, the young votary placed her hand over Mama's on the staff. A flood of warmth flowed from her touch, and Mama looked at her, startled. Amina simply nodded toward the boulder, reminding her of her urgent task. She could now hear the approaching hoofbeats through the rain without the enhancement of the Canon. She closed her eyes again, and—intoning the Canon of the Essence—touched the rock surface with her left hand until the Canon revealed the precise spot of weakness. Nodding to herself in satisfaction, she tapped the specific place on the boulder with two fingers, as if memorizing its location. Then she stepped back, and raised her staff high over her right shoulder, both hands gripping the twisted driftwood.

One of the Barbárs said something that was lost in the storm as their mounts neared the bend in the path. Both slowed to navigate the slippery, twisting climb between the rocks. Just then, with a crack that sounded like thunder, Mama hit the spot and the larger of the two boulders groaned and tipped toward the riders. Their horses reared as the boulder shifted and tilted toward the other rock, and the Barbárs pulled back frantically to avoid the tons of stone. With a shudder, the great boulder settled its bulk against its neighbor, closing off the path between them.

The road now blocked and their horses shifting nervously beneath them, the riders had no real choice in the cold, stormy night but to turn their mounts back toward their camp. Leaning against another boulder in sheer exhaustion, Mama could hear their hoofbeats disappear. She should have felt relief—she had rescued Amina, and they had managed to escape. But all she felt was a bone deep fatigue and the pounding headache from being overtaxed. "Lie down, Mama," Amina panted as the two women collapsed onto the dry floor of a small cave that had been uncovered when the boulder shifted. "I'll tend to the horse."

With a breath, Amina turned and stepped out once more into the storm to find the animal. Mama lay in a heap in the driest spot of the small nook, already almost asleep. The strength-sapping cold, the exhaustion of maintaining the difficult and taxing Canon of Shadows for hours, the panic of flight, and the effort required to move the boulder had all combined to leave her nearly comatose. She surrendered to the inky blackness of the night, trusting her votary to watch over her as the storm continued to rage.

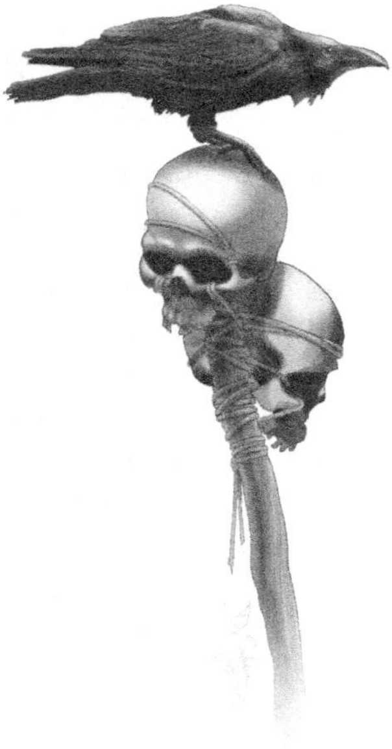

Chapter 28

"Piracy abounds, my dear, and not just at sea. One need only spend a day at court to observe enough blackmail, thieving, bullying, and even murder; why, it puts what we do to shame! At least, we are honest in our thievery. We put a sword point to your throat and demand your gold. There is no question as to motives or desires. We make no bones about our intent. Now, at court, that's another matter. There, they smile and flatter, their words silky and unctuous. All the while, they're slipping a dagger twixt your ribs, taking your land, raping your daughter, and leaving you broken, disgraced, and penniless. And the most amazing part is that what they do is perfectly legal! Truly brilliant! Piracy abounds, my dear. It abounds."

— Captain Tirpak, "The Red Snake"

574 HR—Last month of summer
Mirror Sea, off the eastern coast of the Green Mount

Zsoka

In all her thirty years of life, she had never been this miserable. Crammed into a tiny cabin aboard the square-rigged *Osprey*—the vessel Blood-Tooth commanded—she had spent the past week huddled over a bucket, retching continuously. The ship was familiar to her as it roughly matched the size and dimensions of her uncle's vessel. But then again, most ships that sailed in Orensian waters were sloops of similar size. Periodically, the disgusting man would bring her a thin broth that smelled of fish and grease, which she would attempt to swallow, only to bring it back up moments later. She was feverish, cold, and damp and the cursed boat would not stop tossing and heaving on the stormy northern seas. Adding to her misery was the profound embarrassment that the niece of the infamous pirate, the Black Hand, who had terrorized the coast for decades, should be so unsettled her first time on a ship. Occasionally, she would drift into a kind of wretched slumber, only to be awoken by the violent tossing of the ship, or her stomach heaving in a vain attempt to once again try to empty itself. Her head pounded and she could not control her shivering, despite the heavy and filthy wool blanket in which she was wrapped.

But she was free from her prison. And she knew this illness would pass if she could ever get off this damned ship. She was free!

Her feverish mind clung to this fact like a child clutching a treasured doll against the terrors of the night. Her escape from the island had been surprisingly easy, after all. Following the shaman's instructions, Blood-Tooth's "tengerészgyilkos"—a group of six veteran Barbár sailor-assassins—had left their sloop at the rocky quay and surreptitiously entered the mountain stronghold only an hour after the shaman's passage through the gates. Moving silently, the group had dispatched the various guards and servants, and by the time Zsoka and Blood-Tooth were ready to depart, the way was clear, albeit littered with corpses. She had stood for a moment in mute horror over the body of Vada, a kindly, round, middle-aged woman with a lisp who had tended to Zsoka's needs since childhood and had opted to follow her into exile out of loyalty. Zsoka knelt and closed the woman's gaping eyes, kissed her cold cheek, then—with a determined sigh—moved on to find her escape. She paused only to dash to her chambers and pack a few necessary items into a duffel: traveling clothes, jewelry, and Talon's toy sword, the only keepsake of her son she had been permitted by her jailers.

Climbing aboard the sloop, Blood-Tooth had turned and offered Zsoka his hand to assist her with mock courtesy. Disdaining to touch the man any more than need be, she had refused, consequently stumbling aboard inelegantly. The six tengerészgyilkos had quickly dispersed to their duties readying the ship to depart, while Blood-Tooth had directed Zsoka to a small cabin prepared for her. It was not more than three paces wide and two deep, and had a low, wooden ceiling. A single cot, a small table, a lamp, and a bucket were its only adornments.

"Rest here, Empress," the shaman had said with a sickly smile. "The seas will be rough and you will need your strength."

"Where are you taking me?" she had asked.

"We sail to the southeastern coastline of the Green Mount, my lady," he responded. "Once we are in sight, you can direct our search for this hidden path."

The week since then had been miserable. Zsoka had not once ventured outside her cabin, and her only visitors had been Blood-Tooth bringing that vile broth and one of the sailors who emptied her slops each morning.

She pushed herself back from the bucket, wiping her mouth after the latest round of retching. The muscles of her stomach and ribs ached from the constant heaving. Sitting on the cot, she eased back onto the rough, straw-filled pillow and closed her eyes, willing the pounding in her head to stop. Just as she began to drift into a merciful slumber, there came a knock at the door.

"What is it?" she said irritably.

Blood-Tooth entered, a steaming bowl of fish broth in his hands. "Twice good news, my lady," he said silkily as he set the bowl on the small table beside her cot.

The scent of the soup filled the cabin and she struggled to hold down her gorge. Unable to speak, a raised eyebrow was the extent of her response.

"We near the shoreline," he said, his spider-like fingers curled with anticipation, "and it seems the storm is finally passing,"

After a hard swallow and a moment's further pause, she muttered, "Good news, indeed."

"With the coming of the dawn," he said, in a tone usually reserved for adults speaking to a dull child, "we can begin our search. I trust the worst of your indisposition has passed, and that you shall be fit enough to guide our efforts?"

"I shall do my part," she said thickly. "Please leave me to rest."

"You must eat, Empress." His long fingers gestured toward the bowl. "You will need your strength."

She grimaced as another wave of nausea washed over her.

"You may not feel so inclined," he continued. "But I assure you, your body is in need of nourishment."

"Yes, yes," she said, with a weak wave of her hand. "Please let me rest."

"Of course." His trembling lips pulled back to reveal yellow teeth. "Call out should you need anything."

She barely heard the door close as she struggled against the urge to rush once more to the bucket. Her head pounded, and her vision pulsed with each heartbeat. She took long gasps of breath, willing her rebellious body to ease its convulsions. After several moments, she sat up on the cot, and waited a few moments more for the room to stop spinning. She looked at the unappetizing, gray bowl of gruel and the slimy, mysterious chunks that floated within it and took several more deep breaths. Tears streamed down her wan face as she struggled to imagine eating the contents of the bowl.

"Get ahold of yourself, woman," she muttered to herself, willing her pride and anger to rise to conquer this infirmity. "Is this the Empress that conquered the Southern Steppes? Is this the Queen that expanded her demesnes threefold in three years? Is this the Úrasszony of the Orensian people? Or are you some milk-blooded waif, too weak to bear these burdens? Will you allow Talon to be raised to manhood by someone else, without your guiding hand? Eat, damn you! It's only soup!"

Steeling herself once more, she brought a spoonful of the gray slop to her lips. As the tentacle of some unknown creature slithered down her throat, she gagged, but by sheer force of will and several deep breaths, she kept it down. She took another steadying breath before reaching for another spoonful of the vile stuff.

"Well, it certainly isn't roast beef..." She allowed herself a weak smile.

The dawn's light found the seas calmed beneath a clear, rose-hued sky. Zsoka stood near the prow of the small craft, gratefully taking in the fresh, salt breeze. As foul as it had been, the stew had indeed proven restorative, and after drinking what seemed like a bucketful of water that morning, the color had returned to her cheeks.

"I trust you slept well, Empress?" the shaman asked from too near her shoulder, surprising her.

"I am much restored, yes," she said curtly, flashing him a reproving glance.

Squeezing beside her on the narrow prow, he gestured with one hand toward the shore, where impossibly high, rocky mountains plunged directly into the ocean, stretching as far away to the north as she could see. To her eye, there was not so much as a small cove among the cliffs, nowhere that a ship could possibly approach that rocky coast. But she knew the tales. Her Uncle Alajos had boasted countless times of his secret trips to the Green Mount, through the Long Stair, a path known only to him and his father. It was a steep, brutal stairway carved through the mountains, its origins lost to antiquity—though some said it had been a smuggling route during the decades that Mardin ruled much of the Green Mount.

"There lies the coastline," he said. "We await your instructions."

She stared at the forbidding rock face, her mind awhirl with memories and fragments of meaning through which she desperately sorted. After a moment's frantic scrabbling, she calmed, ignoring the expectant gaze of the sallow shaman. She allowed her mind to drift back into memory and recollection.

Alajos had become a drunkard, and often, when deep in his cups, would share his slurred tales of smuggling and piracy—despite the best efforts of Beatrix, her mother, to silence him. Yet Zsoka couldn't help but idolize the man, clinging to his every word and memorizing the details of his adventures, both from the fireside gossip of servants and friends, as well as from his own lips. His exploits as a smuggler and ruthless pirate were known the length of the coastline. The Black Hand. His banner, flown from his fleet of sleek ships, struck fear and dread into even the most intrepid sailor. Indeed, so great was his notoriety, and so frustrated was the then King of Orense—Zsoka's father—with his efforts to bring Alajos to justice, that a generous amnesty was eventually offered. Not only was he forgiven his many crimes, but he was granted land, a lesser title, and respectability. It was this very respectability that had enabled Beatrix, the pirate's comely younger sister, to catch the King's eye and in time become his mistress. Her subsequent pregnancy had so delighted the King—the Queen being barren—that he elevated Beatrix to the formal title of Royal Consort, thus ennobling Zsoka at her birth.

It had been a meteoric rise in respectability for a family steeped in piracy, murder, smuggling, extortion, and all manner of other crimes. Beatrix worked tirelessly to separate herself from her family's past, and project an image of complete respectability, suitable for a position at court. She strove at every turn to erase the stain of her family's piracy, but to no avail. The drunken ramblings of Alajos undermined this effort and were an ongoing source of embarrassing gossip among the judgmental nobility. Eventually, the King tired of the constant disgrace attached to him as closely as his preferred consort. It was a constant reminder of his own weakness in being forced to capitulate with the pirate. He turned Zsoka's mother out, denouncing her and her criminal kin, and crushing any dreams Beatrix had of elevating the family name. But with no other prospective heirs, the young Zsoka was kept at court, to be raised for the role.

The shame had eventually killed Beatrix, and Alajos had followed shortly thereafter, drowning face-down in a puddle of muck in some back alley. Too drunk even to roll over and save himself.

Zsoka had grown up at court—the heir, unless her father's seed might take root in some other soil and produce a son to replace her. The King was a cold, stern presence, ever disapproving and sterile in his affections. Yet, toward him she presented only duty and obedience, careful never to cross nor disappoint him. Her servants, however, would tell a different tale, if asked. They would tell of a cruel, willful girl, spiteful in her humors, shrill in her demands, and unforgiving of their mistakes. Unwise and petulant in so many choices, yet wise enough to know which reports might reach her father's ear. Her tutors reported that they were consistently amazed by her perspicacity and incisive mind, though they did struggle to keep her focused on her lessons; the girl was ever distracted by tales of adventure. In any interactions she had with her father, she was circumspect and careful, respectful, and to all outward appearances, ever the dutiful daughter. It bought her time—time to plan, for Zsoka never forgot the fatal insult to her mother and the hateful disdain heaped upon her uncle.

At Midwinter in her thirteenth year, Sanyi—the King's prized hunting dog—had to be put down after a life of boldly leading the pack. Zsoka spied upon the castle midwife, Ilya, as the woman gathered nightshade from her private stock. She watched Ilya mix the herbal tincture with death cap mushrooms, noting the dosage and the method the woman employed to muddle the fatal herbs. She watched carefully as Ilya mixed the tincture into the sausage that Sanyi so adored. As the Midwinter Festival approached, Zsoka stole into the midwife's shed to gather all the remaining nightshade and two of the mushrooms—more than thrice the dosage used for the dog. She then slipped into the busy kitchens during the feast preparations, under the guise of wanting to help the overtaxed kitchen staff. The King was overly fond of chestnut stuffing braised with the drippings from the boar, and the cook always prepared a separate portion just for His Majesty. It had been surprisingly easy for Zsoka to find an opportunity to mix the poison into the stuffing unnoticed. Despite being but thirteen, the agony of her father's convulsions and spasms did not touch her. She watched his demise with the same dispassionate coldness with which he had turned out her mother. No other child had been born to the King's many mistresses. She was, undeniably, the heir. And as her father thrashed on the floor, foam bubbling from his mouth, she smiled inwardly knowing that she would inherit the throne. The niece of the Black Hand would show them what it meant to be a queen.

A gust of cold wind brought her back to herself. The shaman stood beside her expectantly, wafts of his rancid odor eddying about her on the cold breeze. She focused on the forbidding coastline, trying desperately to recall the phrase she knew Alajos had shared when she was but a girl of eight or nine. *What was it?* After so long idolizing the man, it seemed a cruel twist of fate that she could not recall his words now. Something about three great hooks or stones or… *What was it?* She had to remember. If she failed to locate Alajos' stair in time to reach the Green Mount before the Equinox, she knew Blood-Tooth would not hesitate to kill her. Her worth to the Grand Hadvezér was both limited and complicated, and he was known to be impatient of complications. She had negotiated her freedom based on her assurance that she could locate the path. No amount of romantic nostalgia would soften Vajk should she fail. No matter that they had been lovers. No matter that he had given her Talon, the son she adored more than the spring. To him, she was a tool to be used to further his vaulting ambitions. She was certain that he had given instructions to the shaman to kill her, should she not live up to her side of whatever bargain they had struck. It would all come down to her being able to dredge up a clear enough memory from the ramblings of an old, drunken pirate when she was but a girl.

"Well, Empress?" the shaman prodded.

"Sail north along the coast," she answered, with more confidence than she felt. "Slowly."

"I assumed as much," he said condescendingly. "For what do we search, specifically?"

"I'll know it when I see it," she said dismissively, then leaned forward against the railing, turning away from him to hide the doubts and fear cascading across her face.

Chapter 29

In stark contrast to the practices in Sudland, Lachland has, since the days of King Armel II, held open the possibility within its military for merit-based promotion, allowing the practice of elevating common soldiers to become officers and on exceedingly rare occasion, knights. This procedure was initiated after the "Lord's Pox" decimated the ranks of the young nobility during the latter years of Armel's reign, leaving countless holes in the ranks of the junior officers in the army. Given the ongoing conflict with the Mardish, the military had no choice but to allow for the possibility of commoner elevation, and though the practice was initially greeted with hostility from the senior officers, and many of the non-commissioned officers, it has proven its value over time, allowing individuals of undeniable merit to advance into leadership, notably improving the ranks. So compelling is this opportunity for social advancement, that the military of Lachland experiences only a fraction of the desertions of the Sudlandic or Aestherian armies. And, though it is true, that those commoners so promoted are said to experience endless social difficulties within their new stratum, nonetheless, the very possibility of elevation and its attendant prosperity plants a seed of hope in the heart of every young soldier. Indeed, my late husband, Col. Sirus Tymer, was, himself, a commoner elevated for distinguished bravery against the Mardish raiders. This elevation changed not only his life, but I dare say, my own, as well.

— Lady Gwyndalyn T. Tymer, Professor Emeritus in Socio-Anthropological Studies at the Académie Royale des Arts Militaires

574 HR - *Last month of summer*
Wetheral Castle, Deep Mere, Lachland

Justiniere

Major Justiniere was not happy. The various palace servants that he passed as he stormed angrily through the corridors of Wetheral quickly found purpose elsewhere to avoid his notorious temper. In the past hour, he'd covered most of the castle, searching for the Princess to no avail. His men were out scouring the palace grounds, the stables, the battlements, and the surrounding hillsides. He had better things to be doing, but the news he had just received needed to be passed on to Darienne without delay, and neither she nor her arrogant bodyguard were anywhere to be found.

Blasted woman! he thought. *How am I supposed to keep you safe if you keep sneaking out of the castle?*

He couldn't understand why she needed a personal bodyguard anyway. The Lake Jacks were a formidable cadre of elite troops that took great pride in protecting the castle and its royal occupants. Bringing in an outsider—and a mercenary, no less—was a slap in his face.

What was the Queen thinking? he mused angrily. *Does she no longer have faith in us? In me? And how in the world did she talk St. Fiacre into it?*

Leaving the dining hall, he rounded a pillared corner and headed toward the servants' chambers in the hopes of finding someone who might have an inkling of where she'd gone. He spotted a gaggle of serving maids at the far end of the corridor, at the intersection with another hallway. Before the women could spot him and scatter, he called out, "You three there, hold!"

His voice echoed in the hallway, punctuated by the staccato click of his boots on the slate floor. The women looked up with wide eyes, like children caught stealing treats from the kitchen after hours. Despite their obvious discomfort, they waited obediently in a cluster for the major to approach, at which point, they all curtsied dutifully.

"Where is the Princess?" Justiniere demanded sharply. The servants looked uneasily at each other, before one of them spoke up. She stood a full head taller than the other two, and was wearing a peach-colored dress that stood out against her smooth, dark-umber skin. Her hair fell in gentle ringlets around her face and her eyes were a piercing green that arrested the major's temper.

"Beg your pardon, sir," she said in an exotic accent that suggested she was from the Southern Reaches. "The Princess does not share with us her comings and goings."

"Of course not," the major muttered, suddenly feeling unsure of his righteous anger in the face of this serene beauty. "Forgive my peremptory tone. It is quite urgent that I find Her Highness, and I hoped that one of you might have some clue or hint as to her whereabouts." He softened his demeanor with a slight smile and an open gesture with his hands.

The maid looked to her companions and was about to speak again when a short, pale, plump one put a restraining hand on her arm.

"She'll be angry with us, Maddie" she whispered urgently, her mottled cheeks flushing bright pink at her own temerity.

"We must tell him what we know, Ingrid," Maddie insisted, her green eyes flashing briefly at the major before looking down, almost abashed.

Justiniere felt a concomitant rush of blood to his cheeks at the brief glance. *Who was this woman?*

"The Princess," Maddie began slowly, as though gathering courage to speak, "routinely goes riding in the hills with Captain Kaiso. Where they go is anyone's guess, but her riding clothes are always filthy when she returns… Sometimes they have blood on them, but there is always sand and much sweat."

"Blood, you say?" he pressed, with alarm in his voice.

"Yes, Major," Maddie replied calmly. "Twice now, she has required minor medical attention upon her return." She paused for a moment, frowning. "We are strictly forbidden to speak of it, though I feel obligated to tell you. She has made it clear that if any of us mention these things to anyone else, we will be summarily dismissed. Please, Major, do not tell Her Highness of my—"

"You have my assurance," he interrupted.

"It's just…" She faltered briefly. "It's just that the blood concerns me."

He nodded, and mused quietly for a moment. The Princess' rides from the castle were not a secret, but this business of blood, sweat, and sand was alarming. *What the devil was she up to?*

"Your secret is safe with me, ladies," he said eventually. If I may ask, when do you expect her back?"

"I really can't say, sir," Maddie replied matter-of-factly in her rich, accented voice. "On a normal day, her outings last no more than three or four hours, but lately she has been out much longer."

"Do you know when they departed?" he pressed, striving to focus his mind on the matter at hand rather than on the full lips of the beauty he interrogated.

"It was early this morning, Major," Ingrid interjected eagerly, glancing at the third servant, who wrung her hands nervously, looking utterly perplexed. The poor, bland woman was utterly out of her depth and looked flummoxed by this conflict of duties—serve her Princess, or serve her Princess' safety. Ingrid, however, seemed to have gotten over any reticence to speak about the subject, as if the discomfort of keeping a secret had finally burned its way through her self-control. She pushed in front of Maddie as she continued. "She had me up before the sun, sir. Fetching her breakfast and laying out her riding clothes."

Justiniere glanced out the window at the afternoon sun. *Eight or nine hours, at least, then.*

"I thank you all," the major said courteously. "Please send word to me, immediately, upon her return. It is quite urgent that I speak with her."

With a slight inclination of his head, he dismissed the servants to their duties. He watched the women, and particularly Maddie, depart... his mind playing over those dark loose ringlets and emerald eyes. With a shake of his head, he reminded himself of his rather urgent duty, and once again was washed with indignation at the Princess' irresponsible behavior. Reminded of the impossible situation in which she had placed him, he stood fuming for a time before turning crisply and storming back down the corridor to find Brigadier St. Fiacre.

Darienne

Darienne and Kaiso were exhausted. It had been another long and fruitless day of chasing down leads in Deep Mere in an effort to root out the identity of the mysterious Lady Ormond of the Westhaven. Darienne was convinced that this was not the real name of their quarry, but until they knew her true identity, the *nom de guerre* would have to suffice. The Lake Jacks had spent days searching the titles and ownership records in the Land Offices of Deep Mere, trying to determine who owned the town house where Kaiso had confronted the mysterious lady. Eventually, they had found a name: Pierre Brodeur, a well-to-do fabric merchant from the south of Lachland, who had only recently moved to Deep Mere and opened a shop on High Street. Kaiso had informed the Lake Jacks that he would follow up with Mr. Brodeur personally, and had promptly visited the merchant at his place of business. Sadly, that had proven to be a dead end. Brodeur had purchased the home intending to house his family there, but their arrival in Deep Mere had been delayed, and he had decided to take a small apartment near his shop until their arrival. He had leased the vacant town house to a man named Levecque, who supposedly would only be in town a short while visiting a sick relative and needed a residence in a respectable part of the city. The man had paid in full up front and Brodeur had thought nothing more of it. The merchant's memory of Levecque was not clear, but he did say that he suspected the man to be in his fifties, and—the merchant had added approvingly—carried himself in an elegant and superior manner, using highly educated turns of phrase, and had a "rich, melodious voice."

"Clearly a man of means," Kaiso had told her. "Perhaps a noble in disguise? Couldn't be a seasoned spy, to have made such a glaring impression."

Darienne had pressed her various contacts in the city for any information on this Levecque, and had largely come up empty, until Madame Lorraine—the proprietress of the Salty Mermaid—had said that she vaguely remembered a gentleman matching that description who had been making inquiries some weeks earlier.

"What kind of inquiries?" the Princess asked.

"Oh, Mistress..." The madame looked befuddled. "I don't rightly remember the details, but he seemed like a displaced gentleman, in need of respectable-appearing companionship, if you get my meaning."

"A courtesan, you mean," Darienne said, gleaning her intent.

"Exactly." The matronly woman produced a short clay pipe from within the folds of her dressing gown and lit it from a nearby taper. "No street whore for this gent," she added through a cloud of smoke.

"Had you ever seen this man before?" the Princess asked.

"No, Mistress," Madame Lorraine responded. "Though he did return a few days later, if memory serves. He hoped I might have thought of an appropriate young lady for his needs." She idly tapped the stem of the pipe on her brown-stained teeth as she searched her memory. "And I set him onto Orly."

"Orly?"

"She's one of the girls frequently requested by Duke Comtois," she said helpfully. "Carries herself right well, she does. Dress her up right, and she could pass for royalty."

Duke Comtois? Darienne thought, horrified. *"Frequently"? No, not Nuncle!*

She shuddered at the thought that the beloved, avuncular man who had bounced her on his knee as a child, might have visited courtesans often enough to have a favorite. She forced herself to continue her questioning.

"And this Levecque," Darienne said, "he paid you for this referral?"

"Two gold scepters!" the woman exclaimed. "Easiest gold I ever earned."

"And he no doubt asked for your discretion…" the Princess stated.

"Of course, Mistress. Of course. If it weren't Your Highness asking, tweren't no power short of torture would make me spill on my clients. Discretion in my business is the chinks, if you get my meaning." She laid a finger on the side of her nose as she blew twin jets of smoke from it.

'Chinks,' Darienne mused silently. The sound coins make in a pouch or purse. Another hint that the matron expected payment for this information.

"Did he leave a card or any other means by which you might contact him?"

The matron laughed. "Gents don't usually leave any proof of their visits behind… except the type that shows up nine months on." She winked at Darienne and tapped out her pipe.

The Princess thanked Madame Lorraine for her time and information, slipping her two gold scepters and a half buckle. "You will say nothing of this," she stated as she pressed the three coins into the woman's plump hand.

"Of course, Mistress," the madame replied earnestly.

Outside the Salty Mermaid, Kaiso turned to her. "So, we have a gentleman—most likely a disguised noble—called Levecque, who rents the town house from this Brodeur fellow, then seeks to procure the services of a courtesan. This 'Orly.'"

"Yes," Darienne replied, deep in thought.

"Then," Kaiso continued, "this same town house is the one in which I find the Lady Ormond sequestered with a raft of dockyard scum, one of whom tries to kill you."

"And nearly succeeded," she added, her eyebrows raised in mute accusation of her bodyguard, who had allowed the attack to happen.

Ignoring the look, Kaiso continued. "I would lay any bet that this Orly and the Lady Ormond are one and the same."

"My thoughts as well," Darienne said.

"Which points the finger of suspicion toward this Levecque character." Kaiso scratched the scar on his cheek thoughtfully.

"Yes, precisely." She turned to gaze up and down the length of the avenue, scanning the windows for spying eyes.

"I would also venture," Kaiso added, "that if we find either Orly or Levecque, we will come close to unraveling this plot."

"Many threads to pursue," Darienne responded as she glanced back at the familiar door of the brothel, before turning brusquely and striding toward the stables.

They spent the rest of the day in fruitless pursuit of any clues as to the mysterious Levecque. They found the luxurious apartments of the courtesans near Canal Street, and despite much cajoling of the women there, could glean nothing of import as to the identity or whereabouts of Orly. It seemed she was a recent arrival from Sudland, having lived in the capital city, Barris, where she had evidently been well-educated in genteel—even courtly— manners, if the other women were to be believed. The other courtesans knew little of her life before Canal Street, but from comments made, Darienne gathered that there was more than a little jealousy directed toward her. Within days of her arrival, she had attracted the coveted attention of the aging Duke Comtois, who—to Darienne's continuing horror—apparently had quite an appetite for women and enjoyed variety, making a practice of rotating through the courtesans.

The duke was one of the most powerful men in the kingdom, and a staunch political ally of the Queen. He was a regular guest at her mother's table and Darienne had grown up listening to him regale the Queen's guests with rambling stories, lessons, and parables. He was like an indulgent uncle to her. She would forever remember his gift to her of Sparks, her first pony, when she was but a girl of nine. She could still see his eyes sparkling with mirth, his lips disappearing beneath his bold mustache, his hand on his rotund belly as he chuckled at her overjoyed discovery of the beast, secreted beneath a copse of trees with a red ribbon bow affixed to the saddle.

Not Comtois!

His family was linked by both blood and affection with her mother's. She prayed to the Five he wasn't involved in this plot… She would need to tread softly with this inquiry, lest she endanger the long-held amity that existed between their houses.

The courtesans shared that his proclivity for variety had all changed when Orly arrived and promptly became his favorite, bewitching the old duke with her erudite conversation and shockingly bold manners. She had quickly eclipsed the other women in his eyes. Day after day his carriage would arrive, and the ladies would wait to see who was summoned to the duke's hunting lodge. But it would always be Orly, they related with bitterness. The other women blamed her for their lost fortunes, and would gladly have given the Princess any additional information about her whereabouts, but Orly had not been seen for over a week, and despite Darienne's and Kaiso's multiple questions, the women could offer nothing more helpful.

"I do find it curious, though," one of the courtesans had offered as an afterthought, "that the duke no longer sends his carriage to fetch anyone. Perhaps she's staying there at his lodge, and he has no further need."

The sun was low above the Westron Mountains at the western end of the Mere when Darienne and Kaiso reined up before the gates of Wetheral Castle. Darienne sat and stared as the south-facing main gate was lit by the last rays of the sun. Kaiso stroked the neck of his mount and waited patiently for the Princess to speak.

"We will need to approach this matter with care," she said finally. "He is a close ally and a beloved friend to my mother… and me."

"Of course," the captain replied. "How far is his hunting lodge?"

"Perhaps an hour's ride east of the city gates," Darienne responded.

"This may be something best attended to by me," Kaiso suggested. "A nighttime reconnaissance of the lodge."

"I agree, Captain," the Princess replied. "Let me know what you find."

Kaiso nodded. "Of course."

Darienne spurred her mount toward the gates, arching her back to ease a muscle strained by riding. She was famished and planned nothing more adventurous for her evening than a hot meal, a hot bath, and a full decanter of wine. As she neared the gates, however, she could see Major Justiniere waiting for her, fists on hips and a look of fierce impatience on his stern face. Somehow, she knew her plans for the evening were about to change.

"What do you mean, 'He'll be here in the morning'?" she demanded as she strode purposefully through the castle corridors, Justiniere walking beside her. He had just brought her the news that her cousin, Pietr van den Berg, the newly anointed Viscount of Valais, was paying a visit and would arrive tomorrow. He was her only cousin, the son of her mother's younger sister Alais, who had married Pietr's father and moved to his demesnes in Aesthir. Darienne had never met Pietr, though the young man had maintained a regular correspondence with the Queen, through which he had repeatedly mentioned his mother's lands and titles within Lachland, seeking—rather transparently—to maintain his ties to the throne in his mother's homeland.

Darienne felt an urgency to continue her investigation, but with her mother gone, a royal visit would demand all of her attention for days. This was unacceptable, and very inconvenient. "Why wasn't I told of his coming?"

"We received word this noon, Your Highness," the major replied in a long-suffering tone. "We spent the rest of the day searching for you to bring you the news, but since Your Highness did not deign to inform the commander of the palace guard of your whereabouts, we were unable to notify you until now."

"Major," the Princess said, stopping suddenly in the sunlit corridor. She looked at him for a moment, clearly weighing how to address his irritation. Major Justiniere was tall, strong, and swarthy with a rugged handsomeness marred only by a somewhat flattened nose that had clearly been broken at some point—perhaps more than once. She considered for a moment his journey to this position of authority and responsibility. She vaguely recalled having heard his story. He was the bastard son of a western baron and a foreign serving maid. Unwanted by his sire, the copper-skinned lad had made his way up through the ranks of the cavalry, starting with only a single horse and a sword with which to make his way in the world. He had found a home and a purpose in the military, earning first an officer's commission, and eventually a coveted posting with the Lake Jacks at Wetheral Castle. Through diligence and a bracing zeal for duty, he had risen to become the day-to-day commander of the Jacks, answering directly to Brigadier St. Fiacre himself. He had a forthright manner that encouraged people to either trust him or dismiss him as naive. With an assassin on the loose, and the country at war, she could not afford to lose him as a potential ally.

As second-in-command of the Lake Jacks—perhaps the deadliest cavalry force on the continent—he was charged with her safety, and the safety of all who resided within the castle. She had been keeping him at arm's length due to the friction between him and Kaiso. But now, looking into his earnest face, she realized that had been a mistake. She needed him as a friend, not an obstacle.

He glowered at her, clearly prepared to be chastised for the sarcasm of his comment. She could see true concern behind the resentment in his eyes, and knew that his irritation was justified. She smiled, and placed a hand on his arm familiarly before speaking.

"I know it isn't easy," she said, "being charged with the safety of a headstrong princess who pursues a private agenda."

Apparently taken off-guard by Darienne's self-deprecation, the major's mouth opened as though he might respond, though words seemed to fail him. He looked down as she continued.

"I will endeavor to be more forthcoming with my plans, and not to make your already difficult job any more trying." She smiled up at him. "Let us not be at odds. In the days to come, I will have need of friends."

"If Your Highness would allow me to send a squad of Jacks with you on your various jaunts," he offered, "I would sleep more soundly at night."

"Perhaps, Major," she patted his arm lightly. "Perhaps." Then, turning in the direction of her chambers, she added, "Now, if you will excuse me, I have much to prepare for my cousin's unexpected arrival in the morning."

She left the major and continued to her chambers, where she immediately sent Ingrid to summon Kaiso. He would no doubt be departing soon for his planned reconnoiter of the duke's hunting lodge, and she needed to speak with him before he left. Her rooms were west-facing, and the large, arched windows overlooked rolling hills that descended to the north leg of the Mere, beyond which stood the Westron range of the Hawless Mountains. Though she had grown up looking out of those windows at that view, it was a vista of which she never tired—especially just as the sun dipped behind them, as it was at that moment. Some alchemy existed between the purple of the mountains, the steel blue of the lake, and the golden rays of the setting sun that lit her room each day at this time with a swirl of vibrant colors. It was her favorite time to bathe and ruminate as she stared out of the three windows. But the bath would need to wait at least a few minutes. Maddie and Dominique continued their toil with buckets of hot water as Darienne's mind whirled with details of the visit to which she now had to attend.

"Dominique," she said as she pulled off a boot, "when you are finished there, please notify the steward that my cousin, the Viscount of Valais, is arriving tomorrow and will be staying.... I don't know how long he'll be staying. But inform him that tomorrow's evening meal will be a state affair. All the finery."

"Yes, ma'am," the middle-aged servant responded dutifully.

"Oh," Darienne continued as she struggled with the other boot, "and have supper brought up for me. And—"

"Wine, ma'am?" Dominique finished Darienne's thought for her with a smile and a wink.

"You know me well, Dom," the Princess said, sitting back in her chair despite having failed to remove her remaining boot. She caught Dominique's eye and held up her foot hopefully.

"Of course, ma'am." Dominique left Maddie to tend to the bath and came over to help remove the stubborn boot. After a moment's straining effort from both of them, the intractable footwear came loose in a rush, evoking a deep sigh of relief from the Princess.

"Anyone who says that trousers and boots are more comfortable than corsets and petticoats has not spent days in the saddle," Darienne remarked, closing her eyes in pleasure as she wiggled her toes.

"Speaking of which, ma'am," Maddie remarked, "would you prefer the green or the royal-blue gown for tomorrow?"

Darienne grimaced at the thought of wearing gowns all day and evening, but in her mother's absence, she was now the hostess and must play the part. With a sigh of resignation, she responded, "I think my summer gown, the rose one, would be appropriate to greet the Viscount. And let's go with the deep-blue one for supper, eh?"

"I'll lay them out for you in the morning, ma'am," Maddie responded with a slight bow of her head.

There was a knock at the door and the Princess gestured for Dominique to open it. Captain Kaiso stepped in two paces and stood formally before Darienne.

"Change in plans, Captain," the Princess remarked. "I'll explain in a moment. Maddie, are you finished there?"

"Just, ma'am," the tall, green-eyed woman said, straightening up from the bath.

"Good," Darienne said. "Thank you. You and Dominique may go."

"Very good, ma'am," the two women responded in unison before exiting the chamber.

The door clicked shut, and Kaiso looked expectantly at her.

"It seems my cousin," she began, "the Viscount of Valais, will arrive in the morning for a state visit. With my mother gone, I am required to host him."

Kaiso rubbed the scar on his left cheek and began to pace the long room. He paused by the furthest window, ostensibly looking out at the sunset, but she knew from the set of his shoulders and the way he traced the scar with his finger that he was deep in thought.

"You should go ahead and look over the duke's hunting lodge," she said, after watching him for a time. "But perhaps go tomorrow night. It's been a long day, and I'm sure you're as weary as I."

"No," he responded, without changing his focus. "I'll go tonight. The sooner we find this Orly, the sooner we can determine if she is our mysterious Lady of the Westhaven. But something bothers me, Highness," he said, turning to face her.

"You mean something other than the fact that there's a mysterious assassin on the loose who wants me dead?" she asked wryly.

"Yes," he continued seriously, not noting her sarcasm. "This visit by your cousin seems conveniently timed, wouldn't you say?"

"How so?"

"He is your *only* cousin, am I correct?"

"He is," she responded flatly.

"The Queen decides to go on campaign," he said, his pacing resuming, eyes looking downward, but not focusing on anything in front of him. "Within days of her departure, you by an assassin, and your cousin —the only person, other than you, in the line of succession—conveniently shows up a week later for his first ever visit. Don't you find that strange?"

"Oh, surely you don't suspect Pietr?" she asked, shocked at the thought.

"Princess." Kaiso stopped his pacing and looked at her frankly. "Until we get to the bottom of this, and have uncovered who and why, I suspect everyone."

"Yes, but…" she stammered, struggling to recall everything she knew about Pietr.

"Let us imagine for a moment," he continued, interrupting her objection, "that your assassination had been successful. The kingdom would be in an uproar. Dispatches would have been sent via the fastest sailing craft possible, notifying the Queen and requesting her immediate return from Autun. Into this chaos conveniently glides the viscount and— Just bear with me, Highness," he said, momentarily stalling another objection from Darienne. "Imagine that he was able, strictly by dint of his presence and his blood, to restore some semblance of order to Wetheral. The Queen, upon her return, would have no choice but to install him as the new heir to the throne. The first rule when trying to solve a mystery is to see who stands to gain the most from it."

Darienne's objections melted away as she pondered the scenario he described. After a long moment, she looked to the captain and said, "It makes a devious kind of sense, I'll grant you."

Kaiso nodded grimly.

"But," the Princess continued, "that doesn't mean that we act on this suspicion, nor does it mean that I embrace this theory. Everything I know of Pietr is that he enjoys a soft life in Aesthir, filled with parties, drinking, and hunting. He doesn't seem like the sort to come up with a scheme like this, let alone put it into action."

"Agreed," Kaiso said. "But assuming this Levecque is the true mastermind, might it not be possible that he has suborned your cousin's involvement?"

"If you are right, Captain," Darienne said after another moment's reflection, "then this would be a conspiracy that reaches further than we had imagined."

"The viscount has not communicated directly with you?" the captain asked.

"No." She shook her head and sat down, deflated. "Which is, in itself, strange, isn't it?"

"Yes, it is," Kaiso affirmed.

"He would know that Mother is away," she continued, following her line of thought, her words gaining intensity as she went along, "and protocol and simple etiquette would demand that he write to me directly to request a visit, not simply notify the castle steward of his imminent arrival."

The captain nodded, allowing her to come to her own conclusions. "I would think so."

"It is almost as if…" Darienne paused, almost unable to speak the words. "It's almost as if he didn't expect me to be here."

"Precisely, Highness," Kaiso said firmly.

Darienne's hands began to shake as the realization flooded over her. "Damn!" she shouted, her hand slapping against the wood of the table. She felt lost. "What should I do?"

"Nothing," Kaiso said, plucking a chair from the side of the small table and positioning it in front of her. He sat leaning forward with urgency, his elbows on his knees. "Welcome him with gracious hospitality. Seem oblivious to the entire affair. If any mention is made of the attack, laugh it off as having been nothing more than the act of a drunken dockworker up to no good."

Darienne nodded, taking in his instructions.

"Whatever you do," Kaiso stressed, "do not in any way indicate that we believe this to be a conspiracy."

The Princess clasped her hands in her lap, making a conscious effort not to reach for the handle of her dagger. Her lip curled defiantly as she considered the plot that seemed to be unfolding before her.

"Be, in every way, the dutiful Princess," the captain said, standing. "Watch for any note of surprise in his face when you greet him. I'll check in with you in the morning and let you know if I've discovered anything at Comtois' lodge."

Darienne forced a smile as the captain turned to leave. But just as he opened the door, she stopped him with a last question.

"Kaiso," she said in a timid voice. "Whatever led you to consider such a horrible possibility, a conspiracy like this?"

He paused for a moment before responding. "Highness, in my experience, nobles are often the same—greedy and ambitious. They aspire to power but have become too fat and happy to be merciless enough to see their grand dreams through. For matters like this, they hire a professional, like Levecque or perhaps the Lady Ormond, to achieve their goals. And that person will be clever, shrewd and cruel." He stroked his scar as he spoke. "I have to say, this scheme has a certain elegance to it, and I am confident we do not yet see all of it."

"You say that as if you admire what this assassin has put in motion," Darienne noted.

"It's what I would have done," he said, his dark words filled with implications that reverberated in her head long after the echoes of the heavy door closing behind him had ceased.

Chapter 30

Over the past century, the Church of the Five has become a dangerous power in international politics. Extending its insidious reach from its main sacrarium on the isle of Cantabria, the Church's hegemonic ambitions—rumored to have first been shaped and enumerated in secret conclave by Pentatarch Julio IV over ninety years ago—utilize financial, political, theological, educational, and charitable means to "persuade" and "influence." These venomous tentacles, many of which seem so benign on the surface, extend and coil about the vulnerable spines of monarchs, magistrates, bankers, commanders, and the lords of virtually every realm north of Asland. When the influence of these various types might prove ineffective in bending an intransigent ruler or region to their will, evidence of apostasy is invariably discovered, and the Holy Knights are sent in to "cure" the disease to the body politic. All of this has allowed the Church to grow and spread most effectively. However, the Church has found their efforts to grow southward stymied at the shoreline of Asland, despite a well-publicized Crusade some thirty years ago. That misadventure ended in disaster when an entire brigade of mercenaries from across Daffyd—led by a charismatic and idealistic young Highlander from the Green Mount called Coinneach MacLir—changed sides at a critical juncture, handing victory to the forces of the Silken Emperor and routing the crusaders. Besides

Asland, and the even more distant Southern Reaches, the only two regions that have thus far resisted the Church's expansion are parts of Daffyd: Lachland and the Green Mount. But, in both cases, it is considered only a matter of time.

— Excerpt from "The Apostate's Guide to the Churchof the Five: Noting the Spread of Evil,"an anonymously published pamphlet widely distributed throughout Sudland and southern Lachland

574 HR - Last month of summer
Bay of Autun, Small Claw, Lachland

Archbishop Mormand

The archbishop leaned back from the table to allow his valet to remove his plate. He had only eaten a portion of the roast pheasant and smoked eel that his chef had prepared so masterfully, but the day's events had tired him and affected his appetite. The plate was the finest porcelain, with gold-leaf detailing that matched the golden fork and knife resting on it. Dinnerware of this caliber was an ostentatious luxury that he only allowed himself in secret on his yacht. He was very aware of appearances, and would never want word to get out that he indulged in such decadence. But after enduring weeks of the siege of Autun, he felt that he had earned the right to some small measures of comfort in the evenings as he rested on his private ship. It rocked gently beneath him as he gazed out the window at the lights of the town. Thus far, they had successfully repelled the enemy's daily assaults, but the Barbárs were tenacious, and—despite a dwindling assault force—showed no sign of relenting. Their resolve was matched only by that of the annoying Queen of Lachland, Isador. His skin crawled at the thought of all of those fawning men taking orders from her. *Well, she does have a certain grit,* he allowed. *But the kingdom and the Church will both be better off once we replace her.* He hoped that the other plans he had put into motion were bearing fruit. If so, things in Lachland, and indeed all of Daffyd, were about to change. Dramatically. The Pentatarch had given him strict instructions: bring the island continent under the sway of the Church by whatever means necessary. He grinned at that. If the naive old fool only knew just how far reaching his plans actually were. After a moment's rumination, his thoughts drifted back to Isador.

It was exhausting, constantly smiling graciously at the woman and seeming to be at her beck and call—even fighting to defend her on the city walls, as had happened that very day. A group of Barbárs had breached the defenses and gained a section of wall just north of the tower. They had been led by a single Räuber, a monstrous scarred brute with a missing nose and hands the size of a cucumis melon. In the past few days, the defenders had seen fewer of the shock troops among the enemy, though of course, Mormand was fully aware of the reason there were fewer of the brutes… Plans within plans. The Räuber had scaled the ladder with almost preternatural speed, quickly dispatching no less than six archers and two royal guards as over a dozen Barbárs had flooded the parapet in his wake. Two of the archbishop's own Holy Knights had fallen before the monster as they defended the Queen, though they managed to kill the brute in the process, and Mormand had been forced to join with Brigadier Dixon and Captain Zachar in a desperate but ultimately successful effort to hold back the mass of barbarians long enough for help to arrive. Eventually the enemy was repelled and the wall was once again secured. Dixon had been gravely wounded in the encounter, and the chirurgeons feared for his survival. He was an honest man, something that Mormand typically found tiresome, but Dixon was an effective—if not inspirational—commander, and the city's defense would suffer in his absence.

"Would you care for more wine, Your Grace?" the valet asked in his slow way, rousing the archbishop from his reverie.

"Just leave the carafe on the table, Grimaud," Mormand said with a weary smile, and watched as his servant set down the carved crystal vessel and left the cabin with his customary shuffling step.

The archbishop had taken the man into his service years earlier when Mormand was still an up-and-coming bishop. At the time, he imagined that the man would only be in his service for a matter of weeks until he could dispose of him and choose a more astute aide. But something about the servant's efforts had grown on the cleric, and now—over a decade later—Grimaud's consistent presence was as comfortable to him as a well-worn boot. Grimaud was an even-tempered simpleton. As a child he had fallen into a well and suffered a head injury, and he had never recovered his full faculties. Mormand had selected him, very publicly, from a lineup of equally challenged candidates. The then-Bishop Mormand had quoted the holy verses about being charitable to the lowest and how every person, regardless of their capabilities, was valued equally in the eyes of the Five. It had been a simple and somewhat transparent ploy to curry favor with the Eventide Watchtower, the one branch of the Church run by women and focused on acts of charity. Politically, it was the weakest branch, by far, but in order to be elevated to archbishop, one needed unanimous support from all five branches. And his support among the other four was already solid. Despite his challenges, however, Grimaud had proven a trusted and reliable valet, attentive to a fault, and quietly consistent in his work, never questioning orders. He was not the most efficient servant, and ofttimes needed reminding of details, but he had the quality that Mormand valued most: discretion. As the man tasked with expanding the Church's hegemony into all of Daffyd, the archbishop's role was equal parts spiritual leader, diplomat, general, spy, and, at times, assassin. It was therefore critical that his personal staff be trustworthy and discrete. Grimaud's damaged mind handled tasks well, but understood little of what was discussed around him. He was the perfect valet for a man such as Mormand.

Taking on Grimaud was the smallest of many gestures that the ambitious priest had made to impress the Eventide Watchtower's governing council, and most importantly Lady Fearn, the wily old bitch that had chaired the council for decades. She had originally been suspicious of Mormand's quick rise to bishophood and even quicker nomination to archbishop within the Boreal Watchtower, where he would become one of the three men who commanded the Church's formidable Holy Knights. She had pointedly and publicly spoken out against the dangers of vaulting ambition, and how avarice was a peril to the soul and an infection to the body of the Church—all thinly veiled references to Mormand. For months, the shrewd bishop made various public displays of charity—hospital visitations to the poor and destitute, hard labor alongside those convicted of vagrancy, personally serving meals to the hungry—all in an effort to soften the stubborn old woman's opinion of him. The turning point had come when Mormand arranged to fund two orphanages in the Sudlandic capital, Barris, and one in Lachland, in the southern city of Morvan, from his own sizable personal fortune. The orphanage in Morvan was the first the Church had ever opened in Lachland, and the bribes to secure the permits alone had cost him dearly. He had been forced to sell a small estate in the south of Sudland, but ultimately the chests of gold had been well worth it. That act of magnanimity had earned him the lasting gratitude of Fearn's daughter, Lady Maiwenn, who also sat on the council and whose portfolio entailed the care of unfortunate children—fully one quarter of the Watchtower's activities and budget. She had been the lynchpin, as she had Fearn's ear, and once he had earned Maiwenn's enthusiastic support, Fearn's few remaining objections had melted away. The other five members of the council quickly fell in line.

He grinned at the memory of how easily he had manipulated the women, though not without one small complication. Lady Fearn had summoned him to a private interview after the council had given his nomination their blessing. As his elevation had not yet been formalized, she still outranked him in the Church hierarchy, and her summons could not be denied. In diplomatic terms, she had made it clear that she had seen through his various machinations, yet had still given her assent to satisfy Lady Maiwenn. Fearn had done quite a bit of digging into his personal finances—apparently employing multiple spies and detectives—and had uncovered a few embarrassing details about his past dealings that he would have preferred to remain hidden. She had even gone so far as to suggest that this knowledge might give her ongoing leverage over him in his new position. He sighed now at the recollection. But within a fortnight, Lady Fearn had been found dead at her loom. Poison was suspected, but no assassin was ever identified or caught.

Looking out the broad window of his cabin at the bobbing lights of the town, he sipped his wine, shook his head and smiled wryly. *Stupid cow.* He arched his back, stretched, and massaged a sore muscle near his right elbow. The daily call to arms was wearing on him, though he would be damned if he would allow anyone to see that. To the eyes of the Queen and her advisors, he must seem to be a stalwart and indefatigable ally, earnestly wading into conflict to protect the borders of Lachland, as any true friend would. He noted that the Queen's early objections to the Church's overtures seemed to be weakening as he continued to endear himself to her, both in battle and in person. He was not unaware of the way women looked at him and responded to his charms. Though in his mid-fifties, he was still considered handsome, dashing even, and knew how to use those looks and his mellifluous, deep voice to his advantage. The Queen, for all of her royal affectations, was but a silly female—no more, no less—and he had yet to meet one that he could not conquer or outmaneuver.

Despite the battles, he still found daily opportunities to talk privately with her, careful to never overstep propriety, yet always attentive, gracious, and conveying a true interest in her as a person. At first, she had been so formal with him, but a few well-timed glances and smiles, coupled with quiet private inquiries as to her well-being and a consoling demeanor, seemed to be melting her formality. Just the day before, he had encouraged her to call him by his given name, Arnauld, and she had agreed, blushing uncharacteristically at the familiarity. It wouldn't be long now, he knew, before her remaining defenses would fall entirely. This would be a conquest he'd remember. Oh, she was a stately and beautiful woman, with that sharp nose and elegant features to be certain. He would enjoy the sheer carnality of bedding her, but more delicious to him was the thought of subjugating her will to his—which women *always* did once topped. He would continue to play his part, and sometime soon the stresses of command, the loneliness he knew the widowed Queen felt, and the passions stirred by combat would combine to tear down her resolve, and she would ask for him. *That part is critical,* he thought. *She must ask for me, willingly.* Only then would she truly be his. He sighed in anticipation. *Besides, if the other plans don't work out, there are worse outcomes than marrying a queen.*

He chuckled softly… Plans within plans within plans.

Then, of course, there was always Zsoka, the former Empress. Now there was a delicious morsel. Willful and headstrong, yes, but all the more enticing for that, and so young! After his trying Midwinter visit to her island prison and what he had shared with her, she was now beholden to him. He chuckled quietly. If only she understood the part she was playing in his greater plan. He clucked his tongue as he thought.

By now, he suspected she would have maneuvered Vajk to free her somehow. She might even have been trying to help him reach the Green Mount herself. She was desperate to regain her throne and her son. But she didn't realize that once Vajk's forces reached the Gate, her usefulness would be minimal. The archbishop had already secured Talon, though she didn't know that either. *Naive whore. She still assumes her son is being raised by the cousin who supplanted her. Foolish, foolish woman! So easily maneuvered.* Once the Gate was secured, they would work to regain her throne, but with many strings attached. It would be quite useful to the Church to have a nation as powerful as Orense fighting alongside the Holy Knights to support its expansion. And the Empress would do whatever she was told. Talon was all the leverage he needed to guarantee that.

The thought of the Empress' son reminded Mormand of a detail he had overlooked.

"Grimaud!" he called.

After a brief pause, his valet shuffled slowly into the room. "You called, Your Grace?"

"How is the boy faring with his new tutor?" the archbishop asked.

"He seems well, Your Grace," Grimaud said, seemingly confused by the question. "Shall I fetch the tutor?"

"No need. Is he taking to his lessons, to your mind?"

"He is learning the language, sir. Today, he asked me for a cup of juice, as clear as you could want." The servant smiled proudly, though whether he was proud of the boy, or proud that he had thought of a meaningful answer, the archbishop could not tell.

"And is the tutor satisfied with her cabin?"

"She has not said anything to me, sir, either way," Grimaud replied. "Shall I fetch her?"

"No, no, thank you. Very good." Mormand dropped his napkin onto his plate and Grimaud turned to leave.

"Grimaud," the archbishop called in a low, corrective tone before the valet exited the cabin. The servant turned back with his customary placid smile. Mormand pointed at his plate and raised his eyebrows meaningfully.

"Your Grace?"

"We've talked about this." The archbishop's tone was gentle. "When a gentleman or lady places their serviette upon their plate, that tells you what?"

Grimaud stared at the plate for a long moment before answering. "That they are finished, my lord?" Again, the proud smile.

"Yes… and what should you do?"

There was a long pause before he answered. "Remove the plate, my lord." Grimaud lowered his head in shame.

"Don't fret, old man," Mormand said as he poured himself another glass of wine. "You'll catch on, one day."

"I'm sorry, Your Grace," Grimaud said as he shuffled back to retrieve the plate, muttering under his breath as he left. "Dull Grimaud! Stupid Grimaud! Dull, dull, dull!"

The archbishop watched him leave, then turned to stare out the cabin window at the lights of Autun as he considered his next move.

Zach

He was exhausted. He couldn't remember the last time he had truly slept. Sick with worry for his wife and his own situation, his nights had become a torment of fears; he would toss and turn, dozing briefly, then waking with a start, his sheets drenched in sweat. The fatigue—both physical and emotional—increasingly weighed on him, and this past week he had barely been able to attend to his duties. The days were a blur of crazed activity and battle with long stretches of enforced boredom as he stood beside the Queen through mind-numbing meetings with her officers. Three times in the past days, he had found himself alone with the Queen. Each time, his trembling hand would find the handle of the Barbár dagger tucked beneath his tabard. Each time, however, his resolve had faltered just long enough for someone to interrupt the Queen's solitude, and his hand quickly returned to gripping the banner staff. He was in torment at the thought of his sweet wife's predicament, but something in him—reverence for the monarch, patriotism, or perhaps even cowardice—prevented him from striking his Queen.

That very day he had allowed yet another opportunity to pass. During the chaos of the fighting in the tower, when Brigadier Dixon had been injured, Zach was kicked backward and had crashed into the Queen, the two of them falling in a tangled heap. It would have been a simple matter to quickly slip the dagger's point beneath her armor as they struggled to disentangle themselves, but somehow he just couldn't do it. He knew Loeiza's captors would not be patient much longer, but the conflicting priorities of his dilemma struggled violently in his mind. There were times, in the small hours of the night, when he considered using the dagger on himself, thus escaping this impossible choice and sparing the Queen, but even that would condemn Loeiza to death. In the end, the image of his wife's terrified face as her captors had dragged her away would invade his thoughts and rob him of his resolve.

Dimming the oil lamp, he sat—still fully dressed for battle—on his cot in his quarters, rolling the handle of the barbed dagger from hand to hand as his mind searched desperately for some escape from his quandary. There came a light tap at the door and he quickly returned the blade to his belt, adjusting his tabard to cover it.

"Come," he said, rising and turning up the lamp's light.

A messenger from battalion headquarters poked her head in meekly before entering and standing at attention. "A parcel arrived for you today, sir," she said crisply, holding out a small rectangular box wrapped in coarse linen and tied with hemp. His name and the name of his unit had been carefully written on the linen in a woman's hand.

Zach thanked her, nodded her dismissal, then sat again on his cot to examine the mysterious package. Though mystified as to what could be contained within, his hands shook violently as he unwrapped it. He carelessly tossed the linen and hemp wrappings to the floor and looked with dread at the carved, wooden box. It looked to be the type of case in which one might send a necklace or some other small jewelry, but something told him this box contained nothing so pleasant. He stared at it for several moments, flushed with sweat despite the cool evening. His hands trembled more violently and his breath caught in his throat as he undid the clasp and slowly levered the lid open, revealing a rich blue velvet lining… and the severed finger of a woman, still bearing a wedding ring—Loeiza's ring.

Corruption had already begun, and the sickly sweet smell of his wife's severed, rotting flesh was an assault on his senses for which he was not prepared. His eyes widened in horror and he covered his mouth to stifle the involuntary gasp that came at the ghastly sight. Quickly setting the box on the small bedside table, he dashed for the chamber pot and vomited, retching until nothing more could come up. Pale, weak, and sweating, he collapsed back to sit on the floor, leaning against the wall of his small room. He held his breath for a moment to listen, hoping desperately that no one had heard his reaction. Hearing nothing to suggest his distress had been noted, he gingerly picked up the box once more and stared at its contents. He clenched his jaw and sobbed silently, unable to pry his eyes from the still-bloody digit. He shook his head and silently apologized to his wife again and again, tears dripping from his nose and chin. It was several more moments before he finally noticed a small note, folded and tucked near the base of the finger. Setting the box carefully in his lap, he lifted and unfolded the small note. It contained but two sentences, written in the same florid script as the address on the parcel:

We grow impatient. Let this be a spur to your resolve.

He sat staring at the box and its gruesome contents well into the night, alternately weighing his options, scheming, pausing to weep anew for his dear wife's plight, and then for his own. It was near dawn before he was finally able to close the box and sequester it deep within his new footlocker, which had been replaced following the fire and no longer contained nothing of personal value. Now, though, it contained a piece of his heart.

Realizing that any thought of rest or sleep was futile, he removed his boots, tabard, and mail and quickly stripped out of his clothing—which was all filthy with sweat, blood, and grime. He took a moment to wash his face and freshen up with a wet towel before dressing in clean trousers and a shirt. He then once more pulled on his hauberk, coif, and tabard, and cinched his belt into place, taking a moment to adjust the saber at his side. Finally, with a deep breath and a resigned sigh, he reached for the barbed dagger and slipped it into its customary place on his belt.

Despite the early hour, he left to pace the still-dark and empty streets, trying to gird his resolve for what was ahead.

Chapter 31

Positioned at the narrowest point of the vast, upward sloping meadow known as Monarch's Pass, Eagle's Gate had stood for hundreds of years as the border between Mardin and the Green Mount. Until the year 567 HR, the fortress had been garrisoned by Mardish troops who historically despised the Highlanders. Over the centuries, Mardish armies repeatedly marched north with territorial ambitions against the fertile Green Mount. Further back in history, the Mardish had even occupied large swaths of the lands of the Tor, including the largest towns of Esper and Stilling for over a century. The Highlanders finally unified their martial efforts under the leadership of Conal of the White Cleft—the last man to bear the title of High King of the Green Mount—successfully expelling the Mardish. So significant was this event, that a new calendar was begun, thus marking year one of Highland Reckoning, the year of liberation. In an effort to punish the Mardish for their depradations, High King Coral even sent a raiding army down through the pass into the northern reaches of the Lowlands. It marked the only time in known history that the people of the Green Mount had sent an offensive force south. Conal burned towns and looted much of northern Mardin before his forces were finally turned back at the fortified capital of Grado. In response, King Judikael I, shaken by how the northerners had laid waste to much of his country, commanded that a fortification be constructed at the mouth of

Monarch's Pass to prevent any subsequent raids. That bulwark was garrisoned by the Mardish for over five hundred years, right up until the invading Barbárs seized Eagle's Gate in 567 HR in preparation for their own invasion of the Green Mount, having already gutted the rest of Mardin and butchered King Offa.

– *Encyclopedia Daffydia,* Third Edition

574 HR – Last month of summer (10 days before the Equinox)
Eagle's Gate, Glenfolk region of the Green Mount

Corvus

It was nearing dusk by the time Corvus rounded the bend in the road at the southeasternmost corner of the Green Mount and beheld once more the ruins of Eagle's Gate—the fallen stones and destroyed battlements that had been the handiwork of his own troops, seven years earlier. A lone raven croaked at him from where it was perched on the jagged remains of a tower that rose asymmetrically above the broken walls like a finger pointing to the heavens. He nodded respectfully at the bird, his namesake, and stopped his horse at the high point in the road to survey what would be the field of battle. From his vantage, he could see all of Monarch's Pass to the south of the ruins, and his sharp eyes could see no sign of an army approaching as yet. There was, however, a lone rider in the distance moving slowly toward him. The mounted figure was still too far away to make out any details but it was clear that they seemed to be in no hurry. He watched the figure for a moment as it shimmered in the late summer heat. Its shoulders were slumped, and the horse stumbled with exhaustion. He would wait here to see who it might be and if they carried any news of the approaching invaders.

Another croak from the raven brought his attention back to the ruins. Though the stonework had been largely destroyed, what remained would still allow an army some cover. And, given that the ruins stood at the mouth of the pass with jagged and steep cliffs to the east, and nearly vertical, forested mountainside to the west, trying to flank a defending force would be nearly impossible once they were entrenched. He wished he knew the numbers of the enemy so he could plan more effectively. If his fyrd arrived and occupied the gate before the enemy, the archers could be quite effective from behind the shelter of the broken stonework and hidden among the trees of the wooded mountainside. With a shield wall arrayed to the south, spanning the mouth of the pass, they could potentially hold it against an invading army of about twice their number while they waited for reinforcements. Even if the enemy came in much greater numbers, the fyrd could delay them long enough for the rest of their allies to arrive, though he shuddered at the thought of that butcher's bill. The enemy would be mounted, but no mounted charge could prevail directly against the spears of an established shield wall, regardless of the numbers involved. The Barbárs would be forced to dismount and form their own wall. Then it would be hammer and tong in the breathless clutch of bodies. Corvus uttered a silent prayer that all the training he and Yazid had done with the fyrd would be enough. Many would die, horribly. But he shook that thought from his mind. *Can't linger on that before the battle. There'll be muckle time to mourn and bury the dead. Keep your eyes on what's afore ye, lad.*

He looked to the steep mountainside on his right, remembering where he had positioned Toren's archers last time. He had kept them hidden until he had succeeded in drawing out the Barbárs from behind the safety of their walls. It had been a gamble, but after frigid days of fruitless attacks against those battlements—and hundreds of Highlanders dead—he had to draw them out before all was lost. His warriors were hearty, but the early snowfall had not been supportive of an attack against a fortified position, and the casualties from both blade and cold had been high. Corvus had judged the nature of his enemy correctly; a force that was accustomed to moving quickly, utilizing speed and brutality to ravage villages and towns, rapidly conquering vast swaths of countryside from horseback, chafed behind walls where they were warm, safe, and had the advantage. As another long, frozen day of fighting was concluding, he had staged a bit of theatre for the benefit of the Barbárs watching from the ramparts. Planned scuffles had broken out between the Glenfolk and the White Cleft forces, culminating in a loud shouting match between Mannon and Fergus. As evening had fallen, King Mannon had ordered his troops to pack up their tents ostentatiously, and march away—presumably back home—abandoning the joint effort. Sometime in the dark of night, King Fergus' forces and those of the Midlands had likewise packed up and left, leaving only Corvus' fyrd to face the enemy. Nonetheless, Corvus had sent his troops once more against the walls in a desultory effort, which ended with his forces suddenly breaking ranks and fleeing up the road, out of sight around the bend—to the very spot where Corvus currently sat astride his mount surveying the land. The gambit had worked and the Barbárs, smelling blood, mounted up and galloped out of the fort in pursuit, no doubt anticipating a slaughter. It was a slaughter, indeed, though not the one the enemy had imagined.

As the screaming barbarians had rounded the bend in the road, they came face-to-face with the full, united, allied army arrayed in a broad arc. The Barbár charge suddenly stalled, causing them to mill in confusion at the unexpected sight. That was when Toren's archers had begun the deadly attack from their hidden positions among the trees on the mountainside. As the fatal rain of arrows fell, the enemy was momentarily confounded and unsure how to respond—whether to dismount and form up, retreat back to the safety of the fort, or attempt a suicidal mounted charge against a prepared shield wall. Those moments proved decisive. A skilled archer with a longbow can fire over ten arrows a minute with accuracy, and Toren's three hundred archers rained down thousands of arrows with lethal effect onto the Barbárs, decimating them. By the time the Green Mount shield wall charged, the battlefield was already strewn with dead and wounded men and horses. The few that had survived the trap tried in vain to flee back to the battlements, but a relatively small force of some fifty members of the fyrd had been hidden in the rocks of the hillside and quickly formed a shield wall to block the enemy's retreat. Corvus' forces had swarmed the Barbárs, leaving none alive.

How the battle would play out this time was entirely dependent on how quickly the allied armies would arrive, and whether they reached the ruined fortress before the enemy. Corvus sat astride his patient mount running calculations in his head, estimating travel times and troop numbers. Fergus' forces would probably take the longest, given that they had to march from the White Cleft in the northeast, while Cailean and the Glenfolk should be able to get here within two to three days—depending on how quickly his son was able to assume full command and mobilize. His own fyrd should arrive within the same time frame as the Glenfolk, he imagined. Though the storm may have slowed them. The Midlands were a question. Would Lady Donella withhold her troops yet again? So many variables.

As he stared at the fallen fortification, his thoughts drifted back through its history. It was a place steeped in blood and bitter battles, and Corvus knew its story would gain another grisly chapter in the days to come.

Seven years, he thought. *We rose to the challenge then. And again two years later. Can we do it once more?*

"Seeing the past, Raven?" a voice asked unexpectedly from behind him. "Or the future? Both are bloody."

Corvus turned in his saddle to find the Fool, Latrans, sitting on the lowest branch of a nearby oak tree, his little dog perched beside him looking forlornly at the ground below. How Corvus had missed them as he rode up was a mystery, as the Fool's clothing was brightly colored and stood out clearly against the gray bark and dark leaves.

"You've returned once again, Fool," Corvus said, by way of greeting.

"You," Latrans replied, pausing to nimbly hop down from the branch, "have a gift for stating the obvious." He then turned and beckoned for his dog to jump into his arms. "Has anyone ever told you that?"

"Better obvious than opaque," Corvus replied.

"Is it though?" the Fool replied quickly, setting his dog on the ground. "Sometimes the most powerful details are the ones that are hidden, no? Nay? Not? Maybe?"

"Once again you speak in circles, Fool," Corvus said.

"Do I…?." The ragged man flashed a rueful smile and placed a hand over his heart. "I do."

Corvus sighed. "What brings you to the Gate, Latrans?"

Instead of answering immediately, the Fool reached into his threadbare vest and somehow produced three balls, which he immediately tossed into the air and began juggling deftly in the familiar circular pattern. Paying no attention to the flying balls in front of him, Latrans looked at Corvus as he answered. "So many pieces, so many details…" Somehow, he had added a fourth ball to the mix, though Corvus hadn't seen him retrieve another sphere. "Regardless of their journey," he continued, and a fifth ball was now miraculously circling amongst the others as the Fool changed the pattern of the legerdemain. Two balls circled on either side, while one flipped on a vertical path between them. "Regardless of how many pieces are moving…" A sixth and seventh ball now joined in an even more complicated pattern. "They all come together eventually." With that, he stopped, somehow catching all seven spheres in his hands at once, and slipping them back into his vest.

"This is the place then?" Corvus asked, hoping he had grasped Latrans' meaning.

"Much will be decided here, though not all," the Fool responded, reaching into his vest once more and producing a long flute, which he held before him as he continued. "This a song with many parts. And you, Corvus Corax, will influence much—perhaps most—of this melody."

With that, he turned and began walking into the hills playing his flute, his dog prancing merrily to the tune. Not satisfied, Corvus spurred his horse and rode up onto the hillside in front of the departing Fool, barring his path.

"What do you know of the invading force?" Corvus demanded. "How soon will they arrive? What are their numbers?"

"Questions! So many questions!" Latrans responded. "Never small talk with you, just questions, questions, questions!"

"For the love of Ilian, speak plain, man!"

"Ah, the Golden Hand," Latrans said with an air of nostalgia. "Did you know He hated the taste of clams? I never understood that. No accounting for taste, I suppose." He lifted the flute once more to his lips.

"Stop playing your damned music and answer me, I beg you," Corvus pleaded.

Pulling his flute from his lips, the Fool seemed to consider his answer for a moment. "One is coming that was moved by my music to visit you. Another is coming who is born for music... one who is loved by you. There are those who will soon arrive who are driven by another type of music... the music of torment and suffering. They seek to undo you. You stand on a rock as the flood waters surround you. You must find your way, leaping and deftly stepping across the flood, without being taken by it."

"Must you speak ever in riddles?" Corvus said, barely containing his frustration. "Too much is at stake for your games!"

"No games, Corvus Corax. Coinneach MacLir. Raven. You may not have the strength to face this foe directly, but face him you must. You haven't the knowledge to find the answers yourself, so you must ask others to help you... and you haven't much time, though time is what you will desperately need. Very soon, the battle is joined."

Seemingly satisfied with his answer, Latrans ducked under the neck of Corvus' mount and proceeded on his way into the forested hills. Before Corvus lost sight of him behind a stand of birch trees, the Fool called over his shoulder, "Protect the Tor, for it is everything!"

The words struck Corvus and stopped him from pursuing the departing figure. They reverberated through his memory, as if he were recalling them from a dream. As he sat puzzling, his mind grasping at vaguely remembered shadows, he heard the familiar voice of his Aslene friend call out from behind him.

"There you are! I had hoped we would find you here!"

Turning, he saw Yazid and Ligulf just riding into view at the bend in the road. He took a glance back to see how far Latrans had progressed, he was somehow not surprised to see no trace of the Fool at all, though the wind still carried echoes of his flute. As Corvus spurred his mount down to meet Ligulf and Yazid, the raven croaked loudly and swooped directly in front of him before flying off again. Startled, Corvus watched it for a moment as it flew into the wooded hillside, another question dying on his lips before he shook his head and turned to greet the others.

Guiding his horse between them, Corvus said, "Glad I am to see you both." He accompanied the words with handshakes and embraces on both sides —first his son, then his friend.

"I wish we brought better news," Yazid said, his smile fading.

"No. She denies us again?" Corvus asked incredulously.

"It's not so much Donella, Da," Ligulf interjected, "but her bastard husband, Aengus."

"True, my friend," Yazid agreed. "He is as narrow-minded a man as ever I have met, jealous of your acclaim and determined to deny you, regardless of the cost to us all. What did you call him, Li, a cockwomble? Accurate, very accurate." The big man chuckled ruefully.

"So," Corvus said, digesting the news, "once again we must make do without the Midlands."

"Aye," Ligulf said somberly. "I wish it werna so."

Yazid looked out over the plain of Monarch's Pass. "Any sign of the enemy, yet?"

"Not as yet," Corvus answered, then gestured at the lone rider making slow progress toward them. "Only that rider approaches. Perhaps they'll be able to tell us something more. Come, let's build a fire and wait. With the evening comes a chill."

The three men rode down to the ruins where they were able to shelter from the mountain breezes among the fallen stones. Corvus and Yazid tended to the horses while Ligulf fetched wood for a fire. Yazid told him the details of their meeting with Donella and Aengus. As he described Aengus' insults, Corvus' hands balled into fists and he turned his face away from his friend. In a quiet, steady voice, he said, "There'll be a reckoning for him." Then, once his breath had calmed he nodded to Yazid and said, "Come let's prepare some food and tea. That rider will want a welcome."

Yadira

She swayed in the saddle as the sun set, exhausted from long hours riding up the difficult switchbacks of the Devil's Hoof. One arm clutched the sleeping Argant, the other loosely held the reins of her weary mount as it staggered onward toward the ruins at the mouth of the pass. Yadira's bleary eyes could make out a flickering of firelight between the stones, and she prayed to the goodness of the White Halls that whoever awaited her there might be friendly. She had lost sight of Lupe hours ago, when her fellow votary had doubled back to scan the road behind them for any sign of Mama and Amina. But Yadira was beyond the point of worrying any longer.

For two days they had ridden north, sick with worry but following Mama's parting instructions to carry on without her as the aging teacher rode south alone to rescue Amina. It was a suicidal mission, Yadira had argued. No one could ride into the heart of an enemy encampment, rescue a prisoner, and hope to escape with their lives. But Mama would not be dissuaded, quoting the sacred text that spoke of the duty of the shepherd before tearfully blessing each of them and sending them on their way into the icy storm. Cold, wet, and miserable they had ridden for hours as the daylight waned behind the heavy clouds. Lupe had first spotted the wolves keeping pace with them. Gesturing with her chin, she subtly pointed them out to Yadira, whose horse was becoming increasingly jittery. Finally they sought shelter in a spittal, or way house, that they happened upon by the side of the road. The one-room stone building by the highway had clearly served many travelers; the thatching on its roof was in dire need of attention, and its door sagged on its hinges. But to the three shivering and soaked wayfarers, it felt like luxury, despite having to crowd inside with the horses to shelter them from the wolves.

Twice, Lupe had tried to turn back to aid their teacher. Each time, Yadira reminded her of the importance of their mission, and their sacred pledge to Mama that it would be fulfilled.

"How can we fulfill the mission," Lupe argued, "when Mama has the staff that we're supposed to deliver to this Corvus?" Indeed, there had been much discussion on that point, but ultimately Mama had felt that her odds of successfully retrieving Amina would be enhanced by carrying the staff, telling them that they must be the harbingers of her approach.

"We can be the word of warning," Yadira responded tiredly. "It is the most we can do, and we must press on."

Ultimately, it was worry for Argant that had kept Lupe with Yadira. As the dawn broke the morning after the storm, Yadira had been unable to rouse the boy. Checking his forehead, she had found him burning up with fever.

"We must press on," she told Lupe, "and pray that we might find a village or town in which to shelter."

Yadira prepared a thin broth for the boy, and liberally added medicinal herbs from her satchel. They were pleased to see that despite his fever, Argant drank the soup eagerly.

"He will sleep now," Yadira had pronounced. "Let us make our best time up this valley."

Lupe agreed and they quickly saddled their mounts and departed, Yadira holding the bundled, sleeping child while Lupe ranged widely to either side of the road for as long as the terrain allowed, watching for dangers and possible game. The broad triangular valley narrowed as they neared the steep rise at its northern edge. As they approached the sheer climb out of the Devil's Hoof with its daunting switchbacks, Lupe had paused, telling Yadira that she planned to double back for a short distance to watch for Mama or any possible pursuit. Yadira had agreed. That was the last she had seen of her companion.

The climb up to the pass had been difficult, and her horse struggled with obvious fatigue. Were she not cradling Argant in her arms, she would have dismounted to make the climb gentler on her mount, but even though the boy's fever seemed to have passed, his small body had been through so much in the previous days that he simply was unable to ride on his own up the sheer switchbacks.

They crested the final rise late in the day, and Yadira's spirits had sunk when she saw no settlements or shelter. Only the broad, sloping meadow of Monarch's Pass, and in the far distance, something that looked to be a jumble of rocks and broken spires. Their horse was exhausted, but Yadira saw no alternative but to make for the stones before nightfall. The heat of the summer's day was rapidly dissolving and bitter, mountain winds were already slicing through her robes.

After an hour, Argant had stirred in her arms, seeming uncomfortable once more. Touching the skin of his neck, she noted his fever had returned, though it seemed less intense than it had been. That was when she spotted the flickering lights in the ruins, as darkness began to fall. She estimated she still had another hour or so before they reached whoever or whatever awaited them there. She glanced behind her once more, hoping for any sign of Lupe, but was rewarded with the sight of nothing but the wind stirring the gorse of the valley. She noted a kestrel riding the steady breeze and hovering, nearly motionless above the grassland, the last glimmers of daylight coloring its brown wings a rosy hue. For a moment, she remembered soaring above this very terrain herself, in her dreamlike journey three nights earlier. Had it only been three nights? She shook her head in wonder. It seemed like moons ago, so much had happened in the interval: Amina being captured; Mama leaving to save her; Lupe, Argant, and Yadira suffering through the icy wet of the storm as they traveled north; climbing the endless switchbacks to reach the pass. After so much hardship, everything was falling apart. She wondered wearily what had happened to Lupe, and whether she would ever see her, or Mama, or Amina again. She sighed resignedly. *Trust the Ancestors. Carry on.* Argant stirred restlessly in her arms, and Yadira stopped her mount to adjust her grip on the boy, pausing to shake out her left arm which was entirely numb from holding him for hours.

"I know, little one," she cooed softly. "Not long now. Be brave for just a little longer."

As the sensation returned to her arm with a fierce burning, she sighed, repositioned Argant, and once more spurred her exhausted mount on.

Corvus

Corvus and Yazid looked up from the fire as the rider finally approached. The light of their small blaze ruined their night vision, preventing them at first from discerning any details about the traveler, but as the horse neared, Corvus recognized the mounted figure to be a woman. He stood, Yazid and Ligulf both following his lead, and offered her a welcoming smile.

"Welcome, traveler," he said warmly, gesturing to the fire. "We have food and warmth to offer, though I fear our hospitality is a bit limited."

"By the White Hall!" Yazid gasped. "She wears a jimas!"

Corvus stood for a moment in confusion as Yazid hurried to the mounted visitor's side.

"Blessings of the Ancestors upon you," Yazid said in Aslene. "You are welcome to our fire."

Corvus was stunned when the weary rider replied in Aslene, "Blessings upon you, friend. I am afraid we have need. The boy I am holding is feverish, and we are weary to the bone."

Ligulf looked at his father in confusion, not understanding what was being said. Corvus gestured for his son to steady the horse and assist Yazid. With a quick nod, Ligulf moved to take the horse's bridle.

"Here," Yazid offered, holding up his arms. "Hand the boy to me while you climb down."

She seemed to hesitate for a moment, but relented in the face of Yazid's open arms and gentle smile. Something about her voice and manner arrested Corvus. Did he know this woman? Familiarity seemed to hover at the edge of his perception, dreamlike, though for the life of him, he could not grasp the connection.

As she dismounted, Ligulf led her exhausted mount away to be brushed and fed, and Yazid busied himself serving up the tea. The woman tended to the boy first, serving him small spoonfuls of rabbit stew, which Yazid gladly provided, and into which she mixed some herbs that Corvus assumed to be medicinal. The boy eagerly ate the food, his unsettling eyes searching the new faces around him with a febrile intensity. Afterward he drifted into a deep sleep, no doubt aided by the herbs. Once he was tucked in by the fire, she gratefully accepted a steaming mug of tea for herself.

As the woman settled in, Corvus addressed her in fluent, if accented, Aslene. "You have traveled far. We do not see many travelers from your land here in the Highlands."

The woman seemed startled to hear him speak her tongue, and she stared at him for several moments before she responded, eyes narrowed as she searched his face.

"I imagine not," she replied eventually. "How then do you speak Aslene?"

Corvus and Yazid exchanged a knowing glance as Yazid handed the woman a bowl of stew. She smelled the food, prepared and seasoned by a fellow countryman, and her shoulders relaxed. She closed her eyes, reveling in the familiar scents. Corvus thought he could hear her muttering a prayer of thanks behind her veil.

"I had the good fortune to travel to your country in my youth," he told her. "I experienced many wonders there, and hold many of your people dear to my heart."

The woman smiled briefly behind her jimas, which she adjusted modestly to allow her to eat. It was customary for

Aslene women to eat separately from men, and he was chagrined to see this weary traveler struggling to spoon up the soup while holding her veil in place.

"You'll pardon me," he said, rising from his place by the fire, "but I suspect my son may require some assistance with your horse. Please be at ease at our fire."

He nodded to Yazid, who understood perfectly and joined him in stepping away to provide their guest a moment of privacy to eat and drink, free from the presence of men.

After a reasonable interval, during which Corvus explained to his confused son why they had both come over to assist with the exhausted mount, Corvus coughed loudly to announce their return, then the three men stepped out from behind the shelter of the ruins. Their guest had finished eating, and looked up at them expectantly upon their return. Corvus had always found it difficult to read the facial expressions of a woman in a jimas, but he thought he detected a look of gratitude in her eyes. He gestured at the sleeping boy beside the fire.

"Is this your boy?" he asked quietly.

Ligulf looked at his father in bemusement, clearly not understanding a word of the conversation.

"No," said the woman. But apparently noting Ligulf's confusion, she answered in Sudlandic, the common tongue throughout Daffyd. "We found him hiding after the barbarians slaughtered his family and village."

"We?" Yazid asked. "Are there more of you?"

"There were four of us," she replied, "not counting Argant here. We became… separated."

Corvus and Yazid exchanged looks. There was much more to that story, but Corvus noted the woman's trembling hands and stooped shoulders and decided against pressing her for more details just now. She was clearly exhausted, both physically and mentally.

"This sounds like a tale worth hearing," Yazid said, before Corvus could reply. "But perhaps it is best saved for morning. You are no doubt weary from your ordeal. Please rest by the fire. We'll keep watch."

Tears welled in her eyes as she looked at Yazid with such clear gratitude that the big man became flustered and promptly busied himself preparing a bedroll for their guest.

"I must ask," the woman said after a moment's pause, staring intently at Corvus, "and forgive me if I am too bold, but why do you seem so very familiar to me? I feel as though we have met, recently… and yet that is impossible."

A cold chill ran down Corvus' spine and he swallowed thickly before responding, "I have the same feeling, though I canna say why."

Setting aside her empty bowl and cup, she stood and approached him, as he rose to meet her. She stared intently at him, searching his face for several moments as if grasping for some lost memory. With a sudden gasp of recognition, her eyebrows shot up and she placed a hand on his chest as if to steady herself. Corvus' hands gently gripped her shoulders to keep her from staggering.

"The Man of Iron," she whispered, and another chill spidered its way down Corvus' neck, raising gooseflesh on his arms.

Corvus and Yazid exchanged a confused look as she blinked more tears from her eyes, shaking her head. The men stood expectantly, waiting for her to recover herself and continue. He dared not say anything that might break the fragile moment. After a time, and several deep, shuddering breaths, she looked up into his eyes and spoke.

"You are Corvus Corax," she said firmly, no hint of a question in her tone. "Protégé of Master Ashahl, and the defender of these lands."

"By the Ancestors!" Yazid whispered.

"How in the wide world…?" Ligulf began, his words fading into wonder.

"And you came into my dream three nights hence, and spoke to me of grave danger," Corvus replied softly, his brow furrowed with realization and concern. "What sorcery is this?"

"It is not sorcery," she said quickly, seemingly aware of how strange and potentially threatening all of this might appear to the men. "My teacher, Nabila Warad, was tasked by Ashahl to warn you of a terrible danger. We have traveled these last eight moons from Asland to find you."

Corvus shook his head in wonder as he stared into her dark eyes. "I am amazed at what you say, but forgive me, that doesna explain how you entered my dream."

"Mama Warad sent my spirit ahead to find you," the woman said weakly. Her legs suddenly gave out beneath her, fatigue from her ordeal finally overcoming her.

Corvus caught her weight and gently moved her to a comfortable place by the fire. Standing protectively over her, he paused for her to collect herself, then said, "This Mama Warad is a woman of unique talents, apparently. I look forward to hearing more about her and how in all the world Master Ashahl could be involved this, and what he may require of me after so very long. But first, you speak of a terrible danger. We are aware of the Barbár army that approaches. Is the peril more dire than that?"

She looked up into his sea-gray eyes and was about to respond when Yazid interrupted them.

"A rider approaches," he said, picking up his staff and moving out of the ring of firelight. Ligulf sprang to his feet, hand to the hilt of his needle-like sword as he moved several paces to Corvus' right. The group watched as a mounted figure emerged from the gloom. It was another Aslene woman, younger than their guest, and stout compared to her bony frame. The rider moved with an assurance, clutching a recurved bow in her left hand and eyeing the three men suspiciously. It took Corvus a moment to realize that there was a body draped over the rear of her horse: a dead Barbár, the beads and ornaments in his tangled hair tinkling with each stride of the mount.

"Lupe!" their guest said, her voice flooded with relief. "Thank the Ancestors!"

Before anyone else could speak, the rider dismounted with a martial grace that Corvus recognized at once. Mulakima. The powerful woman seized the corpse and flung it to the ground beside her horse, wiping her hand on her robes before speaking.

"This one was watching you from the hillside," she said, curtly. "There were three others, but I lost them in the dark."

The men took turns keeping watch as the exhausted women slept, though the new arrival, Lupe, was slow to relax her guard. Before sleep took them, however, the votaries shared the highlights of their odyssey, why they had been sent, and the few details they knew of the mysterious "Key" which Ashahl had tasked Mama with bringing to Corvus.

"Does any of this make sense to you?" Yazid whispered to Corvus as the two sat together later, far from the fire on a section of fallen wall.

"I dinna ken," Corvus said, wiping a hand across his face. "It's all a great puzzle to me. You?"

"I am at a loss," Yazid began, "but if Ashahl truly has stolen one of the Blessed Tools and sent it all this way to you, there must be a great purpose, indeed."

"Aye..." Corvus nodded wearily. After a moment's further consideration, he said, "I am sure more will become clear with the dawn. Muckle a mystery here, Yazid." Then, with a light pat on the burly man's knee, he added, "Get some rest, I'll take first watch."

"No, old friend," Yazid said with his customary smile. "You sleep. Your days have been long, and I see how they wear on your spirit. I fear the coming days will afford little rest for you. I'll watch, you rest."

Not able to find the strength to argue, Corvus sighed. "I dinna know what I'd do without you, old friend."

"Not another word," Yazid said with a wink, and Corvus stumbled off to find his bedroll.

Chapter 32

"Hello, little blackbird," said the snake. "Give me your eggs and nest."

"But this is my nest and these eggs are my young," answered the blackbird.

"Yes, but I am hungry," replied the snake.

"No!" And the little blackbird attacked the large serpent, driving him away from the nest.

— Children's fable

574 HR - *Last month of summer*
Wetheral Castle, Deep Mere, Lachland

Darienne

She endured the ministrations of her attendants with remarkable patience, all things considered. Ingrid and Dominique busied themselves lacing up her boots, while Maddie applied rouge to the Princess' cheeks and painted her lips the color of ripe cherries. Darienne *hated* makeup. She hated all of the cultural frivolity of women having to paint themselves, and on most occasions, she would have long since shooed Maddie away. But today was not about her own feelings. Today was a day to make as powerful an impression as possible. Pietr would be arriving within the hour, and she wanted there to be no scintilla of doubt as to who held the reins here in her mother's absence. Besides, the last time she had seen Pietr, she had been a freckled, muddy tomboy chasing the staff's children about the castle kitchens, waving her toy sword and screaming against any sense of decorum. She smiled at the thought that so little had changed, yet it was an image she wished to dispel from his mind with prejudice.

"Your Highness," Maddie said in her rich, accented voice, "would you care to see the results?"

"I'm sure you've done a wonderful job, Maddie," Darienne said with a relaxed wave of her hand, and yet curiosity still drove her to take the proffered hand mirror. She gasped at the image reflected in it. The face looking back at her from the glass was truly breathtaking.

"Your mouth will show to better effect, Mistress, with your lips closed," the tall woman said with a sly wink.

Snapping her mouth shut, Darienne felt a slight blush rise in her cheeks, making Maddie giggle softly. "Hush, you!" the Princess replied with a playful slap at her attendant's hip.

She stared at the mirror. Not a curl was out of place. The makeup had been applied subtly, yet deftly, creating a radiance around her eyes, a delicate shading that emphasized her firm jaw, and just the right amount of kohl lining her lashes. *In a thousand years,* she mused, *I could never have achieved this.*

"Maddie," she said, dropping the mirror into her lap, "you're a genius."

"Yes, ma'am," the servant replied with a quick curtsy. "I know."

Ingrid snorted in disbelief from her kneeling position and seemed about to say something tart, when a knock sounded at the chamber door. It was Kaiso's typical knock.

"Enter," Darienne said loudly enough to be heard through the oaken door, then gestured to Ingrid and Dominique to finish up. Kaiso slipped in the door, glancing over his shoulder as he did.

He looked rough. Besides having not shaved, he was still wearing his "slinks," as he called them—the black trousers, shirt, and waistcoat he was prone to wear for surreptitious nighttime activities. Even the leather of his sword belt had been blackened and dulled. His eyes looked haggard and sunken, his hair was unkempt, and a swelling on his left cheek was starting to purple. He stood unevenly, as if nursing an injury, and his right arm was clamped tightly to his side.

"You look awful," she said bluntly.

"The other man looks worse," he replied tiredly. Then an eyebrow shot up as he seemed to notice Darienne's transformation. "I take it you have news, as well?"

"I'll explain in a moment," she said. With a wave, she dismissed her servants, who curtsied and exited in a pack.

"Tell me what you found," she said, once the door had closed and they were alone.

"It is both as we feared," he began, "and worse."

She leaned back and steepled her fingers beneath her chin, focused on the captain.

"Duke Comtois is dead," Kaiso said flatly, and Darienne gasped. "As far as I can tell, he's been dead a week or more."

"Start at the beginning."

"I rode to the duke's lodge," he reported as he eased himself into a chair by the hearth, "only to find its gates guarded by unknown soldiers wearing civilian attire. They were dressed in casual, nondescript clothing, but they were large and clearly had some sort of armor beneath their shirts. Staying out of their sight, I circled the lodge and managed to slip over a wall and into the back garden. I was pleased to note the chandeliers were all still lit, despite the late hour. This provided me a clear view of much of the downstairs, and I was able to slip from window to window, unnoticed. I moved to the back portico, where I could see more of the guards roaming the grounds and prowling the interior. I managed to slip behind a hedge, where I could peer through the drawing room window, and there I found our prey. The Lady

Ormond was sitting in a large, leather chair before the hearth, wearing a satin dressing gown and drinking wine from an ornate goblet like she was the mistress of the house. Though dressed differently than in my previous encounter, there was no mistaking her. I watched her for some time. The guards would periodically enter the room and report something to her deferentially, which she would acknowledge before dismissing them. She was obviously in command, and there was no sign of the duke."

He continued his report in this sequential, organized manner. He told of how, just as he was turning to leave his perch by the window to search for a quiet way into the lodge, he heard a disturbance from within that drew his attention back to the lady. A guard had entered the drawing room, this time pushing a haggard-looking woman before him. She seemed to be in her early thirties, and in better times was likely attractive, though of a somewhat mean station. Her hair was distressed, her skin begrimed, her clothing torn and soiled, and her left hand was wrapped in a thick bandage, pink with blood. Her eyes were bloodshot and tears had left tracks through the dirt on her face. The woman began to shake and sob in terror at the sight of Lady Ormond, who waited patiently for the fit to pass. After a few moments, she spoke to the bedraggled woman, though Kaiso could not hear what was said. The woman responded by falling to her knees, both hands covering her mouth as she shook her head and pleaded loudly enough for Kaiso to hear her cries through the glass.

"No, I beg you!" she cried. "Not again, not another!"

The lady had replied softly, her voice but an indistinct murmur. At this, the woman dissolved into racking sobs, collapsing fully onto the carpet before the hearth. The guard seized her roughly by the neck and, with little effort, hoisted her to her feet. The lady then gave some instruction to him. He nodded curtly in response, then dragged the howling woman away.

At this point, Kaiso had moved to begin his search for a quiet entrance: a servant's door, or perhaps a cellar. He had yet to learn the fate of the duke, though he was beginning to fear the worst. After a few minutes creeping around the perimeter of the lodge, he was rewarded with the sight of a cellar door, the handles of which were wrapped in thick chains and locked. The slivered moon had withdrawn behind a thick blanket of clouds, so he had to proceed entirely by feel, but in short order, his picks were out and he soon heard the satisfying click of the lock opening. As he gingerly drew the chains away, a guard—no doubt drawn to the sound—rounded the corner of the building. Kaiso's knives came out and a deadly duel ensued. Despite the man's size and apparent training, he was hampered by whatever armor he wore beneath his clothing, and the large blade he wielded was not suited to the tight confines of the surrounding shrubbery; Kaiso was dressed for nimble, deadly work and his knives quickly found their target.

Or so he had thought. Side-stepping a vicious backhand slash from the guard, Kaiso had leapt forward, burying his knife to the hilt in the guard's eye. A fatal blow. There was a blinding flash of light, and Kaiso was pitched backward with such force that he crashed into the stone wall of the lodge, bruising the side of his face. Stars swam in his vision and he gasped for breath, struggling to regain control of his limbs. Some providence alerted him to danger, and he fell immediately into a backward tumble just as the guard's sword crashed into the wall where Kaiso's head had been. He couldn't begin to understand how his opponent had somehow survived having a knife buried in his skull, but there wasn't time to ponder the question. He leapt onto the man's unguarded back. A garrote that the captain kept hidden up his right sleeve was out in a trice, and around the guard's throat. The man thrashed, slamming Kaiso into the wall two, three times, until stars once again swam in his eyes and he heard something within his torso crack. Just as Kaiso's efforts were about to fail, the guard went to his knees, gasping and clutching at the merciless wire cutting into his neck. Gritting his teeth against the fire in his ribs, Kaiso redoubled the pressure on the garrote, and the thin wire sliced deeply into the flesh of the guard's throat. With a gurgle, the man collapsed dead at his feet.

Kaiso's vision swam and he was forced to take a knee until the searing pain subsided. He crouched there for several moments, listening to the night's sounds for any indication the altercation had been overheard. Finally, satisfied that he was undiscovered, he rose with difficulty and looking about, recovered his dropped knives.

Feeling exposed and unready for another fight should he be discovered, he quickly finished unwrapping the chain from the cellar door. Without waiting to check if the place was unoccupied, he pitched the corpse with some difficulty down the stairs into the dark, then followed it and closed the door behind him as quietly as possible.

After a few moments of groping about, his hands were rewarded with a hanging lantern, which he lit with a flint from his pouch. There, in that cellar, he found that for which he had been searching: the body of Duke Comtois, wrapped in blood-stained muslin and reeking of the corruption of flesh.

Remembering the rapidity with which Lady Ormond had vacated the town house, emptying its contents and removing all clues, he knew what he had to do. Part of him wanted to press on, perhaps rescue the poor prisoner and learn more of Lady Ormond's plot from her. But if the guard was missed, a search would ensue, his body would be found, and the lady would know she had been discovered. His prey would once again vanish and the search would have to begin anew. With difficulty, he wrapped the guard's body in a rolled carpet he found moldering on the cellar shelf, and with great and painful effort, heaved the rug and its grisly contents back into its place. Pausing to listen at the cellar door for some moments until he was satisfied that the path was clear, he exited, chained up the opening once more, and locked it.

A short, limping dash through the garden, then over the wall and back through the woodlands to where his horse was tethered, and then Kaiso had gritted his teeth and ridden hard for Wetheral.

"Well," Darienne said after hearing his tale. "An eventful night."

A knock sounded at the door before she could continue.

"Your Highness?" Ingrid called from outside. "Your cousin is arriving."

Darienne stood on the marble landing beneath the grand receiving portico of Wetheral Castle. Brigadier St. Fiacre stood to her right with Major Justiniere behind him, both backed by an honor guard of Lake Jacks resplendent in their polished steel cuirasses and helmets with bright red plumes. Several steps down from the landing, a bright red carpet extended some two hundred feet to where the carriage would stop. Lining the red carpet were more of St. Fiacre's polished soldiers, standing at rigid attention facing inward. It was all a bit much, she thought, given that her cousin was only the viscount of a small territory in neighboring Aesthir. But he and his mother were her only living kin, and as such had some link to the royal family. She'd allow them this honor, for now. But should Kaiso's suspicions prove true… she would destroy this man.

The ornate carriage—white with purple trim, the colors of Valais—was pulled by four glorious black horses with long, plaited manes and tails, purple ribbons woven into the braids. Its driver wore a crisp military uniform with a black, broad-brimmed hat, the left side pinned up and a long purple feather sticking up from the left side. Darienne's brow furrowed at the seeming incongruity of that ostentatious hat with the otherwise dignified uniform. The carriage pulled to a stop, and a footman who had been riding on the rear of it—again dressed in similar fashion to the driver—hopped down and opened the door. Out stepped a young man in his late twenties, his pale complexion peppered with bright orange freckles. Pietr, dressed in a spectacular white military uniform with purple braids, sash, and epaulets, flashed a radiant smile in her direction before turning back to the carriage. He wore white leather gauntlets that bore purple embroidery as trim on the cuffs. With seeming ceremony, he donned a ridiculously ornate white hat of the same style that the driver and footman wore, but this one was decorated with purple embroidery and a splash of purple feathers where the brim was folded up and pinned.

"What a perfectly ridiculous outfit," Darienne muttered behind a pleasant smile, just loud enough for St. Fiacre to hear. The brigadier sniffed and wiped his mustache, his customary way of masking an undignified snicker.

Having donned his chapeau, Pietr turned and extended a hand back to the carriage to help his mother, Darienne's Aunt Alais, exit gracefully. Alais was dressed in a gown of white satin with both rose and purple trim. The two colors did not complement each other to Darienne's eye, but she understood the rose to be an obvious reminder of Alais' link to the throne of Lachland. Clearly, much preparation had gone into this visit. Darienne had not seen Alais or Pietr since her childhood, and she had forgotten the resemblance between her aunt and the Queen. Though where Isador was stately, tall, beautiful, and carried herself with an ineffable elegance, Alais' frame was more stocky, short, and somewhat awkward. Her complexion, despite far too much powder, was ruddy and lined as though the harsh winters of Aesthir had taken their toll upon her skin. Her silver hair was pinned up and tucked into an even more ridiculous and outlandish hat than that worn by her son. Made of white satin, it was adorned with curls of purple and rose ribbon, and had a brim broader than the woman who wore it.

"I take it back," Darienne muttered again. "*That* is a perfectly ridiculous outfit."

The brigadier snorted audibly, shifted his stance and suddenly found something on his right cuff quite fascinating.

After exiting the carriage, Alais nodded her gratitude to Pietr, took his proffered arm and the two processed up the long red carpet to the base of the steps at Darienne's feet. Beaming down at the two of them, the Princess offered her most gracious smile and opened her arms wide before speaking.

"Viscountess," she said warmly, "Aunt Alais, and Viscount, Cousin Pietr, it has been too long. You are most welcome at Wetheral Castle."

Alais smiled back at Darienne, seeming a bit nonplussed, before speaking. "Thank you, my dear," she said finally, her tone carrying a brusk hint. "I see you have flowered beautifully. Please show us to our rooms. We are fatigued from travel and would like to refresh."

The slightest tilt of Darienne's head was all the cue Brigadier St. Fiacre needed to step forward, as rehearsed, and offer prompt correction.

"Your Royal Highness," he said curtly.

A surprised and hopeful look flashed across Alais' face before she realized she was being corrected and not addressed with the royal title herself.

"I beg your pardon?" she sputtered.

"You will address Princess Darienne as Your Royal Highness," he explained.

"The impudence!" She flustered in outrage and seemed about to say a good deal more, but Pietr held up his hand.

"Mother, please," he said softly, before turning to Darienne to continue. "Forgive Mother, Your Royal Highness, the journey has been long and wearing. We are both overjoyed to see you again, my *royal* cousin, and we welcome your gracious hospitality."

A slight tilt of Darienne's head to the other side brought forward the royal steward. Still wearing the placid smile of welcome, the Princess said, "Armand will show you to your rooms. Perhaps after an interval and refreshment, we might all enjoy a walk in the gardens? Until then?"

With that, she turned and preceded the assemblage into the castle—*her* castle—doing her very best to "glide" as she walked, just like her tutors had vainly striven all her life to teach her, and as her mother seemed to be able to do effortlessly in all circumstances.

Well, this will be entertaining, she thought as she caught the brigadier's eye and offered him a slight wink of gratitude.

Without turning back to see to her guests, Darienne glided up the grand staircase and back toward her chambers. Maddie, Dominique, and Ingrid fell into step behind her as she exited the foyer. She could see the raised eyebrows on all three of them at her uncustomary behavior. They were all too aware of the lengths to which she had gone through the years to resist being a "graceful" princess, and now they seemed quite amazed by her transformation.

"Not a word, ladies," Darienne muttered. "Not a word." And she glided all the way back to her rooms.

Chapter 33

From green rolling hills
To mountains majestic,
Icy blue waters on lakes pure and deep,
The mane of my steed
Flows with winds of the free
As I ride cross the land to hold and to keep!
Lachland! O Lachland!
Your banners lift high!
The destrier rampant so bold!
The rose-colored flag will never descend
'Til the tale of our country is told.

– Lachland national anthem

574 HR - *Last month of summer*
Autun, Lachland

Zach

He was alone with the Queen and the stone of dread once more rested in his stomach. He hoped she hadn't noticed that he was sweating, despite the morning chill. They were in their customary positions in the north tower, surveying the battlefield below. His morning's reflections and wanderings had yielded no definite decision regarding his quandary, though he felt his heart settling toward a direction… one that he may regret for the remainder of his days. He gripped the banner staff more tightly and concentrated on his breathing to try to bull through his exhaustion. He had not slept in days, and the grisly gift that had arrived the night before had wiped away any possibility of rest. He blinked his eyes against the haze that seemed to have settled over his vision and tried to focus on the battlefield. The enemy was making only desultory raids with mounted archers, keeping the defenders busy and sheltering. Yet to Zach's eye, no concerted attack seemed imminent. Both the archbishop and Sir Reginald had excused themselves from the Queen's presence to attend to other matters, leaving only Zach and the monarch in the small tower overlooking the front gate and the field to its north.

He stood at attention, presenting the banner forward out of the tower, while the Queen paced behind him. She was muttering something to herself and fidgeting with her hands. She always seemed to toy with a particular ring in moments of indecision. He assumed it to be her wedding ring, and he found that endearing in the woman. It made her more human, somehow. Then the memory of Loeiza's wedding ring came crashing back, causing him to swoon. He pressed his thighs firmly forward against the battlement wall to steady himself and hoped the Queen hadn't noticed.

A breathless messenger from the hospital ward rushed through the door, interrupting his thoughts. Zach ordered the flag and turned to face the newcomer. With no one else present, he was also her bodyguard, and couldn't afford to have his back to a new arrival. The messenger's white apron was spattered with blood and grime. The look in his eyes belied grim news.

"Madame," he said, trying to catch his breath. He wiped a hand through his graying beard, discovering, and abashedly removing, a piece of human gristle that had somehow gone unnoticed thus far.

"Speak your news," the Queen said, turning to give him her full attention.

"Brigadier Dixon has succumbed to his injuries, ma'am." His eyes were downcast and seemed shameful, as though he were somehow responsible. "He died this past hour."

"Oh, dear man," she said, raising a trembling hand to her lips.

The messenger waited a moment longer to see if there might be any return message from the monarch, but receiving none, he bowed awkwardly and exited, leaving Zach alone with the Queen once more. Her back was turned to him as she dealt with her grief and the broader ramifications of the general's death.

Is this the moment? Should I strike?

His breath caught in his throat at the thought. His quivering hand started to reach for the dagger hilt, then stopped, seemingly of its own volition. With a suppressed groan, he gripped the banner staff once more with both hands, knuckles whitening as his thoughts warred within him. He returned his attention to the battlefield. The battle for Autun had fallen into a grinding stalemate these past weeks. The enemy casualties were staggering as the defense of the town had been stiff and resolute, but the Lachlanders' numbers were dwindling as well. Many warehouses and a significant part of the merchant quarter had fallen to the fires set by the Räuber saboteurs, though the damage had been somewhat mitigated thanks to Sir Reginald's prompt response to the alarm bell. Nonetheless, the townsfolk grew restive. Not a day went by without a delegation from the town's merchants demanding the Queen send for more reinforcements and put an end to the Barbárs, once and for all. *As if she isn't already bringing every viable resource to bear!* Or failing that, the delegations insisted, negotiate a peace. *Unthinkable!*

He stole a glance at the troubled Queen. He noted that her hands continued to tremble as she reached to grip the tower railing. She seemed, in that moment, somehow frail. Not a regal monarch with absolute authority, but just a person striving against terrible odds to do what was best. Perhaps it was his fatigue that allowed his eyes to fill with tears of pity for the poor woman at that moment. He shook his head to clear it. His exhaustion was clearly getting the best of him. He was falling apart. With a snap of his head, he fixed his posture, arching his back slightly against the dull ache that holding the banner produced.

Becoming the banner carrier for the Queen, attending her throughout each day in her various meetings and councils, had been quite enlightening for Zach—hearing reports of the disposition of available troops guarding various sectors of the country and how quickly they might be brought to bear, or the many reasons why, strategically, sending for those troops would be inadvisable as it would leave other portions of the nation vulnerable. It was all well above the unit level logistics and tactics with which he was familiar, and though he found those strategic considerations fascinating, he felt somewhat at sea. He was well versed in the details of ground units—light versus heavy cavalry, the value of pikemen in a company of foot, where to deploy crossbowmen for maximum enfilading fire, etc.—but there was so much that he did not know, concerns that were new to him, things he hadn't ever considered: supply lines, medical inventories, capabilities of various types of naval vessels, the importance of clean and secure dry goods storage, the seasonal possibilities for an army to forage on the march, and so on. Day after day, he watched the Queen work to solve the puzzle of how to defend Autun, while not jeopardizing or weakening the defense of the rest of her kingdom. He heard the reports of limited supplies, of unrest in the northern Claws and foul weather in the south that slowed the arrival of critical troops and materiel. Challenge after grinding challenge, he saw the iron in this woman as she refused to yield before the barbarian threat, and yet struggled to find the means to overcome it. Dixon had borne much of that weight; his seasoned mind masterfully grasped complex logistics and his detailed understanding of the available resources was invaluable. He was the pillar upon which so much of their efforts rested. With him gone, the defense of Autun, and indeed, all of Lachland, threatened to collapse.

Sir Reginald could be of much help, but all too often he was entirely absorbed with the day-to-day logistics of troop positions, requisitions for medical supplies, rationing food, arrows, the transport of water to extinguish fires, and so much more. Now, much more rested on Isador herself, and from the stoop of her shoulders, he could see the crushing weight of that realization settling upon her. Yet, somehow, he knew she would rise to the moment, as she had so often in the preceding days and weeks. Her presence, her sure hand, was the entire reason this defense had succeeded this long. Without her, he feared the city would fall entirely. And then what would become of his country? The invaders would have unfettered access to the Claws, and through that, they could and would rain destruction down on the all-too-lightly defended interior. Images of entire villages and towns burning danced in the exhausted haze before him.

His mind returned to his own dilemma. Loeiza was the most dear thing in the world to him, yet he could not condemn an entire country to rapine and conquest to save only her, could he? *Perhaps,* he thought, feverishly, *there might be a way to accomplish both goals?* Could he possibly find a path to see the defeat of the invaders and still kill the Queen as well? His heart recoiled at the thought of striking Isador, this remarkable tower of strength and fortitude that he so admired. Could he live with himself if he did that? The knot of tension in his stomach suddenly became a gripping pain as his mind leapt again to his poor, abused wife who would die horribly should he fail. He grimaced in pain as his tortured mind wrestled anew with this impossible quandary.

"Captain!" the Queen said sharply.

"Your Majesty?" he replied, shaking his head to clear it.

"You did not respond to us," she said. "Lost in thought, were you?"

"My apologies, Your Grace," he responded. "Our current straits have me preoccupied. It will not happen again."

"Relax, Captain," she said with a wave. "Why don't you sit for a time, drink some water? Rest yourself. You seemed to be in some discomfort. I'm sure the enemy and our defenders will understand that the banner carrier requires a moment's respite." She gestured to a pair of chairs near the rear of the tower and indicated a pitcher of water on a small table nearby. Zach gratefully nodded his head and, propping the banner against the back wall, sank into one of the seats. Weariness flooded his body.

"Our brigadier has fallen," she said after a moment's pause. "Our defenders dwindle and their spirit falters. I fear we approach the nadir of this defense."

"As long as Your Majesty remains steadfast," he told her, "we cannot lose."

She smiled at him over her shoulder. "You flatter me, Captain." Her steely gaze was then once more on the enemy horsemen brazenly riding near the wall, daring the Lachland archers to try to hit them.

"Not at all, Your Grace," he said tiredly, and something in his voice caused her to turn back to regard him. "I have watched your sure hand oversee this city's defense. I have seen you on the battlefield and the battlements. Your very presence makes each of our defenders fight like two men. You are a wise and good monarch, Madame, and this nation is fortunate in you."

She stared at him for some moments, seemingly trying to discern if this was indeed flattery or frankness. After a time, she sighed and turned away to once more survey the battlefield.

"You are a good man, Captain," she said quietly.

Seeing the Queen's back to him again, his fingers reached for the hidden dagger beneath his tabard. *Perhaps now?* Could he do it? Loeiza's tear-streaked face danced before his eyes, her bound hands forward, pleading with him to rescue her from her torment. Acid flooded his stomach and crept into the back of his throat. His hand gripped the handle of the dagger so tightly he felt his knuckles crack. He blinked at the sound, and with some effort, released his grip on it, reaching instead for the cup of water beside him. Loeiza's image drifted away, her head downcast, as though she knew he couldn't do it. Not even to save her.

My love, forgive me!

With a breath, he girded his will and made his decision: He would confess all to the Queen. He would tell her everything, and fall upon her mercy and pray that she might see some way out of this conundrum in which he was trapped. He stood and straightened his uniform.

"Majesty," he said, his voice unsteady. "I have something important to tell you."

"What do you suppose that is?" she asked, ignoring his comment and gesturing toward the field.

The Queen's question interrupted his resolve, and his gaze followed hers to the center of the battlefield before the town gates. There, just out of bowshot, a cluster of enemy warriors were setting up a trestle table. A stoop-shouldered, bald headed man of ill-favor stood on the far side of it, facing the city walls. Zach stepped up beside the Queen and watched as a bound prisoner was unceremoniously flopped onto the table before the bald man, who smiled up at the north tower and pointed directly at the monarch.

"What the devil is he up to?" the Queen asked.

"Majesty, I…" Zach tried to say the words once again, but his will faltered as he watched the bald man place his hand over the face of the quivering prisoner. Immediately, soul-wrenching screams from the victim filled the entire field and echoed over the town. Forges stilled, the hustle and bustle of the town's streets paused. Merchants haggling stopped to listen as the sound of a man's very spirit being shredded filled their ears.

Zach watched in horror as the bald, stoop-shouldered man performing this torture seemed to grow in stature. Even from a distance, it was apparent that his pallid complexion was becoming more robust, and his garments—which had hung on him like loose sackcloth—now were stretched by firm muscle.

"By the heavens!" the Queen muttered.

The Barbárs that surrounded the man suddenly crouched and covered their ears. The Queen and Zach exchanged a bemused look at this inexplicable behavior. The man stepped around the trestle table and began striding directly toward them. His step was confident and buoyant. A feral grin overtook his face as he once more pointed at Isador and inhaled deeply. Too late, Zach sensed the danger and cried out.

"Your Majesty, get back!"

There was a piercing sound, like the cry of ten thousand hawks coupled with a cacophony of brass bells, and the world went silent, muted suddenly, save for a steady high-pitched whine. It took Zach a moment to realize that he had somehow been thrown against the back wall of the tower, and he found himself on his knees looking forward into wreckage. The entire front face of the structure had disintegrated; jagged bits of stone and wood were all that was left of the face of the tower. A moment's further blinking and confusion yielded the realization that the Queen was no longer there. Still struggling against the ringing in his ears, Zach surged forward to the edge of the ruined platform and gazed down upon the bent and twisted body of Isador IV, Queen of Lachland, lying at the foot of the wall, a broken and bloody shard of wood piercing her breastplate.

"No!" Zach cried, though he could not hear his own voice. "No!"

He grabbed the banner and, without thought, leapt down from the tower to the field beside the fallen Queen. He landed hard, his knees and ankles protesting, but he ignored the discomfort as another wave of exhaustion overtook him. Looking down at the body beside him again, he couldn't be sure if it was the Queen or Loeiza. The two faces seemed to dance over one another. He placed his trembling hand upon the body's neck, searching for a pulse, and the Queen's face came into focus. No heartbeat. Her skin already graying with death.

Zach glanced about in desperation. *No! This cannot happen! Not now!*

He saw the strange, bald man approaching, far ahead of any Barbár support, with a swaggering bounce in his step and a hungry smile that revealed brown teeth dripping with slime. Zach looked back at the wall, and by chance happened to lock eyes with Sir Reginald, who was peering over the battlement near the south tower, horror and shock writ upon his face. The two stared at one another for a moment, then Zach was overcome with rage. A fierce, red rage. As though the knot of tension and dysphoria that had been his constant and painful companion these past weeks, had suddenly been released into tendrils of fire and lightning, seeking to burn their way out of his body, demanding release. He was suffused with a mindless fury that overwhelmed his fatigued mind with but one, clear and resolute directive: revenge!

With a scream of defiance, he grasped the banner and charged the smiling, bald man.

Sir Reginald

He watched from the battlements as Captain Zachar leapt down to the Queen's side from the ruined tower. Her fate was clear was clear from the position of her body, but nonetheless it was the captain's look up at him, carrying all his grief and rage, that confirmed the death of Queen Isador. Sir Reginald blanched and gripped the rampart with both hands, shaking his head in mute denial. He could hear cries of horror and outrage from the soldiers around him as if from a distance. After a moment, a nearby archer exclaimed something in amazement. And he looked up to see the brave captain charging alone against the foe, bearing only the Queen's banner as his weapon. In that moment, Bleiz *knew* that now was the time, or all would be lost. Turning to his men, he shouted in a battlefield voice that carried over the ramparts and into the town, where troops and citizens milled in preparation for the day's struggles.

"Lachlanders!" he called, his voice filled with a passion and fury he could not remember ever knowing. "They have struck at our Queen in a most cowardly fashion! She has given her all for the defense of this city, for this country. Will we allow them now to defile her body? Will we allow this foul act to go unavenged?"

A roar of outrage and defiance was the response.

"Mount up! Ready yourselves! This act will not go unpunished! Today is the day! Today we fight for all Lachland. Today we put an end to this! This is the final push! For the Queen!"

An even louder roar sounded from every throat as the townsfolk and soldiers echoed his cry together. Bleiz saw arms and weapons raised in the air as men and women cheered. He noted merchants, servants, women, and even children, with fury and outrage written upon their faces, arming themselves with whatever was at hand: tools, farm implements, clubs, wooden planks, stones for throwing. This would not be a charge of the army, nor even of the able-bodied. No, this would be all of Autun rising against the invader as the citizenry of the town, wearied by weeks of siege, cast aside their fears and worries and rose up as one in defiance of those who would dare to strike their beloved Queen.

Turning to the archers along the walls, he issued quick orders for them to remain vigilant and protect the gates, then he dashed down the stairs into the courtyard where his horse was being held by a young stable lad—who now gripped a pitchfork in his other hand. With a leap that belied his years, Bleiz was in the saddle, drawing his sword.

"Open the gates!" he roared as he pushed on his helmet, and led the final charge against the Barbárs in the battle for Autun.

Zach

He had no plan, no thought for his own safety or well-being. He only knew that this creature before him was the source of his grief and outrage. Screaming as he charged forward, he thrust with the butt end of the banner staff at his foe's chest. To his amazement, the man reached out with one hand and, almost casually, captured the staff, wrenching it out of Zach's grip like an angry parent seizing a belligerent child's toy. With his other hand, the man struck Zach with a powerful backhand blow that sent the captain tumbling back toward the walls, despite the momentum of his headlong rush. Zach heard something in his face crack, and darkness enveloped him.

He came to, moments later, to find himself lying in a heap some twenty feet from where he'd been struck. His left arm was bent at an unnatural angle beneath his body and his legs lay akimbo. His cheek was swelling rapidly from the blow, and he knew it would only be moments before the puffiness would block the vision from his right eye. He struggled to stand, and was alarmed to feel movement in his ribs, suggesting at least some of them were broken. He cried out as he rose, his left arm falling limp to his side, grinding the broken bone. A wave of nausea rolled over him and he fell to a knee, retching.

The strange, bald man had turned back to the enemy forces and was waving the banner over his head, triumphantly. The ringing in Zach's ears seemed to be abating, as he could now hear the Barbárs roaring in approbation as they started to gather for an assault. Struggling again to his feet, he searched the ground near him for a weapon, anything. His eyes fell again upon the Queen's body, which lay not ten feet from him. His vision swam for a moment as another wave of nausea and weakness overtook him. He sank once more to his knees. Tears of futility and helplessness overcame him. He had failed. He had failed in so many ways.

"I'm sorry, my lady," he sobbed. "I'm so sorry."

A new roar roused him, as a defiant cheer rose up from the city. Zach looked up in wonder as the gates began to open. Did they mean to attack? Was this an attempt to retrieve the Queen's body? He watched in confusion as the opening gates revealed a mass swarming forward. Not an organized assault by soldiers. Instead, it looked as though the entire town was charging out. Soldiers and citizens, women and children, rushed forward pell-mell, armed with whatever was at hand. The entire populace of Autun was attacking, finally venting their weeks-long pent-up rage at the invaders. Sir Reginald galloped at their head, his battered helmet gleaming in the morning sun.

Zach looked around again, desperate for a weapon. He spotted the Queen's longsword, still strapped to her side. It was always her practice to go about armed and dressed for battle. He limped to her body and with another brief apology, drew the royal sword from its sheath. He would not die, sobbing in the dirt, while women and children fought for their homes! The Queen would be avenged or he would die with her sword in his hand!

He scanned the battlefield, searching for the target of his hatred. The rush of bodies blocked his view of the bald man, but he could still see the banner swinging about. He staggered forward, willing his broken body into motion. If he could gain some momentum, he might still have some effect. He paused, however, when he suddenly saw bodies flying through the air around the banner, pitched by incredible strength. *More sorcery!* He had to put an end to this creature, or untold Lachlanders would die this day.

He once more willed his body into motion, but now he began to trace a wide arc to his left, skirting the edge of the action. The sorcerer was facing the oncoming attackers, and Zach planned to approach him from behind. Staggering along, he hugged the periphery of the rush, staying near the north wall. In his injured state, he couldn't keep pace with the charging bodies. He hoped any enemy warriors that might see him would dismiss him as too injured to be an immediate threat. After thirty agonizing paces, he could finally see the sorcerer through the hubbub. The creature was wading through the attackers like a bear stepping into a tide, the waves breaking before him. He swung the banner staff one-handed until it broke, then he cast it aside and—using only his hands—he shattered bodies, broke shields, crushed skulls. Though bleeding from a dozen wounds, nothing could slow the man. A sword pierced his side, and the creature simply grinned with those brown, slime-covered teeth, and crushed his attacker.

Some vagary of the wind shifted, or perhaps it was merely that the ringing in his ears finally stopped, but he suddenly heard the roar of the defiant people of Autun more loudly. The sound stirred in him a fierce determination as he looked upon the wretched wizard whose sorcery had cut them all so deeply. *No, Fiend. We do not fall today. Today, we fight for Lachland!*

Zach's gait steadied as he began to rush toward the creature, weaving a path laterally against the flow of Lachland attackers. His approach was from the sorcerer's rear-right.

"My poor Queen," he said aloud as he charged. "Grant me the strength to avenge you!"

When Zach was still some fifteen paces from the creature, he saw a mounted cavalryman try to engage the man from the far side. Before Zach could take three strides, the sorcerer inhaled and unleashed that unholy shriek toward the horseman, a cacophony of ten thousand hawks accompanied by brass bells. A cone-shaped furrow of dirt was pitched from the ground by some wave of force that emanated from the creature. The horse, and dozens of combatants behind it, were ripped in two as the wave rushed outward. Before the stunned rider hit the floor, the creature grabbed him by the leg, and used his body as a cudgel against a cluster of soldiers rushing toward him. Zach faltered in his advance. How could he hope to overcome such a creature?

Then he heard, quite clearly, the Queen's voice—as though she stood nearby.

Captain! she called, startling him and causing him to look about. *Strike, Captain! Strike now for Lachland!*

A wave of strength filled him and, ignoring the various agonies in his body, Zach charged the final distance, ducking beneath the swipe of a blade from a passing Barbár. The sorcerer's back was to him, and his focus was on the attackers from the town gate still rushing him. With a leap, Zach brought the Queen's sword down across the exposed neck of the creature.

A great *WHOOM* suffused the battlefield, and dozens of combatants were knocked to the ground by a huge wave of force centered on the sorcerer. Miraculously, Zach remained standing, still gripping the Queen's sword in his right hand—though the arm had gone completely numb. The creature's decapitated, and suddenly shriveled, body lay at his feet.

There was a pause in the maelstrom of battle as all eyes turned to take in what had happened. In the lull, Zach clumsily slid the sword into his belt and staggered to the broken banner staff. Plucking the begrimed flag from the muck, he held it aloft once more, his numb arm burning in protest.

"For the Queen!" he shouted, his voice raw.

The effect was immediate and profound. The Barbárs, to a man, lost heart and quailed at the turn of events, while the Lachlanders' resolve redoubled. With a roar, the action recommenced. But it was no longer a battle—it was a rout, with the doughty townsfolk and the soldiers of Lachland exacting a fierce revenge upon the now cowed invaders.

Zach stood trembling in place, holding the banner aloft. Had it been minutes? Hours? He doubted he had the strength to walk even a few more steps, but he would rather die than allow that proud flag to dip once more. He grimaced as his arm shrieked in agony, holding the banner high. He floated in a haze of blind pain and exhaustion, alternately sobbing for Loeiza and crying aloud his gratitude to the Queen's spirit for her aid. The cacophony and cries around him seemed distant. His entire focus was on willing his body to remain standing. *Keep that banner up!* Time had no meaning, and yet finally he felt a gentle touch on his back and realized the world had gone quiet once more. Blinking, he looked up to find a blood-streaked Sir Reginald standing at his side, easing the banner from Zach's hand.

"It's over, Captain," Bleiz said reassuringly. "We won. Thanks to you, we won."

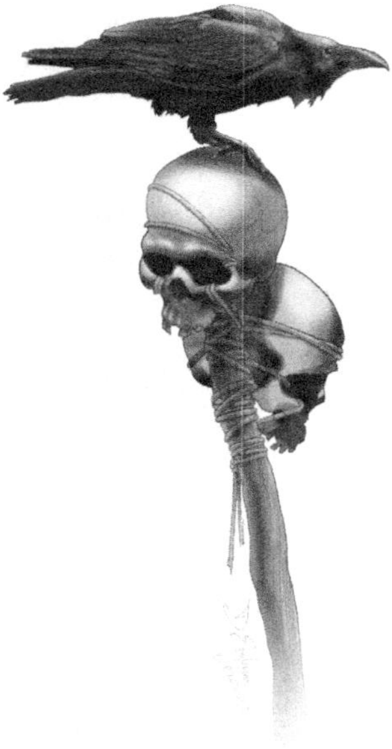

Chapter 34

"The key's the key
To the hidden quay.
Keep it to port, lads, keep it to port.
Mind the big'un, and shave the starboard rail,
Keep it to port, me lads."

— The Black Hand

574 HR - *Last month of summer*
Mirror Sea, off the eastern coast of the Green Mount

Zsoka

She woke with a start. Though her small cabin had no window, she had grown accustomed to the sounds and rhythms of the ship and the sea, and could tell that it was still dark and their sloop was lying at anchor. They were off the rocky coast where they had ended their search the day before. A realization in her dream had startled her awake. What was it?

She had been dreaming about her uncle again. Every night since being freed, she had dreamt of him. She knew that somewhere in his drunken tales he had mentioned the Long Stair to the Green Mount, but the specific recollection eluded her. Mostly, the dreams were incoherent jumbles of memory and fancy. But this night was different. She and her uncle had been sitting at their table in her childhood home. He was rambling on in his sodden manner, but something he was doing while he chattered on caught her eye. He was drawing with his finger in the grease on the table. Nothing he was saying had been of interest or value, but that symbol... She had seen that shape somewhere. It looked vaguely like a keyhole, though the top was irregularly shaped, squared off on one side. She *knew* she had seen that before. Where?

She sat up and reached for her ink and quill. Looking about, she realized she had no parchment. Grunting in frustration and the stupidity of the shaman to have given her ink and a quill but no paper, she drew her knife and used it to hack a roughly square piece of fabric from the bottom of her shift. Trying to move quickly, before the dream image drifted away completely, she sketched the symbol carefully, though the drawing was rough and the fabric kept bunching up as she drew. Once the image complete, she sat back and stared at the strange design before her. Something about it tickled the edge of her memory, though she couldn't quite place it. Sighing in frustration, she stood and opened the small porthole, inhaling the fresh, cold sea air to clear her head. A wave of bitterness came over her. *How low my fortunes have fallen!* Why should she, the Empress of the Steppes, dethroned by treachery and treason, be consigned to a miserable cabin on a pathetic little craft like this? Why should her very life dependent on trying to dredge up some lost memory from her childhood? Was she of no more value to the Grand Hadvezér than this? Their son, Talon, was heir to both her lost throne and the seat of power over the vast Barbár territories—though whether even the vaunted Vajk could ever convince his fractious warlords to recognize the boy as his son and heir was a question. But surely, he could have sent a grander vessel to liberate her, if for nothing more than a gallant gesture to honor their tryst. She should have known better than to expect gallantry from a savage Barbár. Despite his significant physical appeal, he was, at heart, nothing more than a brutish warlord with no feelings for her. Had he felt even a vestige of fondness, he would have welcomed her and offered her succor, committed forces to help her regain her throne. Instead, to show her just how small was his regard, he sent that vile and disgusting sorcerer, and held her on this miserable sloop that pitched and tossed with every cursed wave and tiny chop of the busy sea, her very life under threat if she could not parse out the meaning of this damned symbol from a childhood memory. *Curse the man!*

She gazed out the porthole at the jagged, black rocks of the coastline reflecting oddly in the moonlight, almost like glass. She noted for the first time their unusually sharp lines, as though they had been carved. Then it struck her like a bolt, realization flooding over her. That wasn't a symbol at all. It was a rock formation their vessel had passed late in the afternoon the day before.

"The key's the key
To the hidden quay."

That was one of the nonsensical nautical phrases he had repeated for years, like "Fresh tar and rope, gives a ship hope" or "Never more than a sloop, to slip through the slot." Having never seen it spelled out, she had always assumed that the word "quay" was just another repetition of "key," but now, it made sense. There must be a hidden jetty tucked behind the jagged stones that rose from the sea. She quickly stood and dressed herself, pausing only to splash cold water on her face and tidy her unkempt hair. No matter the urgency or conditions, she was, after all, an empress; it would not do for the sailors to see her looking like some unwashed peasant. She finished pinning up her hair and adjusted the ruffled collar of her dress. Mercifully, there was no mirror. She could only imagine how unsatisfied she would be with her reflection when she had no rouge or kohl. *Well, there's nothing for it. Regal bearing will have to suffice.* With a sigh of resignation, she opened her cabin door and stepped out onto the deck. The slivered moon had already set, and the ship was dark. A storm had passed to the west of them, and now the sky was afire with millions of stars. She stumbled over a coil of rope and bashed her hand on a hanging lantern as she reached to catch herself, before finding her way to the shaman's cabin door. She pounded on it with urgency.

"Blood-Tooth!" she called. "Wake up, man!"

The door eventually opened to reveal the shaman's shadowed figure. His rheumy, black eyes reflected the moonlight, the skin around them puffy from sleep, making him resemble an awakened rodent. A smell like death wafted out of the room, and she covered her mouth involuntarily.

"Empress?" he asked thickly. "Is there a problem?"

"I know where we must go," she answered quickly. "I remembered the symbol."

"Symbol?" he said, confused.

"Never mind." She shook her head. "Just wake the crew and be ready to sail at first light. We need to head back south some hours."

"Very well, Madame," he answered, with a moist smacking of his lips that made her stomach roil in response. "I will see you on deck at first light."

It was still well before noon when Zsoka's search was rewarded with the sight of the oddly shaped stone standing some thirty feet out of the water. Shaped by wind and waves, the massive stack of obsidian or tourmaline had shed plates of stone over the years, creating the unusual, sharp-edged flat face that almost looked as though it had been carved by human hands. It had an irregular top, squared on the left and rounded on the right. A sizable hole in the center of the flat rock completed the image of a keyhole. Zsoka's hands began to tremble as she watched the waves crash against it, white foam splashing around the oblong opening.

"There!" she said, pointing triumphantly across the waves.

"I see no path between the rocks, Mistress," the shaman said doubtfully.

"The way is there," she insisted, infusing her voice with certainty, despite the stone of anxiety in her stomach. He was right. She could see no path between the forbidding rocks either.

The steersman muttered dubiously under his breath to the shaman. The two fell into a lengthy, whispered conversation during which the steersman gestured vehemently at the rocks. The shaman said something final, after which he turned back to Zsoka with an unctuous smile on his face.

"We shall tack closer to the rocks to see if any route between them might be apparent," he said. "It may be that we must anchor here, and take a launch to find our way in."

Zsoka answered with a dismissive wave of her hand as she intently scanned the forbidding stones. There had to be a path! There was something else her uncle had said often. "Quick as you please." Something about this opening allowed a ship in "quick as you please." Or did it? Was she remembering correctly? He would sing the silly phrases like a shanty. How did it go?

> *"The key's the key*
> *To the hidden quay.*
> *Keep it to port, lads, keep it to port.*
> *Mind the big'un, and shave the starboard rail,*
> *Keep it to port, me lads."*

Keep *what* to port? "The big'un"? What did that mean? Shave the starboard rail? It was all nonsense to her, but like a nursery rhyme it had stuck in her memory—so often did he sing it, when deep in his cups.

Just to the right of the key-shaped stone was a massive black rock, well over a hundred feet tall. To her eye, it seemed as though it were connected to the mountain behind it, but as she stared at the water's edge on its right side, she noted a tidal rush. There was a channel hidden behind the rock.

"There! See?" she said to the steersman, pointing at the narrow opening.

"Where?" he responded in his thick accent.

With a series of gestures and an insistent tone, she was finally able to communicate to him how to direct the sloop, and though he never lost his dubious squint, he angled the prow toward the opening, allowing a wide enough berth to swing the craft to port for a direct entry, should her imagined channel materialize.

"Mistress, if you are mistaken, we shall be dashed upon these stones." The shaman spoke with feigned calm as the ship navigated perilously between two jagged rocks, pitching and yawing as they moved closer to shore and the waves rebounded from the black stones.

"The opening is there," she said firmly, clutching her hands tightly to the rail to mask their trembling.

With a fatalistic shrug that seemed to convey they were all going to die, the steersman issued orders to trim the sails, leaving only the foresail to cautiously move them along.

"We must strip away these lantern posts along this side," she said, pointing along the starboard rail.

No longer bothering to question the woman, the sailors moved to obey. A large swell lifted the ship momentarily, and as it descended, the back flow off the mountainous stone pushed them to starboard. The steersman and sailors rushed to the railing, frantically using poles, oars, and lamp posts to stop their craft from crashing against the jagged outcropping. But once the danger had passed, they suddenly could see a narrow channel of water directly before them. *Quick as you please.* The inlet proceeded forward several hundred feet, then disappeared around to the right behind the huge stone off starboard. She could see sunlight near the turn, which confirmed that a bay or opening was hidden by these colossal boulders. The tall rock off the port side descended smoothly into the water all along the channel, while its smaller neighbor, off starboard, had a noticeable overhang. The channel was just wide enough for their ship to pass, though the starboard railing would indeed move beneath the overhang for at least part of their passage. *How many trips did you make here, Uncle, for this to be so burned into your thoughts?*

"It seems your memory has served you well," the shaman said, with begrudging praise. "Though should the tide swell during our passage, the railing will be crushed."

The Empress did not answer as they inched forward. Instead, she backed away, wrapping an arm around the aft mast. The stiff breeze from the open water drove them forward. A cold sweat trickled down her neck, despite the chill from the breeze. *What other secrets went with you to your grave, Uncle?*

Everyone aboard held their breath as the ship eased its way between the massive rocks. Twice, the hull on the port side scraped dangerously along the stone as the steersman tried to avoid the perilous overhang off starboard. He corrected course to avoid a third scrape, which could well have holed them, choosing the lesser danger to slide the starboard railing just under the overhanging rock. Zsoka's fingernails bit into her arm and she gritted her teeth, as the top of the railing scraped along the underside of the stone. After what seemed an interminable passage, they emerged on the far side of the channel to find sunlight and a small bay with a short, stone jetty extending from a small, pebbled beach tucked against the mountain. *The hidden quay.* On the far side of the landing, the mountains towered directly overhead, soaring thousands of feet in a dramatic, almost vertical climb. And there, obscured somewhat by a fold of the mountain and the lush boughs of pine trees overhanging it, was an algae-covered stone stairway, dripping with runoff. It climbed steeply up the mountainside until it disappeared from view around a shoulder of the mountain.

"Looks like we have our path," the shaman said with a grunt and a brown-toothed grin.

"There is your hidden stair," she affirmed. "Now, I insist that you take me to the Grand Hadvezér to fulfill his promise."

"Oh, I think not," the shaman sneered over his shoulder, still facing the forbidding climb. "You will accompany us."

"You want *me* to climb that?" she said, horrified, her heart sinking and knees suddenly weak. "Whatever for? I have fulfilled my part of the bargain, now you will take me—"

"These men and I will climb that stair," he interrupted sharply, his tone dangerous and feral. His bloodshot eyes flashing with barely suppressed danger. "And you, *Empress,* shall accompany us. We must reach the Tor before the Equinox. I do not have time to ferry you to another destination before returning. And I suspect you shall be of some further service in this effort…"

After gathering their supplies, Blood-Tooth, the Empress, and the six tengerészgyilkos began their ascent up the steep, narrow stairs, leaving the captain and steersman on the ship to make their way back out. The path alternated along its route between agonizingly steep steps, curving stone trails between the towering pines that hugged the edge of the mountain, and perilous vertical notches that had been carved ladder-like into the forbidding cliff faces. Again and again, she marveled at the vision and effort necessary to have created this ancient route and wondered at its genesis. Was it a smuggler's route? Had it been created to side-step some military force, or to allow an army secret passage? It must have taken generations to carve and create. The trail offered no clues, however, only continued on mercilessly up into the soaring mountains.

Zsoka's long imprisonment had done nothing to prepare her for the rigors of the ascent, and throughout much of the first day, she slowed the group's progress, requiring frequent stops to rub the cramps in her agonized legs and arms as the tengerészgyilkos exchanged impatient looks. Twice, she only narrowly avoided falling to her death, as the haze of exhaustion made her steps clumsy. After that, the shaman affixed a rope around her waist, tying the other end to the belt of the sturdiest of the sailor-assassins and telling the man that Lord Vajk would be most displeased if she died. Her exhaustion was so extreme that she could only acquiesce to the rope, mustering just a grunt of distaste, despite the humiliation of being leashed like a dog. As the sun was tucking behind the sheer mountains in the afternoon of the first day, they stopped beside a waterfall. Collapsing against the algae-covered bole of a tree, Zsoka was too tired even to tend to her bleeding shins and fingers, which had scraped repeatedly against the cold stone of the stairs. Instead, she hungrily devoured the handful of dried fish that one of the tengerészgyilkos handed her, after which she drank deeply from the ice-cold waterfall, then wrapped her thin cloak tightly about her and fell quickly into an exhausted, dreamless sleep.

She was awakened by the smell of smoke and opened her eyes to see that dawn had arrived mercilessly, heralding another day of this endless climb. The muscles of her legs and back ached and trembled with a severity she had never experienced. She flexed her sore hands, wincing at the pain as the fresh scabbing tore open with the movement, and examined her broken and torn nails. Looking over the edge behind the tree against which she nestled, she gazed down at a sheer drop of hundreds of feet, with nothing but treetops and stones below. She briefly considered casting herself off into oblivion; anything was better than continuing this climb. She felt herself being observed, and turned to find the shaman leering at her with a knowing grin. Somehow, this ordeal was meant to humble her before him, she realized.

A cold defiance came over her and, refusing to give him the satisfaction of seeing her defeated, she composed and adjusted herself as though she were sitting upon a cushion in her drawing room. She looked about expectantly. One of the sailors had made a small campfire in the middle of the trail—the source of the smoke—and was roasting some type of fowl that he had apparently snared or killed. The smell of the roasting meat made her mouth water, after having survived for weeks on nothing but the shipboard seafood stew and dried fish. Zsoka gratefully accepted a roasted leg when offered, though she could easily have eaten the entire bird. The other six travelers shared the remainder of the meat. It wasn't until after she was finished that she realized the shaman had given her the largest portion, and the six sailors were casting resentful glances at her. Blood-Tooth, on the other hand, seemed quite content with his small portion and smiled a revolting grin at her, bits of meat and bone stuck in his horrifying teeth. The incongruousness of his treatment of her left her confused and feeling unbalanced. His demeanor seemed to vacillate between a grating obsequiousness and a severe, even savage cruelty, unforgiving of any frailty or failing. Why was she being dragged along on this journey? Why had he not allowed her to sail back with the captain? What possible use was she now that she had shown him the hidden stair? She had no interest in this Tor, nor could she discern any advantage to Vajk's plans by having her accompany the shaman. Yet, here she was, the erstwhile Empress of the Steppes, dressed as a common fisherman and being dragged up this interminable climb, tied to a begrimed sailor like some captive prize.

Well, she thought, *I will endure this hardship, and whatever may come after. In my veins flows the blood of kings and pirates. This is all a test of some sort, and after I have survived this, I shall have my revenge on this foul creature! My time will come. I will hear him scream as I watch him dismembered, piece by piece…*

Perhaps sensing her grisly thoughts, the shaman turned from her abruptly and barked the order for them to gather their things and renew the climb. After refreshing themselves at the waterfall and bundling their belongings, they set off again. The climb continued on relentlessly, Blood-Tooth urging the group to take shorter breaks throughout the day and press on.

It was midday when Zsoka finally had to stop. The muscles in her bleeding legs and forearms were screaming and cramping after a particularly grueling ladder-climb that had stretched for more than two hundred feet straight up. At the top of the ladder, there was a small landing, and she crawled over and placed her back against the sheer rock face, closing her eyes. As soon as the shaman crested the top of the ladder behind her, however, he kicked the sole of her ill-fitting boot impatiently.

"Up, *Empress,*" he said curtly. "No time to rest. We near the Equinox, and still have days of travel ahead." His voice sounded strange, somehow deeper, rougher.

"Why?" she pleaded with eyes still closed, sounding more pathetic than she had intended.

"We must arrive at the Tor before the day of balance, else our chance will be lost."

"But—"

"I said, get up, bitch!" he spat, his voice a beast-like growl.

She looked up, shocked at his words and tone, only to note that the pallor of his skin seemed worse than usual. His eyes, normally rheumy and bloodshot, seemed to have a gray film over them. His mouth was desiccated and his lips were split in several places. Dark lines traced a spiderweb of veins across the translucent skin of his face. She blanched at the sight, and felt a chill run down her spine. He looked, for all the world, like a walking corpse.

She glanced at the sailor to whom she was tied, and saw an unease in his eyes before he quickly turned away. She attempted to adjust the rope, pulling it higher on her waist to grant her some relief from its chafing, only to have it settle right back into its familiar place. The shaman loomed above her, impatient for her to continue. Clenching her teeth against her exhaustion and her many pains, she rose and glared at him with as much defiance as she could muster at that moment, though she feared the result came across as more pathetic than defiant.

For hours more the trail rose nearly straight, up a steep set of stairs that had been carved in a maddening irregularity of depths and heights. She lost track of how many times the varying stair dimensions caused her to stumble, barking her shins again and again or slamming her elbows painfully against the unforgiving stone. By the time the shaman called a halt for the day, her hands were a bloody mess, blood ran down both legs inside her trousers, and she could barely bend her right arm due to a painful swelling on her elbow.

"Stop here," Blood-Tooth ordered in an unnatural growl. Gone was any hint of the servile man she had traveled with. He seemed more dangerous, more unpredictable. His already-thin veneer of humanity had fallen away, revealing something savage and unspeakable. The tengerészgyilkos obeyed without question, casting uneasy glances in his direction, clearly as unnerved by his transformation as she was. It felt like the mountains had closed in on them, and for the last few hours they had been climbing in a narrow chimney of rock, the stairs carved impossibly between opposing jagged walls. The spot the shaman had chosen for them to spend the night was not conducive to sleep. There was no landing or path on which they might lie down or even rest their backs against a tree or rock. Instead, they perched awkwardly on the moist steps, some hundred yards shy of their goal. She could see the end of their climb ahead, the last glimmers of daylight lighting the stair's end in a dreamlike halo. *Why have we stopped here?* she nearly whimpered aloud. However, a venomous glance from the shaman kept her from voicing her complaint.

Zsoka did her best to tuck herself into the steep steps and tried in vain to find a comfortable position. She dozed fitfully through the long, cold night, startling herself awake multiple times by sliding down a stair or two as her body relaxed. Tears of exhaustion slid from her eyes as she gazed down the impossibly steep, merciless steps behind her and imagined falling truly asleep and tumbling away down the sheer, brutal chimney. She cast a baneful glance at Blood-Tooth, resolving to remain awake, and positioned herself more carefully.

It was a miserable night.

Chapter 35

...for in the long, long sweep of history, too many tales have been lost. Heroes and queens, kings and fools have lived and died. Empires have risen and fallen. Vast libraries of accumulated knowledge have crumbled to dust, their musty contents moldering and falling to corruption. We cannot hope to be remembered. We cannot hope to change the future significantly. But we can strive to make our lives meaningful in this moment. We can work to improve the lot of those around us, and stand as a defiant wall against the flood of evil.

— Excerpt from an ancient scroll fragment found in the Acidio Ruins, discovered in 907 Age of Waters (325 HR) and translated by Mansour ben Muhannad

574 HR – Last month of summer
(10 days before the Equinox)
Dóchas, High Valley region of the Green Mount

Dallin

"Ach, ye've got a wee appetite, I see," Dallin said to Brochy, as the badger cub worked at devouring the apple slices she set down. The two had been out hunting most of the afternoon in the wooded hillsides to the southeast of their village, and now came her favorite time of day. She and Brochy would sit together at a small, shaded table in the garden. She would have tea and one or two of the fresh raspberry scones her mother had made that morning, along with some clotted cream, while Brochy enjoyed fruit and nuts. She never tired of the spectacular view she had of the ocean over the cliffs of Dóchas. The sea breeze kept off the heat of the day, and the cries of the gulls were ever present. She felt at peace as she affectionately scratched the ridge of Brochy's snout.

It had been a successful hunt, and Dallin had returned laden with meat and fowl, which she had shared with those in the village whose need would be greatest, given the absence of the fyrd. She continued to marvel at the accuracy of the magnificent bow Toren had given her. It seemed she simply couldn't miss whatever she shot at. She knew she had *some* talent with the weapon, but the string of accurate strikes was becoming unbelievable. She stroked the bow staff thoughtfully as she recalled the morning's hunt.

The shot that took the large jack that day had been nothing short of remarkable. She had spotted the hare some thirty yards through the woods, crouching behind a fallen branch. Though his ears stuck up above the log, giving him away, she had no clear shot. When the jack had inched forward, she could just spot his eye through the crook in the branch of the log. Having surprised herself with multiple successful shots over the past week, she decided to test just how accurate she was becoming. Hitting a hare's eye from thirty yards through branch and bush was a shot she might imagine Toren successfully making to great acclaim, but she had no reason to believe she could do it. *Still, why not give it a go?* When the shot hit its mark perfectly, she whooped and ran to her kill to prove to herself that she hadn't imagined it. There was the dead hare, the arrow stuck straight through its skull.

"Can ye believe it, Brochy?" she shouted in her excitement. "I ne'er thought I could make a shot like that for all the world!"

She danced about in amazement, slapping her thighs in joy. The young badger trundled up alongside her, unimpressed with her marksmanship, and went about snuffling in the underbrush for grubs. With no one else to witness the feat, Dallin carried on chatting to the badger, expressing her wonder.

"Sure, this is the finest bow e'er made! Dinna ye ken?"

No response from the cub who seemed quite intent on digging out a recalcitrant worm.

"That's four hare and two grouse today, and both of them in flight!" She sat on the fallen log. "Who'd have thought that poor Dallin would become a hunter? And a right good one, I should say. Though dinna ye repeat that to anyone else. Hear? I wouldna want any in the village thinkin' I'm gettin' too big for me britches." She chuckled to herself in amazement as she strung the hair, then gathered up Brochy in her arms and headed for home, her kills proudly hanging over her shoulder.

Now, hours later, as she sat in the garden quietly enjoying her scones and tea, she felt a sense of belonging—of real value to her village—and she allowed herself a proud grin. A bold herring gull swooped near the small table, eyeing her remaining scone.

"Ach, be off wi'ye!" she shouted at the annoying bird, waving her arm. "Or I'll grab me bow and see if I can drop you in flight, eh?"

As she settled back and raised her cup once more to her mouth, she saw something that made her momentarily doubt her faculties. A figure—a man—was somehow hurled from the rocky beach hundreds of feet below the cliff's edge, and was flying overhead. He then crashed to the ground on the moor, just south of her house. She jumped to her feet in shock, upsetting the table and its contents and tipping poor Brochy into her bluebell thatch. With a shout, she grabbed her bow and quiver and dashed onto the moor.

There, some thirty yards from the cliff's edge, the man's body lay in a heap, unmoving. Assuming him to be dead, she ran to look over the precipice, trying to see what could possibly have hurled him such a distance. A small, single-masted ship lay at anchor some half mile out in the bay, though from this distance she could not determine if there was anyone aboard. Directly beneath her, she could see a tiny launch that had been dragged onto the pebbled beach, and near it, another body. Were there any path down the cliff, she would have made her way there to investigate. Instead, she could only stare and wonder. *What in the world just happened?*

A grunt from Brochy brought her round. He had liberated himself from the flowering bush and followed her to the cliff's edge. He was quite curious about something, sniffing the air and looking in the direction of the fallen man.

"Aye, strange, eh?" she said, allowing her gaze to follow his.

The man was stirring. Impossibly, he was *stirring*!

"That canna be!"

She began to walk, then jog toward him. As she came closer, she was able to make out the strange and shriveled form of the man. He wore a black robe, belted at the waist, with a simple homespun shirt and trousers beneath it. His skin had a ghostly translucence and his bald head entertained long random strands of black, greasy hair that seemed to sprout in small clusters. He was now sitting up and shaking his head dazedly. He raised a trembling hand to his brow, then scratched his scalp with brown, claw-like nails.

"Here now," she said as she approached. "Ye've had quite a tumble. Dinna move too quickly."

The man blinked red-rimmed eyes and looked up at her, trying to focus. He flashed a rueful smile at her, revealing ghastly teeth—stained, uneven, and... sharpened? A frisson of unease coursed over her at the sight of this ill-favored man, chills and shivers crab-walking along her spine and limbs. *Something's not right here.* Brochy approached and began to growl uncharacteristically. Indeed, she'd never heard him growl before, at anything.

The sounds of the badger startled the man from his dazed state, and he scrambled back from the creature, inexplicably terrified by the cub.

"Brochy," Dallin remonstrated, "what kinda behavior is that, now? Shame on ya, ye wee beast."

Just then, a cluster of people came toward them from the village. It was Liana, the apprentice healer, and old Maclan with his crippled twin sons, Creighton and Craig. Maclan looked unhappy and was holding a kerchief to his left eye. Liana must have given him his eye drops, which always caused him to swear like a wild man. The twins were hobbling along after Liana, who approached at a jog.

"What have we here?" she called as she neared the man, who spun at the sound of her voice and bared his teeth like a threatened animal. She stopped her progress and held out a calming hand.

"There now," she said soothingly, "we mean you no harm." Then, turning her attention to Dallin, she asked, "Where'd he come from, Dal?"

"Ye'd no' believe me if I told ye," the huntress responded, clutching the still-snarling badger in her arms.

Liana shot Dallin a puzzled look as she slowed her approach to the strange man, who had begun hissing and clawing the air, alternating his threats between the healer and Brochy.

"What's yer name, sir?" Liana asked gently.

Maclan called over his shoulder. "Lads, go and fetch Davonna."

As the two younger men turned to obey, the strange man glanced at Maclan with something akin to terror in his eyes, a terror that seemed to transform into some sort of hunger. Before anyone could react, he leapt at the old man, crossing over thirty feet with a single jump and tackling Maclan to the ground. Snarling like a rabid animal, the man ripped the kerchief away from the old man's eye and slapped a claw over his face making Maclan begin to scream and howl unlike anything Dallin had ever heard. Creighton and Craig were transfixed by the horror. Liana rushed to Maclan's side and began tried to pull the attacker off. But with a snarl, the creature lashed out at her with a claw, knocking her to the ground and tearing bloody rents across her shoulder.

Dallin dropped Brochy and scooped up her bow.

"Stop now, mister!" she shouted, but her voice was lost against Maclan's howling.

The creature leaned his mouth closer to the old man's face, baring his teeth. Dallin couldn't tell if he intended to bite the old man or was perhaps just smelling him? Before the creature could get any closer to Maclan's face, she loosed an arrow that took him in the right wrist, breaking his hold on the old man. With a shriek of outrage, the creature tumbled away from his prey and shot a venomous look at Dallin, who already had another arrow knocked.

"The next one's in yer eye. I'm warning ye!" she called, though whether the strange creature understood her or not was unclear.

He glanced hungrily over his shoulder toward the village, then with a final hiss at Dallin, turned and—with a supernatural leap—propelled himself skyward in an arc toward a cluster of people standing near the market. Without a thought, Dallin loosed the arrow. The shot took the strange man in the base of the skull and he fell in a heap in the marketplace. A great *WHOOM* of energy erupted from him, blowing over merchant stalls and tossing horrified onlookers to the ground in a radius of some twenty feet around him.

Liana and the twins rushed to the stricken Maclan, whose face was covered in blisters, blood, and pus. His screams had stopped, and Dallin feared the worst until she heard soft mewling sobs issuing from his blistered lips. As Liana tended to him, Dallin scooped up a very agitated Brochy. She dashed for the marketplace to ensure the fiend was truly dead, arriving at the same time as Davonna, who was accompanied by a cluster of people armed with staves and tools.

"What in the heavens?" Davonna exclaimed, taking in the destruction.

"I canna tell ye," Dallin said, looking on the mangled corpse in wonder. "But this creature attacked Maclan in a most foul manner."

"What type of man is he?" Davonna asked, leaning over the body.

"Angor shaman," said a man's voice from behind them.

Turning to see who had answered, Dallin saw the second strange man in a day, though this man shared none of the ill-favor of the fiend. Instead, he was of indeterminate age, had a wry, contagious smile, shaggy hair, motley trousers, and a matching vest over a bare chest. A small, scraggly dog trotted at his heel, its nub of a tail wagging furiously.

"What did you say?" Davonna asked, stepping forward to address the stranger.

The curious man held his hands up and smiled at the women. "I am no threat to you, Davonna, nor to your village," he said with a nod. "Quite the contrary. I am… Latrans!" He finished his introduction with a theatrical flourish and bow. After a moment's silence, he looked up to see confusion on the women's faces.

"Surely, Corvus has mentioned me?" he said with a slight swagger and a faux-modest grin.

The women looked at each other, but did not respond.

"No?" he said, smoothing his vest with both hands. "Well, that's awkward. I'll need to chat with him about that. Ruined my beat."

A group of armed folk were beginning to surround Latrans, pressing in on him.

"Look, wait," he said with a smile and a wave of his hand. "I came to warn you and explain some things." He attempted a disarming chuckle, though Dallin didn't feel very reassured—and, judging by the faces around her, neither did the others in the small crowd.

"Explain what, exactly?" Davonna asked, her demeanor stern and unyielding.

"Well…" He looked around lamely for a moment, then gestured toward the fiend's corpse. "That, for one thing."

"Then start explaining," she responded.

"Not just like that," he said with disapproval. "Can't we go and sit somewhere, have a little nibble? I hear the cheese you make here in your village is nonpareil!" Then he smacked his lips a few times distractedly, as if trying to identify a flavor. "Yes, I would enjoy that. Cheese, maybe some of that hearty bread you make… Oh, and some eggs and bangers. Wonderful idea! Yes, let's sit and eat and I'll tell you all kinds of things. Before you know it, we'll be fast friends!"

With that, he rubbed his hands together and started to walk out of the cluster of people. The tip of Davonna's staff brought him up short as it prodded into his throat. With an "urk," he stopped his forward progress.

"Bring rope," Davonna told the gathering crowd, two or three of whom dashed off to obey.

"Rope?" Latrans looked genuinely wounded at the thought. "Davonna, Davonna, Da-vonna! There's no need for that! I'm here to help you. I'm one of the good guys… Or at least one of the better guys! Not as bad as some. Better than… some," he finished weakly, with a shrug and a small chuckle.

"Christy," Davonna called over her shoulder. "Fetch a stool, eh, love?"

An eager young boy rushed to obey and in short order Latrans was seated and bound before Davonna, still surrounded by stern and suspicious armed villagers, most of whom were women and old men. Then Davonna turned to Dallin. Before she could speak, however, Liana stepped up, pressing a bloodied bandage over her injured left shoulder.

"Maclan has passed," she said gravely. "The stress and torment were too great a burden for his heart."

Silence fell as all within hearing distance lowered their heads. After several heartbeats, Davonna spoke in a ceremonial tone. "Hail the traveler!"

"Hail the traveler," the crowd intoned in response.

"We shall hold a burial feast for him on the morrow," she said in a loud voice. "In the meanwhile, prepare his body and see to your own wounds." This last she directed at Liana. And after the young healer left the circle, Davonna turned back to Dallin.

"What can you tell me of this day's events?"

"I fear ye'll scarce believe me," Dallin began. "I scarce believe it meself."

"Speak, child," Davonna encouraged her.

Dallin told her how she has seen the man's body fly over the cliff and crash to the ground on the moor. As she recounted the story, she felt a swell of emotion claw its way into her throat. She hadn't allowed herself to feel anything other than urgency, first for the stranger's well-being, and then for the protection of Maclan and her village. Now, surrounded by the concerned eyes of her community and the emptiness of Maclan's loss, she felt vulnerable, bare. She needed to stop her telling several times to clear her throat, clutching and petting the still-agitated Brochy in her arms. Davonna never once rushed her onward nor appeared impatient, but silently encouraged Dallin to continue her tale.

"Yes, yes," Latrans said, lighting up as she described the shot. "A fine shot, Dallin, a fine shot, indeed!" He said animatedly. Then, leaning as far toward her as the ropes around him would allow, he added in a conspiratorial tone, "Remind me to tell you about that bow, sometime. The fella who made it is an old friend. Lots of stories!"

Dallin frowned in confusion at his casual use of her name, as though he knew her.

"That's enough out of you," Davonna said sharply.

"But I thought you wanted me to explain…" he began innocently, before she cut him off with a look. "Oh, alright. I'll just sit here, then."

"I know it sounds incredible," Dallin added, "but I swear it's the truth."

"We all saw his impossible leap," Davonna reassured the young hunter. "This is some strange sorcery, indeed."

"That's what I want to tell you about," Latrans interjected. "But couldn't we do this over supper? Say, some bangers and mash? Mushy peas? Hmmm?"

Davonna sighed and looked at Latrans, long and hard. "There'll be time enough for food," she said sternly, "if ye prove yerself harmless. Right now, though, I have to say, the scales are against ye. The village is attacked viciously by a demon of sorts, and you mysteriously appear, claiming knowledge of the creature. And I find it passing strange that you seem to know everyone's name, though no one knows you. I'm not one to believe too strongly in coincidence, Mr. Motley."

"Latrans," he muttered, shaking his head. "I told you, my name is Latrans. Corvus should have told you about me. *Really* need to talk to him about that."

"So," she said, nodding her thanks to Christy who had brought her a chair. "Tell your tale."

With an exasperated sigh, Latrans rolled his eyes and said "Well, it's about time."

With a sudden spring, he leapt from his sitting position up onto the stool. In the same moment, the ropes fell away from his body, and he was somehow holding his flute. The alarmed crowd started to rush forward to subdue him, but with a spin and a flourish he held up his hands to forestall their assault. The startled villagers paused.

"Now, now, wait… One must set the proper tone." He began to play a mournful and ancient melody. Something in the music seemed to pull his audience toward a distant time, a sense of majesty and power, innocence and darkness. Soon, he began to narrate his tale, while somehow the flute continued to play. Dallin did not think to question how he managed it, since, like everyone else, she was too swept away with the magic of his story.

In the time before time, the world was clear, bright, and innocent. No human lived upon this world. It was a pristine garden, pure and untouched.

Then came the Six. Six friends, comrades, colleagues. The Hexaphiloi, in the tongue of the Ancients. Though an explanation of their provenance must wait for another time, their names, you know: Ilian, his wife Manu, Feryn, Nuada, Cruim and... Fel, though in those days he went by the name Duff, and was much beloved by the group. They found this fertile world, so very like their home, but as yet unspoiled, and they decided to create something here. They envisioned a world peopled by those untouched by darkness. A world free of the bitter struggles of human desire and avarice. On four of the continents, they erected great places of power: towers which they called the Gates of the Wheel. These were both sources of health and well-being, as well as gateways. And these Gates were directly linked to four matching Gates on their homeworld. Through these magical links, they brought carefully chosen tribes from their home to populate this garden, reaching across time and immeasurable distance. Together, the Hexaphiloi labored, as with one heart and one purpose, to fulfill their great dream. The Gates would nourish and give health to the people, the land, and the creatures. Disease and death would still exist, but there would never be plague, nor famine, nor wholesale want. A paradise, free of strife and need.

Over centuries of building and carefully populating this bright new world, darkness began to find a way into the heart of one of the Six. In his dedicated quest to better understand the very source of life and creation itself, Duff exposed himself to the bitter mysteries of the Dark. What they all did not realize, you see, was that at its very core, the spark of creation is fed by both Light and Dark, and in order to understand one, you must understand the other. Over the millennia, these dark mysteries began to unlock further questions in Duff's heart, the answers to which eroded his bright spirit, turning him slowly—oh, so slowly—away from Hope and Light and Joy. Over time, merriment left his eyes, and his dark brow furrowed with resentment, jealousy and, eventually, hatred of his fellows. He began to undermine their sacred trust. At first, in small, understandable, and defensible ways. "Experiments," he called them, "intended to spur their people to greater achievement and harmony." The Five believed him, for they loved him. But in the fullness of time, it became obvious that Duff had embarked on a dangerous and sanguinary journey into misery and horror. The Five were slow to believe this possible of their brother and comrade. Too slow. For by the time they understood the depths to which he had sunk, the evil in his heart had blossomed into a multi-pronged, poisonous plant with vast, foul tendrils that reached into every corner of their beautiful world. Their sweet garden, Hortus, was befouled.

The Five strove to contain him then, to somehow bring him back from the stygian pit into which his heart had descended. For they could not believe their brother and comrade could so turn against them. Had he no memory of their love? But their efforts were in vain, and he lashed out at them, bitterly, using the Gates against them to bring ravenous, bloodthirsty tribes from their homeworld. The Five recoiled in horror as he unleashed war, desolation, and want upon Hortus. He rejected his old name and all associations it carried, and became Fel the Reaper. Not just an arm or servant of Death, but Death itself.

Eight long centuries of war and dissolution followed, in which the Five led vast, glittering armies against those of his dark fortress. Oh, the many grand heroes of those ages past! More than can be recounted, their names lost to the winds of history, each worthy of sagas and legends. The Five raised exemplars from among the idealistic and pure peoples they had brought to this world, who led brilliant armies caparisoned in light and honor against the walls of the enemy's fortress. Oh, they spent such treasure! Treasure not of gold, but of pure and noble hearts sacrificed to hold the enemy at bay. Countless brave spirits, each with unique gifts and promise greater than the sunrise on Winter Solstice. All lost to the winds of history. For there was no broaching his defenses. He had built his great keep around one of the Gates, and had cast the Keys of power to the winds, preventing the Five from using any of the other Gates. For though the Keys were unbreakable in all ways, he was able to ensure they were lost to time and hidden from the world. From his dark fortress far to the south, armies poured forth, ravenous, hungry, merciless, and cruel. And no matter the size and bravery of the armies the Five arrayed against him, he gave no ground, incrementally advancing and advancing, his foul armies treading on an ever-growing pile of bones, spreading his darkness over the continents like an inexorable tide.

In a desperate, final gamble to stop him, the Five determined to spend what power they had left, of spirit, heart, and intent. Each would sacrifice an essential part of themselves to form an irresistible wave of light and health, which would overwhelm and destroy the Dark Keep and the Gate hidden within its walls once and for all. But in doing so, they would neutralize that Gate, forever severing the bond to their homeworld. Even more tragically, they would neutralize themselves, spending all their godlike powers in this one great effort.

But there was no other way to save their precious garden. And so they built a fire. Not just a fire, but a great pyre, the size of a mountain. Greater than any volcano, its flames reached far beyond the clouds and filled the skies throughout the world with ash and sadness. Countless innocent lives succumbed to the falling ash and subsequent winter as clouds of smoke blanketed the sun and hid its beneficence. The flames became so great as to endanger all life on this world. Indeed, it was only then, as they neared the precipice of self-annihilation, that the flames' heat was finally sufficient for their sacrifices. Into this blaze, each of the Five cast a crucial piece of their being, understanding that in doing so, the hexagonal balance of the world would rip a corresponding sacrifice from Fel. Ilian gave up his generosity, symbolized by his golden aura, shedding that which he held most dear, for there was nothing in all of life that he loved so well as showering his people with gifts. As he cast it into the flame, all the world could hear was the corresponding shriek of Fel. Manu, cast away her love of her children, cutting her very heart from her breast—thus transforming from the smiling, beneficent mother goddess to a cold, uncaring, and bitter crone. And Fel's shriek grew louder still. Feryn gave up her luck, her spirit losing all buoyancy and daring; her fearless heart now quailing behind curtains of uncertainty and caution. And Fel's shriek grew. Nuada, the Archer, gave a great shout and tore his right arm from his body before casting it into the flame, forever eschewing the joys of the hunt and competition. Fel cried. And Cruim the Clever shed his sanity, that which he treasured most, entering into an unending twilight of madness. And Fel's power diminished suddenly, the black flames of his might guttering to their nadir.

Their sacrifices made, the Five, clinging to what little was left of themselves, gathered a united army of all the peoples of the world and advanced on Fel's Gate. With the glorious power of the pyre infusing them and utterly diminishing him, they slaughtered his armies, moved on his fortress, and overthrew him. His keep was torn down, the very stones ground to dust and sunk into the ocean. Fel himself was not slain, however. For how can you ever truly slay a shadow? Instead, infinitely diminished, he dripped away into the jungles and pestilential wild lands to nurse his bitterness, and whisper his malevolence to the deafness of the swamps and venomous toads.

Fel's Gate was destroyed, and with the Keys lost, the three remaining Gates soon followed, their powers and bright energy going dun. Though some small fraction of the health and well-being they emanated continues, they are locked against their original purpose—that of allowing travel between the worlds. And after having lived for countless millennia, the Five were now neutered in their might, empty and bitter at their sacrifice, the core of their bright spirits burned off and spent in a fire hotter than a star. They went the way of all things and faded away, like the last glimmers of a glorious sunset. And the people endured. For such was the purpose of the sacrifice, to enable countless generations of innocent, well-meaning people to be born, grow up, live, marry, propagate, grow old and die in this perfect garden, unharried by the evils of the Lord of Shadows.

But Fel's spirit lingers on and whispers still in the hidden places of this world. And there are those who would listen. Oh, curious people. Forever searching for the unknown, the hidden, the forbidden. In time, a scholar from the Southern Reaches uncovered secrets. Dark secrets. She had a brilliant mind, and like so many of the "clever," she bore the arrogance of intellect. Mistaking intelligence for wisdom, knowledge for understanding. She spent a lifetime delving deeper into dark secrets, uncovering forbidden practices, studying arcane texts and never shying from dark deeds if done in the name of her "research." Somehow, her exploration led her to a moment when she heard but a fraction of a scintilla of an echo of the whispers of the shadowed reflection of Fel. But that was enough. Only the tiniest portion of a dead spark from the fractured ash of Fel's defeat found its way into her mind. But that was enough. Such a minuscule fragment filled her with an energy unlike she had ever known. Buoyed and sustained by the dark power that now suffused her, she spent another lifetime diving deeper, never truly aging, though her body withered. And then another lifetime. In time, she drew others around her. In a cruel reflection of the divine Six, she formed a council of twelve. "Shamans" she called them, for they held themselves to be the intermediaries between the physical world and the shadow world of their dark lord. In the jungle province of Angor, which lies beyond the Great Grass Seas of Orense, where humans scratch out a meager existence in the hostile, venomous swamps, she showed these twelve how to bond with blood, agony, fear, and despair to gain sorcerous, superhuman powers. But in sharing this knowledge, she overstepped. By tapping this dark force and passing it on to her twelve followers, she drained herself—for the shadows are jealous, cruel, and treacherous by their very nature. Just as she prepared to unleash and direct the Angor shamans onto an unsuspecting world, her spirit was sucked away, consumed by the very power she hoped to direct. She collapsed into a pile of bitter ash. The shamans cowered in fear and indecision at her dissolution, their grand purpose thwarted for a time.

The Angor shamans have lurked for generations on the edge of the world's societies, empowered by blood and misery and sustained through long lifetimes by that same spark that had so fueled their leader. They each feed on some aspect of the life force of others: love, flesh, fear, pain, joy, or some combination of these. Perhaps fearing a similar fate to that of their mistress' master, they have resisted coming forth and being known for the force they are, for then the people of the world might rise up and crush them, and surely they would, if only they knew. If only.

But something has changed of late. For so long, the twelve shamans were of equal might and influence on their dread council, none holding dominance over the others. A conclave of equals, balanced in their spite. But it seems that one has risen now, proclaiming himself first among them. His name is Sangine, and he has somehow coerced several of his fellows to recognize his leadership. Though not all. This posture has fractured the unity of the council. He has rallied most of the shamans to his side. Oh, do not be confused, for they are all born of blood, pain, despair, and misery, and have long since forsaken the light. But some few resist his command—not out of any noble or brave purpose, but simply craven or jealous self-interest and arrogance. He and those that follow him have joined with powerful armies and political forces now at work in the world. Together, they strive to capture the remaining Gates. But why, you might ask, if the Gates have been rendered dun?

Somehow, Sangine has rediscovered a secret: that each Gate has a Key and, just as critically, a living Gatekeeper within the structure. Once every five hundred years, a Gatekeeper is replaced, and in that moment of transfer—between the old keeper and the new—the Gate is, once again, suffused with power. How he has uncovered this ancient and lost secret is unknown, but Sangine believes that if he can capture a Gatekeeper and a Key and stand at the Gate the moment of transference, he can awaken the Gate from its enforced slumber, and command its untold powers. This possibility was held close and known only to the Five for untold generations. Despite their diminished capacities, they guarded this secret as a final piece only to be played should Fel's power somehow return. But, Sangine has somehow teased out this mystery. Perhaps, though it is the worst nightmare to imagine, Fel has reawakened and is directing the shamans' efforts. The Gates can, indeed, be awakened, and even controlled, and we stand within a hairsbreadth of his success. This Equinox is the day of transference for the Gate of the Autumn, and a Key has been found. It is not yet held by the enemy, though He bends His will toward its capture. Once again, it will fall to humanity to unite in purpose and oppose this evil. Should Sangine succeed in his scheme, he will rain dark terror and misery upon this world the likes of which would make Fel himself smile from His dank, fetid, and noxious hole.

The tale ended, and the people of Dóchas stirred slowly, as if from a dream. With a flourish, Latrans leapt down from his perch and once again sat on the stool, his flute disappearing somehow into his flimsy vest and his dog leaping into his lap, barking his approval of a story well told.

"And this creature," Davonna said slowly, looking at the corpse of the fiend, "is one of these shamans you speak of?"

"Well, yeah," Latrans said with lighthearted sarcasm, all trace of the drama and majesty of his tale gone from his tone.

"Why would he come to Dóchas, of all places?" asked Fulton, the mason, from the rear of the crowd.

"Look," Latrans said, impatience creeping into his voice. He took a deep breath before speaking again, then rattled off his answer as quickly as his nimble tongue allowed. "The Gates of Power are spread around the planet, except for the one in the Southern Reaches. That one was destroyed. The one on this continent, on Daffyd, that's *your* continent, is not far from here. You know where it is, don't you? Don't you?" He waited for a moment, but quickly rolled his eyes at the confused silence that followed. "It's the Tor, people! Okay, so much for mystery and trying to let you figure things out for yourselves. You people are no fun at riddles! Anyway, there's a big army trying to get there from the south. They've got a shaman with them. There's another group, that also has a shaman with them, heading there from the east. No doubt Jumpy here thought he could just hop up from the beach below, scare you folks, kill a few of you, then hop, hop, hop his way over to the Tor from the west. You know, the Tor? The Mount? The Green Mount? From which the Highlands get their name? You people getting this, yet?"

"We get it, Motley," Davonna said quietly, her eyes darting around as she absorbed the gravity of his revelations.

Latrans leaned toward Dallin and said, "So, as I was saying about the bow..."

"And who are *you*, really?" Davonna interrupted, rising from her seat and pointing at his chest with her staff. "How is it you know this history? A history I do not doubt a word of, though I canna say why... How is it you know this story, that was lost to our furthest ancestors' ancestors? I must say, Motley, I am not one given to flights of fancy, but I have witnessed sorcery this day that has shaken me to my very foundation. And I tell you, it's opened my mind to the thought that where one being of myth and fantasy might exist, so might another. And so I ask you again, Who. Are. You. *Really*?"

"Are we ever going to eat?" Latrans responded like an impatient child. He looked around at the crowd as if she had not spoken. "Oh, and the name's Latrans, not Motley. Latrans."

"Cruim…" Dallin's voice was so soft that it went almost unheard, but it somehow reverberated through the crowd like a bell. She stood dumbfounded by the revelation. "By the heavens above, you're Cruim the Clever, aren't you? You're one of the Five… I mean, Six! Dinna ye ken?" she said, looking around, her voice gaining confidence. "He gave up his sanity and entered a 'twilight of madness.'"

Latrans flashed her a smile and wink, then stood and faced Davonna.

"I suppose I'll have to pass on that feast you promised," he said with another flourish. "Too bad! I was so looking forward to some bangers and that goat cheese. Mmm…" Then turning back to Dallin, all semblance of levity and lightheartedness left him. "You, my clever girl, need to get to the Tor right away. Oh, and bring that bow. Perhaps someday I'll have the chance to tell you its history."

"As for the rest of you," he said melodramatically, spinning again to scoop up his dog, then bowing theatrically spoke loudly in a melodramatic and exaggerated voice, "I thank you for your kind attention!"

With a quick flick of his hand, he cast a colored powder into the air—though afterward the people of Dóchas could never agree on what color it was, exactly. After several long moments, Dallin shook her head to clear the haze it created, while the other townsfolk stirred awake as if from a standing slumber or daze. Latrans was long gone, and all they could do was stare at one another in wonder.

Chapter 36

And the great black bird gazed from its perch over the battlefield below. So many dead, so many still dying. So many to guide over the bridge. He had much work ahead of him.

— From "The Raven's Song" as told by Piper the Bard

574 HR - Last month of summer
(9 days before the Equinox)
Eagle's Gate, Glenfolk region of the Green Mount

Argant

Argant's sleep was troubled. He had slept deeply at first, aided by the herbs Yadira had put in his stew, but as the fire dwindled, the steady cold mountain breeze gave him a chill that his blanket seemed unable to prevent. He tossed and turned, and tucked his head under the cover, until he heard someone stirring. Peeking out with one eye open, he saw Lupe adding fuel to the fire. She then draped something over him, another blanket or cloak. He muttered his thanks, then drifted away into a deep sleep.

This time, he awoke to the sound of someone, a man, muttering to himself. It was repetitive, almost like reading a list of items. He looked around and realized he was standing, and warm. There was no breeze. He looked at his feet, expecting to find his bedroll and the remnants of the fire, but neither were there. In fact, as he looked around, he could see nothing. No stars above, and no sounds, save for the continued recitation that seemed just beyond his ability to hear clearly. Just darkness all around him. Realizing he was alone, a chill of fear struck him and he began to call out.

"Yadira! Lupe!"

No response.

He walked in a large circle repeating his calls. "Anyone!" He began to panic, screaming for help, and he began rushing about, this way and that, though he had no real sense of location or direction. "Anyone! Yadira! Help me! Lupe!!!"

After several terrifying moments in which he dashed about until his breathing was heavy and he could feel himself beginning to sweat, he came upon a man, an old man, sitting on a high throne. It was made of stone, though its shape made it look like it had been formed by the branches of an ancient tree. There was a single lantern lit before the man that illuminated his face. He seemed to be asleep. He had long, wispy white hair, and a long white beard and mustache. On his head, he wore a shiny circlet of some kind with a green gem on the front. His face seemed thin, almost gaunt, and he was wearing a multicolored robe that looked very rich and warm, so Argant couldn't quite tell if his body was similarly slender or not. The continued recitation was clearer now. The boy seemed to be closer to the source, and could now understand what was being said.

"Oak... kestrel... gorse..." the voice intoned in a rich bass. "Fox... kit. Hmmm, cute little one." The voice chuckled softly before continuing. "Sparrow... ewe... roebuck... heather... pine..." And so on. The voice was not loud, nor insistent. It was like a dozing mutter, as though some bearded grandfather by the fireside had started talking in his sleep—though Argant could feel its deep tone reverberate in his body.

"Hello?" Argant said meekly to the sleeping man, not sure if he should disturb him or not. But there was no reaction. "Hello!" he said more insistently, reaching up and tugging on the hem of the man's robe. The man finally stirred awake, blinking his eyes several times and looking about before he noticed Argant standing beneath him, looking up expectantly.

"Well, hello," the man said in a mild, gentle voice, accompanied by a smile. "I see you've come, at last."

"Where are we? Who are you?" Argant asked impatiently.

"Yes," the man replied with a soft chuckle, as the intoning list continued behind their conversation. "I imagine you're quite confused."

"Where is everybody? What happened?" the child asked, his voice rising.

"There, there," the man said with an easing gesture. "You're perfectly safe, sleeping beside your campfire. This is a dream, you see."

Argant blinked in confusion and looked around. "A dream?"

"Yes," the kindly old man continued. "You're drawing nearer, and each night that you get closer to me, you will come here in your dreams. Each night, we'll chat together. I'll explain things. I've felt your approach for some time now. The fact that you've finally found me means you've entered my lands. Well done, my boy."

"Who is that?" Argant pointed into the air behind him in a vague effort to identify the source of the intoning voice.

"Oh, that?" The old man smiled and waved a dismissive hand. "You'll grow quite used to that."

"But who is it?"

"It is not so much a *who,* as a *what,"* the man replied cryptically.

"What's going on?" Argant insisted and even stamped his foot in frustration. "I don't understand!"

"No," the man said with that same gentle, almost loving smile. "I imagine you don't. Come again tomorrow night, and I'll try to explain more."

"Why can't you tell me now?"

"You're about to wake up, young Argant."

At the mention of his name, the boy startled awake. Dawn was breaking, and the large, robed man they had met the night before was stirring the fire and preparing to make tea. He was burly, and had a scraggly black beard with streaks of white, and short, unkempt graying hair. He caught Argant's eye, and gave him a friendly wink and a smile, then put a finger over his lips and pointed to the still-sleeping forms nearby. Argant nodded his understanding. He suddenly had to pee, urgently. Standing, he wrapped himself in the spare blanket against the chill and headed off behind the nearby stones. When he returned, the kindly man handed him a small heel of bread and some cheese, and Argant realized how hungry he was. With a nod of thanks, he tore into the food as if he hadn't eaten in a week. The bread was hearty, dark brown and stiff, and the cheese was unlike anything he'd ever tasted. Sharp, pungent, and delicious. He couldn't eat it fast enough. Soon, all that was left were crumbs on his face and chin. He licked his fingers hungrily, trying to savor every bit.

He looked up to see the big man smiling affectionately at him and holding out another hunk of bread and still more of the amazing cheese. With a sheepish grin, Argant accepted the second helping, and did his best to eat more politely, as Mama Warad had taught him. He concentrated on not chewing with his mouth open, and taking smaller bites, though nothing would have made him happier than stuffing the entire hunk of cheese into his mouth at once.

As he was finishing, the man handed him a mug of tea. When he tasted it, he grimaced. It wasn't like the tea that Yadira prepared, with cinnamon and sweet spices, and always a touch of honey for him. Instead, it was dark and bitter, and he wasn't sure he liked it at all. However, the warmth felt good against the morning chill and it did help to wash down the bread.

"You seem to be feeling better," the man said softly in the women's language.

Argant nodded, not sure what to say.

"Good." The man smiled and patted the boy's knee. "We were worried."

Argant smiled shyly before asking, "What's your name?"

"I am Yazid." The man touched his chest and bowed his head slightly. "And this is my friend, Corvus." He pointed at the imposing, bald man who was just approaching the fire. The man smiled at the boy, though something about his face suggested that he didn't smile often. He was clean shaven and muscular and walked with a slight limp on his left side. Despite his injury, it was clear that this man was a warrior. He wore leather armor and seemed very confident.

"Good morning," Corvus said softly as he sat down and accepted a mug of tea from Yazid.

"Good morning," the boy responded quietly, trying his best to remember the manners the women had taught him. He touched his chest with his right hand and bowed his head as he spoke. "My name is Argant."

"It's very nice to meet you, Argant," Corvus responded, placing his hand on his chest and inclining his head to mirror the boy's formal gesture. Yazid grinned broadly. Argant found that smile reassuring and he liked Yazid, instantly. Somehow he felt that nothing could be wrong, as long as Yazid was nearby, which was strange, since he'd only just met the man. He liked Corvus, too, he thought, but Yazid just seemed so warm and welcoming.

Argant grinned back at the big man before asking, "Is there any more of that cheese?"

Yazid laughed quietly and turned to rummage in a bag nearby before producing yet another hunk of bread and a slice of that heavenly cheese. Argant's eyes lit up.

Yes, he was going to like these two.

Ligulf

The morning had gone well enough. Once everyone was awake, he had been formally introduced to Yadira and Lupe and the boy, Argant. There wasn't much for the group to do while they waited for the arrival of the troops, other than scan the southern horizon, hoping for a glimpse of the women's companions.

Perched high in the broken tower, Li strummed his cittern softly as he looked out over the pass. He felt a sense of dread, knowing that soon enough, the broad valley of Monarch's Pass would fill with enemy warriors. He wasn't sure what role he would play once the armies arrived. Help with the wounded, he imagined. Though he had trained his entire life with his father, the sword style in which he was skilled, Sparrow, was not suitable for standing in a shield wall, as it focused on the use of a light, needle-like blade. The movements of the form were quick and feathery, and relied on wide maneuverability and leaping, graceful attacks that seemed dance-like compared to the heavy, bashing techniques preferred by most Highlanders. Ligulf had always been slight of build, his arms thin and his hands feminine and delicate. Early on, his father had assessed his son's stature and determined that Sparrow form for sword work, and Nasim for hand-to-hand, would be the most appropriate styles for the boy. Though Li had tried time and again, he simply didn't have the strength to manage a heavy shield and be of any use in the wall. He was too easily pushed over. It was humiliating. He knew his father loved him. It was expressed often and freely, but deep down, Li worried that he was a disappointment to the great Corvus Corax. Oh, his father would never say such a thing and would be horrified to think that it was actually a worry for Li. But a man such as Corvus deserved warriors for sons, like Cai. He was forthright, strong, a leader.

He shook his head and silently chided himself for such emotional indulgence. He was as lucky as a young man could be! What in the world did he have to worry about? His family was filled with love and acceptance. His father was famous and celebrated throughout the Green Mount, and Li had found romance and love with Piper. The people of Dóchas had long ago accepted Li for who he was, understanding and appreciating that loving another man was not wrong or evil. Of course, at first they hadn't really had a choice. It was either that or face his father's protective wrath. He smiled at that. How many warriors in the world would so fiercely protect, support, and love an openly homosexual son? And now, years on, he sensed no hostility or judgement from the people of his village or any of the villages in the High Valley, for that matter. He lived his life in the open, wrapped in the arms of a loving community that valued his gifts. Yes, he was a lucky young man, and he owed it all to his father, whose perspicacity, wisdom, skill, and diligence had transformed all of the High Valley. His da would never think of Li as a disappointment.

He looked down fondly from the tower toward the campfire below. He could see his father's broad shoulders and bald head, sitting by the fire as Yadira and Yazid prepared the midday meal. His father was laughing at something Yazid had said as he cleaned his sword. Lupe and the boy were busy skinning the hares she had killed that morning. She was a formidable one. Stocky and strong, she looked like she could snap Ligulf in half with one hand, but she was also polite and formal. She seemed slow to trust, and never had her bow out of arm's reach. He noted that even now, focused on teaching Argant to skin a rabbit, she knelt in a position that kept Corvus and Yazid in her sight. Cautious. A good person to have on your side. He resolved to work on befriending her.

The smoke from the cookfire wafted up to his high perch. Ligulf wasn't sure what Yadira and Yazid were preparing, but whatever it was, it smelled amazing. His stomach growled and he started to pack up his instrument to head back down when something caught his eye in the distance.

"Da!" he shouted, and his father stood and turned, looking up at him. "Rider in the pass!"

As Corvus began rushing toward the tower, Li glanced around in the other direction and spotted a dust cloud that heralded an approaching army.

"Troops coming from the north!" he called out.

Corvus

His leg complained as he ascended the spiral staircase of the ruined tower. The stairs ended on a landing some thirty feet up. The walls of the tower had broken away above that point, leaving a jagged point on the eastern wall that extended above the landing some fifteen feet.

Patting his son on the shoulder as he arrived, Corvus first glanced north to gauge the approach of the army. This would most likely be the fyrd as they'd had the most warning and had set out days ago. The army was too far to see any details beyond the dust cloud, but still, its approach heartened him. Turning to the south, he shaded his eyes to try to see the rider.

"You've sharp eyes, indeed, Li," he said admiringly. "That's naught more than a speck on the horizon. Well done, lad."

Ligulf beamed in response. "Should I saddle a horse and ride to meet her?" he asked, eager to be of use.

"I suspect Lupe's well ahead of you in that," Corvus said, nodding to their right just as the woman galloped off southward on her white mare, riding bareback. "But she may need support. Go after her."

Ligulf dashed down the stairs and in a matter of minutes was galloping after Lupe, his lithe, speckled gelding leaping nimbly over a fortress stone in his path. He had taken the time to saddle his horse, allowing Lupe to gain quite a lead, but he trusted that Luath could catch her. Though Ligulf never competed in games of strength at festivals, he was a masterful rider, and together with Luath, he had never lost a horse race.

Mama

Despite the rugged travails of the past days, and the exhausting switchbacks climbing up to the pass, the powerful gray destrier that Mama had stolen from the Barbár encampment soldiered on without notable signs of fatigue. Amina rode behind her, the girl's thin arms wrapped around the older woman's waist. Mama patted their mount's neck and encouraged him, thanking him for bearing them both so nobly. The stallion tossed his head in response, seemingly eager to run. Perhaps soon, she'd need to accept that offer.

The enemy was pressing behind already. No doubt, their warriors were beginning to thread their way up the switchbacks toward the pass. But she knew it would take time for a force of that size to scale the narrow trails upward, and she was hovering on the verge of illness. Somehow, despite the exhaustion, the freezing rain, and the stress of the past days, she had avoided catching a fever, and she was not eager to spend any additional energy that her body—and her mount—may well need in the days ahead. She thanked the Ancestors for their obvious intercession on her behalf, and then thanked them again for Amina. Without the girl's talents and clarity, the two would not have survived. The boulder she had toppled with Amina's aid had slowed the enemy by several hours, allowing the women time to crawl out of their cave, wring out their sodden robes, and escape. Enemy arrows and threats flew at their backs, despite the blocked road. She shuddered to think of what Amina had been through, how terrifying and painful it must have been. She patted the girl's arm affectionately, careful only to touch Amina's sleeve and avoid the skin-on-skin contact that so unnerved her votary. Amina responded with a squeeze.

The stallion snorted and tossed its head. Mama looked up in response, and in the distance could now make out two riders rushing pell-mell toward her. After a moment, she recognized the lead rider as Lupe, but dashing from behind, and gaining on her, was a man. Was he chasing her? Was there danger? She spurred the stallion into a loping canter and reached down to clutch her staff.

Within a matter of minutes, Lupe reined up and Mama slowed her mount to a walk. Lupe's mare was frothy and blowing with the exertion.

"Mama!" Lupe said. "Thank the Ancestors!"

"All is well, child," Mama said with a broad smile as the two women gripped hands.

"Amina, we were so worried—" Lupe continued.

"Not now," Mama interrupted. "Who is it that approaches?" She gestured at the madly galloping young man, who was smiling broadly as he approached.

"He is a friend," Lupe answered quickly, as he reined up beside the women.

Mama relaxed her grip on the staff, returning it to its tether on the side of the saddle. She nodded to the smiling man as Lupe continued, "He is the son of Corvus Corax."

Mama looked at her in wonder, then turned back to the slight young man, touched her hand to her chest, and said in her broken Sudlandic, "Greetings, son of Corvus. I am Nabila Warad."

Still panting from the ride, the man mirrored the gesture and said "Hello" in Aslene. It seemed like perhaps it was the only word he knew in the language. Then, realizing he still hadn't introduced himself, he tapped his chest again. "Ligulf of the High Valley."

Mama smiled at his awkward introduction and bowed her head, speaking uncertainly in Sudlandic. "Greetings, Ligulf. I hope you are well."

Aware of the pressing enemy behind her, and eager to finish her quest to find Corvus, Mama urged them onward toward the ruins. As they rode together, Lupe explained how Yadira and she had gotten separated, and that by the blessings of the Ancestors, Yadira and Argant had stumbled upon Corvus, Ligulf, and their Aslene friend, Yazid.

Mama looked at Lupe in surprise. "Aslene friend?"

Lupe nodded in wry understanding at Mama's wonder. "Yes, and both he and this Corvus speak our tongue fluently."

"Wonder upon wonder," Mama said, shaking her head.

Corvus

By the time the three riders were nearing the ruins, he could make out clear details of the army approaching from the north. He could just see the green and gold banners of the Glenfolk. *The lad wasted no time,* he thought appreciatively. *It seems the Glenfolk embraced his leadership quickly. That's good. That's very good. I pray the fyrd is not far behind.*

Corvus descended the tower to find the women and the child hugging enthusiastically, all except for a waif-like girl that must have ridden behind the older woman, where he hadn't been able to see her on the approach. No one except the boy hugged her, though all seemed very glad to see her. He noted that despite the reunion, the girl didn't seem to smile much and carried herself with a placid, almost otherworldly air.

Odd, he thought. *Well, based on the tale Yadira told us, the lass has been through an ordeal.*

As Corvus approached the group, Yazid stepped forward and formally introduced him to their leader.

"Mama Nabila Warad," he said, with slight bow of his head, "allow me to introduce Corvus Corax, former student of Master Ashahl."

The short, stout woman beamed up at Corvus, tears springing to her eyes. Then, apparently unable to control herself, she rushed forward and embraced him, sobbing her gratitude and thanking the Ancestors. Corvus returned her embrace awkwardly. Twice, she pulled away from him, gripped his face with both hands, muttered a tearful thanks, then pulled him back to her firmly. Despite the unexpected nature of the greeting, Corvus marveled at the strength in her arms as she pulled him into yet another powerful hug.

As they finally stepped back to look at one another, he smiled at her and said, "I know your journey has been long and difficult, and I am glad you have arrived safely."

With a breath, Mama seemed to suddenly remember something.

"Ah, old woman," she chided herself in Aslene as she retrieved her staff from the saddle of her mount and presented it to him. "Master Ashahl, an old friend, sends this to you. He said you would know what it is and what to do with it, but that you must protect it at all costs."

Corvus accepted the strange staff with a questioning look to Yazid, who shrugged his confusion in response. It looked like a piece of worthless driftwood.

"I thank you for your efforts," Corvus said, struggling to find meaning in the item. "If Ashahl believed this to be so important that he would send you and your group on such an odyssey to bring it to me, we will strive to understand its meaning and purpose." He looked at her hopefully as he concluded and watched as her face fell into despair.

"You do not know what this is?" she asked.

He shook in head in mute response.

"He said you would know…" She looked down in frustration before continuing. "He called it one of the 'Lost Keys of the Wheel.'"

Yazid and Corvus again exchanged helpless, confused looks as Mama scowled. Ligulf whispered to Yazid to translate for him, and when he did, Corvus' youngest son stepped forward.

"Da," he said quietly, "I've heard of this."

Corvus' head snapped toward him.

"There's an ancient ballad—more of an epic poem, really—that tells of the Lost Keys," Li said. "I've heard it, once or twice."

"Do you know the song, lad?"

"I don't," Li said with a shrug. "I'm sorry. Piper sings it on occasion. I've only heard him do it once or twice. But it's haunting and strange. Ancient, from the sound of it."

Corvus nodded. Piper, he knew, was Ligulf's fellow minstrel and friend from Mallaig, though he suspected the two were much closer than that. Mallaig was a journey of several days from Eagle's Gate back toward the High Valley, and with the army arriving, he couldn't afford the time to unravel this mystery right now. He turned back to Mama Warad.

"Dear sister," he said, addressing her with the Aslene affectionate form, implying he held her as family, "we will discover this treasured item's purpose, I promise you. I will not fail Master Ashahl, nor will I cause your long journey to have been in vain. Right now, however, I must attend to the arriving army. Please sit by the fire, eat and rest. The days ahead will be filled with battle and blood, I'm afraid."

"I understand," she responded calmly, mollified by his answer. "The barbarians are close at hand. Even as we speak, I fear, they climb the trail into this valley."

Corvus nodded his understanding, then turned to Ligulf as the women and Argant settled into a cluster by the fire to feed and comfort Mama and Amina and hear all of their travails.

"Back up the tower, lad," he said quickly. "Keep a sharp eye out for the enemy to the south and watch for the fyrd to the north."

"Will we have time to deploy the troops, you think?" Yazid asked somberly as Ligulf dashed away.

"It'll be close, my friend," Corvus said, his eyes scanning the pass. "It'll be close."

Chapter 37

Long had young Taavi worried at the ropes that bound his wrists. His teeth were sore, and his wrists bled from the effort, but finally—slowly, so slowly, my children—the knot began to unravel. A great booming and a roar told of the imminent return of the dragon. Taavi frantically worked to finish untying his wrists.

"Where is my prey?" The dragon's voice rumbled through the cavern. The urchin's heart sank as he searched the cavern for a place to hide. Then suddenly, with a roar that shook the bones in Taavi's small frame, the dragon thundered into view, his eyes fury, his grin savage hunger.

Just as the realization came that he was about to die, Taavi felt a breeze on his neck from behind him, which was very strange as he was standing against the cavern wall. It was as if the mountain itself breathed upon him.

– Taavi and the Dragon, Aslene children's tale

574 HR - *Last month of summer*
(9 days before the Equinox)
Eagle's Gate, Glenfolk region of the Green Mount

Corvus

Cailean smiled broadly as his father rode up to greet him. The younger man wore a green and gold tabard over his battle leathers. The two exchanged an affectionate handshake, then Corvus turned his horse to ride alongside the new commander of the Glenfolk.

"They seem to have taken to you quickly," Corvus remarked.

"Aye, no worries," Cai responded lightly. "Had to knock a few heads, but nothing I couldn't handle."

"I'm proud of you, lad," Corvus said softly, before adding in a wry tone, "though I didn't expect you to dress in their colors quite so quickly."

Cai laughed. "Well, you canna expect me to lead them if I dinna dress like them. And I think the green goes well with my eyes, dinna ye ken?"

Corvus leaned his head back and laughed loudly, both in genuine amusement at the comment and to hearten the soldiers nearby. It would not do to convey any signs of nervousness or worry at the oncoming battle, or its preparations. As far as the soldiers needed be aware, their commanders were confident and things were proceeding as planned.

As the Glenfolk army arrived at the ruins of Eagle's Gate, Cailean and Corvus were greeted by Ligulf on his gelding. After a quick, fond greeting between the two brothers, Ligulf reported that he had sighted the enemy beginning to arrive at the southern end of the pass. Corvus' face fell, and he nodded.

"Any sign of the fyrd?" he asked his younger son.

"Aye, sure," Li responded with a quick grin. "They're but two hours behind this sorry lot." He winked at his brother, and earned a sharp whack on the shoulder from the glove Cai was holding.

"Ah, that's a relief," Corvus said with a sigh, wiping his brow with the back of his hand.

"I've sent riders back to keep an eye out for Fergus' troops and report their progress," Cai said. "We should hear from them before dark."

Corvus nodded. "Good thinking. Li, ride to the fyrd. Urge them to make all speed. We have to have them in position quickly. After that climb, the enemy will need to rest the night, but I suspect tomorrow will be a busy day."

"Sure, Da," Ligulf said, then galloped off.

"Cai, position two of your sharpest-eyed scouts in that tower," the Raven continued, all business now. "I need enemy numbers as soon as possible, and send more riders north to find and urge on Fergus. If he can get here before dawn, his troops will be shagged, true, but perhaps we can surprise the enemy with a last-minute swell of our numbers."

"Corvus!" Yazid shouted from the camp. "When you have a minute…"

Corvus waved in response and nodded, then turned back to Cailean. "Send your logistics people to my camp for troop disposition as soon as you're able. I'll want you on the right flank."

"Sir!" his son responded crisply, and rode off to attend to matters.

Corvus dismounted and headed for his camp. He had not taken three steps, however, before he realized why Yazid had summoned him. There, standing by his fire, was the tall form of Toren. He quickened his pace.

"Toren!" Corvus said with a broad smile and a welcoming hand extended. "I thought you said you wouldna make it in time."

The taciturn archer accepted the handshake quietly and merely nodded his head toward the mountain behind them before saying, "I took a shortcut through the hills."

"You'll have to show me that shortcut, someday," Corvus said in amazement. "Right glad we are, though, to have you here. The enemy approaches, and I've been told there's a handful of their spies on that slope."

"Not anymore," Toren said simply.

Corvus did not need to ply the archer for more information. Though the man rarely showed any emotion, Corvus had learned over the years to read the subtleties in his expression. The slight furrow of his brow told the commander that this peerless hunter had found and dispatched the intruders. *Good. One less worry.*

Corvus nodded his thanks and patted the tall man on the shoulder gratefully, before turning to the business at hand. "When your archers arrive, I'd like you to position them on either side, well-hidden but in clear sight of each other." He indicated the wooded mountain slope to the west and the cliff face to the east.

"Difficult to hide on the cliff face, but we'll make it work," the archer replied.

"Good man," Corvus replied. Then he indicated that Toren should sit. Corvus outlined his plan for the coming day, which forces would be positioned where, and how their signaling should be handled. Toren nodded in understanding of each detail and said very little, asking concise questions only when necessary. As their conference was concluding, the men stood and shook hands just as a breathless Ligulf rode up with another man behind him on his horse, and a broad smile on his face.

"Da!" he called as he approached. "You'll never guess who I found marching with the fyrd."

Corvus' peered at the other man.

"It's Piper!" Ligulf said, as he dismounted. "My friend from Mallaig. The one who knows the ancient song."

Corvus had been so wrapped in the preparation for battle, he had almost forgotten the curious staff Mama had brought him. He stepped forward to greet Piper apologetically. The man was some ten or fifteen years older than Ligulf. He had a lean, athletic build and a dark complexion, and was shorter than Corvus expected. He carried an instrument strapped to his back, much the way Ligulf was prone to do, and bore no weapon.

"Glad I am to meet you, Piper," he said, shaking hands. "Though I must apologize, as events are pressing."

"I completely ken, sir," the bard replied with a winning smile. "I wouldna fash ye for a tick, but Li explained the circumstances and th' unusual item that wis given tae ye. Ah think ah kin hae a clue."

Corvus blinked at the surprisingly thick mountain dialect, but answered in a businesslike tone. "If you can tell it quickly, lad, then do. Otherwise, I'm afraid it'll have to wait until after the battle."

"That's just it, sir," Piper replied. "I dinna think it can."

Corvus frowned in confusion at the bard's cryptic response, but before he could follow up, Lupe came thundering toward them in a mad sprint.

"Corvus Corax!" she called as she ran. "Come quickly!" She was gesturing to the north side of the ruins.

"Come along, lads," Corvus said, and the group started jogging toward Lupe, who turned and sprinted back around the ruins. "Lass can move!" he commented wryly in appreciation of the votary's impressive burst of speed.

As they rounded the ruins they found the Aslene women clustered around Mama, who was staring to the northeast, seemingly transfixed by something only she could see.

"What is it?" Corvus called as they jogged up.

Mama did not answer. Instead, she was chanting something under her breath.

"She is using the Canon of Perception," Yadira said in a hushed voice, apparently wary of disturbing Mama's concentration. When Corvus looked confused, she added, "It grants many gifts, among them is Longsight."

Corvus understood that. In centuries past, Aslene mystics and martial artists had followed the same path, shared the same mysteries, but sometime in their distant history, there had been a rift, a schism. The mystics chose to pursue a more spiritual path, while the martial artists focused on their fighting prowess. However, many of the mysteries crossed over and were still utilized by practitioners on either side. Just as Eagle form granted Corvus Longsight, he knew that those who followed the Path of the Divine Halls of the Ancestors could access it through their own means.

"What could she see to our north?" Corvus asked, nonplussed. "The enemy is to our south."

"The army, yes," Yadira responded. "We must wait until she finishes to find out what she has seen, but I believe there is a danger that demands your immediate attention."

Corvus looked to Yazid who shrugged in response. After a few dozen more heartbeats, Mama lowered her head, wiped her brow, and leaned on Lupe's shoulder. Corvus knew the nausea and disorientation that followed his own brief uses of Longsight, and could only imagine how difficult and taxing it might be for an extended period such as this.

Mama turned to him and spoke gravely. "The enemy is behind you, Corvus Corax." She gestured to the north, across the raging Gomul River a mile distant, at the broad, seemingly peaceful plains of the White Cleft's southern territories.

"What enemy?" he asked with urgency. "What have you seen?"

Yazid was quietly translating for Ligulf and Piper, who stood nearby, fascinated by the exchange.

"I cannot explain what led me here," she responded. "I can only say I felt something on the wind from that direction. At first, I saw nothing, but as I sharpened my perception, I saw a small band of Barbárs emerge from a cleft in the mountain, there." She pointed at a spot in the far distance, then continued. "Six warriors, a woman, and, I fear, a blood sorcerer. They emerged from that spot and began moving quickly northwest across the field."

"A sorcerer?" he responded incredulously. "How can you…?"

But Mama's raised hand forestalled his comment. "I faced one of his brethren during my trip to rescue Amina," she said quickly. "Please, you must trust what I have seen. There is no doubt. He is a being of dark power. I cannot guess their intent, as I do not know this land. What would lie to the northwest of that spot?"

Corvus' mind raced, but it was still largely filled with strategy, troop placement, and tactics. He couldn't focus on this problem. *Not now!*

"The Tor!" Piper shouted, as soon as Yazid finished translating. Corvus' blood ran cold. Of course. The Tor. It would be a week's journey on foot, but yes, it was northwest of that spot.

Mama read his expression and gripped his arms with undeniable urgency. "They seek this Tor!" she said, her eyes seeming to plead for him to understand.

"A small band, you say?" he asked, turning his entire focus to this moment.

"There are but eight of them," she responded firmly. "I do not know the extent of the sorcerer's powers, but I fear them. If he is as strong as his fellow that I faced in the enemy camp, he is mighty."

"And you faced him?" Corvus asked, surprise in his voice.

"I was able to hide us from his power," Mama replied.

Corvus nodded, his mind racing. He turned to Piper. "You understand this Key and its link to the Tor?"

"Not really, sir," he said, taken aback by the question. "Th' song haes hints 'n' clues that kin be helpful, bit ah wid need time 'n' mair speirins tae truly ken its meaning. Bit ah dae ken that it's critical that it gits tae th' Tor."

"What did he say?" Yadira asked, confused by the minstrel's thick dialect and rapid speech.

"He'll need more time and information to understand the song, but the Key has to get to the Tor quickly," Li supplied.

Yadira nodded sagely, then translated for Mama and Lupe.

"Well," Corvus said, reaching his decision. "There's no question they're up to no good. I've been told repeatedly to 'Protect the Tor,' and that's a charge I canna ignore." Turning back to Mama, he asked "Are you and your group up for further travel and danger?"

Mama straightened her shoulders, standing as tall as her short frame allowed. She looked at him proudly. "Corvus Corax, Ashahl trusted that you would know what to do. Give us a command, and we will fulfill it."

Corvus' heart melted as he looked at this proud, defiant woman and considered asking more of these travelers who had already suffered through so much in their efforts to bring him the curious staff.

"I hate to ask any more of you than what you've already been through," he began, "but as you can see, I have my hands full here with a slavering army at my doorstep. I have to stop them. I will send a company of thirty troops with you and these two..." He nodded at Piper and Ligulf. "You must get to the Tor before the enemy. I don't understand their plan or what they think they can accomplish, but you're the only one who has seen one of their sorcerers at work, and I suspect you have more of a chance of stopping him than anyone else I might send."

Mama nodded grimly, then looked at Piper and Ligulf. "We can leave at once," she said, simply.

"I'll arrange for the boy to be cared for among the healers of our baggage train," Corvus said, prompting Mama to turn and cast an assessing eye over Argant.

"No," she responded, with a finality that surprised Corvus. "Again, I cannot tell you how I know, but he has some role to play at the Tor and should accompany us."

Strangely, though he had known this woman for but a few hours, he trusted her judgement completely. He nodded his acceptance of her decision. Turning to Ligulf and Piper, he said, "Gather your things, you'll leave before dark." Then he spoke to Yazid. "Dispatch thirty of your Adders to ride with them to the Tor. They'll go via Esper and ferry across the river there. I'd send more, but I fear I'll need every available sword here."

Yazid nodded.

"One more thing, Corvus Corax," Mama said in her formal tone, and he turned back to her. "I will need to carry the Key with me. It has powers that enhance my own, and will give me the best chance to succeed should I face that sorcerer."

"Understood," he agreed. "May the Ancestors guide and protect you all."

As the small group turned to leave, Yadira lagged behind, as if she had something she needed to say.

"Something troubles you, sister?" Corvus asked.

She stood, blinking, as if she was trying to recall a memory or a dream. With a start, her head snapped up, her eyes wide, and she stepped up to Corvus, placing a hand on his arm.

"There is something you must know, Corvus Corax," she said, her eyes ablaze with an almost febrile urgency.

"Speak," he responded.

"In my vision, the one in which I entered your dream, I saw a place that is important."

He nodded. "Yes, the Tor. You told me as much when you shared your vision with me."

"No," she said, "not the Tor. A place… just there." She pointed to the southern edge of the ruins.

"I don't understand," Corvus said.

"Come with me, now, I'll show you."

Before Corvus could protest that he had many demands on his time, she stalked off toward the fallen south wall. With a shrug at Yazid, Corvus followed.

"These votaries enjoy leading us about, I think," Yazid said quietly as he followed.

"So it seems…"

As they rounded the remains of the south wall of the fortress, the two men found Yadira kneeling in the field some fifteen yards away, examining what looked to be a small mound. As they approached, Corvus could see that the south side of the mound was actually an opening or small cave, perhaps large enough for a child to enter. As he leaned toward the opening, he sensed a steady breeze emanating from it.

"There," she said, pointing at the cave's mouth.

"I'm afraid I still don't understand—" Corvus began.

"I traveled into this cave," she said, interrupting him. "It goes far, and has many fingers that stretch the width of the valley."

"Are you suggesting we sequester men in there?" Corvus asked, incredulously.

"The opening is too small, I think," Yazid said.

"Men would not live," she responded quickly, clearly frustrated at her inability to explain her vision more clearly. "The air is not good."

"I'm afraid you'll have to explain what you mean," Corvus said, his patience wearing thin. "And quickly, as I have much to do."

"The breath of the mountain..." was all she could say, shaking her head in frustration.

Yazid looked up sharply.

Corvus looked from one to the other before raising his hands in defeat. "I'm afraid this will have to wait." He turned to leave, calling over his shoulder, "I have a battle to prepare."

"Corvus, wait!" Yazid called after him, sharply.

Something about his friend's uncharacteristic tone made Corvus turn back.

"There is a myth among my people," Yazid began. "A story of a boy captured by a great wizard and taken to a mountain far in the south of Asland, where he would be sacrificed to a terrible dragon."

"Yes," Corvus replied quizzically. "Taavi and the Dragon, I have heard it."

"Do you remember how young Taavi escaped the beast?" Yazid asked him, excitement in his eyes.

Corvus strove to keep the impatience from his tone. "He lit a fire, as I recall. Though I don't see what this has to do with—"

"Not just any fire, I think," Yazid interrupted him. "He found a small cave, out of which the mountain 'breathed,' and he put flame to the breath itself, causing a great conflagration. The dragon was consumed along with a large part of the hillside."

"Breath of the mountain..." Corvus looked to Yadira, who was nodding her head vigorously, her hands to her mouth in a prayer-like gesture. He moved once more to the cave mouth, putting out his hands to feel the breeze. Then, as realization dawned, he stepped over to Yadira quickly, gripping her shoulders and searching her eyes. "And you're saying the same breath comes from that hole?"

"Yes!" she responded.

He turned and stared for a moment at the small cave, then with a glint in his eyes, he turned to Yazid.

"Call all the captains to my tent in half an hour, and prepare a rider to take word to Fergus."

Chapter 38

For it is in the silent watches of the night that our hearts are free to speak our true desires.

— Emil Tremblay, "Reflections in the Garden"

574 HR – Last month of summer
(9 days before the Equinox)
Autun, Lachland

Zach

Zach woke in a private room in a brewery that had been converted to a hospital ward for wounded soldiers. A separate hospital had been set up in the merchant district for wounded civilians. The healers were stretched thin, serving between the two, and he knew that following that battle, both hospitals would be crammed beyond capacity. So why was he in a private room?

He looked around the small chamber, which might have once been an office. Sunlight was streaming in through a high window, and he felt disoriented, unsure of what day it was and how long he'd been out. Outside the room, he could hear the moans of the injured and the bustle of the healers as they tended them. His head and face were bandaged, his left arm was in a splint, his chest was wrapped in tight linen straps, and his mouth felt like a desert, cracked and parched. His left eye was crusted over and he had to blink multiple times before he could open it enough to focus and look around the room gingerly, careful to not move his head too quickly, as it ached like the devil. To the right of the bed was a small table with a pitcher of water and a tall cup. He started to reach for it, but his ribs protested sharply, causing him to grit his teeth in pain. Another bad choice. His cheekbone too was apparently broken, and gritting his teeth sent waves of agony through his head. He passed out.

When he came to again, there was a figure standing by the door, off to the left side of the bed. It took Zach several seconds to focus and finally identify Sir Reginald Bleiz.

"You're awake. That's good," Bleiz said.

Zach tried to work some saliva into his mouth to respond, but all he could do was croak.

"Here," Sir Reginald said, moving to the pitcher of water. "Allow me."

He poured a small amount into the cup and helped Zach drink. The water had a peculiar taste and Zach looked up in confusion.

"Ground willow bark has been added to the water to ease your discomfort," the knight commander explained.

Zach nodded his head gently in understanding, grimacing against the ache even that small movement produced.

"You did well, son," Sir Reginald said, setting down the pitcher and returning to his position near the door. It seemed to be the one place in the room Zach could look without having to turn his head. He was grateful for Sir Reginald's consideration.

"The enemy are gone?" Zach asked in a rough whisper, after a moment.

"Routed and destroyed," Bleiz said with finality.

Zach sighed in relief and closed his eyes for a time.

"The healers tell me that they anticipate you will make a full recovery, though I'm sure it will be some time before you regain strength in that arm."

"That's good," Zach responded, his eyes still closed. Then an image of the Queen's broken body at the base of the tower flashed before him. "The Queen?" he asked in alarm, his eyes springing open.

Sir Reginald placed a comforting hand on Zach's left foot before speaking.

"I'm afraid Her Majesty is no longer with us," he said gravely. "But your bravery on the field was singular. I watched you leap to her aid, then single-handedly charge the enemy wizard. It's a wonder you survived. Quite foolhardy, really. That creature tore through our ranks like a hungry wolf."

"Yes, I saw," Zach replied, his mind replaying the events of the battle. "What *was* he?"

"No one knows," Bleiz replied thoughtfully, "except perhaps the Barbárs, and the few prisoners we were able to take either don't speak our tongue or are simply not talking. If you hadn't struck him down, I fear the day would have gone very differently for us."

"Glad it worked…" Zach said quietly, the image of the dead Queen still hovering in his mind.

There was a moment of quiet before Sir Reginald said, "I should tell you that I've recommended you for knighthood."

Zach looked up in confusion. "But—"

"Now then, none of that nonsense about being of common birth. When a man displays such uncommon and selfless bravery as you did, and his actions turn the battle so significantly… Well, the rules of attaining knighthood really become more like guidelines, shall we say?"

"Thank you, sir," Zach said weakly, still struggling to grasp the enormity of Bleiz's words.

"Of course," the knight commander continued, "the actual elevation would have to be approved by Queen Darienne, once she's been crowned. So, beyond making the recommendation, I'm afraid the matter is out of my hands."

Zach's brow furrowed. Of course, Princess Darienne was the next in the line of succession. It simply hadn't occurred to him that there would be a new queen. From what he had heard of her, she would be a very different monarch than Isador had been. *Queen Darienne...* He rolled the name around in his mind. *Have to get used to that.*

"However," Sir Reginald continued, after allowing Zach a moment to absorb his previous comments, "there are certain things that are well within the auspices of my position."

Zach looked again at the knight commander, an unspoken question in his eyes.

"I am promoting you to major," Sir Reginald, leaning forward and pinning a silver badge onto the left breast of Zach's gown. "Effective immediately. Battlefield promotion, you know."

"Sir, I..." Zach stammered. "I don't know what to say."

"You don't *say* anything, boy." Sir Reginald tapped Zach's foot lightly in mock-reprimand. "You salute."

With a deep breath against the pain in his ribs, Zach lifted his right hand to his forehead, touching the backs of his fingers to his right eyebrow in the Lachland salute. Sir Reginald returned the salute crisply, clicking his heels together and accompanying the gesture with a reassuring wink.

"Now," Bleiz said, adjusting his helmet in the crook of his arm, "I'll let you rest."

"Thank you, sir," Zach replied as Sir Reginald turned to leave, but the knight commander quickly stopped himself and turned back.

"Oh, there was one other thing," he said. "I should like you to accompany the Queen's body back to Wetheral. It seems only appropriate that the Queen's banner carrier should escort her."

Zach was confused and looked in consternation at his broken body.

"You needn't worry, lad," Bleiz said, obviously reading the concern on Zach's face. "Her Majesty's remains will not sail for Wetheral for some time. It will take that long for us to prepare a suitable catafalque. The city is in shambles, I'm afraid. We must tend to the living before seeing to the dead. She has already been embalmed and her body rests, temporarily, in the catacombs beneath the Great Temple. When all is ready, and that includes you, the archbishop has agreed to use his personal ship to transport you and the Queen's body back to the castle. That will give the Princess time to be crowned and to receive the body of her mother, one queen to another."

Zach nodded, and immediately regretted the motion, white stars exploding behind his left eye.

"Get some rest, Major," Bleiz said again, then departed.

Zach woke to the sound of screaming and it took him several moments to orient his mind and understand what he was hearing. A soldier was crying out in agony as the healers tended to him. From the sound of the screams, it was an amputation. Since his arrival, he had listened to more than a few of them. Soldiers whose limbs were damaged beyond repair were held down by burly orderlies as a bedraggled healer or chirurgeon with a bone saw and tourniquet did the grisly work. The pleading and begging from the victims seemed universal. No matter how strong a soldier, they all seemed to cry and beg the moment the saw came out.

It was nighttime; the flicker of lanterns was apparent through the crack beneath the door. Another scream of agony. Zach tried to will the sound away and turned his head gingerly toward the pitcher of water. He was parched. Having learned the folly of reaching too quickly, he stretched out his hand toward the pitcher carefully. Concentrating on keeping his mouth open as he grimaced from the pain in his protesting ribs, he succeeded in sloppily pouring himself a cup of water and replacing the pitcher carefully. As he sipped the bitter water, the screaming finally stopped. Either the operation had concluded, or the poor soul undergoing it had slipped unconscious, or worse.

Replacing the cup on the side table seemed somehow easier. As he settled back into as comfortable a position as he could manage, his thoughts drifted to Loeiza. His dear Loeiza. He remembered a clear moment in which she had utterly botched a dinner, scorching the meat and fouling the bread with the smoke from the burned mutton. The two had sat at their modest dining table, staring at the ruined meal, trying small bites of the meat only to spit it out in disgust. He had spent the day in the training yard with a company of recruits, and had come home, exhausted, sweaty, and famished. She had looked at him over the ruined meal with tears in her eyes.

"Zach, I..."

He had simply leaned across the table and stopped her apology with a kiss. "There's always wine," he had said with a wry smile.

The image of her crying laughter wrung his heart, and he prayed that whatever gods there might be would protect her from further horrors.

The screaming in the hospital had ceased and the bustle from the ward had stilled for the moment. Zach turned his head carefully and looked out of the darkened window at the faint glimmer of stars, just visible through a haze of thin clouds. Tears streamed down his cheeks, as he sobbed, alone in the night.

"Loeiza..."

Chapter 39

The time has come, my friends. All of your training was for this moment. This land's history is written in blood, and today we will add another chapter filled with merciless cruelty. Remember your positions and patterns. There can be no failure. There will be no steps backward. Our wall will advance unto the annihilation of the cowardly enemy. Today, we win for glory, we win for the Emperor, we win for our brothers in arms! And tonight, you will enjoy their wine, their riches, and their women!

— GrandArch Lucania, address to the legions at the Battle of Borysthenes, the Rape of Cantabria

574 HR - Last month of summer
(8 days before the Equinox)
Eagle's Gate, Glenfolk region of the Green Mount

Corvus

He thanked the young guard that woke him with a silent hand to his shoulder in the pre-dawn dark. He rose from his cot and dressed in his leather trews and a white cotton shirt. He stretched and twisted his back, listening to the variety of pops and clicks that his aging body made as he moved. Picking up Raven's Tooth, he glanced across the tent to see if his activity had awakened Yazid, but his friend was not yet stirring, his breathing still slow and regular. Corvus took a healthy bite of the dwindling bitter root that Shanna had given him and slipped the remainder into his pouch for easy access as the day went on. Taking a full waterskin from a hook by the tent flap, he smacked his lips and grimaced at the dry mouth that instantly set in from the root. Still barefoot, his shirt not yet tucked, Corvus Corax, the Raven, slipped outside.

He nodded to the two guards on watch as they warmed themselves by a fire. Then he walked around the tent into a patch of heather and gorse that he had requested remain open and unoccupied. Stepping to the middle, he drew his sword and stood for a moment, eyes closed, before he began the breathing exercises that were the prelude to his forms. Once his mind had stilled and focused, he began his movements.

The first form was always Willow, as the arching and bending required eased the stiffness in his back from days in the saddle and sleeping on his unforgiving cot. After several minutes, he transitioned smoothly into Badger. Its percussive movements and spinning blade attacks had become second nature after decades of this daily work. Next was Eagle, the graceful leaps and spins warming his body. He then transitioned to Ocean to connect with the inexorable, tidal force of his ruhon, filling him with potential. Finally, he transitioned into the quiet solidity of Mountain. Of all the forms, nothing brought him such peace and connectedness as Mountain. Whereas each of the movement styles had special gifts—Willow's unique bending and whipping of the body, Badger's rapid sighting and attacking of vulnerabilities, Eagle's gift of Longsight, Ocean's immeasurable power, and Mountain's immovability—only the last added an almost spiritual link to his homeland. When moving through Mountain's subtly shifting stances and postures, Corvus envisioned great, stone plates, extending like roots downward from his legs, reaching and bonding to the subterranean heart of the great peaks that ringed the lands of the Green Mount. He felt as one with the stone: ancient, patient, mighty. This was a change from how he had felt when first learning the form in the deserts of Asland, so far from any mountain range. There, he had struggled to physically understand and actualize the form's power. Ashahl had drilled the notional potential into him repeatedly, only to scowl with frustration as his gifted pupil continued to fail to connect to the land through the form. Upon returning to the Highlands, however, Corvus found that the form *spoke* to him as no other did.

Over the years, through the grief of Greer's death and the stresses of raising two boys and striving tirelessly to inspire the image of the fyrd in the minds of the people of the High Valley, Corvus had found a growing connection to the land through Mountain form. His roots had grown deep, and through his daily practice, they had changed him. Ancient mysteries from unseen depths flowed when he immersed himself in the movements and their parallel meditation. He had gradually changed from a headstrong and physically talented youth to become, in time, the very *rock* of the Highlands. All who dealt with him could sense it, on one level or another. His spirit had become entwined with the foundation of this land, firm and unshakable, yet generous and giving. Regardless of any exertion or fatigue, he always finished Mountain form calm, relaxed, and in a state of readiness, with a serenity that was visible in his eyes and instantly noticeable to those close to him.

As he slipped back into the tent, a light patina of sweat covered him, though his feet were wet and numb from the cold morning dew. He smiled at Yazid, who was awake now, and standing shirtless over a basin of frigid water.

"All is well, my friend?" his comrade asked.

"As well as can be expected," Corvus replied quietly, "for an old man."

Yazid chuckled, then asked, "How fares the leg, do you think? Will it support you today?"

"There's a stiffness to it, I canna lie." Corvus began his own ablutions over a matching basin. "But I suspect it'll hold me. I had only scant problems with the spins in Badger, and the left-side Eagle leaps are right out. My kicks on that side are lacking power as well, but..." He chuckled ruefully. "It isna like our preferences enter into things, eh? Today's the scrap, so we fight as we are today."

Once cleaned and dressed, both men readied their separate altars for pre-battle prayers. Yazid set out a small silver bell and a matching dish with a mound of white sand in the middle. He poured a thimble of oil from an ornate porcelain pitcher into a tiny cup, carefully placed a glowing coal from the brazier on the pile of sand, and sprinkled a modest amount of incense over it. Kneeling, he rang the bell twice, its soft tinkle almost imperceptible, then touched his finger to the oil, then to his forehead and began muttering his prayers softly. The familiar, gentle smell of the incense wafted through the tent.

Corvus had just arranged the items on his altar, lit a small brazier and candle, and was preparing to kneel when a soft scratching came at the tent flap. He looked up just as Cailean's head poked in.

"Cai, come in lad," Corvus said, concern on his face. "Is there a problem?"

"No problem, Da," his son responded as he entered the tent. He was dressed in his battle leathers, but not yet wearing his mail, tabard, or weapons. "Just hoping I might be able to join you for prayers before the day."

"Of course," Corvus said with a proud smile as he slapped his son's back. "It wouldna feel complete or right without you."

Unlike Yazid's supplication of the Ancestors, Corvus and Cai's ancient words asked the blessings of the Five. They burned small offerings, with the intention that the smoke would carry their prayers to Ilian, Nuada, Manu, Feryn, and Cruim. They asked for Ilian to once more stretch out his golden hand and protect his people; for Nuada to make their aim true; for Manu to help them protect the homes, hearths, and children of the Green Mount; for Feryn to bring them luck; and for Cruim to sharpen their minds and give them acuity during the confusion of battle. As they finished their invocations to the Five, they prepared the black candle and brass charms to also beg Fel's mercy.

"Oh, I wouldn't do that," a voice from within the tent said, causing all three men to spin in alarm, their hands reaching for the nearest weapons.

There, seated on Corvus' cot, leaning casually back against the tent pole and eating an apple, was Latrans. His scraggly dog looked up at him, clearly hopeful that the apple wasn't the only food on offer.

Cailean was instantly on his feet and moving toward the intruder, having never met the Fool before. "It's alright, Cai," Corvus said, before his son could attack. "He is known to me."

"I have seen this man, I think," Yazid said, recognition dawning. "He was the one that warned you of this impending attack, yes?"

"It's true," Corvus said, rising slowly. "Cailean, Yazid, this is Latrans. A most curious and unusually knowledgeable fellow."

Cai relaxed back a step, though his posture suggested he was alarmed and disturbed at how this strange man had managed to enter their tent so silently and position himself directly behind them. Yazid merely touched his hand to his chest and bowed formally.

Latrans smiled and winked at Cailean mischievously, then turned to Yazid with a smile.

"Blessings of the Ancestors be upon you, good man," the Fool said in fluent Aslene, causing the three men to exchange surprised looks.

"And forever upon you, good sir," Yazid responded in kind.

"Forever is such a long time," Latrans said with a sigh, then sprung to his feet.

"What's your business, Fool?" Corvus asked. "I'm not sure we have time for your riddles this day."

"No, I imagine not. Much to do, much to do." Latrans reached into his vest and produced a small morsel of jerky. He tossed it to his dog, who leapt up and caught the piece in mid-air, while performing a perfect backflip. This so delighted Latrans that he clapped rapidly and began cooing over the scraggly little animal, scruffing its forehead, seeming to have completely forgotten the three men.

Cailean looked at his father quizzically, and Corvus just shrugged then cleared his throat.

At the sound, Latrans stopped petting the dog, stood up, and looked around the tent, seemingly confused as to where he was. Noticing the three men staring at him, he blinked momentarily. He raised his hand to his forehead as if he suddenly recalled the purpose for his visit. "Oh, you three. Right!"

"I ask again, Fool," Corvus said quietly, "what's your purpose? We have a battle to prepare for."

"Yes, yes you do," he said, pointing at Corvus, then shifting his pointing finger to Cailean. "Straight to it then! You, young man, should stand on the far right." He waved his hand as he suddenly raised his voice, sounding like the crazed priest that had visited Dóchas years earlier and held a rally before the bemused villagers. "Eschew the center!"

"I directed such last night," Corvus said, his brow furrowing as he tried to discern the Fool's meaning. "The Glenfolk will line up on the right flank,"

"Not the Glenfolk!" Latrans suddenly snapped his crazed attention back to Corvus. "I'm talking about him. Him! On the far right. The far, *far*, right." With each word, the Fool stabbed his index finger painfully into Cai's broad chest, and Corvus' son only barely bore this indignity, staring at his father with a look that seemed to beg for permission to cuff this motley man, soundly.

Corvus stifled a grin at his son's discomfiture, then replied, "And why would I position a commander so far from me, might I ask?"

"You'll do it," Latrans replied, suddenly spinning with a theatrical flourish into a kneeling position, his dog leaping into his open arms, "if you're not a fool." He paused for a moment, as if expecting applause. When none came, he dropped the dog and stood up, sighing in disappointment and brushing off the knees of his trousers. He raised a finger to Corvus as if he had more to say, then hesitated for a moment, finger still raised, then said with resignation, "Typical Corvus, always ruining my beat. So serious!" He then scooped up his dog once more and flounced out of the tent through the flap, leaving the three other men staring after him in bemused silence.

"What in the bloody…?" Cai started, but his words faded away.

Corvus chuckled and looked at Yazid, who rubbed his face with his hand, which Corvus knew to mean his friend was struggling between amazement, amusement, and outrage. Many a time in the training of the fyrd, a young recruit would make a blunder so extreme and ridiculous that it would earn the "face wipe," as the lads came to call Yazid's familiar gesture.

"Well, I dinna care what some mystery motley man has to say," Cailean said firmly, "I'll line up front and center of my troops."

Corvus looked down, pensive.

Perhaps sensing his father's change in mood, Cailean asked, "Don't you agree, Da?"

After a moment, Corvus turned and placed a hand on his son's chest. "He's a strange one, I'll grant ye. But perhaps there's meaning here. I disregarded the Fool's advice once already, years ago, and the people of Cairgean paid dearly for it. Perhaps this is a warning you should heed."

"But Da…" Cailean looked incredulous. "Surely you're not paying any mind to that blathering gowk?"

"I've lived long enough," Corvus said softly as he moved to finish dressing, "to know that not every wise man is wise, and that many a fool's not a fool. Latrans can be maddening, I grant ye. But he's never offered me counsel that wasna true. Take the advice, son. Line up on the far right of your men."

"'It is madness to look into the very heart of the gods,'" Yazid added, quoting the familiar Aslene aphorism.

Cai rubbed his arms, as though reacting to a sudden chill, then nodded. "Sure, Da, I'll do as you say."

Corvus patted Niall on the shoulder good-naturedly as he walked along the front line of his beloved fyrd.

"Alright, Corvus?" Niall responded with a huge smile that was more appropriate for a festival day than what they faced.

"I can't be other," Corvus responded loudly, "with you and Quinn to keep me straight." That was met with loud laughter from the ranks.

Corvus stepped off to the left of the fyrd toward the ranks of the White Cleft, leaving his troops to finish buckling and checking their gear as light conversation rippled among them. *Good,* he thought. *They're not afraid. Not cocky, either. Just ready. Good.*

He had to step around the remnants of a small wall to reach the first of the White Cleft soldiers. The difference between the two armies was startling. Where the fyrd looked rested, fed, and ready, the White Cleft troops looked haggard, nervous, and exhausted. They had force-marched much of the night, arriving only three hours before dawn. Too tired to even pitch tents, they had dropped their bedrolls in a meadow to the north and collapsed in the open, seeking an hour or two of sleep. A bleary-eyed King Fergus stepped out from his ranks and approached Corvus, his red beard tangled and askew. Dark rings hung beneath his reddened eyes.

"Don't you look spry and chipper this fine day?" Corvus jibed at his old friend.

"Well," the King responded in his customary light-hearted manner, though the fatigue was clear on his face, "I wouldna have said no to another hour or so of sleep, but we can't let you lot have all the fun!"

Corvus laughed and clapped the King on the shoulder before leaning in. "Remember the vaulters," he cautioned quietly. "Keep the spears handy in the middle ranks."

"Aye," Fergus responded, with a wink that seemed to imply that he appreciated the discreet reminder.

"And remind your lads to move to the second position when the yellow signal flies."

"They've been told and shown twice," Fergus said firmly.

"I'm positioning half my reserves behind your men," Corvus continued in a low voice, so the troops couldn't hear.

"The White Cleft will hold," Fergus responded indignantly, as though Corvus had touched a nerve. They both clearly remembered the rout that had occurred at the battle near Esper five years ago.

"I know they will," Corvus reassured his old friend. "I mean no disrespect, nor distrust of the valor of your troops. It's just that your men are shagged and may need some support. If they're less than spry getting to their second position, my reserves can cover their movement."

After a moment, Fergus nodded stiffly, accepting the wisdom of Corvus' comment.

"I look forward to raising a glass in victory with all of you when this day is through!" Corvus shouted to the White Cleft troops, who responded with a heartened cheer, though he could see clouds of doubt and fear in the eyes of various soldiers.

He strode back to his position, and turned to address the fyrd.

Cailean

The young commander stepped in front of the Glenfolk soldiers to address them. He busied his hands with his gloves, to mask the slight tremble from nerves. He envied his father, who was always so relaxed when he harangued the fyrd before a scrap. Cai was typically very comfortable speaking in public, or before the troops as they trained, but today, his guts were filled with butterflies. This was his first real command opportunity in battle. He so wanted to get it right. To set just the right tone. He caught his father's eye just as he prepared to address the fyrd off to his right, and the two exchanged a quick grin. That smile from his father, so full of trust and pride, seemed to wash over Cai, erasing his nerves and reminding him that he could *do* this. If his father, the Raven, had such trust in him, then he had no reason to be nervous.

"Proud soldiers of the Glenfolk," Cai called loudly, noting that every eye was on him, a mixture of hope, worry, and pride in them. "The soldiers of King Mannon have a storied and well-earned reputation for being stalwart on the battlefield, unshakeable before any foe. You held the line at Esper, at Gomul, in the hillsides north of Cairgean, and here, years ago, at Eagle's Gate. You stood against this Barbár menace time and again, and despite their fearsome demeanor, you slaughtered them!"

A spontaneous cheer went up from the troops. Cai could see that the worry in their eyes seemed to be melting away, being replaced with a fire.

He continued, "Your glorious King has sadly passed, and truth be told, there was never a braver or better ally for all the peoples of the Green Mount. I am not King Mannon, nor do I pretend to his greatness. But I have fought these brutes and I can tell you, though they seem like fearsome giants, savage and cruel, you stick a blade in their belly and they die as quick as any man."

Another cheer, louder than the first.

"Remember what we talked about yesterday. Keep the spears handy in the middle ranks. In addition to the danger from their mounted troops, the enemy will send runners who will use their height and size to try to vault over the shield wall and sow chaos amongst you. Spit them on the pikes and close up the ranks! And remember, when the yellow signal goes up, move quickly to your second position, and re-form the wall without delay."

His soldiers nodded in silent assent.

Cailean turned and pointed at the black banners over the fyrd. "You see those black banners? Those signify that today, we'll take no prisoners. No sorry, shaggy, loupin' Barbár will wander home with tales of the Green Mount. Let them wonder what became of their precious Räubers. Let them tremble in fear of what terrors might wait for their kind in the Green Mount. Sure, they're bigger than you or me. Sure, we're outnumbered by a bit. But we have discipline, skill, and training, and friends, in my experience, that wins the day every time. Today, it is my great honor to lead you, for you are as fine a fighting force as e'er I've seen. And we stop them, here, lads. We stop them *here*!"

A huge cheer erupted as the soldiers of the Green Mount began to chant Cailean's name, smacking their swords on their shields rhythmically. With a shy grin back at Corvus, Cailean turned and walked to his position on the far right of his troops.

Corvus

The Raven had likewise fueled his own force with his characteristic mix of charm and seriousness. They understood the danger of the Räubers, and had adjusted their tactics accordingly. Every alternate soldier in the second through fourth ranks of each of the three forces was armed with a long spear in anticipation of the giant warriors vaulting the shield wall as they had at the Battle at the Gomul. Once the walls closed and the bloody business began, it would be the added responsibility of the second rank to attack the faces of the foes, preventing the tall enemies from being able to stab down over the shields of the first rank, while the front line's swords searched for groins, legs, and bellies.

As Corvus stepped back from his speech, he heard the cheering from the Glenfolk, and the quieter, though no less heartfelt cheering from the White Cleft troops. He took pride, however, in the fact that the cheers of the fyrd were the loudest of all. It would be a bloody day, he knew, but the fyrd would acquit itself well. *Now,* he thought, *let's hope the enemy comes on true to form.*

Looking off toward the cliff face to the east, he caught eyes with Toren, who was well hidden behind a large rock. The two men had split the archers of the fyrd to either side, while those of the Glenfolk and the White Cleft were behind their respective armies, perched on the various levels of the ruins, ready to rain death down upon the enemy.

Corvus looked to the enemy line. His scouts had reported a number in excess of ten thousand, Räubers all from the look of them. He had never seen so many of the shock troops massed together. In all, the Highlands' forces numbered just over six thousand, but fully fifteen hundred of those were the reserves, positioned in the rear and only to be brought forward if the line faltered or needed support while repositioning. He noted five distinct groupings of the foe. On either flank, the mounted archers had divided their number, with five hundred or so per side. Their short bows could never hope to match the range and power of the Highlander longbows, so they would need to ride in at a gallop, getting close enough to fire as they looped in front of the Green Mount forces. Standing out in front of the shield wall were some two hundred warriors, scattered across the field just out of bow range. The first runners. They would rush in as the mounted archers distracted the Highlanders. No doubt the fastest of the Räubers, and those with the highest leaps, they would strive to avoid the rain of arrows, vault the shield wall, and disrupt the cohesion of the defending troops. A suicidal attack, but if even a handful got through the rain of arrows, it could be disastrous. Directly behind the first runners was the enemy wall. Corvus estimated their numbers at roughly three thousand. They would follow quickly after the runners and archers in an attempt to strike the disrupted Highlander walls before they could re-form. Looming behind them was perhaps the greatest threat of all: over five thousand mounted Räubers, just waiting until the Highlander wall broke, when they would gallop forward and overrun the fleeing troops. No amount of training could protect scattered infantry against a cavalry charge, and the Barbár cavalry had a fearsome reputation. Corvus knew all too well the brutal efficiency with which those riders would dispense death. Their massive destriers were bred and battle-trained on the brutal steppes of Orense until they learned to respond to their riders' very thoughts, seemingly without guidance, and they attacked in concert with their riders, teeth and hooves flashing as they fearlessly trampled anyone unfortunate enough to be caught in their path. Despite the distance, he could see the hunger in the milling ranks of cavalry as they waited impatiently for their turn. *The line canna break,* he thought grimly, *or it'll doom us all.*

He noted some activity just ahead of the enemy's west flank, but it was too far away to make out. *Well,* he thought, *now's as good a time as any to take a closer look.* He would use Longsight to see what was happening and assess the enemy lines, while he still had enough time to shake off the accompanying nausea before the battle began in earnest. He settled himself, calmed his breathing, shifted his weight onto his bent left leg, and drew his right foot back into Cat stance: heel off the ground, just touching the left ankle. He breathed in Eagle form and, with a disorienting swoop, his perception lifted above the battlefield, his sharp eyes picking out new details in the enemy formation.

Knowing he had but moments to maintain Longsight, he focused on the enemy's right side. There he saw two men arguing: one a tall Räuber, his white shaggy hair bouncing as he gestured angrily, and the other, a much shorter man, bald and pallid, and ghoulish in appearance. The shorter man had set up a folding camp table on which a bound prisoner was tied and squirming. Corvus willed his sight to draw closer, feeling his spirit eagle surge forward. The shaggy Räuber bore a commander's necklace and was shouting at the shorter man, who grinned an eerie smile in response to the imposing giant, apparently unafraid. Though the shorter man's shoulders were slumped and he appeared sickly and pale, he looked at the commander with naked contempt. The prisoner on the table had been stripped and bound, and a set of serrated and rusty knives were set out beside him. As Corvus' sight drew closer still, the ill-favored man suddenly looked over his shoulder directly into the eyes of the invisible spirit eagle. He waved his clawlike hand in a violent gesture. Corvus felt a shock like a blow to the head, and with a disorienting suddenness, found himself once more in the front rank of the fyrd. Yazid's strong hands steadied him as his knees buckled momentarily and he was overcome by a powerful wave of nausea, much stronger than was typical.

"Steady, friend," Yazid said softly. "It would not do to have the fyrd see sudden weakness, I think."

Breathing deeply, Corvus nodded in agreement, straightened his back with great effort, opened his eyes, and flashed a reassuring grin to his friend, though he knew his face was pale and he could not mask the sudden sheen of sweat. He kept his hands hidden behind his shield to cover their trembling.

What sort of power was that? he thought, shaking his head to clear his senses. *To sense my spirit eagle in Longsight and knock me back…* He realized with a start that this was, no doubt, the sorcerer that Mama Warad had encountered. *Mighty indeed. This will add a challenge to the day.*

A raven's croak pierced the hubbub of the gathered army, and Corvus looked up to see it perched near the tip of a towering fir sprouting from the mountainside. The bird's black eyes seemed to bore a hole in Corvus as it stared intently at him. A frisson of *other* washed over him, and a momentary breeze whisked down off the mountain, from the direction of the raven. It carried on it impossible scents, of woodsmoke and kitchen spices favored by Greer. He clenched his eyes tightly closed as the familiar smells filled him with an unexpected comfort and warmth, easing his nausea and weakness. The lavender oil she used in her hair, the sharp clove of the pomander she always tucked in the pocket of her apron, the moist, starchy steam from a pot of potatoes boiling as she tended it.

"My Coinneach…" The words were as clear as if she stood before him now. *"You carry with you the trust and reverence of all the people of the Green Mount. Remember all you have yet to do, my love. Protect this land. Protect my boys."*

"Greer," he whispered through unbidden tears, "I miss you so."

The breeze gone as quickly as it had come. He blinked his eyes open, and arched his back, looking to the sky with gratitude for the brief visitation. But something was different. Something had changed in him. He looked to his left leg in surprise, flexing and stretching it. The stiffness was gone. He moved through a few stances, testing his limb, and found that all residual soreness from his injury had fled. His legs were solid beneath him. He turned to share his revelation with Yazid, but just then, the enemy horns sounded, drawing his focus back to the battlefield.

He had only moments before the attack began. With a sense of wonder, he cuffed the tears from his cheeks and flashed a grateful smile at the bird, who croaked once more, then took flight. Filled with newfound warmth and certainty, he glanced around at his troops, nodding and winking assurance. He spotted Cai attending to last-minute details with his soldiers. So tall and strong, his long blonde hair playing in the breeze. *He'd make you proud, Greer. They both would.* His eyes played over the majestic landscape, drinking in the soaring, dramatic beauty of this land. This was *his* land, *his* home. No one would take it. Not while he lived.

"Right," he called over his shoulder to the fyrd. "Stand ready with those pikes! And dinna forget your second position when the yellow flag rises!"

Bone-Eye

Who was that spying on me with Longsight? he mused. *The witch again? It would make sense, but somehow it had felt different. Another on the battlefield with talent? Perhaps…* He smiled at the thought, welcoming the challenge.

"Don't you dare smile in my presence, you foul little shit!" Gaszi screamed.

Bone-Eye was wearying of this boorish, loud man. He had the gall to stand there yelling at the shaman to get back behind the lines. He simply didn't know how things must unfold, didn't understand Bone-Eye's talents, didn't realize what danger he was in if he continued threatening him. His annoying clamor was spoiling Bone-Eye's enjoyment of the delicious aroma of fear on the breeze. *So much! Yes.* He could feel his body responding—muscles growing taut, blood flowing in his veins with abandon. *This will be a glorious day!* His hands flexed and tingled with new power. Oh, how he loved the moment of effusion! And this boorish brute was spoiling it!

"Are you listening to me, shaman?" Gaszi screamed again. "You will not interrupt my plans! I am talking to you!"

"No, you're not," Bone-Eye replied calmly, grinning up at the commander. "You're bellowing. You've mistaken something, Gaszi. I don't answer to you. Go, tend to your army. I have work to do." Bone-Eye turned his hungry, feral grin to the victim on the table. "Now, shall we begin?"

Gaszi grabbed the wizard's shoulder to turn him back. His final mistake. With a snarl, Bone-Eye spun back, infused with the might of all that fear, he lashed out with an open, clawlike hand. There was a loud crack accompanied by a ripping sound, and Gaszi—commander of the Räuber invasion force and Third Stone Bearer to the Great Hadvezér—fell to the ground, arterial blood spurting from his throat. His jaw, which had been ripped from his head, sailed through the air—the long, braided beard connected to it waving gently in the morning breeze like a banner—and landed some thirty feet from the rest of his rapidly bleeding-out body.

There was a sudden shocked stillness among the Räubers, who had been preparing for their charge. Thousands of horrified eyes fell on him. Hands involuntarily touched talismans, and lips recited silent wards against evil.

There it is. The fear of thousands. I knew these savages would give it to me. Thank you! He closed his eyes and rolled his shoulders, feeling them stretch and broaden in response to the wave of horror directed at him.

Opening feral eyes, the shaman looked over the army—*his* army now. Then in a preternaturally loud voice that boomed over the battlefield, he shouted, "What are you waiting for, fools? Begin!"

The horns sounded.

Corvus

Despite the distance, Corvus heard the sorcerer's voice clearly as it echoed across Monarch's Pass, and though he couldn't understand the man's words, the meaning was clear. *So now it begins.*

First would be the mounted archers, who would gallop in sinuous lines down the outside of the battlefield on either side, looping in front of the Highlanders and loosing their arrows into the Green Mount forces. His own archers would be hard pressed to hit them at a full gallop, though with around five hundred on each side there should be enough targets for the Highland arrows to do some damage. His eyes shifted to the two great iron spikes some thirty yards ahead of him. His men had quietly driven them into the ground during the night with mallets wrapped in burlap. Each was as thick as his forearm and as long as his leg, and had been driven deep. He hoped this first gambit would work, as it would set up the rest of the battle.

True to his expectations, the enemy archers began galloping down the edges of the valley, while the runners began their mad sprint up the middle, the line of the enemy shield wall advancing more steadily behind. He glanced over and caught Toren's eye. The huntsman's curt nod indicated that all was in readiness. Looking to his right, Corvus caught the eye of Isla, the young woman carrying the signal flags. She stood nervously at the right edge of the fyrd, staring at him, ready to give the signals that would coordinate the Highlanders' actions. She was an earnest lass, whose weak weapons work had denied her a place in the fyrd, but whose reliable nature had recommended her for the critical role of signaling.

Corvus first held up one finger, then two, indicating she should ready the blue flag followed by the red. She nodded and clutched the desired signals to her chest, waiting for his command.

"Shields high!" he shouted to the fyrd, and they responded promptly by readying themselves for incoming arrows. He could hear Cai and Fergus giving similar commands to their units.

The first of the enemy's mounted archers were within range and began to loose their shafts, firing, nocking, and firing again in rapid succession, all while steering their madly galloping mounts with their knees. Despite their savagery, he had to appreciate the skill. However, in their eagerness to attack, the Barbár archers were bunching up, galloping too closely together, each racing to be the first to engage the Highlanders. Good. He was counting on that. As they approached the point at which they would need to begin their looping turn, Corvus gestured to Isla. The young woman lifted the first signal flag high, turning to each side to ensure that all of the relevant soldiers saw the colored flag. With a snap, two ropes leading diagonally from the iron spikes back into the ruins behind the Highlander line pulled taut at thigh height, and were quickly tied off to waiting buckles affixed to the massive, fallen stones. The lead enemy archers saw the sudden obstacle too late, and their galloping horses fouled on the rope, snapping legs and going down at the head of a rapidly developing pile of screaming horses and archers. The lines of the galloping enemy quickly stalled and bunched behind the wreckage wrought by the trip lines. A few were able to peel off and loop around, but the majority were caught in an unexpected cluster, their horses colliding and biting one another, archers forced to lower their bows to manage their confused mounts. Corvus gestured again to Isla and she raised the red flag. At once, hundreds of Highlander bowmen hidden on either side of the battle line, and many more positioned behind the troops in the ruins, stepped out and began to rain down death upon the tangled enemy.

The sky darkened as clouds of arrows sailed overhead. Within moments, the mounted Barbár archers were decimated and scrambling to flee the deadly trap. Toren had given instructions that those bowmen hidden on either side were to focus on the mounted archers, while those in the ruins behind were to try to stop the runners from reaching the shield wall, and Corvus saw multiple runners fall as they too came in range of the deadly rain. He allowed himself a grim smile as it looked as if few would reach the shield wall, and those mounted archers that had survived were fleeing back to their lines, wounded and humiliated. The enemy would have no choice but to advance their wall and engage. Hopefully, the "breath of the mountain" would live up to Yadira's tale. So much was riding on the dream-vision of a woman he had only met two days ago.

He looked to Isla and gestured low with three fingers, indicating she should be ready with the yellow flag. Her eyes wide with nerves, she nodded acknowledgement of his signal as she clutched the flag to her chest.

Most of the runners were down now, but some fifteen or more were still dashing for the shield wall. The largest of them had three arrows stuck in him, one in his thigh, one in his shoulder, and one buried in his exposed belly. Corvus was just wondering how in the world the man continued to run when an arrow took the Räuber in the throat, finally dropping him. Corvus grimaced as the remaining runners hit the lines. Four leapt into the White Cleft troops, two into the Glenfolk, and another six attempted to vault the shields of the fyrd to crash down and sow mayhem behind them. Corvus' blade lashed out at the nearest runner just as the Räuber leapt, stabbing the man's hip, and rotating him in mid-air to be impaled on Yazid's waiting spear, which caught the leaping giant in the upper chest. With a twist of his arms, Yazid deftly removed the spear before the Räuber's dead weight could wrench it from his grasp. Though four of the runners that had attacked the fyrd had been impaled on waiting pikes, one had somehow managed to get through relatively unharmed and was slashing about with his vicious, hooked sword off to the left of the line. Too far away to intervene, Corvus watched the chaos unfold for anxious moments before the giant was felled by an axe to the face. It was hard to see from his vantage, but Corvus thought the killing blow had come from Annis, a powerful woman who gathered wood for the village of Arisaig. He nodded in grim satisfaction, then looked to the Glenfolk and White Cleft lines to see how they had fared. Receiving reassuring nods from Cailean and Fergus, Corvus breathed a sigh of relief. The pikes had worked. Runners foiled, enemy archers routed. Now came the shield wall.

The enemy mass was advancing quickly, though—true to form—they were maintaining their lines. No undisciplined rush. They had covered roughly half the distance to the Highlanders, and were holding their shields high to fend off waves of arrows. The bowmen would run out of arrows soon enough, but their continued rain was slowing the enemy advance, and the Räuber shield wall now resembled a hedgehog's hide.

"Look to the right!" Yazid's voice was filled with alarm and was accompanied by an urgent squeeze on Corvus' shoulder. Following Yazid's direction, he saw the sorcerer moving ahead of the approaching enemy wall. His body seemed somehow larger, more muscular. He held the still-living, naked torture victim by the neck in his extended left hand, the victim's feet dangling well off the ground. The sorcerer's eyes seemed crazed and his face was filled with a demonic light as he held the man effortlessly, as though the victim weighed no more than a hare. The Highlanders watched in horror as, with a cackle, the creature tightened his grip on the man's neck, squeezing off the head like the tip of an overripe squash. With a careless gesture, he flung the body aside, and began to run toward the Glenfolk line. The Highlanders let out gasps and shouts as they watched the sorcerer move far faster than a galloping mount. With a leap, he cleared the tangle of dead and dying horses and archers, crossing over thirty feet in an effortless bound.

"He'll tear the Glenfolk apart, I think," Yazid said urgently.

Greer's words echoed in Corvus' head. *"Protect my boys..."*

"Cai!" Corvus shouted, and stepped forward out of the wall. With a quick nod to Niall and Quinn to close up the formation behind him, he dashed toward the Glenfolk line, where chaos now reigned.

The sorcerer had crashed directly into the center of Cai's troops, pitching the broken bodies of soldiers in all directions. *Right where Cai would've been standing had he formed up in the center, as planned,* Corvus realized. Like a starved wolf suddenly loose among a clutch of hens, the creature thrashed about hungrily, batting aside weapons and tearing the soldiers apart. Broken shields, cleft helms, shattered armor, and torn limbs all flew from him as he grabbed and ripped, with no weapon but his empty, clawlike hands. To their credit, the Glenfolk soldiers did their best to stand their ground before this aberration, but their weapons and strength were no match for his fury. No sword seemed to reach him. Spears were batted aside, their hafts shattering at his touch.

Corvus was sprinting toward the chaos when he saw, with horror, that Cai would reach him first. He saw Cai's determination as the young man dashed toward the mayhem, sword and shield ready; he couldn't stand by and watch his troops get savaged like this.

"Cai, no!" Corvus shouted. "Stay back!" But his son's focus was entirely on the creature that was killing his men. With a burst of speed, and an Eagle-form leap on his now-restored left side, Corvus intercepted Cai, slipping behind his son in a circular movement and throwing him to the ground away from the wizard. Cailean, reacting quickly, went with the throw, tumbling flawlessly into a fighting crouch.

"This one's not for you, lad!" Corvus shouted and rushed toward the sorcerer.

The soldiers had backed away to form a defensive cordon holding the creature, at least momentarily, at bay. The Glenfolk troops were too brave to break and run before this monster, though Corvus could tell from their postures and wide eyes that it could happen. The fiend had paused and was sniffing the air and cackling at the surrounding troops as Corvus attacked, Raven's Tooth moving so quickly as to be no more than a series of silver flashes in the air. Spinning with unnatural speed to face this new foe, the creature seemed surprised by the ferocity of Corvus' blade. Despite his preternatural gifts, the sorcerer was actually forced back a few steps, batting ineffectually at Raven's Tooth as the razor-sharp edge opened several cuts along his arms and chest. In apparent frustration, the sorcerer leapt suddenly to the side, crashing into a group of soldiers and hurling their bodies at Corvus one at a time, like so many rag dolls.

With a series of tumbles to each side, Corvus managed to avoid the flying bodies and shields, but the sudden need to duck had halted his onslaught. He and his opponent eyed each other warily, Corvus panting from his mad sprint and assault, the sorcerer standing with muscular legs wide in the center of a mass of fallen soldiers. This was a being unlike any Corvus had faced before. Never had he seen such strength. The creature's eyes were locked on him as though it recognized something truly unusual. With a snarl, the sorcerer squatted down and plucked up the corpse of a broken soldier. Without breaking eye contact, the creature ripped the head off the corpse's body, and bit down into the meat of the neck, blood and viscera running down his chin as he watched Corvus for a reaction. The observing soldiers gasped in revulsion and took an involuntary step back away from the fiend, prompting a smile on the sorcerer's face. Corvus remained crouching, ready, calm. The creature's grin widened further, revealing brown-stained, jagged teeth, dripping with slime and gore.

"You don't fear me…" The wizard spoke calmly, his voice unnaturally clear and loud, despite the tumult, though his thick, wet accent made his words somewhat difficult to decipher.

"You're as foul a demon as e'er I've seen," Corvus responded, rising from his crouch. "But no, I fear you not. You bleed as any man does." He nodded toward the various small cuts and gashes on the creature.

"How novel," the sorcerer said. "These men fear me." He glanced around at the soldiers nearest him. "Makes me strong.

When they watch me rip you in two, they'll break and run, and the day will be ours."

Corvus stood for a moment, noting the broken and dismembered bodies around him, the shattered weapons and armor. He listened to the moans of the injured. He could see the fear in the faces around him. The sorcerer was right. The soldiers were on the verge of breaking, and if they did, all was lost. Not just Cai or the battle, but all of the Green Mount. He would have to show them it could be done, that this creature could be beaten.

The Mountain is immovable…

He had never attempted something like this, but the briefest wisp of lavender and cloves on the breeze reassured him. With a carefree sigh, he cast his shield to the ground behind him, then to the obvious surprise of all around him, Corvus sheathed Raven's Tooth and opened his empty hands in a welcoming gesture, inviting the creature's attack.

Its roots are deep and ancient, reaching to the very core of the world…

The sorcerer looked at him, confusion writ on his pallid features. Corvus began the subtle movements of Mountain form, envisioning broad, unbreakable shafts of stone reaching downward from his legs, merging with those of the mighty peaks around him. *His* peaks, the mountains of *his* ancestors, *his* people. No foreign creature, sorcerer, or army could move *his* mountains. He breathed deeply as his hands and feet subtly shifted through the movements of the form. In his mind's eye, he took in the soaring majesty of the range of impenetrable, rocky peaks that surrounded the Green Mount. Their bones reached deep into the crust of the world. Unbreakable bones. He would *become* the immovable mountain.

In its majesty is peace…

A wave of warmth spread over Corvus as he felt his heart rate slow, his breathing ease.

In its immensity, strength…

The sorcerer sneered at Corvus and began to stalk from side to side like a caged animal. "You think to fight me, little man?" he snarled through dripping teeth.

"Avaunt, demon. You will not prevail here today," Corvus responded calmly, his eyes half-lidded, his stance wide and solid.

With a shriek of disbelief, the creature launched itself at Corvus, aiming a powerful, sweep of his extended right claw at his chest. The suddenness and speed of his attack elicited a cry of alarm from the soldiers. There was a sound like the shattering of a spear haft. The wizard's attacking and still outstretched arm had broken against Corvus' immovable frame. The gesture of the block was known in Asland as the "Serving Posture." Corvus held his hands out before him, elbows bent, as if holding an imaginary tray of food. The incoming blow was received on the forearms below the hands. It was a passive block, exerting no force against the incoming strike, yet it had somehow stopped the wizard's mighty attack, and shattered the creature's arm; bones protruded from the wounded limb in a ghastly mix of black and red blood. Given what the soldiers had witnessed already of the might of this creature, they had no doubt expected to see Corvus' broken body fly through the air as so many before him had. But Corvus had not been moved an inch. He had not met the incoming blow with force, but had instead become the stone of the mountain, and the creature's arm had shattered against him.

The bones of the Mountain are mighty…

With a howl of pain and wonder, the creature staggered back a step, clutching his broken limb to his side, before launching another series of vicious attacks with his remaining claw. With a calm gesture that looked for all the world like Corvus was merely scratching his ear, he blocked that attack, then the next, and the next. Though each blow landed with a force that would have cast a war horse to the ground, Corvus remained unfazed and unhurt. The wizard staggered back again, his left arm battered and bruised from flailing against this immovable foe.

"How is this possible?" he slurred in apparent bemusement and exhaustion. The muscle tone in his body seemed to deflate visibly as the soldiers saw their champion untouched by the fiend's frenzy.

"These are *my* mountains, creature," Corvus responded, an air of peace and firm resolve coming from him. "You willna prevail this day."

The sorcerer snarled and resumed his circular stalking, turning occasionally to hiss and spit defiance at the soldiers, striving to stir fear in them on which he could feed. Corvus pivoted with the creature, keeping the monster before him. The Raven's hands and feet continued to shift subtly through the movements of Mountain form, a half-smile on his lips. As they rotated within the small circle to the point where the sorcerer's back was to the battlefield, Corvus shifted into Ocean form, his feet carving small semicircles in the spongy gorse as his hands began the circular motions to summon up his ruhon. To attempt to shift so quickly between forms was difficult and spiritually costly, but he had no choice.

The creature rushed as soon as he saw the shift in Corvus' stance, attempting a tackle.

The might of the Ocean is limitless…

A sound like a series of waves smacking against the cliffs of Dóchas reverberated through the battlefield as Corvus halted the creature's headlong rush with what seemed to be but a small push of his hands against the sorcerer's chest. The creature stopped dead as if struck by a thunderbolt. Then in a rhythmic motion, Corvus shoved again, first with only one hand, and then the other, then again with both. Each push, though seemingly small in effort, produced the thundering sound and visibly shocked the sorcerer's body, as though he was being kicked by a powerful stallion. Corvus exhaled loudly on the final push, dropping into his deepest stance, a peaceful calm upon his face. The wizard flew backward, flailing in the air before landing in a crumpled heap atop his broken arm. The fiend moaned and began struggling to rise, clutching his chest in agony.

"Your turn, lads," Corvus said loudly, gesturing to the gathered soldiers who rushed toward the fallen creature like hounds released to the hunt, stabbing down viciously with swords and pikes. Blades rose and fell in a frenzy.

A great *WHOOM* suddenly filled the air, and the cluster of soldiers was blown back and knocked from their feet. Corvus stood, blinking, as the dust settled and the dazed soldiers began helping one another to their feet. The creature lived no more. But just beyond it, the Barbár shield wall had advanced and was almost upon them.

Struggling through profound and sudden exhaustion, Corvus shouted, "Fall back to position two!"

He looked about urgently to see if he could catch Isla's eyes. Then he found her. The reliable lass had moved perilously forward of the line to keep sight of Corvus. He gestured urgently for her to raise the yellow flag, praying that Toren would see the signal. He shouted again in his loudest battlefield voice, hoping against hope that the entire line would hear him.

"Fall back to position two!"

The enemy wall was almost upon them when the entire line of Highlanders—Glenfolk, fyrd, and White Cleft—suddenly broke formation and turned to flee to the north side of the ruins, every soldier repeating the cry, "Position two!" A shout went up from the approaching Räubers as they saw victory before them, their enemy apparently fleeing in disarray. Breaking their disciplined formation, the Barbárs dashed forward to pursue the fleeing Highlanders. But just as the first of their number passed the mound Yadira had shown Corvus, with the breath of the mountain issuing from it, a single flaming arrow from Toren's bow found the mouth of the cave. A sudden flaming cloud ignited and swirled down the throat of the mound, into the depths below. And then, with a groan like the death of some enormous beast, the world exploded.

Many of the Highlanders dashing back to their second position were knocked to the ground as a series of blasts like the fury from the mouth of a furnace washed over them. The earth shook, tumbling stones and soldiers from their roosts among the ruins, and archers from their hidden perches on the cliff face. Wave upon wave of bellicose thunder engulfed them. The air was sucked from their lungs and replaced with a foul taste, like bitter ash, leaving them gasping and clawing at the ground. Then there was silence, punctuated only by distant moans and cries of confusion that crept through the ringing in their ears.

Adorjan

The senior war chief among the mounted Räubers had watched in frustration and fury as the strange wizard lashed out and killed the mighty Gaszi with a single blow. *May his name be remembered.* Had the army not immediately advanced, Adorjan would have ridden the puny shaman down, punishing him for such an insolent violation. He had no truck with so-called wizards, and this vile, sadistic creature had filled their camp for weeks with the sounds of torment from his near-constant torturing of prisoners. Better to kill a man in battle than excruciate the weak and helpless for no purpose. Adorjan had no qualms with torture generally, of course. It had its place—to quell and terrify the enemy, gather information, tame unruly women, and punish the treacherous or those too proud to submit—but the nightly screams of agony from the tent of this "Bone-Eye" had pushed the proud Räubers of the invasion force to the very edge of madness and mutiny. But today, Adorjan had watched in amazement as the sickly shaman had suddenly grown visibly in stature, assumed command of the army against all protocol, and then dashed ahead of them all, moving faster than any galloping stallion. *Powerful magic, indeed.*

Adorjan instinctively touched the iron talisman at his neck three times as a ward against evil. He would wait to see how the battle played out, and once they had completed this conquest, which should be a simple affair, he would put a blade in the back of the treacherous shaman—though he was sure there would many other loyal Räubers clamoring to do the same. Perhaps he would find the fiend on the battlefield and strike him down from behind. As the senior war chief, Adorjan was next in line for full command. With Gaszi dead, only the sniveling shaman stood in the way of him earning the right to bear a stone for the Grand Hadvezér. His mind filled with the possibilities this day would bring, and his heart soared with anticipation of his elevation. *But first,* he cautioned himself, *the sorcerer must die.*

The mounted Räubers waited impatiently as the proud shield wall advanced. The riders were unaccustomed to the gyalogos katonák, the '"warriors on foot," gaining glory before them. Räuber riders were the apex killers of the Barbár forces, and it galled them to allow any to advance to glory before them. But Gaszi's strategy had been sound enough. The Highlanders were known for the strength of their shield wall and the lethal accuracy of their archers. Better to hold the riders back and let those on foot soak up the arrows. When the enemy line broke, then his riders would bathe in blood. The reports from the spies suggested that the land beyond this pass was undefended. Fat villages and towns just waiting, unguarded. He smiled hungrily at the thought.

From his position, he couldn't see what was happening beyond the warriors on foot. Adorjan held up his hand, signaling patience. Any moment now, the enemy would break. This would be a glorious day and Adorjan's reputation would grow apace with the Grand Hadvezér's dominion.

"Prepare yourselves!" he shouted. "The enemy will break soon, then we strike! Wait for my command."

This was greeted by the familiar rumble of impatient growls and the kóstoló, or "tasting," the traditional Barbár practice of extending their blackened tongues to show their gods a fearless hunger for the blood of the enemy. His riders—five thousand fierce Räubers—adjusted their positions as one, moving their restless steeds to the line and preparing for the charge. He could sense their anticipation, their lust for the kill. He smiled and extended his own tongue, growling loudly.

"Adorjan, uram!" his scout called from his vantage on the far right of the field. "The enemy breaks! Now is our time!"

Adorjan raised his war staff high, the ram's skull that adorned it clacked with the many bones that dangled from it. He would wait a moment longer to give the Räubers on foot a chance to begin the chase. But as he looked back at the enemy lines, something unexpected happened that defied explanation. His brow furrowed in confusion at what he saw.

Then the whole world turned to fire, screams, and death.

Epilogue

The Fool stepped from the copse of trees by the lakeside into the clearing near the road. His scruffy dog wagged its nub of a tail furiously and sniffed about the ground, quite fascinated by a small pile of deer scat. A fluttering on a low branch of the oak tree just behind him announced the arrival of the raven.

"Well, it's about time," Latrans said over his shoulder to the bird, who croaked in response. "Excuses, excuses," he said, turning to face it with a shake of his head. "At least I was on time."

The raven croaked twice more, ruffling its feathers and looking for all the world as if it were irritated at the criticism. Latrans gave a smug smile and turned back to the clearing with a flouncy step, as though he were about to begin a dance. However, he was interrupted by the barking of his dog, who was now on the far side of the sward, where the road cut along it.

"Alright, alright," the Fool responded with mock irritation, marching purposefully across the grass and pulling out his juggling balls. "I'm coming, I'm coming! Sheesh!"

He stepped up beside the dog and began juggling the colorful spheres just as a lady rider rounded the bend at a quick canter, her chestnut mare sweating and blowing as though she had maintained that pace for some time. The woman was all alone, which was unusual, though the Fool seemed unsurprised at this. She was dressed in a high-necked green jacket that buttoned in the front with a plaid sash pinned at the shoulder, and beige trews which were tucked into knee-high black boots. At the sight of the Fool, she reined in, her gaze taking in his unusual appearance and odd activity.

"Well," she said in surprise, "I must say, that's an unexpected sight!"

"Donnella!" The Fool exclaimed, tossing one ball higher than the rest and spinning to catch it.

"Yes, I am Lady Donnella..." she replied with a quiet curiosity in her voice. "Have we met, sir?"

"Not yet," Latrans replied, slipping the juggling balls inside his vest and pulling forth his flute. "But can we just chat for a moment about your husband?"

Donnella looked nonplussed as she suddenly was surrounded by a haunting melody. The raven croaked once more in satisfaction and took flight, soaring out of the oak and high above the clearing. Smoke from the cookfires in the town of Stilling were visible to the west as the bird turned to the southeast, toward far-off Eagle's Gate, its wings working against a notable headwind.

There was much to do.

Author's Note

Welcome to the world of Hortus. I first began this book in the spring of 2020. It seemed like an appropriate use of my suddenly abundant and isolated time. Little did I realize the Pandora's Box I had opened as Corvus, Mama Warad, Latrans, Darienne and all the others sprang so completely to life before me, fully formed.

To clear up any confusion regarding the calendar and Highland Reckoning — on the world of Hortus, there is no standardized calendar, each region or nation having its own method of tabulating the years. So, it seemed the best choice was to make all date references in the book into HR or Highland Reckoning, which measures the years since the territories of the Green Mount achieved their complete independence from the nation of Mardin. Of course, the people anywhere outside the Green Mount would not use Highland Reckoning, but I've done so here in an effort to keep things clear.

Countless thanks are due to my alpha readers, Miranda Wiley, Catherine Doersch and Gigi and Dave Paddock. Their consistent and tireless investment in these chronicles kept me going, kept me believing and kept me writing. Thanks also must be extended to my brilliant editor, Kate Nascimento for her painstaking and detailed work, squeezing every ounce of potential from the text. Also, my endless thanks to Duncan Eagleson for his brilliant artistry. I've known Duncan and drooled over his artwork for over twenty years. So glad to finally get to work with him.

Untold thanks are due to my friend and comrade, David Blixt, a successful and brilliant author of highly literate historical fiction. He inspired me, encouraged me, and answered far too many questions with patience and grace. Thank you, David.

Finally, I must extend my deepest gratitude to all of you, the readers of this story. Writers work in isolation and weave our tales, but that effort is meaningless and ephemeral without all of you investing in the story, getting to know the characters, sending emails, asking questions, etc. So, thank you, and keep those emails coming!

Protect the Tor!

About the Author

David Doersch lives in the mountains of North Carolina with his wife, Cathy and their two cats, Harriet and Winifred. Ensconced in his living room, writing, surrounded by the unrivaled beauty of the Smoky Mountains, one would imagine it to be a quiet life. But in addition to being an author, David is a fight director and stunt coordinator for live action spectacles, a touring musician playing bagpipes with his Celtic Rock band, and a theatrical director, specializing in the works of Shakespeare. All of these competing interests try to pull him away from Daffyd and the adventures of Corvus. But then Winifred curls up on his lap, purring, and he simply surrenders once again to the call of the Green Mount.

Made in the USA
Middletown, DE
21 January 2024

48224202R00308